ZANE PRESENTS

Ruthless

Dear Reader:

Pasha Allen is back and this time her vindictive nature is at its extreme: she's on fire to eliminate her enemies one by one—particularly she's on a mission to destroy the team who kidnapped, tortured and violated her in a basement. Retribution. Vengeance.

She's also on a cat-and-mouse game with her baby's daddy, Jasper, and they're both seeking to exact revenge. He's still disgusted that she cheated on him during lockup, and that she has obtained a restraining order and is denying him access to his son.

Watch how this vixen goes to the ultimate to pay back all those who attempted to terminate her.

I appreciate the love and support shown to Strebor Books, myself, and our efforts to bring you cutting-edge stories.

Blessings,

Zane

Publisher
Strebor Books
www.simonandschuster.com

ALSO BY CAIRO
Retribution
Slippery When Wet
The Stud Palace (original e-book)
Big Booty
Man Swappers
Kitty-Kitty, Bang-Bang
Deep Throat Diva
Daddy Long Stroke
The Man Handler
The Kat Trap

ZANE PRESENTS

A NOVEL BY

CAIRO

SBI

STREBOR BOOKS

NEW YORK LONDON TORONTO SYDNEY

Strebor Books
P.O. Box 6505
Largo, MD 20792
http://www.streborbooks.com

© 2014 by Cairo

ISBN 978-1-59309-513-0
ISBN 978-1-4767-3358-6 (ebook)
LCCN 2014935330

First Strebor Books trade paperback edition November 2014

Cover design: www.mariondesigns.com
Cover photograph: © Keith Saunders/Keith Saunders Photos

10 9 8 7 6 5 4 3 2

Manufactured in the United States of America

For information regarding special discounts for bulk purchases, please contact Simon & Schuster Special Sales at 1-866-506-1949 or business@simonandschuster.com

The Simon & Schuster Speakers Bureau can bring authors to your live event. For more information or to book an event, contact the Simon & Schuster Speakers Bureau at 1-866-248-3049 or visit our website at www.simonspeakers.com.

This book is dedicated to
All the cock 'n' cum lovers who love having their throats gutted.
Swallow the heat 'n' enjoy the cream…
This one's for you!

ACKNOWLEDGMENTS

Aiight, my Juice Lovas 'n' freaks…once again, I'ma keep it short 'n' sweet. Eleven books in 'n' countin'. And I'm still pushin' out the heat, one keystroke at a time! And *whaaat?!*

To the sexually liberated and open-minded: Thanks for spreadin' the juice to ya peeps 'n' continuin' to wave ya freak flags. I appreciate ALL of you. Let's keep it wet, keep it sticky, and always keep it ready! Real freaks know how to turn up in the sheets! No questions asked!

To all the Facebook beauties 'n' cuties and cool-ass bruhs who make this journey mad fun: Real rap. I couldn't do this without ALL of you! Y'all my muthaeffen peeps! Thanks for vibin' with ya boy!

To all the closed-minded & sexually repressed peeps: Bless ya lil raggedy, whack-fuckin' hearts!

To Zane, Charmaine, Yona and the rest of the Strebor/Simon & Schuster team: As always, I hope you all know how much ya boy appreciates the never-ending luv!

To Sara Camilli: You are everything I could ever want in an agent. Thank YOU!

To the members of *Cairo's World:* Be on the lookout for a new look 'n' new shit poppin' over on the other side real soon. I'm finally about to turn the flames up for y'all nassy-asses!

And, as always, to the naysayers 'n' silent haters: Keep poppin' shit. Ya thoughts n opinions don't move me. So go have several seats 'n' lick these nuts! The Cairo Movement is here to stay!

One luv~
Cairo

Prologue

Remorse and guilt don't exist in an empty heart...

I wasn't born a killer.

And I hadn't initially planned on becoming one. I had hoped that if I had to murder anyone, Jasper would be first on my list. Not Felecia. Not my flesh and blood.

But here I am.

In the flesh.

A killer.

A murderer.

Still clutching the gun in my hand, I stare into Felecia's dead face. Her eyes wide and frozen in fear, her curled lashes still wet with tears, what's left of her bloody mouth is gaped open, front teeth cracked and knocked out, smoke still floating out of her lying dick suckers. I feel a surging rush of adrenaline pumping through me, yet I feel *nothing*—for her, for what I have done. I am numb to this, to her current state. Slumped over and lifeless. In a flash, Felecia, along with every mental snapshot—an entire lifetime of memories—of everything we've ever shared, gone. Her last breath snatched by the bitch she tried to do in. Me.

By choice.

I stare at the gun in my bloody hand, then look up toward the ceiling as if expecting the roof to open up at any moment, to only get struck by a bolt of lightning. This bitch betrayed me. She hurt me. She disrespected me. She fucked me over. And she *fucked* my man. Regardless of whether it's over between Jasper and me or not, this bitch fucked him, sucked him, while things with him were good—even if they were only in my own head. And the bitch continued fucking him on the sly—*after* shit between him and me went downhill.

So *I* killed her.

By choice.

Because I wanted her dead! Because she deserved to be dead! Because she ran her mouth and popped shit.

Sadly, I feel not one ounce of sorrow. No regret. No remorse. No guilt. Nothing. And no goddamn tears.

I'll admit. Killing this bitch wasn't my initial intention. No. I planned on confronting her, allowing her the chance to confess, to redeem herself—not that anything that came out of her cum trap was going to change the damage already done. She and I would never be close again. Then I was going to slip out of my heels and beat her ass real good. However, somewhere in the back corners of my mind, I knew it was a slight possibility that I would take it to her skull—not with my fist, with a bullet—if the bitch came at me sideways and crazy.

And she did.

The more she tried to lie and deny her way out of shit, the stronger the urge became. The more reckless she talked, the deeper my conviction became. Then the bitch had the audacity to tell me she was pregnant. The admission of who planted his nut in her became scribbled in the fear shown in her eyes. It was Jasper.

So, for that, I took her life. There was no blackout. There was no lack of judgment. There was no temporary moment of insanity.

I didn't just get caught up in the moment. I was clear *and* in my right frame of mind when I reached in back of me and pulled out my 9mm, shoving it down into her motherfucking throat.

And I was fully cognizant of the look in her eyes when I pulled the trigger.

I am *still* very much aware of what I've done. *I've* murdered her.

And the scary thing is—standing here taking in the splattered blood on the walls and the loose teeth knocked out of her big-ass mouth—I know, deep down in the pit of my soul, I am very much certain, I'll have no problem doing it again, if I have to, *when* I have to… *if* I am forced to.

Bitch wanted to be me. Thought she was going to snatch my spot. I'm convinced she wanted me dead. Wished it. Hoped for it. Shit, the bitch admitted she didn't give a fuck. That she didn't care then. And damn sure didn't care now. I'm glad I didn't allow her up to the hospital to hover over my bed, secretly gloating that she'd had a hand in doing me in while I clung to my life, and sanity.

I glance over at the clock: 10:38 P.M. Then step away from her body. I walk into the bathroom and wash off the blood on the gun and my hands, carefully drying them. Then I wash my face, glancing up from the sink at the reflection staring back at me in the mirror. I don't like what I see.

I don't even know who I see.

The bitch staring back at me has my face, my complexion, my hazel eyes. But she is still a stranger to me. I don't like her.

I don't like me.

But this is who I am.

This is what I've become.

Thanks to Jasper.

Thanks to Felecia.

Thanks to every motherfucker who took his turn at fucking my throat raw.

I flip off the light and walk back out into my office over to my desk and pull out one of the burner phone's Lamar had given me, then place a call. "Who this?"

"Pasha."

"Oh, what's good? You still need that remodeling work done?"

"Yes. I'm ready for that paint job," I say, unlocking and opening my office door, then walking into the staff lounge, going over to the counter and pulling out the top drawer. I grab a steak knife, then shut the drawer. "And I need the carpet pulled up and tossed along with all the *dead* weight in the room."

"Oh, aiight."

He understands, clearly. She's dead. He's the only person I told about my meeting with her tonight here. The only person who I let know things might get ugly between us. He was the only person I let hear the extent of my rage toward her. And when I told him out of anger that I felt like killing her ass, he said, "Then maybe she should catch it. What she did was some real grimy shit. You didn't deserve that. So, whatever you decide, I'ma ride it out with you. Real shit, ma, I know that's ya fam 'n' all, but I think you should handle her."

He said it with no expression, no emotion. Then leaned into my ear and whispered, "I have a professional cleanup crew *in case*... things get bloody. I can get you a piece that won't ever trace back to you. You won't have to do anything except pull the trigger."

He walked me through it. Told me to make sure to turn off the security cameras just in case I decided to handle her—*permanently*, so no one would see her coming in if anyone were to ever ask to see any footage. Not that they would have reason to. But I needed to be three steps ahead. He told me to be sure to meet with her in my office, where it's soundproofed. Then handle my business.

"Right after you pop her top, hit me up and I'll handle everything else. I *specialize* in these kinds of jobs. Security work is my other gig." Without him saying more than that, it was evident at that very moment that there was a whole lot more to my armed-security stud. "You wanna rid ya'self of a poisonous snake before it has a chance to strike again, chop off its head."

The seed had been planted. Her slick mouth sealed her fate.

Hate me? Bitch, please!

There is no room in my life for snitches and snakes. Felecia really thought she'd reap some hefty reward by snaking me. Thought she had snatched her the door prize, along with a quick come-up by backstabbing me. Ha! I showed that bitch. She couldn't have possibly thought she'd get away with it. She almost did.

Almost.

But getting caught happens to the best of us. Eventually she would have to pay her dues. It was only a matter of time. And, tonight, her time had come.

It's over. When I walk out of here tonight, I will go home, grab a bottle of wine, run a bubble bath, then soak away any memory of tonight. Then I am going to pop two sleeping pills and sleep the rest of the night away free from any chance of being plagued with nightmares of what I've done. And, before the crack of dawn, I will wake up with a smile plastered on my face. Catch my flight to Los Angeles to spend the day with my son. Catch the red-eye flight back. Then Tuesday morning, bright and early, I will step up in my salon, facing the day with the same renewed purpose. To shut down *everyone* else who had a hand in hurting me.

And I will go on with my life as if nothing ever happened tonight. As if I hadn't laid eyes on this bitch in almost two weeks. I will pretend she never existed. As if, minutes ago, I'd never pulled the trigger, blowing a hole in the back of her head.

I grab a pair of latex gloves, then the toolbox from under the cabinet and take out a wrench and a pair of pliers, then place the toolbox back in its place.

"Oh, aiight. You still there?"

I walk back into my office. "Yes." He already knows where to park his trucks. Around the back of the building as we discussed. He knows to enter through the emergency exit door on the side of the building where the staff lounge is. I snap my fingers, suddenly remembering something. *Yes, that's exactly what I need.* A large bag of ice and a cooler. I pull out the key to my storage closet, unlocking it, then taking out what I need. One last piece to finish this bitch off.

"Aiight, bet. I got you. I'ma holla at my crew now. They're already on standby. We should be there in a few." He tells me they'll work around the clock until they have shit right. That by the time I land in Newark on Tuesday morning from L.A., everything will be in order. My office will be good as new.

"Perfect. You're a lifesaver, literally."

"I tol' you, I got you. It's *whatever.*"

Nothing else is said. I turn off the phone, removing its SIM card before smashing the phone into pieces. I scoop up the pieces and dump them into the wastebasket that will go out along with the rest of the *trash*. I slip on the gloves. Then call Felecia's cell. Wait for it to roll over into her voicemail, then leave a message. "Felecia, this is Pasha. I've been at the salon waiting on you for almost two damn hours now. Bitch, the least you could have done is called and told me you changed your mind, or something else came up. Whatever."

I smirk, ending the call. Then stalk back over to her body, narrowing my eyes. "Gossiping bitch," I snap, slapping her face with the wrench. Her neck snaps to one side where it stays. I hit her upside the head, banging what's left of her skull in. "Fucking bitch! I don't hear you popping shit now! Worthless bitch! What was that you said about being pregnant? Oh, wait. You're dead!"

I kick her in the stomach. Then reach into her mouth, grab a hold of her tongue, yanking it out, then start hacking into it with the knife. I saw and cut into the still-warm organ until I finally have it sawed off. Then I take the pliers, twisting and yanking out every last one of her teeth.

Unfazed by the pool of blood surrounding her head, soaking into the carpet, splashed all over me, I glance at her body, one last time, sighing. "Now look at you, stupid, dead, toothless bitch!"

I spit in her bloody, mangled face, then lean in and finish her off.

One

*The game of seduction can turn deadly
when temptation gets in the way...*

Wednesday morning, as I'm walking into the salon quarter-to-eight with Lamar and Mel behind me, my cell rings. I reach down into the side pocket of my purse, pulling it out, glancing at the caller ID. It's Thick Seven.

In spite of what's going on inside my head, I smile. Hearing his smooth, dreamy voice on the other end of the line is a welcomed distraction. And if I'm completely honest with myself, I really like him. But I know he's a diversion I don't need right now. I can't risk it. After the things I've done over the last weekend—and the things that I'm about to do, I need to stay on course. Can't lose perspective. So this thing between us is going to have to end, sooner than later. Besides, he's someone else's nigga who I've been regularly borrowing for the last several months.

"Hey," I say, answering before his call gets sent to voicemail. I leave Lamar and Mel up front, heading toward my office. I unlock the door, immediately greeted by the smell of fresh paint and new carpet. The walls are now a soft pink. The carpet is a rich chocolate brown. Everything is put back in its place. Any signs of my bloody deed from Sunday night have been scrubbed down, painted over, pulled up, and discarded.

"What's good, beautiful? How you?"

I yawn in his ear. "Ooh, excuse me," I quickly say, apologizing.

"Oh, you good, baby. Sounds like someone had a late night."

"Yeah, I did." I sit my bag on top of my desk. "I didn't get much sleep."

Fact is, instead of flying back from L.A. Monday night like I had intended to, I stayed an extra day to spend it with my Jaylen, giving Sophia and Greta a break. So I took the red-eye last night instead. And landed a little after seven this morning. Then, instead of going home, I had Mel pick me up from the airport to get my car from Lamar's boy's body shop, then drove straight here with him following behind me.

So here I am...at the salon, pretending.

That I hadn't initiated burning down three of Jasper's stash houses; that I'm not planning to burn down three more—this week.

That I hadn't sucked Stax's dick and swallowed his creamy nut Saturday night; that I hadn't allowed him to rock my pussy with his tongue and fingers, then his hard dick right here in my office, enjoying every last thick inch of him.

That I hadn't turned on my laptop, logged into my Deep Throat Diva AOL account and reached out to the nigga who attacked me in my yard, then harassed me for not sucking his dick, making plans to slice off his fucking balls.

That I hadn't murdered Felecia, taking a serrated knife and hacking out her tongue *after* shoving a gun in her mouth and blowing a hole in the back of her skull.

The first person on my list to take down.

Yes, I am pretending. The curtain is up. The stage has been set. The script is written. The spotlights are on. The scenes are playing out quite nicely. And there's nothing anyone can do or say to stop what's about to happen next. So onlookers might as well sit back, relax, nibble on their proverbial popcorn, and wait for the drama to unfold. Because shit's about to get real.

Images of Stax's hard dick pop into my head. I grin, licking my lips and pressing my thighs together. Whether he likes it or not, shit between him and Jasper is about to change quickly. No matter how hard Stax tries, it'll never be the same between them. How could it be after I put it on him? To think, the divide that is about to come between them is by my own doing. And all it took was a few shed tears and a good dick suck to break his resolve.

Yes. Coercive manipulation. All a part of the plan. To milk him, suck him, edge Stax, into giving me what I need. I haven't heard from him since I sucked the nut out of him, and coated his tongue with my pussy cream. And right now, it's probably for the best.

I open my bottom drawer, grab my handbag and pull out the slip of paper with the list of names Cassandra wrote out, then reach for a pen and write the nigga AJ's address she'd given me next to his name. Then I add two more names to the list, under-scoring each one.

KILLA

JAH

The two names Stax had given me. I stare at the paper. He refused to tell me any more than this. Refused to rat out the rest of the niggas Jasper recruited in his sick, twisted attack on me. But I'm fine with it. He's told me enough, *for now.*

Until I suck him down into my throat, again. And there will be a next time. No matter how hard he tries to fight it, Stax will come back for more.

I glance at the paper again. These two niggas are the ones who kidnapped me. Now, altogether, I have six names, not including Jasper's. And one of the niggas is already handled thanks to Booty killing him. I draw a line through JT's and Felecia's names.

And this bitch, along with JT, is also considered missing, thanks to me! No. Thanks to her fucking mouth!

Two down!

Even if I can't track down every last one of the motherfuckers who played a part in my assault, I'm okay with getting at the ones I do know. One by one, they're going to get dropped. Until the only one left standing is Jasper. Saving the best for last.

"I wanna see you, yo," Thick Seven says, slicing into my thoughts. "But I know shit's hectic right now so I'ma be easy and let you do you."

"I appreciate that," I say, running a hand through my hair. He wants to know when I'm going back to L.A. I don't tell him I just returned this morning. Or that I'm going back Sunday morning. It's none of his business. Being away from my son is killing me. Has me feeling empty and alone. I know it's only been six days since I moved Jaylen and Sophia out to L.A. and asked Greta to be his temporary caretaker until this mess with Jasper is over. Until I am free of him, once and for all. Still living without my son, no matter how short term it is, is one of the hardest things I am dealing with. The aching in my heart is like no other. But I know it's for the best.

And sucking this nigga's dick isn't going to fill that void. Nor is giving him some pussy. And it isn't going help me do what needs to be done.

He lets out a slight chuckle. "I can't get enough of you, baby. Seems like goin' to Cali is the only way I'm gonna be able to get at you and that magical tongue of yours again." He lowers his smooth voice. "I wanna feel them pretty-ass lips up on this dick, soon, baby. Damn. Every time I talk to you, my shit gets hard."

I smirk, looking up when someone knocks on my door. I cover the mouthpiece and tell whoever's on the other side of the door to come in. "Well, I'm glad to know I have that kind of effect on you," I say, avoiding his initial question.

"You definitely do. But look, baby, I gotta bounce. Just wanted to hear that sexy-ass voice of yours. And let you know this dick's hard for you. Stay sweet, babe."

"I always do," I say, ignoring the remark about his hard dick. I end the call as Lamar walks in, a black backpack slung over his left shoulder, shutting the door behind him.

Two

Trust no one without knowing their agenda, or end up their next perfect prey…

"What's up?" I say, quickly glancing up at the surveillance monitor. *Now keeping this nigga's dick in my throat is definitely going to get me what I need…and want.*

Lamar drops his backpack to the floor, taking a seat in one of the chairs in front of me. He glances around the office, then lands his gaze on me. "So what you think? E'erything good?"

I nod. Tell him everything's perfect. That his crew did a phenomenal job patching up the bullet holes and repainting the walls and tearing up the old carpet. I thank him, pulling out my handbag.

"I hope you know how much I appreciate you," I state, getting up from my desk, then opening my closet and going into my safe.

"You good, Pasha. I tol' you, it's whatever."

I pull out fifty thousand dollars in stacks of hundreds banded together, stuffing the money into a black gym bag. Then shut and lock the safe, walking over and handing the bag to him.

He looks at the bag. "Yo, what's this for?"

"Compensation for handling that situation Saturday night. Then taking care of the mess I made in here Sunday night." He made sure Jasper's stash houses were burned down to the ground early Saturday morning. Then handled disposing Felecia's butchered body late Sunday night for me. I don't know what he did with her. Okay, okay…I do know. But all I say for now is, like JT's body, she won't be found.

He unzips the bag, looking inside. Then quickly zips it back. "Nah, you good, Pasha. Handling that nigga for you is on the house, ma; feel me? That pussy-ass nigga had that shit coming, and then some. Besides, we copped all the work and weapons that nigga had up in them spots. So we good."

I nod knowingly. The deal was, he got to keep whatever drugs and weapons they confiscated before burning each stash house down. But whatever money they find comes to me. I meant what I said when I said I am going to take every dime of Jasper's I can get my hands on. I'm going to leave that nigga penniless and broken—or damn near close to it—by the time I'm done with him.

Lamar eyes me. "So how you? You *good*?"

I swipe my bang over my forehead, nodding. "Yeah. I'm as good as I can be, considering." I lower my voice, glancing up at the security monitor. "I mean, it's not every day I blow my own cousin's head off, have her body disposed of, then arrange to have three of my future ex-husband's stash houses burned down."

He nods knowingly. "I feel you. But you good, though, right?"

"Bitch! You want the fucking truth? Then here it is raw and uncut: I love you. But I fucking hate you more! And, yes, I sucked Jasper's dick! There, you satisfied! I sucked his dick, okay! Why? Because I fucking wanted to! You didn't fucking deserve a nigga like him! Bitch, you had it good. Jasper gave you anything you wanted, and that shit still wasn't enough for you. You still went and shitted on him. It's always about you, bitch! Pasha this, Pasha that! The fly bitch who always gets what she wants. Who always gets all the right niggas eating outta the palm of her goddamn hands!

"And bitches like me, who know how to treat a good man, gotta stand

on the sidelines and watch bitches like you fuck over all the good men...."

I blink, shaking that two-faced bitch's voice from my thoughts as I take in Lamar's smooth, dark skin. Then gaze at the way his biceps flex as he runs his thick hands through his locks. "I'm more than good. What was done needed—no *had*, to be done. And I *don't* regret it. None of it."

He cups his chin in the palm of his hand, tugging lightly at his close-cut goatee. "That's wasssup. Like I tol' you, the only way to get rid of a snake is to chop its head off."

"And that's *exactly* what I did when I took that bitch's head off." I shift in my chair, crossing my feet at the ankles.

"No doubt. You handled that shit like a real pro."

I toss him a dismissive wave. "Please. I don't know about all that. I simply reacted. And gave that bitch what she had coming to her."

"Yo, I hear you. Still, it was impressive."

An awkward silence fills the space between us. He licks his dark-chocolate lips and, instantly, the memory of what they felt like on my nipples, on my clit, suckling and nibbling, taunting my pussy lips, causes heat to spread through my thighs. Flashes of his hard dick gliding in and out of my throat shoot through my head, triggering a pulsing in my tonsils. I swallow back the lusty thoughts, shifting the flames slowly flickering in my pelvis.

"But dig, Pasha. I wanted to talk you about something serious."

I tilt my head, pressing my legs together. "Okay. I'm listening."

He leans forward, rubbing his chin. "Yo, on some real shit. I think you got serious skills, ma. I dig how you move. You mad classy and real discreet. And you have a lil' street edge to you underneath all that sophistication. On some real shit, my peoples could really use someone like you on his team."

I raise a brow, narrowing my eyes, indignation written all over my face. *How dare this motherfucker!* There's no office decorum for how to address him for coming at me like this. Besides, professionalism went out the window the day I invited him to my home and sucked down his dick, then rode his tongue.

"*Skills?* Your peoples' *team?* Nigga, I *know* you are *not* implying what the hell I think you are? And I don't appreciate you disrespecting me or discussing my…"

He raises his hands, palms out, in mock surrender. "Whoa… hol' up, hol' up, Pasha. Where you going with this?"

I narrow my eyes. "No. Where the hell are *you* going with it? You're sitting here referring to my skills, like I'm taking dick-sucking referrals or some shit. If your *peoples'* is looking to recruit a few good dick suckers for his squad, I am *not* interested. Sucking dick is something I do when I'm in the mood. And being somebody's damn on-call dick sucker will *never* be what the fuck I do."

He grins, then cracks up laughing. "Oh, shit! Damn. You just went in."

My nose flares. "I don't think the shit is funny, Lamar."

He tries to regain his composure. "Yo, my bad, Pasha. But word? You really think I was talking about *those* skills? Nah, ma, I'd never play you like that. Damn. I mean, shit. Yeah, ya skills ain't no joke. Ya head game is serious. Hands down. You most def the truth in that department, but I'm not even talkin' 'bout no shit like that. I wouldn't do you like that, Pasha. C'mon, ma. That's not how I get down. I don't play them kinda games. I can't believe you'd actually think I'd handle you like that."

I relax a bit, tucking a strand of hair behind my ear. "Oh, okay. But those are the only *skills* I know I've shared with you. It's not like I've done your hair. And I haven't cooked for you. So what *other* skills could you possibly be talking about?"

He shakes his head. "I'm talkin' 'bout that work you put in on Sunday, yo. I dig how you handled that situation."

My heart drops. "*You* assured me," I hiss, leaning up in my seat, "the utmost discretion. *No* one can know about that, or anything else. There's a lot at stake here. Do you not understand that? I've put all of my trust in you, Lamar. *Please* don't make me regret it."

He gives me a serious look. The muscles in his jaw tighten. "Yo, hol' up. My word is my bond, Pasha. On my life. Don't ever doubt that shit. I'ma man of my word. One thing I *don't* do is front on anything I say or do. I got *you*. I already know what it is. If you go down, ma—we all go down. And real shit, I ain't goin' down for *you* or anyone else. So, yeah, I know what's at stake. Real shit, e'erything me 'n' my peeps handle is airtight. And what we discuss 'n' *what*ever pops off between us, *stays* between us; period, point blank."

I narrow my eyes at him, taking in his words, studying his posture, his facial expression. Once again, I do not see any signs to cause alarm. I sit back in my seat, breathing out a sigh of relief. "Thanks for those reassuring words. I'm glad we're on the same page."

"We've always been on the same page; from the rip. Which is why I'ma put you onto some real shit. I know a lotta muhfuckas, Pasha. I stay connected to niggas who make shit happen; muhfuckas, like *me*, who know how to make shit disappear; feel me?"

I nod. "I'm listening."

"Right now, my peoples only has one female on his team. And she's bad as fuck, and vicious as shit..."

"Okay, so what does all that have to do with me?"

"It could potentially have e'erything to do with you, if you consider what I'm about to spit at you. No bullshit. You're sexy as fuck, Pasha. And you have a fire inside of you that keeps burning with more intensity. The more that nigga Jasper fucks with you, the hotter that shit seems to get. It's a turn-on. But there's something else about you, ma...."

I fold my arms over my chest, pressing them into my swelling nipples, aching for his tongue, his warm mouth. *Oooh, God, I wanna fuck him.* I blink my gaze away from his lips. "Oh, yeah. What's that?"

"Underneath all that fire and passion and beauty makes you potentially dangerous, ma. Muhfuckas sleep on you. And that shit's what'll get them knocked. 'Cause on some real shit, ma. There's a real killer inside of you. And that, Pasha"—he scoots up in his seat, placing his forearms up on my desk, then licking his lips and clasping his hands together—"is sexy as fuck. The way you move, no one would ever suspect you'd be capable of slumpin' a muhfucka. But you proved you got it in you."

I blink. "*Slumping* Felecia, as you put it, wasn't one of the things on my things-to-do list. Being a"—I lower my voice to a hushed whisper—"*killer* isn't what I've aspired to be."

"Yeah, but you thought it. I saw the fire in ya eyes when you spoke on it. Bodyin' that broad gave you life, didn't it? It gave you an adrenaline rush like no other, didn't it? And"—he snaps his fingers—"just like that, it's what you've become."

"Bitch, you sealed your fate!"

Thrrrssp!

Felecia's bloody mouth, her broken teeth, fragments of her skull and brain matter sweep through my head.

I swallow.

Shift in my seat.

"Felecia got what her hand called for."

"And you can get paid out the ass to handle other muhfuckas who gotta get what their hands call for too."

I furrow my brows. "What exactly are you saying to me?"

He tells me he's down with a "work-for-hire" operation that his peoples' runs. A multimillion-dollar business he operates that handles *waste management*—the elimination of unsuspecting marks through contract hits. That he currently has eighteen *contractors* on his squad. Fierce killers who move in silence, swift and unseen.

"I want you on our team, ma. If you'd like I can set up a meeting wit' you and my peoples. He'd wanna snatch you up wit' a quickness."

"To do what?"

"Body muhfuckas…"

Three

*Be careful what you ask for. The truth is sometimes
more than you can stand…*

"Pasha," Kendra says through the intercom, "there's an Andre on line two for you. He says it's urgent. And my nine o'clock is here, so the front desk will be unattended."

I'm not surprised Felecia's long-term fiancé is calling me. I knew this day would come. Still, I haven't mentally prepared myself to deal with him—or Nana, for that matter, when she starts calling, inquiring about Felecia. Pretending won't be the problem. The anxious, relentless probing will be.

"Okay, thanks," I say, relieved she's interrupted us. I look at Lamar. "We'll have to finish this conversation some other time. I need to take this call."

He stands. "No doubt, baby. I have…"

I hold a finger up at him. "Rule number one. *Unless* I have your dick wrapped between my lips, or your tongue is wedged in between the ones between my legs, *don't* refer to me as *baby*."

He holds his hands up. "My bad. It'll never happen again."

I raise a brow. "Good."

"No doubt." He hands me his backpack. "I almost forgot. This is for you." I give him a quizzical look. "Saturday night's catch."

I nod. That quick, I'd almost forgotten myself. It's the money from Jasper's stash houses burned down over the weekend. They were able to collect from all three spots close to two-hundred-

and-eighty-seven thousand dollars. I lick my lips. "Thanks. I'll have to be sure to *really* thank you later."

I make a mental note to have either him or Mel drive me to the Wells Fargo down the street later today, so I can rent another safe deposit box and stuff my new riches inside—compliments of Jasper.

He grins, heading for the door. "I look forward to it."

Oh, I'm sure you do. I take in the way his muscled-ass sits up on his lower back, the way it fits in his jeans, imagining my nails digging into his dark flesh, urging his big black dick deeper into my throat. Sucking Lamar off is so far proving to be one of my smartest investment moves.

My cell vibrates.

I wait for him to shut the door behind him, then glance at my cell. *I knew I'd hear from you, Stax.* A sly smile inches over my glossed lips. And sucking and fucking him will prove more beneficial than it already has soon enough as well.

I let his call roll over into voicemail, lifting the office phone from the receiver, taking a deep breath. I press line two, going into script. "Heeeeey, Andre. This is a nice surprise. How have you been?" My voice is cheery and light, dripping with sunshine and happiness.

"I'm good," he says in his deep voice. "No complaints. And you?"

"You know how it is here. Busy as always. But I know you're not calling me out the blue for an update on my life. So tell me, Andre. To what do I owe the pleasure of this call?"

"Honestly, I was wondering if you've spoken to Felecia. I know the two of you were supposed to meet on Sunday night."

"No. I haven't spoken to her; well, not since the day she called and agreed to meet me. But she never showed up. I called her twice and didn't hear back from her, so I figured she either changed her mind or something else came up." I feign concern. "Why? Is everything okay?"

He sighs. "Damn. I haven't seen or heard from her since she left the house Sunday night around eight to meet you at the salon." The alarm in his voice causes my chest to tighten. He and Nana will both become sick with worry as the days turn to weeks and weeks become months with still no sign of her. The consequence of my dirty deed. "I don't know what to think, Pasha. I'm really starting to get worried."

Poor thing. I wonder how worried you'd be if you knew the bitch you've been fucking the last five years was a lying, conniving-ass slut.

For some reason a conversation she and I had over dinner drinks at P.F. Chang's comes to mind. She had asked me, again, if I had ever cheated on Jasper while he was locked up. Of course I lied. Told her, "Nope. I have no reason to."

The way the bitch stared at me, like she didn't believe me, like she was on a fishing expedition, should have given me pause to question her. But I'd let it go over my head. She sipped her third Margarita, eyeing me over the salted rim of her glass.

"Girl, good for you. I don't know how you do it. Personally, I'd be pulling my damn hair out if I had to go without sex. I'm sorry. I love Andre. But if his ass ever got locked up, I'd have to have me some dick on-call until he got out. Fuck that. I'm not about to deprive myself of some cock just because a muhfucka can't keep his ass out of the streets to handle his business in the sheets."

I licked the salt from around the rim of my own glass, chuckling. "Well, I'm not saying it's been easy because it hasn't. But with the help of a whole lot of batteries and a collection of toys, I get by."

"Hmmph. Girl, if the shoe were on the other foot, do you actually think Jasper would be so quick to keep his dick in his pants...?"

I should have known then that that bitch was up to no good. I wonder if she had already been going down to South Woods sucking the nut out of Jasper's dick when she was sitting there saying this shit to me.

Here that bitch popped shit about me fucking over a good man when she had a good man of her own right in her own damn bed every night. For as long as I've known Andre, he's been a real easygoing, laid-back, and hard-working man who handled all the bills and made sure she had whatever extra money in her wallet. Not once have I ever known him to disrespect her, or even raise his voice to her. He wasn't a street nigga. But he'd grown up in the hood and survived letting its elements become a part of his life. The nigga had good credit, a job with benefits, and knew how to treat a woman. And that bitch thanks him by fucking Jasper—a nigga who was only using her ass to keep tabs on me.

Stupid bitch!

Andre doesn't drink, smoke, or use drugs. And he's never been arrested, or seen the inside of a jail cell, not even for a traffic violation. He's always been good to her. But that still didn't stop that bitch from cheating on him. Once—that I know of, in Jamaica, during one of our many weekend getaways that *I* fucking paid for. She met him on the beach earlier in the day. Then later that night fucked him. As a matter of fact, the bitch fucked him the whole three days we were there. Then boarded the plane back to the States and acted as if she'd never had her pussy stretched open by some long, thick Blue Mountain cock.

Then there were other times, now that I'm sitting here thinking about it, that that ho would disappear for hours anytime we traveled somewhere, then she'd pop back up out of the blue with her lips all shiny, looking all disheveled. That cock-hopping bitch was a whore, too. Yet, she wanted to pop shit to *me* about fucking over a good man. Bitch, please!

"I figured I'd try you one more time before I called Nana," Andre says, snapping me out of my reverie. Truth is, he'd tried calling me several times yesterday, but I kept letting his calls roll over into voicemail. Now the thought of Nana being dragged into Felecia's disappearance almost makes me wish I hadn't had her body tossed in flames. "I called out from work yesterday and spent all day calling the area hospitals in case something had happened to her..." His voice cracks. "Pasha, I know this might sound kinda fucked up, but I kinda hoped something did happen to her and she was in one of those hospitals. At least I'd know where she was."

I twirl a strand of hair through my fingers. "Andre, I don't know what to tell you. There's no telling where she is. Like I said, I haven't heard from her. And as you know she and I aren't on the best of terms right now."

He sighs. "Yeah. I heard. Which is why I was glad to hear y'all were meeting Sunday to talk things out, feel me? The two of you have been too close to let whatever beefs y'all are having now to come in between you."

I roll my eyes. "Well, she was a no-show, so obviously mending fences wasn't on the top of her things-to-do list. I guess she had something more important to deal with."

"This isn't like her," he mutters, sounding as if he's struggling to keep his emotions in check. "She's never not come home. I think something serious has happened to her."

"Well, good luck with finding her," I say nonchalantly. The need to keep up the act of feeling concerned is wearing thin.

"If by chance you hear from her before I do, can you call me?"

I shake my head. He sounds so pitiful. I'm convinced I've done him a favor getting rid of her ass. "Sure," I say, reaching for the backpack Lamar left for me, and peeking inside. I inhale deeply. The smell of sweet revenge fills my nostrils. I hold it in my lungs, then slowly exhale. "What's your number?" He rattles it off, then says something about calling Nana before calling the police. I cringe. "Well, you take care, Andre. It was good hearing from you."

"Yeah, you too, Pasha."

I prepare to disconnect.

"Uh, Pasha?"

"Yes?"

"Listen. Not that it's any of my business. I know how close you and Felecia were. But what really happened between the two of you?"

"What did she tell you happened?"

"She didn't. She danced around the question. Said something about you believing a bunch of lies some chick told you she supposedly had said about you. But none of it made any sense to me. So I'm hoping you'd tell me."

"Mmmph. Are you sure you really want to know, Andre?"

"Yeah."

"The bitch fucked Jasper."

Four

If not weaved carefully, the web of deception can ensnare even its deceiver…

I place the phone back on its receiver, pulling out my laptop. I turn it on, then wait for it to boot up. A few seconds later, I'm clicking into my server, opening AOL. I log into my Deep Throat Diva email account, and I am immediately alerted that I have new mail. There are three emails. All from MydickneedsUrtongue2.

Immediately, the hairs on the back of my neck go up. I pull in my bottom lip, clicking on his first email. *Yo wat's good witchu? U gonna front on dis dick or gonna be 'bout ya business n be ready to put in dat neck work? Hit a nigga back, yo. I got dis hard dick waitin for u to guzzle up witcha freak ass.*

I roll my eyes. *Thirsty-ass nigga!* I specifically told this asshole when I reached out to him on Sunday that I'd send him an email *this* Thursday to confirm whether or not I'd meet him for what he thinks will be for one of my deep throat specials. But this loony-ass motherfucker too stuck on crazy. Mmmph. Yeah, I have something especially *deep* for his ass all right. But it's damn sure not this throat.

I open his second email. *Yo wat's poppin' witchu? U gonna eat da nut outta dis big dik or wat, yo? Don't get back on da dumb shit. A nigga horny for some'a dat throat. Get at me, yo*

I open the third email. There are two attachments. One is of his hard-ass dick. The other is a video sent from his iPhone. I open it. *Ohmygod!* It's a five-minute video of his nasty-ass stroking his long, black dick. His face isn't shown, just his lower body. And instead of turning it off, I sit and watch it until the very last end when a thick wad of white thick cream shoots out of his dick. I play it again, disturbingly turned on by the way his hand slowly glides up and down as he holds it upward, then back and forth as he points it straight out toward the lens and his nut shoots out like a cannon.

The third time I replay it, I try to convince myself that it's simply to look for any clues that might potentially lead me to him. There are none.

I hit the REPLY button, then type. *Oooh, daddy, yessss! You have that big hood dick! Luv, luv, luv watching you stroke that long, black dick! Thanks for video. Yes, I'm still going to suck the nut out of your big, thick dick. This long throat is wet and ready. I can't wait to have you down in my neck. I'm so ready to suck down more than one round of all of your gooey, thug milk. I'll email you on Thurs. to confirm for sure if I can meet you Fri. night.*

I press SEND, then quickly pull out my cell and call James. He picks up on the third ring. "Hey, you. Good to hear your voice," he says, sounding all cheery. "I haven't forgotten about what we talked about last weekend. I got sidetracked. It's a little crazy around here. I should have everything you need later on this evening."

I roll my eyes. Steady my voice to keep the sarcasm from coming out too thick. "Good." There's another email from Mydickneeds Urtongue2. "I need this handled ASAP. Please, and thank you."

"I promise you, I'm on it."

"I really hope so," I say, opening the email. *I need this nigga shut down quick!* I lower my voice to almost a sultry whisper. "The sooner you handle this for me, James, the sooner I can handle *you*." I tell him this with no real interest, but as a little motivation to light a fire under his horny, cheating ass. Some niggas seem to need an extra push to get shit done when it isn't something important to them. "*If* that's what you still want. Or maybe you can't handle it."

"Oh I want it all right," he says, sounding as if he's ready to shove his dick through the receiver and into my mouth in any second. "Consider it handled."

"Don't keep me waiting, James. Or I'll have to find me someone who can give me what I need."

"Now hold on, baby. Not so fast. I got everything you need right here. Give me until the end of the day."

I disconnect, reading Mydick's email. *Yo, freak u got my dik hard AF!! Make dat shit happen yo. NO BS. Ya heard? Real shit yo. I want you suckin' on my shit now, right now!!! But I'ma wait 'til Friday yo. Do whatever da fuck u gotta do to get dis hard dik! Don't front on me yo!! Dis hard dik needs dat tongue up on it!*

"Oh trust, nigga," I mutter to myself, forming a plan in my head fit for a sick motherfucker like him. "I'm going to do everything I can to get at you. When you least expect it." Shutting my laptop, I slide it in my desk drawer, lock it, then push up from my desk and walk into my bathroom. I take a quick look at my reflection in the mirror, shaking my head. *Fucking Jasper! I fucking hate you for putting me through all of this.*

Bitch, you and your dick sucking is what put your ass in this predicament in the first place!

Whatever!

I run a hand along the nape of my neck. Attempt to knead out the tension coiling around my neck.

We've both made choices. We've both drawn lines in the sand. And we've both crossed them. Now this shit between us has gotten messy.

And it's going to get even messier.

Because of him, I've become this hateful, vicious…now *murderous*…bitch!

Felecia.

One bullet. And it was over. The back of her skull splattered open, her brain a bloody, clumpy mess.

Those niggas bodied in the stash house fires—sons, brothers, fathers, lovers, friends—all casualties caught up in the crossfires.

Shot up.

Burned up.

Dead.

Because of me.

Because of Jasper.

I close my fists tight to keep my hands from shaking.

Bile rises in my throat and I feel the rushing need to vomit.

The realization—the weight of my own actions, the knowing that more than likely, they'll be more bodies dropped before this is all over—causes my stomach to churn. I flip up the toilet seat, and toss my guts up, clutching the sides of the bowl.

Maybe I should rethink this. That's what a part of me fights with. To leave everyone else out of this, so that no one else gets hurt or loses their life for something that really has nothing to do with them. This ugly war is between Jasper and me.

He's the real target.

Yet, there's the other part of me that says they all deserve to get it too. All of them. Every last one of them niggas on Jasper's team made conscious decisions to jump into a fire that had nothing to do with them.

So now they all have to get burned to ash.

I know, even if I wanted to there's no turning back now.

It is the only way poetic justice can be dished out.

It is the only way it will be served.

When I am done throwing up and dry-heaving, I flush the toilet, then walk over to the sink, washing my hands and rinsing out my mouth. I brush my teeth, then rinse, keeping my gaze locked on my reflection in the mirror.

Despite flying all night, despite trying to deal with all of these conflicting emotions, my face, my eyes, defy what's really going on in my heart and head.

I sigh, fussing with a few strands of stray hair, then shut off the light and head out into the front area of the salon. I honestly feel like I'm spinning in a vicious wheel of tit-for-tat.

I suck dick behind Jasper's back. Jasper finds out. He feels betrayed, which he was. Feels hurt, which he should. Then becomes vindictive.

And now I am retaliating.

The wheel is spinning fast.

We are both playing a far more dangerous game than Russian roulette.

It's a game of vengeance.

In the end, I can only wonder who'll really win.

"Pasha Nivea Allen, will you marry me?"

"Yes, baby."

"I'm givin' you my heart, Pasha. Whatever you do, don't play me, yo."

"I promise, baby. I won't."

But I did.

And now look at us. Look what we've become.

Two warring ex-lovers hell-bent on destroying the other.

Shaking the thought of what used to be from out of my head, I take a deep breath and finally step into the spotlight, smiling, pretending—already plotting my next move.

Five

Sometimes it's the ones you love who hurt you the most...

At a quarter to three in the afternoon, Booty comes strutting into my office in all of her dramatic ghetto-fabulousness. I haven't seen or spoken to her since Saturday when she came in to get her hair done. She shuts the door behind her, bringing in with her one of her signature scents, Viva La Juicy by Juicy Couture.

"Yes, *FahverGawd*, we got shit to do, Miss Pasha, girl. And the clock is tickin', sugah-boo." She claps her hands together for emphasis. "Tick-tock, tick-tock. Where you been? I couldn't get ahold of you for the last two days."

I tell her I had some last-minute business to handle out in L.A. There's no need for her or anyone else to know that I've temporarily moved Jaylen out there until this shit with Jasper is over with. Or until Jasper drags me into court for visitation and I'm court-ordered to return him. I know what I've done by relocating Jaylen to California without Jasper's permission, since he is his father, could technically be considered criminal under different circumstances. But, given what's rapidly unfolded over the last week, my actions are justified.

She twists her lips, taking a seat in one of the chairs across from me. "And you ain't think to return any of my calls, either, huh?" She rolls her eyes, tossing her thirty-eight hundred-dollar Marine monogram tote bag in the chair next to her. The bag came out in 2011 and is hard to come by now as it's a limited-edition piece. But this hood diva comes in here with it draped in the crook of her arm. She tosses her bang from over her left eye, peering at me. "You need to get ya mind right, Miss Pasha, girl."

"That Louis bag is sharp," I say, changing the subject. Flattery always sidetracks this attention whore. "I am so hating you right now."

She waves me on, crossing her legs. "Oh, this old thang. Sugah-boo, you know how I do it. I had to pull out a classic 'n' give it to these thirsty coon-bitches real good today. You know these low-budget bitches ain't used to no high-end, exclusive shit."

I shake my head. "You're a real mess."

"But I ain't ever messy, sugah-boo."

"Unh-huh." *Chile, please! If you wanna keep believing that lie, then go right on ahead.* "So what'd you end up doing over the weekend?"

She smacks her glossed lips. "Well, I ain't get me no damn ding-aling, that's for sure. Miss Pasha, girl, I had to take me a quick road trip down to D.C."

"Oh, I'm sure that must have been a nice little ride."

She grunts. "Nice my ass. Not with a buncha bad-ass kids who can't sit they asses still 'n' goddamn quiet for less than two seconds. Next time I'm flyin'."

I chuckle.

"Miss Pasha, girl. That ride tore my drawz."

She tells me she drove down to Howard University to visit her son Da'Quan. He's either her third or fourth child out of her ten kids, I think. She simply has too damn many to try to keep up with. But what I do know is, he's in his third year of college trying to make something out of himself.

"Miss, Pasha, girl, that dark-chocolate nigga was stressin' me out so bad 'bout not comin' to see him that I had to finally roll me a blunt 'n' get my mind right. That lil' nigga gets real crazy when he don't see me when he wants to. And I ain't want him comin' home for the weekend 'round none of these niggah-coons. So to shut his ass up, I packed up the kids and we all took that long-ass drive down there to see my baby with his big-dick self. He better be glad I had just come in 'n' got my hair did on Saturday or he woulda been shit outta luck. But you did me right, goddammit. And you know I had to go up on campus 'n' turn it up a taste."

"Oh, Lord. I'm scared to ask. What'd you do?"

"Sugah-boo, we ain't gonna get into all that. All I'm say is, I thought I was gonna have'ta step outta my heels 'n' take it to one of them lil' nigga-boos' heads 'cause her lil' boyfriend was tryna holla. I tol' that ho, 'Booga coon, *boom!* Sit yo' young hot-ass down somewhere.' Shit, Miss Pasha, girl, you know this booty shake keeps all the niggas' stompin' on the yard. They better be glad I was keepin' it classy 'n' I had the twins with me, otherwise, I woulda turnt up the flames real right. I woulda popped this booty heat up on one'a them young dingdongs 'n' sucked him right on up in the fire."

I laugh, shaking my head as my cell rings. I hold a finger up, answering the call. "What do you want, Jasper?"

The fact that I have a temporary restraining order on this nigga still doesn't faze him one bit. And the *only* reason I'm accepting any of his calls instead of ignoring them is because Lamar suggested I do. He reasoned it's always better to keep the lines of communication open, even if a restraining order is dangling in front of him.

"Where the fuck is my muthafuckin' whip, yo?! You really muthafuckin' testin' me, Pasha. And *don't* fuckin' lie, yo. What the fuck you do wit' my shit?"

Last night, while I was at the airport waiting to board my flight, I got a call from one of Lamar's *night watchers* who's been keeping tabs on Jasper's every move. Jasper made it very clear that he has eyes everywhere. And *now*…so do I.

So when I got the call that he was over in East Orange on South Arlington at some random bitch's house, I called Lamar and asked him to have his people tow his shiny SL550 Benz. I wanted it towed away before the sun came up. I didn't have to use Booty's connect she'd given me last week. Lamar handled it for me with no problem. So far, the way he's been handling everything else.

Even this pussy.

"Yo what the fuck is really good wit' you, Pasha, huh? You really tryna escalate this shit, right? Is that what you tryna do, huh? You still think I'm playin', right? You keep testin' me, Pasha, real shit. You really think a muhfucka won't get at you, don't you?"

"Is that another one of your threats, Jasper?"

"Yo, fuck outta here! Take that shit however you wanna. You should know by now I don't make threats. I make promises. You fuckin' really feelin' ya'self now, right? You think I give a fuck about bein' behind the wall, huh? I'll eat that shit. Now where's my fuckin' whip, yo?"

"I had it towed. *That's* where it is."

"Yo, what the fuck you do that shit for?"

"Jasper. Do I need to remind you that I have a restraining order against you? And technically I shouldn't be talking to you?"

"Yo, fuck outta here, yo. I'm callin' you 'bout my shit, yo. Fuck a restrainin' order. Don't fuckin' play me, Pasha. I want my muth-afuckin' shit! You hear me, yo?"

"That's too bad. Because you're not getting it."

"Whaaat?! What the fuck you mean, I ain't gettin' my shit? Don't have me bust yo' ass, Pasha. And where's my muthafuckin' son at, yo? I wanna see him. And why the fuck he ain't been at daycare, yo?"

Booty eyes me, folding her arms across her chest and twisting her lips. She flicks imaginary dirt from beneath her fingernail, clearly bored.

"Jasper, we have court on Friday morning at nine. You did get the memo, right?"

He sucks his teeth. "Yeah, I got that shit. What the fuck that got to do wit' anything, yo?"

"Anything you want to know, ask in front of the judge when we go for the final restraining order hearing."

"Oh, so you really gonna keep this shit on me, right?"

I frown. "Jasper, you *can't* be serious. Of course I am. Nigga, I'm done with you. And thanks to you, Jasper, I am *not* putting up with any more of your shit. That Benz, the one *I* own—in *my* name. And the house, again, in *my* name—is mine, free and clear. I have the title and the deed, in my name. And the day you thought it was okay to walk up in here and toss me around, you lost all rights and privileges to either."

The nigga starts screaming on me, like a lunatic. I pull my ear away from the phone.

Booty huffs, rolling her eyes up in her head. "Look, Miss Pasha, girl. Tell that nigga-coon to eat the inside of ya ass cheeks, then hang up on his black ass, goddammit! He's givin' me a goddamn headache 'n' I ain't the one on the phone with his no-good coon-ass. Ole stank motherfucka."

"Look, Jas—"

Booty reaches over and snatches the phone away from me, shocking the shit out of me. Boundaries, as always, are clearly nonexistent for her. "Nigga-bitch, stop motherfuckin' harrassin' Miss Pasha. She's done with your sneaky, lyin' ass. She said she gonna see ya no-good ass in court. So, boom, nigga-coon, boom! See her in court! Puttin' yo' goddamn hands on her. Is you crazy, nigga-bitch? You ain't no real nigga. Real niggas don't beat on no high-end classy bitch. They fight a hood bitch who ain't scared to sit in the county jail for knockin' ya goddamn eyeballs in." She hits the END button, handing me back my cell. She sits back in her chair like nothing ever happened. "There. Motherfuck that coon!"

I blink. Open my mouth to say something. My phone starts ringing again. It's Jasper calling back.

Booty puts a hand up. "Don't do it, sugah-boo. Fuck that nigga-bitch. You got a restrainin' order on his ass, so it ain't shit else to talk about. Fuck chitchat. Fuck tryna argue with that coon-nigga. It's a wrap for his ass. You gonna see him in court. You said you done with his ass, so be done. It's time to get down 'n' dirty, Miss Pasha, girl. Not tomorrow, not next week...*now*, goddammit!"

She pulls out her phone and starts scrolling through it.

"We still gotta get that nigga-coon, *L*, handled. And I spoke to Dickalina's old dizzy ass 'n' she said that coon's real name is Legend. Then we gotta do that AJ nigga. Now if you stay focused, Miss Pasha, girl, 'n' keep the fire lit under ya ass, we should be able to have them two nigga-coons down on they backs by the end of the week. Then the rest of these niggas should be shut down by next week. I'ma let my kids stay with they *fahvers* for the rest of the week, so I ain't gotta worry 'bout rushin' home. It's time, goddammit! So who's first? That nigga-coon AJ? Wait. Ain't you s'posed to be seein' that bitch, Miss FeFe, soon?"

I quickly dart my eyes from hers. Land them on the bookcase, the space where Felecia was thrown. The image of her being swung into the case flashes through my head. My fists, my feet, pounding her face and body; my anger toward her swelling in each punch, in each stomp.

"*...You always somewhere tryna act like you so much fucking better than me when you're the one who was out there sucking all kinds of different niggas' dicks in dark alleys and fucking abandoned buildings and wherever else you could go to drop down on your slutty-ass knees....*

"*Bitch! You want the fucking truth? Then here it is raw and uncut: I love you. But I fucking hate you more! And, yes, I sucked Jasper's dick! There, you satisfied! I sucked his dick, okay! Why? Because I fucking wanted to! You didn't fucking deserve a nigga like him! Bitch, you had it good. Jasper gave you anything you wanted, and that shit still wasn't enough for you. You still went and shitted on him. It's always about you, bitch! Pasha this, Pasha, that! The fly bitch who always gets what she wants. Who always gets all the right niggas eating outta the palm of her goddamn hands!*

"*And bitches like me, who know how to treat a good man, gotta stand on the sidelines and watch bitches like you fuck over all the good men. You fucking slutted yourself out on Jasper and that nigga still wanted you...!*"

I blink, bringing my focus back to Booty. "I was supposed to see her Sunday. But she never showed up." The lie rolls off my tongue with ease. My heartbeat doesn't even skip a beat as the words float out of my mouth. "I left her two messages and I still haven't heard back from her. That bitch had me sitting around here waiting for her dumb ass."

Booty grunts, shifting in her seat. "Mmmph. Stink bitch. Don't worry. We gonna do her stank-ass real good 'n' goddamn dirty. I'ma get Day'Asia and Dickalina's daughters, Clitina and Candy, to gang-bang her face in wit' they fists. They gonna give that ole messy booga-coon bitch a new face by the time they finish with her ole man-sharin' ass. Miss FeFe messy like them ole whorin' triplet cousins of yours, but she stayed talkin' shit about 'em 'n' she doin' the same damn thing. Mmmph. I can't stand no messy bitch."

I blink. "Cassandra, listen. Leave my cousins out of this. They have nothing to do with Felecia's shit. That bitch snaked me."

I unlock my desk drawer, then open it and pull out the folded sheet of paper from earlier. I slide it over to her. "But let's focus on these two niggas here. The two names underlined are the niggas who snatched me up from the mall."

"See. Now you talkin' my talk, goddammit! Let's serve 'em, sugah-boo. Let's take it to they goddamn skulls."

She reaches for the folded paper, then opens it. She glances at the underlined names. She squints. Blinks. Then blinks, again. She grabs her neck. Her mouth drops open. Every ounce of color in her caramel-colored face leaches out. I've never known Booty to look shook about anything. She looks as if she's seen a ghost as shock and horror register on her face.

She lets go of the paper, causing it to flutter back onto the desk. "Nooo, *FahverGawd, noooo*, goddammit!" Her voice fades in and out. She holds her head in her hands, shaking her head. "Fuck. Fuck. Fuck. *FahverGawd*, nooooo… this can't be right. *Fahver-Gawd*, I know you ain't gonna do me like this, goddammit! Don't do me, *FahverGawd*."

"Cassandra, what is it?"

She peers up at me. "I-I… think I know who one of these niggas is."

My eyes widen. "Which one?"

"*Jah*," she whispers, leaning forward, grabbing her chest as she points to the name on the paper. Her gaze drops back to the sheet of paper. She shuts her eyes and starts rocking and hyperventilating. "Oh *FahverGawd*, nooooo! For the love of big black dingaling, this gotta be a mistake. This shit can't be true. Are you sure, Miss Pasha, girl? I *need* you to be absolutely positive, goddammit."

I nod. "Yes. I'm very sure. It came from a reliable source." I decide not to mention my visit with Stax last Saturday night, or that I've sucked him and had my pussy smeared all up on his lips—that piece of information isn't any of her concern. Besides, the less she knows, the better. She and I may be in an alliance, but that doesn't mean I trust her to keep her mouth shut about every-thing.

She starts heaving. "Please, *FahverGawd*, no! Why you tryna do me, goddammit?!"

"Cassandra, tell me. Who is he?"

Her lips quiver. "I t-t-think that n-n-nigga-coon's my son. *Jah'Mel*."

I fall back in my chair, feeling everything in the room start to spin.

Six

The difference between friends and foes, you always know who your enemies are…

It takes me a few minutes to pull myself together, so that I can digest what's come out of Booty's mouth—that *her* twenty-one-year-old son, *Jah'Mel*, is possibly one of the niggas who kidnapped me.

I'm literally shocked beyond words.

Feeling sick to my stomach, I race into the bathroom, clutching the toilet bowl as I toss up this morning's yogurt and fruit salad. When I'm done, I flush the toilet, wash my face and hands, then rinse out my mouth.

I glance up at my reflection in the mirror. *Ohmygod! I can't believe this shit! What kind of niggas would be okay with getting involved in kidnapping and sexually assaulting someone?*

Ruthless niggas who don't have any regard for anyone else, niggas without a conscience who simply don't give a fuck; that's who!

Then again… How does what I've done so far make me any different from any of them? No matter how I justify it, after all the dicks I've sucked, the lies I've told, I'm no less grimy than Jasper. And, now, after killing Felecia and having those stash houses robbed and set on fire, I'm clearly capable of being equally as ruthless.

I sigh, running my hands through my hair. *This shit is getting crazier by the minute.*

I brush my teeth, then take a deep breath and walk back out into my office. I buzz out front. When Anna, one of my nail technicians who's covering the front desk answers, I tell her to please hold all of my calls and that I am not available for any walk-ins, then hang up.

"I need me a goddamn blunt," Booty says, rummaging through her handbag. "I'm so fuckin' sick, Miss Pasha, girl. I heard you in there throwin' up your guts. I feel like I'm 'bout to have the shits, my stomach's so tore up. I can't believe this. I don't wanna believe it. No, no, not Jah'Mel. That nigga-bitch wouldn't do me like this. Yeah, he might not pay his child support. And his ass might even drive on the revoked list 'cause the nigga stays gettin' his license suspended. But I know goddamn well I ain't spread open my legs 'n' push that long-dick nigga-bitch outta my cootie-coo for him to become some motherfuckin' kidnapper. I woulda aborted his ass if I woulda known this is how he was gonna do me. Oh, *Fahver-Gawd*, for the love of sweet black dingaling, I know you ain't gonna do me like this. I know you tryna learn me for slicin' off that nigga-coon's dingaling. But you know he was tryna do me, *Fahver?* You know I ain't have no other choice but to shut him down." I eye her as she shakes her head, having a personal conversation with herself. "No, no, no, no…I know he ain't do me like this, Miss Pasha, girl…"

I feel bad for her. But the shit she's going through at this very moment is not my concern. He's a grown-ass man. The nigga knew right from wrong and made his choice, as we all have. And now, son or not, he has to get it, too.

But how he gets it is another story.

Truth is, I have no real plan. And never really thought out what I would do to the niggas who snatched me from the mall if I ever found out who they were. Or what I'd ever do to The Calm One if I found him. The only niggas I've focused on were the ones down in that basement shoving their dicks down in my throat, cumming in my mouth, in my face, disrespecting me. And the nigga who had been harassing me, calling me here at the salon with his threatening and condescending voice, threatening me, doing whatever he could to make my life a living hell. Then attacking me in my own yard.

He had become a thorn in my side. I had fleeting thoughts of how to dispose of his menacing ass if I ever found out who he was. I imagined myself, setting him up, agreeing to suck his dick since that's what he was so pressed for, then thrusting a blade up into his balls. Sometimes I'd imagine taking a scalpel and slicing off his dick. I still might.

"You sucking this dick?"

"I told you…Hell. Fucking. No!"

"I guess having the back window of your whip knocked out of that fancy whip of yours still isn't enough, is it, ho?"

"Fuck, you!"

"Yeah, like how I'm gonna fuck that throat of yours. I'ma call every day. And I'ma ask you the same shit. And every time you say no, I'ma give your dumb ass something to remember me by…"

Yeah, that dirty nigga definitely has it coming to him. Until then, the minute I learn of his whereabouts, I'm going to toy with him, tease him. Keep him wanting and waiting. Then when he least expects it, I'm going to swoop down on him the way he did me.

In the still of the night.

Caught off guard.

I reflect back on the memory of him acting all thirsty when I sent him an email last Sunday, telling him I wanted to reach out and touch, suck, lick that dick. I could practically see him nutting on himself at the idea of getting some of this throat work. Little does he know, it's all a ploy to reel him in. Then do him in.

Yeah, dirty motherfucker. This just in: By the time I'm done with you, you're going to wish you'd never fucked with me!

"I can't find my shit," Booty says, cutting into my thoughts. I glance at her. She takes a deep breath, placing her hands in her face, shaking her head. She takes a moment, then looks up at me. "Why this nigga do me like this?"

I try to keep my face expressionless. But I feel like snapping, "Bitch, he didn't do shit to *you!* I'm the one he snatched up. I'm the one he hit upside the head with a gun. I'm the one who got tossed inside the back of a van, driven to some unknown destination, then dragged down to a basement, kept tied up until they were ready to force me to suck their dicks. So stop talking about how the nigga done did *you.* The only thing he's done to *you* is, embarrass your ass!"

Let it go, Pasha. Let this bitch have her victim moment. I bite the inside of my cheek, getting up and walking over to the locked closet door. I unlock it, pulling out a CANCUN shot glass and another bottle of RÉMY xo that I'd been given as a gift from one of my clients last year. The bottle hasn't been opened, yet. But seeing Booty all broke down is cause to crack it open. She obviously needs something to soothe her.

I pour her a drink and hand it to her, sitting the bottle next to her. "Here, take this. Maybe it'll help calm your nerves a bit."

"Sugah-boo, I got me a long throat. I'ma need me somethin' a lil' bigger to coat the back of this neck—after this shit right here. But, thanks."

She tosses it back before I can even get back in my chair good. She reaches for the bottle and pours herself another shot.

"I can't believe that nigga-bitch would do some shit like this. Kidnappin'? Mmmmph. That nigga-coon done lost his mother-fuckin', goddamn mind." She looks up at me, then tosses her drink back.

"Cass, girl, I'm sorry you had to find out that he was a part of this shit."

She pours another drink. "*You?* Shit, this done tore my drawz down to the seams." She takes a deep breath, looking up at the ceiling. "No, *FahverGawd*. I don't wanna believe this shit." She brings her attention back to me, shaking her head. "Miss Pasha, girl, I ain't raise his ass to be caught up in no grimy shit like kidnappin'. I raised him in a clean, good goddamn home.

"No, I ain't do a whole buncha prayin' 'n' maybe I shoulda did a lil' more huggin' 'n' a lot less beatin' his ass. But I ain't ever abandon his ass, neglect his ass, or goddamn abuse his ass. So he ain't got no excuse for doin' some coon-nigga shit like this. I'ma beat his skull in, goddammit! This nigga-coon done embarrassed me, Miss Pasha, girl." She starts digging through her bag again. "Ooooh, where's my motherfuckin' stash? I know I packed me a lil' somethin' in this goddamn bag. I need me a lil' get-right to ease the ache in my damn bones. This nigga done cut me deep."

I watch as she dumps the contents of her bag out onto her lap. I blink, surprised at the things that come toppling out: a can of mace, brass knuckles, a sleek chrome pistol, a bottle of Platinum Wet, and a butt plug.

I'm too through!

I think to ask her about her essentials but decide not to. *It's none of my business.* "Cass, are you sure this *Jah* is your son? I mean, it could be someone else with the same name," I reason, taking in the pained expression on her face.

"No, Miss Pasha, girl. Ain't no other nigga 'round here goin' by *Jah*'cept for Jah'Mel Theopolous Goddamn-Simms. I don't wanna think it's him. I swear I don't."

She pours herself another drink, then guzzles it down. "I've always tried to do right by my kids, goddammit. Yeah, I did a lil' boostin' here 'n' there to keep my fashion up when I ain't really have my stacks 'n' sponsors up. And, yeah, I even had me a lil' credit card hustle goin' for a hot minute. I even pussy-popped these hips up on tables when I had to. But I ain't never teach my kids to be no goddamn criminals."

I blink. *Is this bitch serious right now?*

"I've laid on my back 'n' dropped down on my knees to keep a roof over my kids' heads. And, yeah, I done some shit that I prolly shouldn't be proud of. But guess what? I ain't livin' with regret 'n' I'm damn sure not fuckin' with guilt. I did whatever I had to do, by choice, goddammit. I ain't *never* let none'a my kids be without *shit*. I ain't ever let 'em be homeless, or hungry. And this is how Jah'Mel do *me?* He out there kidnapping bitches. I feel like that nigga-bitch done sliced me in the face with a rusty goddamn blade."

I don't know what to say to her, so I don't say shit. I figure it's best to let her talk it all out before we move on. I glance at the clock on my wall, relieved that I have another two hours before my appointment gets here.

"Cass, I know you're hurt, girl. If this is your son, what he did—what all of them niggas did—was dead wrong."

She pours herself another drink, this time filling the shot glass all the way up to the rim. She leans forward and slurps some down to keep it from spilling over, then lifts the glass to her lips and slings it back. I can tell by the glassy look in her eyes that the brown elixir is working its magic, making her more relaxed.

"Miss Pasha, girl. Tell me what them niggas who snatched you at the mall did to you, so I can get my mind wrapped around it. I need to know e'ery-goddamn-thing. Don't hol' ya drawz back on me either, Miss Pasha, girl. Peel 'em all the way back so I can see it raw."

She asks if I can remember anything about the two niggas who snatched me that night. I close my eyes, tightly, recollecting every conscious moment of that night. Starting with the phone call from Jasper as I walked out of the mall toward the parking garage with him asking me if I was still at the mall, telling me how horny he was, telling me to hurry home, then to my head being yanked back and the click of a gun being pressed against my temple.

I replay in vivid, excruciating detail how one of the niggas punched me in the mouth and the other nigga in back of me pressed a blade up under my throat and told me he was gonna slice my fucking throat. The haunting memory spills over into being gagged and bound and blindfolded, riding in the back of a vehicle, then being dragged out by two other niggas.

I blink Booty back into view as she's pouring herself another drink. Her sixth shot. She tosses it back. "Aaah!" She shakes her head. "Yes, goddammit. Miss Remy is doin' me right, Miss Pasha, girl. I needed me a lil' bit of this dark 'n' lovely devil juice to help get me together right quick. Now I can think straight, sugah-boo." She closes her eyes and shakes her head from side to side. "Yes, gawd, I feel it heatin' my bones." She opens her eyes, fixing her gaze on me. "Miss Pasha, girl, did them niggas really take it to your head out there in that parking lot?"

I nod, wincing from the memory.

"I need you to tell me, Miss Pasha, girl. Did you see what them nigga-coons looked like before they dragged you into that van?"

It looks like she's holding her breath as she waits for my response.

I shake my head. Tell her they were both wearing black ski masks, and that they were both tall, like six-two, six-three. That one of them was taller than the other. I tell her I remember one of them having a deep voice.

She bites her bottom lip. I can tell she's still genuinely all broken up over the information I've shared, over the possibility of her son having been involved—even though I know she's trying hard not to show it.

"Cassandra, if it's true that it really is your son, how do you wanna handle?"

She narrows her eyes. Clenches her teeth. "I pray to *gawd*, it's not him, Miss Pasha, girl. But, he's the only nigga I know in the streets called *Jah*. So I know it's him. I know it in the pit of my cootie-coo, it's his black ass. So, I'm sorry, Miss Pasha, girl. That nigga-coon gotta get it like e'ery goddamn body else. *If* Jah'Mel had his goddamn hands in any part of what happened to you, then…" She takes a deep breath. I can tell she's fighting back tears. "We gonna have'ta do his ass good, Miss Pasha, girl. But you ain't wanna kill 'im, did you?"

She twists in her seat.

I close my eyes, then slowly open them, shaking my head. "No, girl. I don't want anyone else's blood…" I pause, catching myself. Hoping she doesn't catch the almost slip-up. She seems too distressed over not having a blunt tucked in her bag to have noticed. I press on, "I don't want anyone else getting killed. Maimed, *yes*. Beat up real bad, *yes*. But nothing more than that—unless someone tries to take it there."

She nods slowly. Her chest heaves in and out. She reaches for the bottle again, pouring herself another drink. I watch as she swishes it around in her mouth, then swallows. "Thank you, *Fahver-*

Gawd! I'm glad you ain't wanna take his life, Miss Pasha, girl. I don't know if I coulda cosigned no shit like that. But I'ma kill the nigga-coon for you."

I gasp. "Cass, killing him isn't going to solve anything. You already have one bod…" I stop myself from saying the rest. There's no need to mention JT's murder.

"And I'ma 'bout to have me another one on these hands in a minute. I brought that nigga-bitch into this world. And I'ma be the one to takes his black ass outta it; the minute his black-ass get outta the county, I'ma welcome his no-good ass home with a hometown beatdown."

She wipes a single tear that falls from her eyes.

"Cass, you don't have to do this, girl. This is *my* fight. Not yours. You've already done enough. Hell, you're the one who struck the match under my ass to finally make shit pop. Your son can be spared. All I want him to do is tell me everything he knows about that night."

"No, Miss Pasha, girl. I won't stand for it. That nigga gets it, too. Son or no goddamn son, what he done did is…oooh, I need to roll me a blunt to get my mind right, goddammit. That nigga done got my drawers twisted 'round the inside of my ass."

She tosses everything back into her bag. I can tell she's fighting back her tears. Something I've never seen before. "I don't know what I'ma do, right now. I'ma do my best to keep it classy. But I wanna swoop down on his ass like he did you. Then learn him goddamn good! What he did was messy. And you *know* I don't do messy. I promise you, Miss Pasha, girl, I'ma peel the skin off that nigga-coon the minute he gets out. And when I'm done with him, he's gonna wish he ain't ever lay his goddamn eyes, hands, or anything else on you. I'ma do his ass up right, goddammit."

She hops up and starts pacing the floor, punching a fist into the palm of her hand. "And I hope he ain't have his dingaling in ya throat, Miss Pasha, girl. Please tell me he ain't skull-fuck you like the rest of them niggas did you."

I shake my head. Tell her no.

"Thank you, *FahverGawd!* I don't know what I woulda did if you woulda had ya lips wrapped 'round his dingaling, Miss Pasha, girl. Oooh, I wanna fight that nigga-bitch. I'm ready to bust his eye sockets outta his goddamn head. I wanna sling that nigga into the streets 'n' fight that coon good. Yes, gawd! He done tore his motherfuckin' drawz with me, goddamn him! Let's go bail his black ass outta jail, so we jump on his ass *tonight*, Miss Pasha, girl."

I won't lie. Cassandra getting hyped to set it off tonight has me practically sitting on the edge of my seat, leaning forward. I feel blood and heat rushing through my body. Shit is really moving, fast!

I still haven't been able to digest everything that's already transpired over the last week. I need to think. I take a few deep breaths to calm myself. I tell her tonight's too soon. That we can't move hastily. That we can't move impulsively off of emotions. Or we'll get sloppy.

She glances over at the sheet of paper still on my desk, tossing another drink back.

"Cass, really, you *don't* have to do this. I'd understand."

She shoots me a look. "Oh, noo, sugah-boo. He wanna be 'bout that life, then he gotta get a taste of his own damn medicine. I done tol' you I ain't raise his ass to be no shiesty nigga." She digs in her bag, pulling out her compact. She takes out a tube of lipstick, then glides a coat over her lips.

"Miss Pasha, girl, I can't even think straight right now. I'ma go home and roll me a blunt, feed my kids 'n' get them ready for school tomorrow." She tosses her compact back into her bag, letting it hang in the crook of her arm. "Then I'ma go out for a taste 'n' have me a few goddamn drinks. And if I'm lucky, I'ma be ridin' down on some good hard wee-wee to beat the stress outta this cootie-coo. Then maybe my mind'll be right."

"Umm, Cass." I sit on the edge of my desk. Think before I speak. Knowing how she can go from zero to hundred in a blink of an eye, I choose my words carefully. "I need to trust that everything that is said between us, stays between us."

She gives me an annoyed look, planting a hand up on her hip. "Oh, no, Miss Pasha, girl. Don't do me. I got loose lips for some good damn dingaling. My lips ain't ever been loose for no gossip. You know I ain't messy. But I see you tryna say I am. You stay tryna do me. And *I'm* the bitch who has your back. *I'm* the bitch ready to roll up on every nigga-bitch who did you dirty, even my own goddamn son. *I'm* ready to take it to his skull for you, goddammit, Miss Pasha, girl." Her voice starts to crack. "And you standin' here with your dick-suckin' ways tryna tear my drawz down to the seams."

I take a deep breath.

"Booty, I mean, Cassandra, girl, I know you have my back. And I appreciate that. I mean, it's a little unexpected. But it really means a lot."

"Uh-huh. Then why you tryna stand here and do me, Miss Pasha, girl? Standin' here sayin' I'm messy. You better go back through your newsfeeds and get your facts straight. Ain't shit messy 'bout Booty, sweetness."

"That's not what I'm saying, girl. Maybe it didn't come out right. All I want to ensure is that you exercise discretion at all times, that's all."

"Sugah-boo," she says, slinging her bag over her shoulder and tossing her bang over her forehead. "Like I *said*, I don't flap my gums for nothing but dingdong 'n' cream... like *you*." She gives me a look, raising an arched brow for effect. "So instead of tryna do me, let's start doin' them niggas who had you gaggin' on they goddamn dicks. Now like I said earlier, it's Wednesday. I wanna have all these nigga-coons shut down by the end of next week. We ain't got no time for games."

I give her an incredulous look. "Now wait one minute, Cassandra. I beg your pardon, hon. I know you're upset and all, but you need to pump your damn brakes. The last time I checked, Miss Thing, *this* was *my* fight. Not yours. So if you're not happy with the way I'm handling things, then fall back and stay out of it."

"Sugah-boo, *boom!* I ain't ask you for no goddamn pardon, *hon*. And I ain't givin' none out. I'm *tellin'* you to get ya mind right, goddammit. And I ain't fallin' back from shit. Not when my son done got his coon-ass all wrapped up into kidnappin' dick-suckin' bitches."

She opens the door and flounces her ass out, as my phone rings, leaving me standing in the middle of my office, speechless, wondering how the hell I got entangled in her messy-ass web of drama. And how the hell I'll ever get out of it.

In one damn piece.

Seven

There's no turning back, no way of rewinding time.
Once it's over, it's over...

"Hey," I say the minute Stax picks up. It's a little after three in the afternoon. I finished up my two o'clock about five minutes ago. Now I'm in my office, shoes off, stretched out across my sofa, with the door closed. "I got your message. What's going on?"

"Cool. How you?"

"I'm okay. Your message said you needed to talk to me."

"Yeah, yeah. I wanted to check on you; that's all. You know. Make sure you aiight."

"And?"

He sighs. "C'mon, Pash. Why can't I just be checkin' on you?"

"You can. But if that were the case, Stax, you would have said that in your message. But you didn't. So, again, *and?*"

"Aiight, aiight, real shit. You right. I called for another reason *and* to check on you."

"Mmmph. I knew it. So what is the reason?"

"Before you start snappin', hear me out, aiight?"

I sigh. "I'm listening."

"Yo, I just left Jasp 'n' he's buggin' real hard 'n' shit."

"Oh well. What does that have to do with me?"

"For the last two days, he's been beatin' me in the head to holla at you."

I frown, feeling my attitude kick up a notch. "For *what?*"

"He wanted me to try to get you to let him see his son 'n' try'n convince you to drop the restrainin' order on him, but I been kinda avoidin' it; feel me?"

I roll my eyes. "And what does he think having you talk to me is going to accomplish?"

"He wants to get back home, nah mean? He wants to see his son. That nigga's poppin' mad shit, but I know he misses his family, Pash. But you really got him goin' through it."

I let out a sarcastic laugh. "Oh, really? Exactly when is he *going through* it, Stax? Before, during or *after* he's fucking his whore over on South Arlington?"

"That shit ain't 'bout nothin', Pash. Jasp's head's all fucked up. He's all over the place. I know my fam, Pash. That nigga…*loves* you. Despite all'a the shit y'all put each other through, you the only woman he's ever loved, yo."

I scoff. "Oh, please, Stax. Love hell. Yeah, he loves me all right. He loves me so much that he'd stage a kidnapping, have me tied up in a basement, have me repeatedly sexually assaulted, then come down and beat me half-to-death, then have niggas toss me out in a park half-naked in the middle of the fucking night. Yeah, that sure sounds like *love* to me. Yup. Jasper loves me enough to hire niggas to shoot at me, make threats to have me killed, and rape me anytime I refuse to give his ass some pussy. Yeah, Stax. You're right. I'm so *loved* by his crazy, sick ass."

"Pash, I checked him on that shit; real shit. He knows he's fucked up. That nigga don't think straight when it comes to you. It's all or nothing with him. He gets mad reckless."

"Mmmph. Well, that's his problem. I'm done. So you can tell him I said he *can't* see his son. And I'm *not* dropping shit. Whatever shit he's going through, he put it on himself. He should have thought long and hard about all of that *before* he did what he's done. After he found out I was out there sucking dick behind his back, he should have beat my ass real good, or fucking packed his shit and left me.

"But, nooooo. The nigga gets all psycho on me, threatening to kill my unborn baby—the *son* he now claims to love so much. Then he threatens to have my grandmother harmed if I ever tried to leave him, rat on him, or play him again. The nigga forced me to marry him, Stax, then turned around and made my life a living a hell. Did you know that?"

"What the fuck?" he mutters. "Nah. I didn't."

"Well, now you do. So, no, I'm not dropping shit. Jasper's black ass can get rolled in gasoline, then dropped in a pit of fire for all I care." I pause, swiveling back and forth in my chair. "Speaking of fires, wasn't it tragic what happened to those three houses that got burned to the ground last weekend?"

"I'd rather not talk about that," he says solemnly.

The tone in his voice confirms what I already knew. I'd hit them hard. Shook up their little playhouse. If he's going through it, then I know Jasper's ass is really feeling the weight of what went down. I decide to keep twisting the screw.

"You know they're saying that all three of those houses were known drug spots."

Silence.

"Stax, you still there?"

He clears his throat. "Yo, Pash; real shit. I think we need'a change the subject, aiight."

I smirk. "Fine by me. If they *were* known drug spots that caught fire and got burned down, the community will be much better for it."

"Yo, Pash. Let's drop it, aiight?"

I feign shock. "Oh, God, no! Stax, wait! Don't tell me!"

"That shit hit hard, aiight? Some good cats lost their lives in those fires."

Well, you have Jasper to thank for that. This isn't how it was supposed to go down. But Jasper wanted to play dirty. So dirty it is.

I *tsk*. "So sad."

"Yeah. Well, there's nothing we can do about it now. E'erything went up in flames, and muhfuckas are gone. Shit happens. But, uh, I ain't tryna talk about that."

I shift in my seat. "Well, okay...enough about that then." I abruptly hop up from my desk. "Anyway, listen. Since you're passing along messages, I need for you to do me a favor." I walk into the bathroom, flipping on the light switch. The light immediately glints off the four-carat diamond studs in my ears.

"Aiight, I got you."

"Do you really, Stax?"

He lowers his voice. "C'mon, Pash. No doubt. I played it back when all that other shit went down. But I ain't goin' out like that again, yo. I'm not gonna let anyone, not even my own fam, try'n hurt you, aiight? I put that on e'erything."

He sounds so sincere in the way that he says this that I believe him. A sly smile eases over my lips as I tuck this away for future use. I know I'll be able to use this to my advantage at some point.

"I really appreciate hearing that, Stax. Thanks."

"No doubt. So what's good? What you got for me?"

"I need you to let Jasper know that *if* he wants his money in his safes and wants to see Jaylen, then he needs to give me the names of the rest of those niggas who were there that night. If not, I'm going to keep hitting him where it hurts. And, by the time I'm done with him, he's going to wish he'd killed me when he had the chance to."

"Yo, c'mon, Pash. Chill wit' that talk. I'm not gonna tell him no shit like that. That nigga's already on the edge. But I'll pass along it's a no-go wit' court 'n' seein' his son."

"You can pass along whatever you want. But *I* want those names."

"Aiigt, Pash. I hear you. Listen. I got some shit I gotta handle. I'ma hit you up later tonight. I got some other shit I need'a holla at you about, aiight?"

"You know how to find me," I say, ending the call as another call rings through. I glance at the screen. It's Nana. I take a deep breath. Then slowly exhale, answering, "Hello."

"Pasha," she says, sounding distressed. "Felecia's still missing. No one has seen or heard from her since early Sunday afternoon. And I don't think the police are really trying hard enough to locate her."

"Nana," I attempt to reassure, "I'm sure the police are doing everything within their power to find her. I'm sure she'll show up somewhere."

"I'm keeping it lifted in prayer. Has she called you?"

"No, Nana. I haven't heard from her."

"This is not like her…"

Yeah, so you think. I didn't think she'd ever snake me. But the bitch did.

"She's never gone missing before. It's not like her to not return phone calls, or check in. And now her voicemail is full. Something isn't right. She's somewhere lying in a ditch, rotting."

"Nana, don't talk like that."

"She's gone, Pasha," Nana says, her voice quavering. "I know she is. I've been nothing but a faithful servant. And I know my God is an awesome God. But, once again, the devil done gotten his filthy hands on another one of my own. I know he has."

I swallow, hard, fighting back the slow-growing pang in my heart.

Not for what I've done to that bitch. But for what my Nana is going through at this very moment, for what she'll go through in the very near future when she realizes that Felecia's body will never be found. And there will never be any closure. Not for her.

"I saw her body," she continues, choking back sobs, "in my dreams last night. "The same way I did when I saw your father's and her mother's. But I didn't wanna believe what was revealed to me." She breaks down, crying. "Why, Lord? Not another one of my babies!" I tighten my grip on my cell phone, squeezing. "I knew it then. And I know it now. But I don't wanna face it. Not now. I don't think I have it in me to go on. Not this time, baby. I'm tired. I can't bury another one of mine. Not another one of my babies."

My stomach drops.

"Nana, please."

I try to console her the best I can, to no avail. She's too heartbroken. And my heart aches for her. So I let her be. Let her sob for what feels like forever until she finally calms. Nana blows her nose, coughs, then blows her nose, again.

She pushes out a heavy sigh. "My God is an awesome God. I lay my burdens down. Lift up my hands. And praise His name. I'm asking Him to deliver me from this pain. To lift up this heavy heart and carry me on my way..."

I press back tears, fight back the gnawing in the pit of my soul. I knew the minute Felecia walked up in here and started talking shit that there'd be no happy ending. But I hadn't thought it all through when I pulled the trigger and blew out the back of Felecia's skull. I hadn't considered the consequences.

That by killing Felecia, I'd be killing Nana, too.

If something happens to her because of Felecia being missing, it'll be my doing. It'll be something I'll have to live with for the rest of my life.

I *meant* to kill that bitch.

But *killing* my grandmother in the end was never my intent.

"Please, Nana…"

"Pasha, I'm tired, baby. My heavenly Father knows I've fought a good fight. He knows I've given it my all. I'm so, so tired, baby. Your Nana's ready to go home to sit beside her King…"

"Nana, please," my voice cracks. "I don't like it when you talk like this. I love you so much. It hurts me when you talk about dying and not going on, like you're throwing in the towel and giving up."

"I can't keep doing this, baby. I can't."

"You can't keep doing what, Nana?"

An agonizing moment of deafening silence floats in between us. I glance up at the surveillance monitor, then over at the wall clock. My spirit plummets with each ticking second. In my mind's eye, I see the guillotine. I watch the angled blade lift. My body is secured to the bottom of its frame.

My neck hangs slightly under the blade, exposed and ready.

I wait.

"I know what happened to her, Pasha," she says into the chilling quiet, her voice barely above a whisper. I have to almost strain to hear her.

I shut my eyes tighter. Brace myself. Attempt to steady my breathing as the imaginary blade is released and swiftly drops.

"Somebody…done…murdered…my…grandbaby."

Eight

Believe only half of what you see and nothing of what you hear. Everyone's suspect...

"Well, since we're spending so much time on the phone talking, I've been meaning to ask you. Did you know Jasper was fucking Felecia?"

Silence, followed by a deep breath. "Yo, c'mon, Pash. Don't."

"*Don't what, Montgomery?*" I can almost see him cringing through the phone as I call him by his birth name. I smirk.

"Don't put me in the middle of this. I've already fucked up 'n' crossed lines I shouldna."

I *tsk*. "Umm, it's a little too late to be worried about that now, *Monty*, don't you think? You've already had your dick in the *middle* of my lips, so you might as well get in the middle of everything else and tell me what I want to know. So, answer the question, please. Did you know about Jasper fucking Felecia?" Of course he knew. But I want to see if he's willing to admit it.

"Shit," he mutters, blowing out another breath. "Yeah, I knew."

"Mmmph. Wasn't I the silly fool in the room. Here I thought all that time the bitch was giving you the pussy. And, all the while, that trick-bitch was on her slutty-ass knees swallowing Jasper's babies and letting him fuck her in the ass. You and everyone else obviously knew he was fucking that shitty bitch, except me. And all of you were grinning in my damn face."

"Yo, c'mon, Pash. It wasn't even like that. Not wit' me 'n' you, anyway."

I grunt. "Mmmph. Isn't that special. That's what your mouth says. But I can't tell."

"C'mon, Pash. Stop it, ma. I never smiled in your face on some sly shit. What was I s'posed to do, huh? Rat Jasp out? Nah, that's not how I move. You should know me better than that, Pash. No matter how fucked up that situation was, it wasn't my place to say anything. That shit wasn't my business, feel me?"

I roll my eyes up in my head, scrolling through pictures of Jaylen that Greta took of him this afternoon, then emailed to me. I touch the screen of my laptop, tracing his little smiling face. *I love you so much, my handsome, little prince.*

Not being with my son is killing me!

I suck my teeth. "Whatever, Stax, you did what you were supposed to do. Keep their dirty little secret safe."

It all makes sense now. The times when Stax would be here and I'd walk up on the two of them looking all cozy, huddled up in each other's faces, whispering, as if they were conspiring. Then the minute one of them would notice me coming into their space, the body language would shift, the conversation would abruptly stop, or they'd quickly change the subject, making them both look suspect. But I'd always act as if I hadn't peeped it. But it always stuck in the back of my head that that bitch was up to something. And somehow Stax was connected.

I just didn't know what.

Stax sighs. "Pash, on some real shit. I was never down wit' how she was movin'. I ain't gonna front on you, Pash. Anytime you'd peep us huddled up, it was me tryna convince her to get her mind right. Or she'd be tryna cry on my shoulder 'bout how Jasp was playin' her 'n' how she got caught up in her feelin's for him, 'n' askin' me what she should do."

Ohmygod! The silly bitch was really in love with Jasper. Mmmph. Dead, stupid bitch! Isn't that some shit!

"Mmmph. If you say so." I glance up at the surveillance monitor, then over at the clock. It's a little after eight p.m. I watch as Mel unlocks the shop's door, then steps inside. The slutty me can't help but wonder what he looks like butt-naked, or better yet…with his pants dropped down around his ankles and his dick hanging out of the slit of his underwear.

I lick my lips and swallow.

"Yo, what you mean by that?"

"It means what I said."

"Oh, so you think I'm not keepin' it straight up wit' you?"

I click into my browser, log in to my Virgin America account, then book another first-class flight to L.A. for six a.m., this Saturday. "I don't know, Stax. Are you?" I pull out my credit card, completing my transaction.

"Check this out, Pash. I have no reason to lie to you. I ain't ever been beat for lies, ma. I'd rather just say I don't wanna talk about it than lie about it. Eventually the shit's gonna come out so you might as well keep it a hunnid from the rip, nah mean? But since we talkin' 'bout lies, riddle me this, Pash: how many have you told?"

I blink. Surprised by the question. But the truth is, I've told enough lies to know that the more you tell, the more you start to believe them to be true. Like all the times I went out on dick patrol, sucking down a nigga's nut, I lied to myself, trying to rationalize that what I was doing wasn't cheating. That it was only a means to an end. That there was no real harm being done. That once

Jasper was released from prison and sent to the halfway house, everything would go back to normal.

It didn't.

I convinced myself that he'd never find out.

But he did.

Fact is, we all lie—for whatever reasons, some more than others. We lie to justify actions, to escape arguments, to spare someone else's feelings, to avoid potential consequences, and even to manipulate. We lie to ourselves over and over, to protect ourselves from our own feelings. Still no matter what shape or form the lie takes on, it is still a damn lie.

And for every lie told, there's always a chance of getting caught, of being found out. Still...the best lies told are the ones laced with truths.

And my truth is, I'm still lying...to manipulate him, Jasper, and anyone else I have to in order to get what I want, need.

In the end, I know we all need to be accountable to the truth. The facts. Not the shit we've conjured up in our heads, convincing ourselves that what we're doing or saying is right. Not the twisted distortions we've allowed to become our realities. No. We need to be accountable—at some point, be stripped down, to the naked truth.

Whatever that may be.

But for now...I'll stay wrapped in lies. Stay enfolded in the pursuit of justice—my *way*; one tortured body at a time.

"I've told my share," I admit. I hold my breath, waiting for a sliver of guilt to creep up in me. But there is none. So I press on. "Everyone has lied at least once in their life, even if it's only to themselves, or to spare someone else's feelings. Hell. Most people spend most of their lives living a lie."

"Yeah, I feel you. But I try not to live that life," he says, conviction coating his tone. "I'd rather be hurt by the truth, than to be cut down by a lie."

I shift in my seat, wondering how many times Jasper attempted to wipe the images of me down on my knees with another nigga's dick in my mouth out of his mind before he decided to have me kidnapped. I wonder how long he plotted, played it out in his head, before he finally executed his attack on me. I wonder how he stomached watching his boys, the niggas he broke bread with, take turns running their dicks into my throat. Or maybe he didn't watch at all. Maybe he simply gave the order with strict instructions.

"Remember, she's not to be hurt..."

"... She's pregnant..."

I swallow back the anger rising up in the back of my throat. *Fucking Jasper!* "Hmmm. How noble of you."

"Nah. It's who I am."

"Yeah, like grinning in my face, knowing what Felecia and Jasper were doing to me behind my back. But, whatever...it doesn't matter now. The lines have already been crossed. And shit's about to get messier than it already is."

"Real spit, Pash, you bigger than that, ma. Be the bigger woman 'n' let that shit go. Walk away, ma. It's not worth it. But since we havin' this conversation, keep it gee wit' me. How you gonna feel any kinda way 'bout me keepin' shit from you when you was out there doin' *you* behind Jasp's back the whole time he was on lock?"

I blink, feeling as if I've just been slapped. And I immediately become defensive, ready to bring it to his ass. *"Excuuuuuse you?!"* I shriek, pushing back from my desk and jumping to my feet, hand up on hip. "Newsflash: I wasn't *doing* shit behind Jasper's back his whole bid. I held out for *two*-and-a-half, sexless, lonely-ass years before I gave in. But that nigga stayed fucking bitches behind my back whenever he felt the urge. You and I both know it. I never cheated on Jasper, not *once*, while he was on the streets. Never even gave it a thought, even after all the bitches he cheated on me with and I had to run up on. I did…"

"C'mon, Pash, you don't have to—"

I pace the floor, cutting him off. "I wanted dick, Stax, *okay?* I wanted Jasper's dick. This pussy needed it. I wanted that nigga home to fuck me, deep and hard. But he couldn't, Stax. His black ass was locked up. I knew going into it that doing that bid with him wasn't going to be easy. Still, I swore to him I wouldn't fuck another nigga while he was on lock. And I *didn't*. As bad as I wanted to have this pussy gutted by a hard-ass dick, I stayed true to my fucking word.

"But there's only so much fucking a bitch with a high sex drive and a neglected, wet pussy can do with fingers and dildos and phone sex before it's no longer enough. Before it breaks her resolve. And guess what, Stax? It *broke* me. It wasn't enough for me anymore. *I* needed, wanted, *craved* more. My pussy wanted more, my pussy begged for more…"

"I hear you, Pash," he says, sounding uncomfortable hearing my declaration.

"I *love* dick, Stax, okay? I love *sucking* dick. Lots of it!…"

He tries to stop me again. Tells me he doesn't need to hear this. That he was out of pocket for calling me out like that. But he's already flipped open the confession box. And there's no shutting it back until I am done. Until I have purged my dirty deeds.

"I held that nigga down his *whole* goddamn bid, okay. Anything he wanted or needed, he got it. Every collect call, I accepted. Every goddamn visit, I was there. With a smile on my face, and an ache in my heart, I was any-and-every-thing Jasper needed me to be. And each time I left those visits, or hung up from his calls, or stepped out of his embrace, I was still an angry, frustrated, horny bitch.

"I *know* what I was doing behind Jasper's back was fucked up. *I* was cheating on him. *I* was lying to him. At that time I didn't think sucking a nigga's dick was cheating, since I wasn't being *fucked*. But it was, it is, cheating; period. Yet, I wasn't doing anything that he hadn't been doing to *me* when he was out on the bricks. Still, two wrongs never make it right. The thing is, Stax, my sucking dick had nothing to do with purposely trying to wrong Jasper. It was about *me* needing an outlet; *me* needing a little something on the side to take the edge off until Jasper came home. But guess what? The closer Jasper was to coming home, the more I indulged. I got caught up. The more dick I snuck out to suck, the more dick I wanted. And the more reckless I became.

"I did what I did while Jasper was locked up. Again, I'm not saying that made it right. Cheating is cheating, no matter what. But I wasn't *fucking* or *sucking* any of his damn cousins. And none of them niggas were grinning up in his damn face, while fucking me like Felecia, you, and everyone else had been doing in mine."

"C'mon, Pash," he laments, lowering his voice. "I don't wanna beef wit' you. My bad if I got you feelin' like I was tryna come at ya neck. I'm just sayin'…how you gonna fault me for fallin' back 'n' keepin' shit on the low? I didn't do it to hurt *you*. You know…"

I push out a frustrated sigh. "You know what, Stax. Don't…" There's a knock at the door. "Hold on a sec."

"Aiight."

I get up from my desk and walk over to unlock the door, then open it. Mel is standing in the doorway holding up two large, take-out bags from one of my favorite Chinese restaurants. P.F. Chang's.

"Since it looks like it's gonna be a long night," he says, a slow grin easing over his lips, "I bought *us* something to eat." He licks his lips. "You *hungry?*"

I step back, letting him in, along with the intoxicating aromas of Asian cuisine. "Listen, Stax. I gotta go."

"Cool. I'ma hit you later."

I raise a brow, glancing over at Mel as he stacks the papers scattered on my desk into a neat pile, opens up napkins, then places containers of food out, turning my desk into a mini buffet.

"For what?"

Stax's voice dips low; his mouth must be pressed closer to the phone because it now feels as if he's standing right here next to me, his lips flush against my ear.

"There's sumthin' else I wanna talk to you about..." I can almost feel his breath on my skin. I feel myself starting to heat.

"Oh, yeah? What's that?"

"I'll hit you up later tonight. What time you headin' home?"

I glance over at Mel. He's moved one of my desk chairs over to the side and is sitting in it with his long legs stretched all the way out; his large feet crossed at the ankles. I strain not to stare at the lump in his pants. Fight to not run my hand along the deliciously thick outline of his dick bulging and stretching against the fabric.

I blink back my filthy, slutty thoughts, stepping out of my heels. I shift my cell from one ear to the other. "I don't know. But you know how to find me." I end the call, then turn my attention to Mel. "Soooo, what was that about being *hungry?* I stay hungry."

He grins. "Then come get fed."

My gaze slowly drops to the center of his lap again, then quickly shifts to the containers of food.

I swallow.

Sweet Jeezus, give me strength!

Nine

*Even the most focused niggas can become distracted by
a dose of good pussy...*

My cell keeps buzzing. It buzzes and buzzes and buzzes, snatching me out of a delicious slumber. I pop one eye open, glancing at the digital clock on the nightstand. 6:42 a.m. *Are you fucking kidding me?* I groan, rolling over onto my side. *Whoever it is, they can kiss my damn ass!*

My back is now facing the annoying sound. I am naked, lying in bed, the scent of last night's—well, early this morning's—fucking still lingers around the room. The sheets still damp from sweat and cum. The taste of Stax's cock still clings on my tongue, remnants of his last nut—the one he popped just before he rolled out of my bed, slipped back into his clothes and let himself out. At 4:12 a.m., that's what time it was when I rolled over and peered out of one eye, watching him watching me before he walked toward the bedroom door. My only words to him, before he quietly snuck out were, "Make sure you lock the door on your way out."

"I got you," he said, glancing over his shoulder at me, then shutting the door behind him.

After about six minutes, the double chirp of the alarm panel in my bedroom alerted me that he had finally gone. That's when I drifted off to sleep.

But now this shit...

My cell starts vibrating again and again and again. Then finally stops. Two minutes later, it starts again. *What the fuck?!*

I am determined to ignore it. I am not interested in hearing shit from anyone this early in the morning.

I am exhausted.

My pussy is well fucked. Sore. And still wet.

I press my thighs together.

Fucking Jasper! Asshole! You fucked my cousin. And now I've fucked yours. Mmmm... And he fucked me soooo good, too!

But we still ain't even, nigga. Not until you feel what it's like to be violated.

I stretch and yawn, pressing my eyes closed tighter. Shit, I had only teased Stax the first time I sucked his dick down at the salon last Saturday night. But, last night, well...this morning, there was no holding back.

I fucked him *raw*. Fucked him every which way without a care in the world. Rode it. Galloped on it. Took it on my knees. Took it on my side. Gave it to him on my back with one leg wrapped around his thick waist and the other up over his shoulder. Thrust it at him pound for pound with my knees bent. Legs up and crossed at the ankles, I let Stax get all up in this juicy snatch.

I fed him my pussy. I rode his face, his lips, his tongue. Smeared my cream all over every part of him, then licked it off.

I sucked his dick, sucked his balls...even sucked the nigga's toes. I licked him all over his rock-hard body. I gave it to Stax good and real freaky. I serviced him the way a real freak-bitch does it. Without limits.

Yeah, he claimed he only wanted to finish our discussion—face to face—when he called last night. And I'm sure he did. But, my mind was already made up by the time I'd ended the call, agreeing to see him.

I was fucking him.

So unless he was coming here to give me the names of the rest of those niggas who had me down in that basement, I wasn't interested in hearing anything other than moaning and groaning and the sweaty sounds of fucking and heavy breathing as we came.

And obviously, he'd gotten sidetracked, forgetting why he'd come to see me in the first place, when I answered the door wearing only a pair of six-inch red bottoms, seductively pulling a big red lollipop out of my mouth, smirking.

Yeah, it was brazen. It was rash. And so out of character of me.

Then again, was it really?

No. I'd been reckless many times before. I'd stepped out of character every time I slipped out into the middle of the night to pop a dick of some random nigga into the back of my mouth.

So what I did in the wee of hours this morning was no different. Well…other than the fact that I tossed discretion out of the window, and threw caution and the fear of getting caught into the wind, and fucked Stax right here—in *my* home, in *my* bed. Something I'd never done with anyone else. Well, okay, lies…aside from Lamar. But we didn't fuck. We sucked. Stax and I *fucked* all up and down these springs.

But who cares?

I was feeling slutty and vengeful. And if Jasper had any of his goons watching me, then I wanted to be sure to give them an eyeful. Yes, I was really crossing a dangerous line last night. Playing a dirty game. But someone has to do it. And it might as well be a bitch like me. Besides, Jasper set out the board game and laid out the rules on how he wanted it played the minute he slid his dick in Felecia.

So now, I roll the dice.

And the minute I got Stax upstairs to my master suite—where, not more than a week ago, he'd walked in and seen me on my knees, ass up, my breasts swaying, as Jasper fucked me from the back—and he stepped out of his boxers, then stretched his naked six-foot-six, chiseled frame out in the middle of my bed, with his long hard dick pulsing and pointing upward, I confirmed what I already *knew*. I was a bad bitch!

"Fuck, yo," he said, grabbing his dick and stroking it while gazing at my naked body. "This shit we doin' ain't right, nah mean? But my dick's so fuckin' hard for you, Pash. But, fuck. This some real grimy shit I'm doin' to my fam."

I let him rattle on, climbing up on the bed. I crawled between his spread legs and flicked my tongue across his huge balls, then slurped each one into my mouth. "Fuck, Pash," he pushed out in between a low moan. "Aaah, shit, baby, that's my spot. Mmm… fuck…you got my balls tinglin'."

I grinned triumphantly. *By the time I'm finished with your fine ass, that's not the only thing I'm going to have tingling.*

I took his dick into my mouth, teasing the head a little. Then swallowed all ten inches, down past the back of my throat. No gag, no hassle, no fuss. I sucked Stax until his whole body shook. The whole time he was coming in my mouth, he kept saying how what he was doing was fucked up, how he was all fucked up for snaking Jasper like this, how he knew he needed to stay away from me; all the while grunting and groaning and busting his thick load and clutching the sheets, telling me how good my head game was. How he didn't know how he was going to stop wanting this, stop wanting me.

Mmmph. Thought that nigga knew. Now he knows firsthand.

The whole time he was wallowing in his guilt and fighting back the rising surge in his balls, I wanted to tell his ass to shut the fuck up, to stay in the moment. But, with a mouthful of dick and nut, the only thing I could do was suck and swallow.

So I did exactly that.

Then when I was completely satisfied that I had emptied all of his nut down into my throat, I climbed on top of him, positioning the shaft of his semi-hard dick in between my slick pussy lips. I leaned into his ear, then whispered, "Fuck Jasper. Everything that nigga's done to me has been grimy. He fucked me over. And *now* I'm gonna fuck him. But first, I'm gonna fuck you and this big dick, big daddy."

I grinded on his dick, sliding my juicy slit up and down the length of him as I stared into his eyes. I leaned in just so, making sure every time I slid back and forth over the shaft of his dick that it hit my clit.

"Tell me you don't want this pussy, Stax, and you can get up and walk out that door, like nothing ever happened. We can both forget how good my lips felt wrapped around this big-ass dick. Is that what you want, Stax, huh? You wanna forget how good I sucked your dick? How I made your toes curl and your eyes roll up in the back of your head? You wanna forget how good my pussy tasted on your tongue? You want me to forget how good your fingers and tongue felt all up in my pussy? Is that what you want? If it is, then get up and stuff all this hard dick back in your boxers and bounce."

He groaned. "Fuck. Nah, yo. We might as well finish what we've started. You got a muhfucka horny as fuck." His hands gripped my waist, then slide over my ass where they stayed. We stared each other in the eyes. Neither saying shit for several seconds until he broke the silence. "But, after tonight, Pash, we can't do this shit again, you feel me?"

I nodded my head, not believing that he really believed what he was saying. Judging by how hard his dick was and the lusty look in his eyes, I knew what was coming out of his mouth wasn't what he really wanted. I reached a hand behind me, lifting my hips and pressing the head of his dick up against the mouth of my pussy. I pushed it inside of me. Leaned back on it, then slowly slid up and down on it until my body adjusted, my pussy opening and engulfing him deep into my wetness.

"Now I feel you. Mmmm...*all* of you."

I bent over and kissed him, riding his dick in long, deep strokes as I imagined Jasper walking in on us, my ass mid-air, Stax's wet dick gliding in and out of me.

"Yeah, give it to me, Stax. Oooh, yes...all this big thick dick, stretching this pussy...you like how my pussy's stretched all over this big juicy cock...?"

He grunted. "Hells, yeah...aaaah, shit, yo...mmmph... Hol' up, hol' up...aaah, shit...you 'bout to make me bust..." His eyes stayed fixed on mine as he reached up and started playing with my erect nipples, tweaking them, lightly rolling them between the pads of his fingers, before squeezing them together, pulling me toward him and placing each nipple into his wet mouth.

I picked up the pace, clutching his dick, determined to fuck the nut out of him. And just as he announced he was coming, I quickly hopped off his dick and sucked his babies down. Then shifted my body and let him tongue-fuck my orgasm out of me.

I moan, reminiscing, savoring the memory.

Now that he's gotten another taste of this sweet pussy and a double-dose of this knee-buckling deep throat service, there's no turning back. The plan is in motion. Yeah, Stax claims it won't happen again. Whatever! If it does, it does. If it doesn't, it doesn't.

He can keep telling himself whatever he wants to if that's going to help him look into the eyes of his partner in crime. The one *he's* now betrayed by sleeping with his wife.

I don't know if it's his big dick and the way he used it—precise and purposeful, with smooth even strokes, deep and long-lasting—that made it so good. Or if it's the fact that I fucked him, knowing how close the two of them are—or *were*.

A sly grin slides over my lips as I lie here in the comforts of my luxurious bed, replaying our night over in my head. The entire evening is etched in my memory. And I'm sure it's stamped in his head as well.

Stax, you should have kept your horse dick in your pants. Little does he know, he'll be back for more! They always want more. And when he does, I'll be waiting with my mouth wide open, wet and ready to give him what he'll never be able to forget. This deep throat.

I smile, replaying more of my night.

"Fuck, Pash," he had said as his hand traced over my body as he spooned in back of me. His touch was gentle. His fingers floated, feathery and soft over my hip, around my waist, over my nipple, then between my thighs, where he searched for my clit. He pinched it. I gasped.

"I can see why you have Jasp goin' through it," he said low in my ear.

I craned my neck, glancing at him, a scowl plastered on my face. "Why you say that?"

"Because you're addictive, Pash. Real shit," he replied, lifting my leg up and in one swift motion, pushing his hard dick, *all* of it, into the slit of my pussy. "And dangerous as hell."

I moaned, arching my back and pumping my ass into his pelvis while reaching around and grabbing him by his hip, pulling him in, urging him to go deeper, to bury himself—along with our dirty deed, as far into my pussy as humanly possible. "This pussy's good, Pash. You'll fuck around and have a nigga ready to snap."

My very last thought before getting lost in the thrusts of his pounding dick and giving into the sweet burn churning my pussy inside out was:

Oh, you have no idea what I'm now capable of! You haven't seen shit, yet…

Ten

Sometimes you have to give a little to get a lot...

"Good morning, Nappy No More. This is Pasha. How can I help you?"

"Yo, so is this how you really fuckin' doin' it, Pasha, huh? You really tryna drag a muhfucka into court for a restrainin' order over some fuckin' bullshit, right?"

I glance at the caller ID, shaking my head. This nigga is calling me from an unfamiliar number. I pull in my bottom lip; bite down on it to keep from screaming on his ass. Yes, I can hang up on him. But I won't, not yet.

"I'm not dragging you anywhere, Jasper. You do know you *don't* have to show up if you don't want to, right? Either way, I'm getting that final order against you."

He huffs. "Fuck outta here, yo. Why is you doin' all this bullshit, huh?"

I sigh. "Jasper, I'm not doing this with you today. We've already been through this. So, moving on. Did Stax tell you what I said?"

"Yeah, why?"

"So are you calling to give me those names or what?"

He sucks his teeth, blowing a frustrated breath into the phone. He remains uncharacteristically calm, too calm. "Nah, I ain't callin' you wit' no shit like that. Them niggas ain't got shit to do wit' what's poppin' off wit' me 'n' you right now. This shit's between us."

"Oh, really?" I let out a sarcastic laugh. "Mighty funny they had *everything* to do with me cheating on you and *you* feeling the need to drag them into it to *teach* me a lesson. Tell me how that works, Jasper? It was okay for you to hire niggas to kidnap me, then rally up your niggas to *sexually* assault me, right? But, now all of a sudden, they don't have shit to do with anything." I *tsk*. "Jasper, get over yourself."

"Yo, I ain't tryna hear all that. Where's my son at?"

"Give me those names, Jasper. I'm serious."

"Pasha. You heard what the fuck I said, right? Dead that shit. Now—"

I cut him off. "Nigga, you must be friends with that bitch, Molly. I'm not *dead*ing shit. We can do this the easy way, or the hard way. Either way, make no mistake, Jasper. I *will* find out who they are. And one by one, all of them grimy motherfuckers are going to catch it. So you better let 'em all know I'm coming for 'em."

"Yeah, aiight, Pasha. Whatever you say, yo. Talk that talk. So you gotta lil' heart now. Good for you. But, I'm tellin' you, yo. You ain't ready for this shit you tryna start."

"Jasper, you don't know what I'm ready for. Or what I'm capable of…"

He laughs. "Yeah, right, right. I didn't think ya ass was capable of bein' a cock 'n' cum-slut, but you fooled me there. So, yeah, you right. I don't. All I know is, you better fall back, real quick 'cause you really pushin' ya muthafuckin' luck."

"Laugh if you want, nigga. And think what you want. I want those names."

"Look, I'm tellin' you, yo. Leave that shit alone."

"Or *what*, Jasper?"

"Yo, whatever, man. You heard what the fuck I said. Don't keep pressin' me, yo. Now where is my son? I wanna see him."

"Oh, well. Not today you won't. Not *ever* if I can help it. Nigga, you think I'm going to let you *anywhere* near *my* son after you had niggas roll up on me last week, shooting at me? Nigga, please! Or did you forget that?"

"Yo, fuck outta here wit' that. You can't keep me from my son. I already tol' you what it was. If I wanted to have them niggas really get at you, Pasha, they woulda handled ya stupid ass. You'd be in a box. Not on this muthafuckin' line poppin' shit."

"Whatever, Jasper. I'll be stupid all day long. But I'm done with being your fool. I gave you an opportunity to see Jaylen down at the police station *before* you tried to shoot me up. But you didn't want that. Now the only way you're going to *ever* see him is through a court order. So I guess you should have had me *boxed* when you had the chance."

In my mind's eye, I can see him pacing the floor, fist clenched, wild and crazed. Muscles in his jaws tightening. *Ten, nine, eight…* count in my head how long before it takes for him to snap. *Seven, six…*

"Yo, Pasha, real shit. Keep talkin' slick, aiight? And I'ma knock ya muthafuckin' sockets in, ya heard? So you better shut the fuck up wit' that dumb shit, aiight? I ain't tryna come at ya fuckin' neck, yo. But you fuckin' really pushin' it, yo. What the fuck I look like seein' my seed down at some muthafuckin' pig spot, huh? Is you fuckin' crazy, yo. You tryna come at me like I'd really do somethin' to hurt my own seed, yo. Fuck outta here wit' that dizzy shit.

"Like the fuck I said, if I wanna have muhfuckas get at ya dumb ass, yo, you'd be got; straight up. Is that what the fuck you want, huh? For me to shut ya muthafuckin' lights, yo? Keep on fuckin' poppin' shit, 'n' ya ass gonna end up boxed, Pasha. Ya heard? Restrainin' order or not, I don't give a fuck! I'm warnin' ya muthafuckin' ass, yo. Keep fuckin' wit' me, Pasha, aiight? And I'ma fuck you up.

"I hit you up, tryna come at ya silly ass like a man, askin' you fuckin' nicely to let me see my muthafuckin' son 'n' you tryna be on some ole spiteful bitch shit. Aiight, damn, Pasha. I get it. You done wit' me. I got it. We done. Fuck it. It's over. Cool. But, fuck, yo, why is you tryna make shit fuckin' difficult, huh? Let me get my muthafuckin' paper, let me see my son 'n' me 'n' you dead this shit."

"Why am *I* trying to make shit *difficult*?!" I shriek in disbelief. "Are you *fucking* kidding me right now? Tell me how have *I* made anything *difficult*, Jasper? Tell me."

"Yo, c'mon. Don't play fuckin' dumb, yo. All this bullshit is poppin' off 'cause of ya dumb ass. Nobody tol' ya muthafuckin' ass to be on some slick shit out there suckin' a buncha random niggas' dicks 'n' shit. *You* fucked us up, yo. Cock-suckin' bitch! *You* fucked us over. *You* fucked up what we had, yo. All because you couldn't stay the fuck up off ya muthafuckin' knees 'n' wait for a muhfucka to hit the bricks. Stupid bitch! All this muthafuckin' dick you had right here 'n' you wanna be on some whore shit.

"Now ya fuckin' ass got me all hemmed up wit'a muthafuckin' restrainin' order. Got me outta my own muthafuckin' crib. Then I asked you to let me get back up in the muhfucka so I can get the rest of my shit 'n' you wanna be on ya bullshit about that. I tol' ya ass to run me my muthafuckin' paper 'n' you still playin' fuckin' games. You stay…"

"Nigga, and I told *you* that if you wanted your money to give me those names and you can have every fucking dime of it. But you have yet to do that. So until you decide to get your fucking mind right and give me what the fuck I want, you're *not* getting shit. And I mean that. So do *what*ever you feel you need to do. But know *this*, nigga: *any*thing you try to do to me, I'm going to have done to *you*. You might have niggas watching me. But guess what, nigga? I got 'em watching you, too. Now *fuck* with me if you want, Jasper. And see what happens next."

I take a deep breath, then calmly, slowly, say, "Jasper, understand this. You are on borrowed time. The *only* reason I haven't had *you* boxed is because I want *you* to watch how the niggas you had disrespect me start to drop. I want you to see *every*thing around you go up in flames. Then Jasper…*I'm* going to see to it that *your* lights get shut. And when you *finally* come to, I'm going to be the bitch standing over you. *Every*thing you've done to me, I'm going to do to you. So get ready to suck a dick, nigga!"

I slam the phone down in his ear. "Fucking bastard!" I hiss, pressing the palm of my hand into my forehead, trying to push back a banging headache. I take several deep breaths. *I can't stand his ass! I don't know why I let that nigga still get under my fucking skin.*

Because a part of you still loves him. Admit it.

I fucking hate him!

Bitch, please. Keep living that lie if you want. The truth is, you don't hate him. You hate what he's done to you. That nigga still has your heart.

The only thing Jasper has is my fucking contempt.

Lies, bitch! You still love him.

Bitch, shut the fuck up! Whatever ounce of love I might have had for Jasper disintegrated the moment he had me shot at! So, no, bitch. I don't still love him. I hate every-fucking-thing that nigga stands for.

I want his ass…dead!

The ringing sound of my cell phone snaps me out of the one-sided conversation in my head. I pull it from my waistcoat pocket, glancing at the screen. *Finally! Please let this nigga have my shit.* "Hello."

"I got that information you needed. When you wanna come get it?"

I flip through the appointment book. I'm booked solid from noon up until seven o'clock tonight. "Can we meet after seven?"

"Can't do tonight. I have to meet the wife in the city at six. To-morrow night's good, though."

I roll my eyes. "Where would you like to meet?"

"Here, at my office. Everyone else will already be gone. So it'll be just you and me. We still good, right? Quid pro quo?"

I smirk. "A deal's a deal, *right?* You give me what I want. And I give *you* what you want."

"That's what I wanna hear," he says excitedly. "Let me give you the address." I grab a pen and take down the information, then tell him I'll see him tomorrow night. "I'm looking forward to it. I have a two-day load I can't wait to share with you."

"Then I guess we'll both walk away with very happy endings."

I end the call just as Mel walks through the door, dressed in a pair of black jeans and black short-sleeved T-shirt with the word: SECURITY stretched across his chiseled chest in big white letters. He shuts the door behind him, his backpack dropping off his shoulder. "What's good, Pasha? How you?"

I smile. "Hey, Mel. I'm good."

"Cool-cool." He eyes me. And for a split-second I think I see something dancing in his gaze at me. Lust maybe. Perhaps a secret that only he knows. I dismiss the craziness of it, turning my back on him as I mindlessly shuffle through the appointment book. "So, e'erything's good around here?"

I nod. "Yup. So far, so good." He wants to know what time I arrived at the salon this morning. I tell him seven-thirty. He grunts. I turn to face him, feigning ignorance. "What?"

He shakes his head. "C'mon, Pasha. Didn't we talk about this last night? You already know what it is. The deal is: when you pull up, I pull up. When you step through this door, I step through this door. Wherever you go, I go. Or if not me, Lamar goes or someone else on security detail. We can't keep you safe, Pasha, if you're going to keep moving like e'ertything's good."

I put my hands up in mock surrender. "I know, I know. Guilty as charged. You're right." I sigh defeat. Then bat my lashes. "I'll do better."

And I'd love to see what's hidden behind the zipper of those jeans, just a little peek to ease the curiosity, big daddy.

Admittedly, last night it was torturous being alone with him sitting up in my office watching him eat. Every time his lips wrapped around his chopsticks, I imagined it was my clit he was slurping into his mouth.

He smirks, shaking his head. "Yeah, aiight. I'ma go heat up my leftovers. You want anything while I'm in the back?"

Yes, nigga. You!

I swallow. "No, I'm good. Thanks." I glance up at the clock. "I have some work to do in my office and need to run some errands before my twelve o'clock gets here."

"Oh, aiight. What time you wanna roll out?" I tell him around ten-thirty. "Cool." I eye him as he walks off toward the staff lounge. I stare at his muscular ass, clutching my neck and swallowin'.

Girl, you need to get your whore meter in check.

Luckily for me, any salacious thoughts beginning to take root in my filthy little head are quickly tossed aside the second Mona bursts through the door, looking disheveled and on the brink of tears.

"Ohmygod," I say, my eyes wide with concern. "Mona, what's happened?"

"Pasha, we need to talk."

Eleven

Sometimes the truth slices deeper than a knife...

"Pasha," Mona states as she steps into my office and I close the door behind us. "You were right." She closes her eyes and shakes her head. When she reopens them, they are wet with tears.

"About what?" I sit on the edge of my desk, folding my arms.

"About JT. That dirty bastard was down in that basement with you that night. Them fucking dirty niggas..." She covers her hand over her mouth, leaning over and clutching her stomach.

I am surprisingly calm hearing Mona confirm what I suspected, what I already knew, in my gut. "What about your cousin, Desmond? Did you hear anything about him being there to?"

I hold my breath, waiting, hoping that the father of my cousin Paris' son wasn't a part of it. That he wouldn't have to be...another name added on my list.

Another nigga brought down for violating me.

I am silently relieved when she tells me she didn't hear his name mentioned.

Still doesn't mean shit...

Mona takes a seat on the sofa, shaking her head as she swipes tears from her face with her hands. "I feel so fucking sick right now. I've been calling you all morning. Didn't you get any of my messages?" I tell her I hadn't checked my messages, but saw where she had been trying to reach me and planned on returning her call later this morning.

"What I want to know is, where or whom did you get this information from?"

She tells me she stopped by her parents' house early this morning to check in on her mom because she hasn't been feeling well the past few days. And when she got to the house, Stax's car was in the driveway.

"Which I thought was odd," she says, getting up from her seat to grab the box of tissue from off the desk, "because it was six o'clock in the morning and he's never over there that early."

"Okay?"

"Well, after I checked in on Mama and made sure she had everything she needed, I went downstairs to say my hellos to Sparks and Stax before heading to work. But when I got to the bottom of the steps to the basement, all I could hear was muffled sounds coming from the other side of the door where Monty lifts weights and has all of this gym equipment. So I thought they were working out, or something. The closer I got to the door, I could hear the two of them talking.

"Then Stax started going off, saying how JT and the rest of them dumb-ass niggas were all fucked up for getting involved in Jasper's bullshit. That what Jasper and the rest of them niggas did to you was some real savage shit. And how it fucks with him every time he has to look at you. That Jasper's fucking reckless. He thinks he'd really try to have you killed for keeping him away from his son and for trying to leave him. He also said something about some money Jasper has stashed at the house that you won't let him get his hands on. I think Jasper is hoping Stax can somehow get it for him without you knowing it."

I blink. *Oh, I know damn well Stax isn't even trying to play me! Then again, if he thinks he is, stupid him.* I smirk, imagining the look on his face when...if...he tries to retrieve Jasper's money and comes up empty-handed.

Jasper's black ass will be in for a rude awakening when he learns his precious safes that he thought were so hidden from me have all been breached. And all of his money swiped by the same bitch he shitted on.

"Oh, really? Well, Stax can try. I'd like to see how he makes out with that.

"And that's all you heard? Stax didn't mention any other names other than JT's?"

She shakes her head. "I only heard JT's name." She pushes out a frustrated breath. "This shit with Jasper is messier than I ever imagined. That fucking nigga is crazy."

I give her an "oh-really-you-think" look. But my expression goes unnoticed.

She shifts back in her seat. "Did you know those three houses that went up in flames last weekend were Jasper's? I overheard Stax saying something about them losing close to a million dollars in product, and over a quarter-million dollars in cash."

"Really?" I say feigning ignorance. "I had no idea. Well, that's exactly what the fuck he gets." I hide a triumphant smile. *And the motherfucker's about to lose a whole lot more than that by the time I'm done.* Jasper really thinks he can shit on me and get away with it. That I'd keep lying down, letting him treat me like some raggedy doormat he can wipe his size-thirteens. "Jasper's going to get everything his ass deserves. Karma's a real bitch."

"It sure is. And from what I gathered from the conversation this morning, Karma is really fucking them good. I heard Monty saying something about having to do some reorganization and cutting some niggas from their team now that they've lost those spots. They think it was an inside job."

I keep my game face locked in place.

"Wow…that's crazy. Then again, I wouldn't be one bit surprised if it were true. Greedy, hating-ass niggas will turn in a heartbeat."

"Yeah. You're right. It's just too bad innocent lives are getting caught up in all of Jasper's drama."

I shrug. "I guess. It's a dirty game they play. Every last one of them niggas knows the risk going in. And they still choose to roll up their sleeves and get dirty, so they all get what they get. When their time is up, it's up. Jasper, Sparks, Stax, and whoever else all know they're gambling on borrowed time doing what they do."

She nods. "You're right. Out of all of them, Stax is the only one who has fallen back from that life."

I nod knowingly. Over the last two years, Stax has opened three fitness centers around the tri-state area. And has invested money in the production and distribution of his own fitness video. "Still, Mona. At the end of the day, it doesn't really matter how he's fallen back, he's still guilty by association. And, push come to shove, if niggas can pin shit on him when the heat gets turned up, they will."

She agrees. "I've been telling Sparks and Stax for years to distance themselves from that shit, to stack their money, then get the hell out. Stax seems to be the only one halfway smart enough to do something to clean his money up. Sparks on the other hand." She sighs, shaking her head. "I don't know. But I think he's finally starting to see that Jasper's a ticking time bomb."

"Well, for his sake, let's hope so."

She lets out another heavy sigh. "Pasha, to be honest with you. You don't know how relieved I am that my brother and Stax weren't involved in that grimy shit Jasper pulled on you. I don't know what I would have done if either of them had been. It's bad enough JT's dumb-ass was involved."

"Yeah," I say ruefully. "And now look at his ass. Missing."

"Correction. *Dead*," she states grimly. "JT was murdered. And there's still no body, thanks to Cassandra. And there's still no closure for any of us." She shakes her head. "And that bitch still wants to play like she doesn't know where his corpse is."

"Maybe she really doesn't. Maybe she had someone else dispose of his body. At this point, it doesn't really matter what they did with it since we'll never know. Besides, there can't be a murder unless there's a body. So technically, JT's still considered missing."

She rolls her eyes, sucking her teeth. "His body may be *missing*. But *we* both know he's *dead*. He's probably somewhere stuffed down in some sewer pipe, rotting."

Right where the fuck he belong—with the rest of the trash. I hope the rats are eating his fucking eyeballs out.

It's two weeks, today, since he's gone *missing*, since his death— okay, *murder*, at the hands of Booty. And the family is still beside themselves with worry, rightfully so. Still, that nigga got what he deserved. However, for the life of me, I still can't wrap my mind around why Booty chose to have his body dumped when it was clearly justified. It was a life-or-death situation. She had to act quickly, or her children would have come home from school and found her dead.

That nigga barged his way up into her home and physically at-tacked her, then tried to rape and sodomize her. As far as I'm concerned, that was an airtight, open-and-shut case. Booty acted in self-defense; period, point blank.

Personally, I would have rather seen that nigga suffer a slow, torturous death, instead of the swift killing he'd gotten. That's the one thing I feel I've been robbed of, exacting my own punishment on his ass for what he did.

Oh, how I would have loved to have seen the agonizing look on his face when Big Booty took that knife and sawed off his dick. I can almost see him now, his eyes wide in shock, his dark skin turning ashen and pale as his blood drained from his face while spurting out from his lacerated appendage.

If it had been me, I would have probably chewed and gnawed until I'd bitten his dick off. Then I would have ripped into his balls with my teeth until I'd torn them off of his body. In my head, I can practically hear his blood-curdling screams as I sink my teeth into his flesh, breaking skin.

I can almost taste his blood pooling in my mouth.

I swallow.

Mona stares at me. "Have you seen Stax?"

I think, decide whether or not to lie or share half-truths. I err on the side of caution, not sure what Stax has told her—if anything at all, and go with lying by omission. "Yeah, briefly."

"Have you tried to…?"

Fuck him?

"Have I tried to *what?*"

"Do what Cassandra's nasty, freak-ass suggested you do to try to get info out of him about that night."

I push out a fake laugh. "What, fuck *Stax*?" I wave her on. "Girl, no. I let that crazy mess Cassandra was talking go right over my head."

She tilts her head, twisting her lips. "I'm not talking about *fucking*. I know you wouldn't do *that*. Did you try to offer him up some of your oral services for whatever information he has?"

I cough, practically choking on my spit. "Ohmygod. There's no way I'm going there. I know what I did while Jasper was locked up was some scandalous shit. And, yes, it is no secret. I love sucking dick. But sucking Stax isn't something I'm interested in adding to my list of sins. Besides, Stax wouldn't go for any shit like that anyway. You know how loyal he is to Jasper."

"You're right. Stax is extremely loyal to Jasper's ass. Always has been. Sometimes I think he's too trustworthy to a fault."

She studies me, narrowing her eyes.

I frown. "What? Why are you eyeballing me like that?"

She slowly shakes her head. "No reason." She leans up in her seat, keeping her stare on me. "You know. On second thought, I overheard Sparks ask Stax something I thought was strange."

I raise a brow, giving her a quizzical look. "Oh, yeah? And what was that?"

"He asked him if he had feelings for you."

My eyes grow wide in disbelief. "Say *whaaaat?!* Why in the world would Sparks ask Stax something like that?"

Mona tilts her head, then shrugs. "I guess the same reason why I asked if you had taken Cassandra's suggestion and sucked his dick. He wanted to know."

I give her a blank look.

"Pasha, please. Stax may not ever cross the line. But it's damn sure no secret, no matter how hard he tries to hide it, that he feels something for you. I've always suspected it long before that loud-mouth bitch put it out there. I just didn't say anything. Everyone sees the way he looks, or tries *not* to look, at you whenever he's around you, which is why that messy bitch suggested you fuck him."

"Well, I'm not going there." I pause, sweeping my eyes and the lies pouring out of my mouth around the room before landing my gaze back on her. "So what did you hear Stax tell your brother when he asked him that?"

Mona looks down at her hands, then closes her eyes.

The room goes silent for a moment, a kind of silence that only a room filled with secrets can take on. Dirty secrets.

I squint at her. "Well?"

There's a long stretch of silence before Mona finally opens her eyes and takes a long, slow breath. She glances in my direction, not quite meeting my eye. "That Jasper's trifling-ass is pressing *him* to fuck *you*." She raises her brows slightly. "Jasper wants Stax to set you up for him."

Mmmph. And here I thought I was the one manipulating Stax with tears when I fell into his arms last weekend, and pressed my warm, soft body into his hard, chiseled frame. I thought I was seducing him, throwing myself at him, reeling him in with a good dick suck. And he'd probably already come here, standing in my office, wrapping me in his strong arms, with a plan of his own, one devised by Jasper.

To fuck me...

In more ways than one.

Twelve

The deadly dance of deception can leave one both tempted and tormented...

"Jasper wants Stax to set you up for him. Jasper wants Stax to set you up..."

I repeat Mona's statement, rolling it around in my head. Yeah, Mona had said that she'd overheard Stax telling Sparks this. But the question, "Do you want to, have *you*, fucked her?" wasn't what Sparks had asked him. He wanted to know if Stax had feelings for *me*.

And he'd dodged the question.

If in fact Stax had come to my office last Saturday night to put a plan in motion to *fuck* me, to set me up, for Jasper. It doesn't matter.

I wasn't coerced or manipulated by him. I lured him that night. No, Stax hadn't come there for pussy that night. I'm certain of it. He hadn't wanted it—not then. But I'd dangled a string of temptation in front of hm. Used tears to break his resolve. Clung to him. Pushed my body into his. Wrapped my arms around his neck and rose on my tiptoes to kiss him. My intent masked, my tongue found his. Yet, Stax pulled out of my embrace, wrenched his mouth away from mine. Held his ground. Then walked out the door, leaving me feeling humiliated, ashamed, for what I'd done.

Until he came rushing back into my office, lifting me off my feet and giving into his own hidden desires.

Yes, I'm certain of it. It was my womanly wiles that manipulated

Stax, seduced him, enticed him, clouded his judgment...until he surrendered.

I sucked Stax's dick with a purpose in mind that night.

In the end, I got two names out of him.

But I *fucked* him because I wanted to, because I needed to.

Because...

In a quick whirl of images, I see Stax's lust-hazed eyes above me as I am lying on my back, right leg up over his shoulder; left leg draped around his waist, his hips moving with the rhythm of the music playing in the background. My hands exploring the thick muscles of his forearms, his chiseled back, as he caresses my pussy, deep and slow; his long dick slick from my juices, my walls gripping the width of him, milking the length of him, with each stroke.

Stax's face is inches from mine, the scent of my pussy on his breath, still lingering on his tongue. I hear my breath escaping in trembling gasps, feel my stretched cunt tightening around his cock as he skillfully hits my spot—a rushing of wet heat sweeping through my pussy.

Every roll of my hip drives him deeper inside of me, widening the want and wetness of my cunt. I breathe Stax in. The faint scent of cologne and sweat commingling with the heady smell of heated sex. His dick feels hot and heavy inside of me, his steady thrust slicing into the warmth and welcome of my pussy, slicing into my spirit, slicing into my heart. And it is in his eyes—as he watches my face, as I am arching my back and coming, his dick fucking into my juices, our bodies fusing as one as he moans out my name—that I see it.

The answer to Sparks' question.

"Hello?" *Snap, snap!* "Earth to Pasha…you there?"

I blink. "Huh? Did you say something?"

Persia shakes her head, chuckling as she eyes me through the mirror. "Girrrrl, I don't know where you've been for the last"— she brings her arm out from under the cape, glancing at her watch—"four minutes, and forty-eight seconds. But wherever you were, you weren't here. Is everything okay?"

I attempt to keep my face expressionless as realization hits me that I need to change my panties. I have come on myself. Soaked through my liner. And my pussy is a wet, tingly mess.

I flick my wrist dismissively, shaking my head as I lay the rattail comb on the counter. "Chile, I'm good. It's been a long day; that's all." I steal a glance over at Lamar, who's posted up front by the door. I make a mental note to serve him my wet pussy for lunch as I excuse myself and quickly go into my bathroom to freshen up.

I return a few minutes later. "Okay, I'm back now," I say, reaching for the curling iron. "Girl, I had to splash some water up on this face and get it together right quick."

Persia keeps her gaze on me. "I know that's right. For a minute there, you were nonresponsive. I didn't know if you were having a seizure or what. I was sitting here just a running my mouth until I looked up and saw you standing in a daze. Then I realized you weren't listening to a word I'd said."

I apologize. Tell her I have so much going on between work, securing the location for Nappy No More II out in L.A., and my court hearing tomorrow that I don't know which way is up.

Truth is, I haven't been right since Mona left up out of here almost three hours ago. My mind has been flitting back and forth from my telephone conversation with Jasper earlier this morning to what she shared with me in my office. I replay the disc in my head over and over. *"Jasper wants him to set you up…"*

The idea, the possibility, of Stax having played *me* instead of it being the other way around is… priceless!

I'm not the least bit surprised at Jasper's request, considering what his slimy ruthless-ass had done, what he willingly allowed other niggas to do, to me. But, what I am shocked at, even a little disappointed in, is the thought that Stax might have really been considering it. And why hadn't he told me?

Girl, get over it. Stax doesn't owe you shit. So what if the nigga uses you. So what if he's scheming with Jasper to set you up. You're doing the same shit, using and scheming.

Yeah, on niggas who deserve it!

And on Stax!

That's different.

Still, I don't think, don't believe, that he'd conspire with Jasper's ass. *Not* to do me in.

Then again…

Everything isn't always what it seems. Everyone has an ulterior motive. Someone is always going to get used. Lies will always be told. And someone is always bound to get hurt, intentionally or not.

Persia waves me on. "Girl, please. No worries. I understand. Between Felecia's scandalous ass and Jasper's mess, I know you have a lot going on right now in your life."

I huff. "Don't even remind me. I'm done."

"So it's really over between you and Jasper, huh?"

I nod. "Yes. It is *over*, girl. I want nothing to do with his ass. And tomorrow morning, fingers crossed, I'll be walking up out of court with a final order of protection in my hand. Then I'm divorcing his ass. And for all those bitches out there that want him, who stayed trying to fuck him, they can have at it. But his ass'll be close to broke by the time I'm done with him."

She gives me a saddened look. "It's really a shame things didn't work out for the two of you, at least for Jaylen's sake."

I grunt. "Girl, please. I tried that. Trust me. Staying for Jaylen, would do more harm than good. My son wouldn't benefit from that. No child does; especially when they have parents who despise each other. And make no mistake. I can't stand Jasper's ass. That nigga's put me through more shit than I care to remember. The only good thing that's come out of all of this is my son, Jaylen. I am so in love with that little boy. I can't stand being away from him. I miss him so much."

That last part slips out before I can catch myself.

Persia gives me a puzzled look through the mirror. "You *miss* him? Well, where is he?"

Shit.

"Girl, don't mind me." I chuckle, attempting to play it off. "Every second that I'm away from him my heart aches. He is my life. You don't know how many times I've thought about begging the owners next door to sell their business to me so I can open up a daycare just so I can have him close by."

She smiles warmly. "Oooh, you and Paris with your beautiful chocolate baby boys and all of your gushing pride, make me want to have a baby of my own."

My mouth drops open. "Shut your mouth. *You?* Miss I'd Rather Choke To Death Before I Ever Have Kids?"

She laughs. "Whatever. That was the old me. But now…" She beams. "I don't know. Something's changed. And I'm open to the possibility." She catches the surprised look on my face through the mirror and puts a hand up. "Now, don't go pulling out bassinets and bottles, just yet. I'm only entertaining the idea. Nothing more than that."

I smirk. "Oh, Mister Man must really be working that West In-
dian magic stick to get *you* to even consider having a baby. Sounds
to me like someone's—in the words of Miss Miki Howard—in
love under new management."

"Girrrrrrrrl, don't even get me gossiping and telling lies." She
shudders. "Who woulda thunk it? *Me.* In love. With a younger
man, no less. But, baaaaby. Mmmph. Royce is everything I could
have ever imagined. Then some. And to think I almost let our age
difference keep me from giving him a chance."

I smile. "Do I hear wedding bells ringing in the background?"
She tells me it's something they've been talking about. He wants
to start a family. Wants to build a life with her. But she's in no
rush. "Good for you. Stay in the moment. Simply live, love, and
enjoy each other."

She lowers her voice. "And fuck like wild rabbits. And, *honnnnney*,
let me tell you. I stay in heat. And that man knows how to keep
my fire lit."

I laugh. "Persia, girl, you're a mess." I turn the styling chair, so
that she's now facing me. "Between you and me," I say in a hushed
tone, leaning into her ear, "I stay in heat, too."

"Girl, it's genetic." We share a knowing laugh before the conversation turns serious again. "Pasha, girl. I hope you know I'm
here for you, if you need me."

"Aww, girl. Thanks."

"I'm serious, Cuz. If there's anything you ever need—an ear to
bend, a shoulder to cry or lean on, I'm here for you. We're *all*
here for you. So don't hesitate to call."

I'm looking at Persia, smiling, as she says this. But, in my mind's
eye, I'm giving her the side-eye. Mmmph. I love Persia dearly.
And, as much as I appreciate the gesture, I don't trust her as far as

I can throw her, which is nowhere. Persia's ass is messy like her mother, and her mother's sisters, Fanny and Lucky. Them three messy heifers love gossip. And they love telling everyone else's business except their own. And Miss Persia is right along with them.

And what really cracks me the hell up is the fact that Persia really thinks I'm stuck somewhere in the middle of silly and stupid to actually believe she woke up and had some epiphany to step up in here two weeks ago simply to cut her hair off.

Yeah, I'm sure she wanted a *new* look, to go with the *new* her. But trust and believe. The *only* reason Persia's ass is sitting up in this chair, spending her dollars in *my* salon, is because the bitch wants gossip. And she can't get shit from Felecia.

One, because she's pissed at her for talking shit about her to Booty, then Booty's messy ass coincidentally runs into her sister, Paris, at the mall and tells her what Felecia said about her.

And, two, because of the obvious—well for me, that is. The bitch is dead.

So here Persia sits, again, eagerly sucking in every little morsel of dirt I so graciously dish out to her. And, trust. The minute she bores, the second there's no more scandal, she'll be sitting her ass back over in one of the stylists' chairs down at Tender Cuts, where she'd been going for the last year-and-a-half.

I unsnap the cape from around her neck, handing her the hand-held mirror. She admires herself, moving her head from side to side. "Yes, girl. You give me life, boo. I love everything this look is. You have no idea how many compliments I've gotten, and heads I've turned, since you cut my hair into this short style two weeks ago."

"Girl, I'm just happy to know you love it. It's definitely sexy on you. And as long as you come in every two-to-three weeks to keep it looking fresh and sassy, you'll continue to turn heads."

She rummages through her handbag, pulling out a leather pouch, before getting up from the chair. She stands in front of the mirror, admiring herself as she applies a fresh coat of lipstick over her full, pouty lips. She blows herself a kiss, tossing her case back into her bag, then follows me up front.

She hands me a hundred-dollar bill. I pull three tens from the register. She waves me on as I go to hand her the change. "Girl, please. That's for you."

"Ohmygod. I knew I was forgetting something. I meant to ask you about Felecia. There's still no word from her, huh?"

"Nope," I respond flatly. "There's no telling where that bitch ran off to, or with whom."

Persia slowly shakes her head. "Mmmph. That's crazy. I'm still pissed at her ass for talking all crazy about me, but I really hope nothing's happened to her. My mother told Paris that she spoke to Aunt Harriet the other day and Aunt Harriet told her that she saw it in her dreams that someone had murdered Felecia."

I shrug, giving her a look of indifference. "Oh well."

Her eyes widen, gasping. "Ohmygod, Pasha. That is so not cool. No matter what, Felecia is still family. I'm done with her as well. But I'd never want, or wish, anything bad to happen to her. I'm praying she miraculously appears, alive and well. Burying another child is the last thing Aunt Harriet needs."

I blink.

"Unless there's a body," I say nonchalantly as we embrace, "it isn't murder. It's her missing."

My eyes quickly meet Lamar's glance over her shoulder. I step back from her embrace, tossing my bang from over my eye.

Persia sets her bag up on the counter, then reaches for her jacket from off one of the coat hooks. "Well, let's hope it's the latter," she says as she slips her arms through the sleeves.

Yeah, good luck with that. "Let's hope."

"Well, sweetheavens," she says dramatically. "Clutch the wheel. Can you be any less enthusiastic about the possibility of something tragic having happened to Felecia? I know she wronged you, but can you at least *pretend* that you care."

I look her in the eyes. "That's the point, Persia. I don't care. And I'm done with pretending. If that bitch never shows her face again, it's fine by me. I'll see you in two weeks."

She blinks, clearly taken aback by my remark. "Well alllllrighty, then. On that note, I guess I'll be on my way." She glances over her shoulder as she heads for the door. "Oh. And I hope everything works out for you in court tomorrow."

I smile. "Thanks. I trust that it will."

Thirteen

It's not who you know that'll get you what you want.
It's whom you fuck over to get it...

Apart of me wished, hoped, like hell that Jasper's black ass would be a no-show today as the elevator stopped on the second floor and I stepped out, making my way down the corridor to Courtroom C-211. But all chances of that happening are quickly dashed the minute I spot his ass—reeking of street money and hood swag, leaning up against the wall talking to a very tall, well-suited, dark-skinned man with a smooth bald head. I can't see who he is since his wide—and what appears to be muscular—back is toward me. But whoever he is, it's clear to me that not only is he well dressed, he's well paid—*very* well, for what he does.

His attorney, I think as I keep my eyes trained on the huge mahogany doors to the left of me. I feel Jasper's eyes on me as I smooth out the imaginary wrinkles in front of my black knee-grazing Diane von Furstenberg wrap skirt. It hugs my curves just right without coming off slutty. My black and white print silk chemise is tucked inside; a wide designer belt cinches at the waist. I shift my oversized handbag from one hand to the other, tossing my hair and lifting my black Louis Vuitton shades up and sitting them atop my head when I spot my attorney, Maria McCartney. A well-heeled, well-versed, white-bred, lily-white woman who is as cutthroat as she is politically correct.

This is my first time actually meeting her face-to-face. But she's come highly recommended as one of the best divorce attorneys in the tri-state. And from what I've heard, she's a no-nonsense bitch who gets a hard-on from ripping new assholes into men who like to beat, mistreat, or cheat on, their wives.

By the time she and I finished our initial consultation call, forty minutes later, followed by a video chat while I was in L.A., it was clear to me I had a winner. Today, she'll handle my restraining order hearing. Then she'll handle my divorce proceedings. And, *yes*, after only several months of marriage, I am filing for a damn divorce!

"Mrs. Tyler." She gets up from one of the leather chairs alongside the wall, extending her hand.

I take her hand in mine and shake it firmly. "Please. Don't call me that. Pasha is fine. Or if you *must* be formal, my maiden name, *Allen*, is even better."

She politely smiles. Her straight white teeth are striking against her smooth porcelain skin. Her beautiful blue eyes look like shimmering sapphires set in large round sockets. "Understood. But for the purpose of this hearing, we'll call you by your married surname. It's a pleasure to finally meet you in the flesh."

"Yes, it is. I can't thank you enough for taking my case."

She squeezes my hand. "I'm glad my schedule made it possible. But after speaking with you in great length a few days ago, I would have taken the case either way." She gestures with a hand toward two seats. "Please, let's sit."

I take a seat. Back straight, legs crossed at the ankles. Handbag perched up on my lap. Jasper stares in my direction. I avoid his gaze.

My attorney opens her leather case, pulling out a notepad and Mont Blanc pen. "I've already checked us in. And I've had the opportunity to speak to your husband's *very* handsome counsel."

Her piercing eyes light up as she says this. *Oooh, let me find out this bitch likes a little dark chocolate swirled in her vanilla cream.* I glance over in their direction. But still can't see who he is. I bring my attention back to my own attorney.

I smirk, giving her one of my "ooh-you-messy-bitch" looks.

She smiles coyly, batting her lashes. "My dear. I may be happily married, but I do recognize a beautiful hunk when I see one. As long as you aren't sampling, it never hurts to look." She clears her throat, quickly becomes all business. "Now I should warn you that in the event a final restraining order is granted today, not only does your husband intend on appealing it—which is his right— he'll be asking the judge to make stipulations within the order that allow him two days out of the week and alternating weekends of parenting time with your son. And that communication between the two of you is allowed strictly in the context of the welfare and interest of your son. He'll also be requesting permission to be allowed into the marital home to get the rest of his belongings."

I roll my eyes, huffing. *"Please.* Jasper is so full of it. Jaylen is the *last* thing on his mind. The only thing he wants to be able to do is, keep tabs on *me.* All he wants to do is control me. And as far as getting the rest of his things, he's more than welcomed inside of *my* home with a police escort. I've already told him this. *That's* the only way he's getting inside." I sigh, shaking my head. "I'm so sick of him. He'll do and say whatever he can to try to manipulate the court, including trying to use our son."

She lifts her eyes from her notes. "Oh, don't you worry; I'm already three steps ahead of him. I'm used to dealing with men like your husband. So he can try to manipulate all he wants. In the end, he'll get exactly what he's entitled to, but not an inch more than that. Were you able to bring what we've discussed?"

I glance over in Jasper's direction. He's standing alone. That quick, the suited chocolate Adonis has disappeared. Jasper's gaze is still burning on me. As if he's trying to undress me. Under different circumstances—during a time when I'd fuck him any-and-every-where, I'd pull open my skirt's split, spread open my legs and show him my freshly waxed pussy. But those days are over.

Still, I'd be the first to say that the nigga looks good as hell standing over there in his dark dress slacks and crisp baby-blue shirt and black Louis Vuitton loafers. The nigga even has on a *tie!* Versace, I'm certain given the print of the fabric. Large, flawless diamonds glisten from both of his earlobes, their sparkle blinding even from over here. For a nigga who just lost three of his stash houses he doesn't look the least bit fazed or hurt by it. Of course it's all an act. Inside, I'm sure he's sick. And he'll be even sicker this weekend, when three more get torched.

I roll my eyes.

"Yes, I did." I open my bag and pull out the photos of my bruises, handing them to her. Bruises of me when I was in the hospital, pictures I secretly asked one of my nurses—an older white woman who comforted me in the wee hours of the night during my hospital stay—to take for me. In fact, she's the one who told me about Maria when I called her a few months back to see how she was. I also have pictures of the bruises that were on my face and wrists from last week, which I took of myself.

She purses her collagen-filled lips together. "Hopefully we won't have to use these, but if your husband's attorney plays hardball, which I'm sure he will based on the way he was speaking earlier, then these will become very useful."

I narrow my eyes. "And if those photos aren't enough to get the final order, I have recordings of him threatening me."

Maria gives me a knowing grin. "Why you sly little diva. That's

perfect. Don't you worry; we'll get you that final restraining order."
She leans in to me. "And tears never hurt, for effect. Turn on the
waterworks at the right time. This judge does not take kindly to
bullies and batterers." She eyes me. "Pasha, are *you* afraid of your
husband?"

I slowly nod, placing a hand up to my chest. *"Very."*

Her gaze locks onto mine. There's a glint of deception in them.
Conspirators. That's who we are. "Good answer." She glances at her
diamond-encrusted timepiece. "We should be called in shortly."

"Good. I'm ready to get this done and over with."

"Oh, before I forget." She reaches into her briefcase, pulling
out papers. "Would you like your husband served before, during,
or after the hearing?"

I glance back over to him. The nigga is still staring at me. I smile
at him through gritted teeth. Seeing him standing there all smug
stirs up unwanted emotions. I've become an angry, bitter bitch
because of him.

"There's no need to put it off. Serve him now." I stand. Then
excuse myself so I can use the restroom. She tells me it's around
the corner, down the corridor to the right.

I strut off. Head up, back straight, sashaying right by Jasper,
pretending he is invisible. I know it's killing him to see me and
not be able to pop shit. Out of my peripheral vision I see him
scowling as I breeze by.

I grin.

But my smirk is quickly knocked from my face when I round
the corner and literally run smack into Mister Tall Dark and Bald.
Both of our mouths drop.

His long, thick, dark-chocolate dick and big, heavy balls flash
through my head. Another one of my online, late-night creeps.

Dark Stallion.

My mind instantly flashes back to our first night together. After he responded to one of my online ads, then sent me a picture of his dick, I agreed to meet him at the Hilton on JFK Parkway in Short Hills. I entered the hotel room, first. Then five minutes later he walked in, finding me undressed and already on my knees in the middle of the room in a negligee. I necked his dick, super-soaked his balls, until he shot out a load of hot, foaming cum. Two hours later—after three rounds of dick sucking and pussy eating, I walked out of that hotel with a well-licked pussy. And he staggered out after me, well sucked and drained to the last drop.

"Oh shit," we both mutter simultaneously.

"*You're* Jasper's attorney?"

He lets out a nervous chuckle, quickly glancing around the corridor. "Yeah, in the flesh. And you're beautiful as ever."

"And *his* wife. I didn't know you were an attorney."

"You never asked."

I take in his smooth-shaven face and dimpled chin. Then allow my gaze to linger over the rest of his six-foot-three frame, before setting my stare back up at him. His cologne licks my nostrils, teasing my senses. It's intoxicating.

Damn him!

"Well, I guess I wouldn't have had the chance," I say, lowering my voice to a hushed whisper, "with your dick down in my throat."

He nervously shifts his weight from one Ferragamo loafer to the other. Beads of sweat instantly pop up across his forehead. "Fuck." He runs a hand down over his mouth. "This is awkward as hell. I didn't know you were my client's wife until I looked over and saw you sitting with counsel. My client told me who you were when I glanced over in your direction."

"In the flesh," I say, repeating his line.

"Shit," he grumbles, glancing at his Rolex. "I probably should see if I can get someone else from my firm to handle this."

I tilt my head. "Why?"

"Well, uh, given the circumstances. I think…"

"You should stay on as his attorney, Wil." I grin. "There's really no need in getting all nervous and pulling out now. It's only a restraining order hearing. I won't tell, if you won't."

"Right, right."

"But if you're planning on representing him in my divorce, then I'd probably rethink passing his case over to someone else real fast because it's going to get real messy." He tells me he's a criminal defense attorney by trade that someone else from his firm would most likely take on his case for our divorce.

"Lucky him," I say sarcastically. "Do me a favor. Since you're a criminal attorney, when you go back over to your *client*, tell him I want the names of all the niggas he had rape me *after* he staged my kidnapping." He blinks, shock registering on his handsome face. "Yeah, that's what *your client* did to me when he found out I was out throating dick behind his back." His mouth drops open. He opens his mouth to speak, but I don't give him a chance to. "By the way…how are the wife and kids?"

He nervously clears his throat. "They're good. Thanks. Listen. I better get going. They'll be calling us in shortly. Is your contact info still the same?"

I nod. "Yup. It sure is."

Fourteen

There's really no difference between gold diggers, ditch diggers or
gravediggers...

"All rise!" the bailiff says in a singsong voice, opening the
back courtroom door. In walks this regal-looking sister
with skin the color of dark fudge. The courtroom falls
silent as she briskly makes her way toward the bench, her black
judge's robe swooshing behind her as she climbs up the stairs to
the bench and sits.

"Court is now in session!" the bailiff barks. "The Honorable Precious Lenora Mobley presiding. All electronic devices are to be
turned off now. Please be seated."

Judge Mobley glances around the courtroom. "Good morning."
She clears her throat, placing her reading glasses on. "We are here
on the matter of Pasha Nivea Tyler v. Jasper Tyler in determining
probable cause for a final restraining order on an existing TRO.
Docket number F2013-01033." She looks up from her papers. "I
see we have counsel here for both parties. Counselors, please
identify yourselves for the record."

Both attorneys stand.

"Maria McCartney for the plaintiff, your Honor."

"William Stratford for the defendant."

The judge nods her head, then gets right down to business. "I
will listen to testimony from both parties, review any evidence
relating to this matter, then make my ruling accordingly. I see here

that a TRO was issued after an alleged altercation transpired between the alleged victim, Mrs. Tyler, and her husband, Mr. Tyler, the alleged aggressor, at her place of business. Is this correct?" She looks up from the bench over at my attorney.

Maria stands. "That is correct, Your Honor. Mr. Tyler entered my client's place of business and assaulted her during a verbal dispute in her office." The judge wants to know if there were any witnesses. "Your Honor, patrons witnessed Mr. Tyler's agitation prior to the events leading up to my client's assault in her office. And they did, in fact, witness her bruises afterward when Mr. Tyler left the premises."

Will stands to address the court. "Your Honor. My client loves his wife. And he wants nothing more than to reconcile their marriage and work out their differences."

Maria scoffs, standing. "Well, Your Honor. What's love got to do with it when you can use your fist to show someone *just* how much you care? There will be no reconciliation. Prior to court, counsel was given divorce papers on behalf of my client to give to his client, Mr. Tyler. Mrs. Tyler has been living in a state of constant fear throughout her relationship with Mr. Tyler. And over the last two years, she reports things getting progressively worse. That the violence has escalated to physical altercations. The most recent one, as stated earlier, a little over a week ago…"

The judge peers over the rim of her glasses. "Mrs. Tyler, is this true?"

I stand, dabbing my eyes. I nod, sniffling. "Yes, Your Honor." I pull out my Academy Award-nominated performance and give her waterworks. "I am terrified of my husband. Ever since he found out I'd cheated while he was incarcerated, he's changed."

"How so?' the judge inquires, clasping her hands in front of her.

"He monitors everything I do. Has people tracking and following me." I choke back a sob. *"He* constantly threatens me. And last week h-h-he c-c-came into my place of business and b-b-beat me."

"Were the police called?" the judge wants to know. When I tell her no, she wants to know why not. Dumb bitch!

"Because I was afraid to. Jasper has threatened that h-h-he was going to have me *handled* if I told anyone what happened."

Jasper glares over at me. "Fuckin' lyin'-ass. Yo, is this how ya snake-ass wanna do it, Pasha, huh? You really wanna get dirty?"

Judge Mobley scowls. "Mr. Tyler! You will watch your mouth in this courtroom, you understand? Or I will…"

"Your Honor," Jasper's attorney interjects, quickly standing to his feet, "if I may address the court for a brief moment. My client insists his wife is fabricating untruths. He denies all accusations of ever being physically abusive. He denies any wrongdoing. And, in fact, my client argues that it is his wife who attacked him in her office once the door was closed behind them. Mrs. Tyler is a scorned woman who is simply trying to assassinate my client's character."

The judge glares at him. "And *why*, counsel, would she want to do that?"

"My client feels…"

"And *your* client," she scolds, cutting him off and pointing a finger at Jasper, "will have a chance to speak what he *feels* when I'm done with Mrs. Tyler. Understood?"

I shoot Wil a dirty look. He clears his throat. "Yes, Your Honor." He sits his fine, chocolate ass back in his seat.

Bastard!

"Good." The judge brings her attention back to me, softening her voice. "Continue Mrs. Tyler."

"Umm, Your Honor," Maria quickly interjects. "I'd like to submit photos of bruises my client sustained during a brutal attack back in 2010. It is believed that my client's husband was behind the alleged attack."

Mister Tall Dark and Bald aka Dark Stallion hops to his feet. "Your Honor, this is all hearsay. No charges were ever filed against my client. My client was by her side during that whole tragic ordeal."

The judge gives him a "nigga-please-sit-your-fine-ass-down" look. "That may be true," she says. "But judging by these horrific photos, it is evident that *someone* was behind this brutal attack."

"And if I might add," Maria says, "I also have photos of my client's most recent bruises from a week ago." She hands them to the bailiff who gives them over to the judge.

I glance over and see Jasper whispering something to Wil. I quickly shift my eyes back to the judge who is shuffling through the photos, every so often glaring over at Jasper.

I grin inwardly. *Fuck with me if you want, nigga!*

I start sobbing louder this time. "Y-y-our Honor. I-I-I j-j-just…" I pause, shaking my head and pulling in a deep breath. Maria reaches for my arm reassuringly. Oh, the stage is set lovely. Maria stands to address the court.

"Your Honor, as you can see, my client is extremely distressed. She wants no contact with her husband. And has asked that he stay away from her, and her place of business, as well as the marital home." Maria requests that Jasper only be allowed supervised visitation with Jaylen down at the local police department. And that he not have any contact in writing or in person with any of my family members, particularly Nana.

Jasper springs to his feet. "Yo, c'mon, Pasha. Are you serious? What the *fuck*, yo?! You'd really stand up in this muhfucka 'n' snake me like this, huh, yo? Tryna keep me from my muhfuckin' seed, yo. What the fuck?! You on tha bullshit, yo!"

Judge Mobley brings her gavel down on the bench. "Order in the court! Mr. Tyler, your outburst will not be tolerated in my courtroom. Another outburst like that and I will have you thrown out of my courtroom. Do I make myself clear?"

Jasper glares at the judge, taking his seat. I can see his jaw twitching from over here. I know him. He's about to blow his stack.

After a few tense seconds, the judge breaks their stare down, looking over at his attorney. "Counselor, I'd advise you to—"

Jasper stands up. Undoes his tie. "Yo, he ain't gotta advise me on *shit*, yo. Fuckin' trick! My fuckin' wife wanna play muthafuckin' games up in this muhfucka, like she scared of a muhfucka 'n' shit. Ya ass wasn't scared when you was out there suckin' a buncha muhfuckas dicks, was you? Fuck outta here wit' this bullshit, yo, wit' ya cum-suckin' ass. How 'bout you tell these muhfuckas how you tried to bite off my muthafuckin' balls, yo."

I hear a few gasps and "ohmygods" in back of us.

"Mr. Tyler, this is your *last* warning. That language will *not* be tolerated in this court," Judge Mobley says sternly. "Now, take your seat."

"Why the fuck you ain't mention that shit, huh, trick-ass? And fuck them muthafuckin' divorce papers, yo. I ain't signin' shit, dick-suckin' bitch!"

I cringe. Feel myself shrinking. This nigga has dragged me for filth for all to see. Turned my indiscretions, before a packed courtroom, into a Public Service Announcement. It takes everything in me to sit, stone-faced, my eyes glued to the judge's bench.

It isn't until Jasper storms out of the courtroom that I realize I am holding my breath. The spectators seated around us get an ear-and-eyeful, causing hushed whispers to fill the courtroom.

"My goodness," Maria says, leaning over and whispering to me. "He's a real ball of fire, isn't he?"

I nod. My voice stuck somewhere in the back of my throat. I feel myself suffocating. Feel myself getting lightheaded. Air. I need air.

"Order!" the judge barks as she bangs her gavel. "Order in my courtroom, I said!"

I gasp, finally breathing, pulling in several deep breaths, stretching my burning lungs, slowly blowing out each breath, until my heart stops racing and I find a calming balance. I blink, glancing around the courtroom. Realization blooms into view. My lips curl into a triumphant smirk.

Jasper has handed me exactly what I wanted. His outburst has proven that he is a danger to my welfare and safety. And Jaylen's.

Dark Stallion attempts to apologize for *his client*. I roll my eyes. "Your Honor, please forgive my client's outburst. He's under a lot of emotional stress. He hasn't been home in over a week. And he hasn't been able to see his son. He misses his family."

"Well, your client has a very strange way of showing it." The judge peers at him, lifting her glasses from off the bridge of her nose. "Counselor, if *this* is any indication of how your client behaves in the presence of the court, I can only imagine how he is behind closed doors. He's lucky I don't hold him in contempt and have him hauled off in handcuffs. I'm ordering that your client, Mr. Tyler, attend anger management."

"Yes, Your Honor. I'll be sure to inform him of such."

"You do that." She clears her throat. "Okay. After reviewing numerous photos of bruises, and given Mr. Tyler's lack of regard for this courtroom, and his aggressive outburst displayed before me, I find probable cause. And do hereby find that an act of domestic violence did occur against Mrs. Tyler…"

A sly smile eases over my glossed lips. *Oh, it's about to get ugly now,* I think as the judge grants me my final order of protection. *Real ugly…*

Fifteen

A weak nigga will be blinded by greed, and misguided by lust…

"D amn," James says, unbuckling his brown leather belt, then unfastening his beige khakis, "I swear I didn't think I'd ever get a chance to feel your beautiful lips wrapped around my dick again. I feel like I'm about to die and go to heaven. This is all I've been thinking about since our phone conversation."

Nigga, please! I fight to keep from rolling my eyes. When I called his ass last Sunday, asking him to track down Mydikneeds Urtongue2's location, the first thing his horny-ass wanted to do was barter. One of my specialty dick-sucks for his IT service. The horny nigga didn't even want money, just my infamous lip, tongue, and throat work loaded with a bunch of this juicy spit and a whole lot of slobbering.

Now I know I could have found someone else to get the job done for me. And I'm sure Lamar knows someone who knows someone who's good at hacking into computers as well as accessing IP addresses, and everything else. But I didn't want anyone else.

I *wanted* him.

I guess, subconsciously, when I rushed back to the salon, tearing up my office to locate his card, a part of me wanted to feel his dick stuffed down in the back of my throat, one more time.

So here I am.

At his office.

Up on the eighteenth floor, overlooking a magnificent view of the city.

Eight o'clock in the evening.

On a Friday night.

With Lamar outside, waiting.

"A deal's a deal, right," I say, pressing him up against the floor-to-ceiling window, then slinking down to my knees. He's concerned someone will see his bare ass cheeks plastered against the glass. I tell him to stop worrying. That the only things that'll see him this high up are birds and planes.

I glance up at him. Flutter my long lashes while roughly yanking down his pants along with his gray boxer briefs. His thick, curved dick is already hard as it springs forward, then swings slightly to the right, bobbing in anticipation. Its veins bulging.

"Oooh, look at this pretty black dick," I say, grabbing it at the base with my right hand, then easing my left hand over the shaft while licking my lips. I stroke it, slow and sensual, caressing it with loving care.

"Yeah, you like that big dick, don't you, baby?"

I nod my head, glancing up at him. Coyly. "Uh-huh. I love it." I stroke it some more. It's hot and heavy. "Oooh, it feels so good in my hands. It's so thick and hard."

"Yeah, what you gonna do for daddy's big black snake, baby?"

I silently roll my eyes up in my head. *Daddy? Nigga, please.*

Niggas kill me with that daddy shit. Then again, I can't really fault him, or them, since it's bitches like me who stay gassing their heads up and keep them believing they're some-damn-body's *daddy*.

Like now…

"I'm gonna make daddy's big black dick throb and pulse. I'm

gonna wet it up real good for you, *daaaddiiiiiie*, then suck the cum out of it. Then I'm gonna smear your nut all over my pretty lips. I'm gonna paint my mouth with your sweet thick nut, daddy."

I slither my tongue along his piss slit. He's already leaking sticky precum. James is a nonsmoker and the fact that he doesn't use any type of drugs is evident in the way his clear, stringy nectar tastes. Sweet.

"Aaaah, shit, yeah. That's what I'm talking about. I want you to freak daddy's big dick with them pretty-ass lips and that tight-ass throat."

Ohmygod, this computer geek is a real undercover freak.

I kiss the tip of his dick. Flick my long tongue over it. Then suction my lips ever so slight over it, allowing my tongue to swirl figure-eights over and around it. His walnut-size balls tighten as my fingers slide behind them, moving in slow, taunting circles. There's something disturbing to me about a nigga having a big dick and a small ball sac. The two just don't seem to fit. Whatever!

I cup them, then tug lightly.

James groans low in his throat. Less than two minutes and I already got the nigga going through it. And, in one swift motion, I unlatch my jaws and swoop my hungry mouth over his dick and gulp him down. His whole dick disappears inside my mouth. I release him from my throat, my lips gliding over the length of him as I pull his dick up to the tip, then gulp him back in.

"Oh, shit. That shit's sexy as fuck. Aaah, shit, your mouth feels better than pussy. Damn…wish my wife could handle my dick like this…"

I proudly spit-shine his pole, throat-fuck his cock. Gurgle and suckle him. Give him an Oscar-winning porn-star performance. My spit glands go into overdrive as I neck him down, gulping and gurgling. My neck, throat and head all working in sync to deliver the ultimate deep throat experience.

"Aaah, shit yeah…" he whispers. "Oh, yeah, baby, suck that dick. Oooooh, sssssssshiiiit…you love daddy's big dick down in your throat, don't you? You daddy's nasty little cocksucker, aren't you…?

Nigga, I think to myself, coating his dick with spit and neck juice, *I'll be whatever you want as long as you handle what I need handled.*

I grunt out my answer, gulping and slurping.

James rams his pelvis into my face and I swallow more of him, all of him. There's nothing left, just his tiny balls brushing against my chin every so often as I bob and neck weave. My pussy tingles and twitches as I swallow and swallow, milking his big dick, coaxing a nut out of it, making it harder and thicker inside my throat.

I focus. Steady my breathing, extending my tongue out, lapping his balls. My clit is on fire. Wet flames roar through my pussy. And I'm not sure how much more of this I can take before I shove a finger—or two, or three—inside of my boiling snatch. Before I am demanding James suck my clit and tongue my pussy. Before I am riding his face down and dirty.

The overwhelming urge, the burning need, to nut pushes its way through my uterus, shakes my walls, causing my clit to throb.

Slowly, I pull James' dick out of my throat, then look up at him licking my smeared MAC-glossed and spit-slick lips while stroking his rock-hard dick in my hand. I lean in and lick around his gonads—smooth, computer geek balls; swollen, cum-filled chocolate nuggets dipped in man musk.

"Oooh, yeah…that's it. Suck them balls, baby." I suck one in, then the other—and I still have room in my wet, slippery mouth for a set of two more. I soak them with spit. Gently roll them around in my mouth.

He shakes and moans and chants how good my mouth feels.

Professes how magical my tongue is. Groans out how wet and warm my throat feels. He holds my face and eases his man marbles out of my mouth.

He grabs his dick, slaps my face, my lips, with it. "Finish sucking on this dick. I'm ready to bust a nut down in your throat."

"Yeah, daddy…mmmm…give me that hot cream…"

I lick up and down both sides of his spit-slick shaft, then glide my lips along the underside of it and kiss his balls one last time.

He moans. "Yeah, baby, lick them shits…ooh fuck…wish my wife knew how to handle them balls the way you do, baby…oooh, yeah…"

I smirk.

"You love this head game, don't you?"

"Hell yeah…you got that demon head, baby. Have a man all possessed 'n' shit."

Demon head? Oooh, I like that. I'll have to use that.

I swallow him into my mouth again, looking up at him as he peers down at me in amazement. I give him my infamous deep-throat special. No hands, all neck, rapid head bobbing, tongue swirling and gliding along the length of his dick.

James moans and pants. His eyes roll up in the back of his head. His face is twisted. His bottom lip pulled in, his teeth bite down into the meaty flesh of his lip. The feeling is getting to him. My throat becomes a rushing waterfall of warm, wet, tight pleasure. "Aaah, motherfuck, shiiit…mmmm, motherfucker…god…daa-aamn…aaah…shit, baby…mmmph…you about to make me bust this nut… mmmm…"

My pussy swells with excitement and lust by his constant moaning and panting and grunting and growling. He cries out. "Aaaaaaaaaah, fuuuuuuuuuuuuck!"

He begins to pound harder with deep, long strokes. His dick

swiftly, effortlessly, glides in and out of my groaning throat. James' hips thrusts as he palms the top of my head with one hand, then inches his hand up his polo shirt and tweaks one of his nipples. I grip his ass, squeezing and pushing it as he fucks in and out of my gaping, gulping throat. My mouth drools. His cock is coated with a mix of spit and precum. Some of it pools out of my mouth, sliding down my chin, then puddles down into the carpet.

"Aaaaaah, aaaaaah, aaaaaah…oooh, oooh, oooh…mmmm…" His ass muscles tighten, the balls of his booted feet lift, he rocks back on his heels, then plants his size-thirteens back onto the carpet, dipping at the knees. He grunts. Thrusts. Then convulses. His body quaking as a torrent of thick, briny cum blasts down in my throat, filling my mouth. I continue sucking, greedily siphoning out every drop of his nut. His pubic hair is saturated in spit and cum.

"Fuckfuckfuckfuck…ohhhh, ohhhh, ohhhh, ohhhhhh…"

He is still coming, another round of hot nut bolting from his dick. My cum-soaked throat becomes an overflowing reservoir of nut and spit. I suck him until his dick softens, then plops out of my gushy mouth. I swallow, hard. Glide my tongue over my teeth to catch any remaining droplets of his nectar, then swallow again.

I stand. Lick my lips. Wipe the corners of my mouth with sticky fingers, then lick them clean. "I believe you have something for me," I finally say, savoring the last drop of him and reaching into my purse, pulling out a pack of unscented wipes. I wipe my mouth, then my hands, discarding the wipes into his trash.

"Yes, I do." He blows out a heavy breath. "Whew, give me a sec to get my head right. You got me spinning."

I smile. "You know this deep throat is dangerous."

"Baby, head that damn good needs to be outlawed. To get sucked into a stupor should be a crime."

I eye him as he reaches for the window, plants a hand up to steady himself from falling as he stuffs his glazed dick back into his underwear, then pulls up his khakis. I can tell by the dazed look in his eyes that I have his ass still weak from the ten-and-a-half-minute suck session I put on him.

He fastens his belt, then wobbles over to his cubicle. He pauses, taking another deep breath. "Damn. I need a cigarette and I don't even smoke," he says as he shuffles through a manila folder on his desk, pulling out a white envelope. "I have everything you need right here."

He hands me the sealed envelope.

I smile, sliding it into my bag. I pull out my compact and a tube of Coral lipstick, gliding a fresh coat over my plump, just-finished-sucking-a-big-black-dick lips. I check myself in the small mirror, popping my lips.

When I am done, I toss everything back in my bag. Then hand James an envelope. He gives me a quizzical look, peering into the envelope. He blinks at the wad of hundreds.

"What's this for?"

"For the hard dick," I say, tossing my hair, then walking off. I don't give him a chance to speak before I am spinning on my heels. "It was nice doing business with you," I say over my shoulder as I maneuver my way around sets of cubicles toward the bank of elevators out in the hall.

"Anytime, baby," he says. "The *pleasure* was all mine."

I ignore him. We've both gotten what we wanted. So there's nothing else to be said.

The only thing on my mind now is getting to the nigga who had been a thorn in my side from the moment he learned who I was. Mmmph. I super-soaked his dick down one damn time, then the nigga turned all nutty on me—after sending me an email a few months later wanting another round of these soft lips and this wet neck—when I kindly told him, "Thanks. But no thanks."

Yeah, he had a long, fat, juicy dick. And, yeah, back then one of my dick-sucking rules was to never give up the neck to the same nigga more than three rounds. So technically I could have spun his top another round, or two. But I didn't. I didn't want to. There was something about that nigga that seemed a little off.

And I was right. The bitch-ass nigga tracked me down and started calling my salon, threatening and harassing me, nonstop. Having niggas bust out my car window, and smash out the window in my salon. Then the nigga took it a step too far when he hid in wait behind a set of bushes in my yard, then jumped from out of them as I prepared to stick my key into my front door—after having been out most of the evening on another one of my late-night dick-suck prowls. The nigga admitted he had been following my every move.

"This shit ain't over, bitch!"

Oh you got that right, bitch! *It's far from over.*

So you best believe. The *only* thing that has my attention at the moment hides behind the screen name MydickneedsUrtongue2.

Watch your back, motherfucker! I'm coming for you...

Sixteen

Some niggas will take their regrets to their graves; others will repent...

"Miss Pasha, girl, I gotta 'hold of this...nigga-bitch! Yes, *gawd!* I bailed his black ass out. Yes, *fahverGawd!* Got his no-good monkey-ass...strung up...like the dirty nigga-coon he is! Greasy muthafucka ain't know what hit 'im 'til his black ass dropped. We..."

We? Who's we?

"...Been takin' it to his muthafuckin' skull all night! Now I need you to get ya high-class ass on over here so we can finish peelin' the black off his back..."

My pulse quickens as she talks a mile a minute, sounding like she's just finished running a marathon. She's breathing heavy in my ear.

"...I ain't wanna do him like this, *lawdGawd* knows I didn't! But he had'a learn, goddammit! He tore his muthafuckin' drawz with me...kidnappin' bitches. He ain't had no business tryna do me like this, Miss Pasha, girl..."

"Ohmygod, Cassandra! Slow down. *Who* are you talking about? I mean, who is *we*? You're talking—"

She cuts me off. "Sugah-boo, *boom-boom!* Is you gettin' dicked in ya ears right now or is you not listenin' to a word I'm sayin'? Who you *think* I'm talkin' 'bout? Don't do me, goddammit! Stop actin' like you gotta brain full of nut. You know I ain't in my right frame of mind right now, Miss Pasha, girl. You know this nigga-coon got my insides all gutted up in shame. Now I gotta hope I don't shit on myself fuckin' 'round with this no-good nigga-coon. I'ma kill his monkey-ass, goddammit…Darius punch his goddamn balls in…!"

In the background all I hear are loud grunts and groans, followed by piercing yelps, like someone's being tortured.

I cringe.

"…He tried to do me, goddammit! He wanna kidnap bitches for niggas… Nigga-coon, you ain't had no goddamn business gettin' involved in no shit like that, goddamn you! And what the fuck you do with the money you got paid, huh, nigga-bitch? 'Cause you damn sure ain't pay ya child support with it. Darius, do him good, goddammit! Soon as I get off this phone…'ma take a blade to his throat! So what if she was suckin' a buncha dick… that ain't have shit do with you…!"

I hear more grunts in the background, followed by groans, then a piercing scream.

I frown. *Is she motherfucking serious right now?!* Now I'm annoyed that this bitch is talking sideways about me and I'm right here on the phone.

"Knock his muthafuckin' teeth out, Darius, goddammit…!"

"Ummm, hello? Hello? Do me a favor, Cassandra, if you're going to talk shit about me, at least *wait* until I'm off the damn phone."

"Now wait a minute, Miss Pasha, girl. Ain't nobody talkin' shit 'bout yo' ass. I respect the fact that you a cum-guzzler, sugah-boo. I'm sayin' shit that's true. Don't do me."

I take a deep breath. Count to ten in my head. Decide to let it go. "Cassandra, where are you?"

She tells me she's at her son's barbershop, Gutter Cuts, on Grove Street in Irvington. I almost swerve off the road hearing that. I quickly regain control of the wheel, glancing at the digital clock. 9:38 p.m.

There is no fucking way in hell I want to be on *that* side of town, on *that* particular street, at *this* time of night—alone, driving a big-body Benz. Grove Street is about as gutter as the name of her son's barbershop. *Gutter Cuts is right! One wrong turn, you might end up getting the* guts *cut right out of you!*

I tell Booty I'll be there in about fifteen minutes, then disconnect, checking in my rearview mirror for Lamar's SUV. I flick on my flashers, quickly pulling over on the side of the road. Lamar stops his truck behind me. I eye him as he gets out and makes his way over to the car, a hand on the handle of his gun tucked in his waist.

I roll my window down.

He has a concerned look on his face, looking around. "Yo, you good? E'erything aiight?"

"I need to make a detour. Do you have plans tonight?"

"Nah, what's good?"

"I have to make a stop by Gutter Cuts…"

"Over on Grove Street in Irvington?"

I nod.

"*This* time of night?"

I give him a blank stare, raising a brow.

"Aiight-aiight, I was only askin'. I got you. How long you think you gonna be over there?" I tell him about thirty, no more than forty-five, minutes. He suggests I park my car and let him drive me in his truck. I agree. He tells me he wants me to follow him to one of his boys' custom-detail shops about fifteen, twenty, minutes away. That he'll pull my car into one of the garages, where it'll be safe.

Thirty minutes later, we're pulling up in front of Gutter Cuts.

He hops out, first, coming around to open my door. I tell him he can wait for me. That I shouldn't be inside for too long. He tells me no worries. That he'll be right here. He stands outside, leaning up against the passenger door, watching as I walk up to the shop's doors, taking in the sway of my hips. I can feel his eyes on me.

I glance over my shoulder, and smirk, catching his stare on my ass. *I knew it.*

I ring the bell, peeking through the glass panes.

The shop is dimly lit by recessed lighting. And judging by what I see through the glass, it looks like it's a really nice barbershop. I count eight barber chairs. There's a long glass case over to the right filled with what looks like CDs and/or DVDs. I spot another glass case that has different types and sizes of plastic bottles, tubes, and jars of what I suspect to be hair care products. Sitting on top of that case is an oblong case filled with what looks to be earrings and or bracelets. *Mygod, theses niggas even selling jewelry up in here.*

I continue scanning the area through the window. There's a clothes rack next to it, and a mounted wall display with hanging jerseys along the wall in back of the glass case. There are several shelves on another wall lined with hats, fitted and probably snapbacks. *Mmmph. Probably all bootleg shit!*

I ring the bell again. A few minutes later, there's someone barechested, clad in sweats and Timbs, coming from the back area walking toward the door. He's a tall, dark-chocolate, broad-shouldered nigga with rippled abs, round brown eyes and dimpled chin. I eyeball him as he unlocks the door, opening it. He reeks of weed, and hood grit. And there's a faint hint of cologne. My probing eyes move purposefully up and down his chiseled frame.

There's blood on his left hand. He tucks it behind his back, hiding his bruised knuckles.

"Yo, what's good?" he says, eyeing me suspiciously, glancing over toward Lamar, then back at me. "You, Pasha, right?"

I nod, looking up into his dark eyes. *Yes. And I love sucking dick.* I swallow. "Yes."

He sweeps his gaze lazily over me, then steps back, slightly, motioning with his head for me to step inside. I step in, trying not to brush by him. He locks the door behind me. "C'mon, follow me. We're down in the basement."

The nigga doesn't introduce himself. And he doesn't need to. Looking at him, I know he has to be one of Booty's sons. He looks like her around the eyes, mouth and nose. *He must be Darius*, I muse, following behind him. I've never seen, or met, any of her children, personally. Never had a reason to. I try not to stare at his muscled back, or the way his sweats hang off his waist. His street swag is on high. And I feel myself losing focus.

I bet his dick is like two king-size Snickers bars. Doubly thick, sweet, and packed with gooey nuts!

Mygod, he has a nice ass!

Bitch, snap out of it!

I blink.

At the end of the hall, to the left, he opens a door, then gestures with his hand for me to go, first. Instantly, I hear Booty cursing and screaming. "Nigga-coon, you tried to do me, goddammit!" Next, I hear the cracking sound of something slashing, then a loud, pained grunt. "I'ma whip the skin off'a ya black-ass, goddamn you, nigga-coon!" *Slash!*

There's more grunting.

Slash!

"No-good nigga-coon! I ain't raise no goddamn kidnappers, goddamn you!" *Slash!*

I grip the railing leading down into the basement. Take one step at a time, bracing myself for whatever I might see.

The basement is thick with weed smoke.

My eyes widen in shock. There he is. Her son. Jah'Mel. Naked. Bloody. A bloodstained pillowcase over his head, his head hangs, his chin resting on his chest. His arms are extended over his head, his wrists tied and bound together by rope to a large pipe in the ceiling. Judging by the dark-purplish bruises around his ribs and chest area, it's obvious he's fucked up real bad. It looks as if he's barely breathing.

There's a puddle in the middle of the floor. Piss, I think. I fight not to stare at his long, thick dick. *Mygod, he has a dick like a horse!* I shift my eyes. Bring my attention to Booty, clad in a pair of pink Juicy Couture sweats that she's cut off into a pair of booty shorts with a pink wife beater, and a pair of high-heeled, brown knee-high Timberland boots. A brown silk Gucci scarf is wrapped around her head, Aunt Jemima style. She's pacing the floor—looking wild and crazy, a half-smoked blunt dangling from her lips, her ass bouncing and shaking, her ass cheeks showing, as she circles around Jah'Mel; the way a starved lioness would circle its prey. She's sweating like a bull. The brass knuckles on her right hand are bloody and she's holding an extension cord.

I cringe.

She stops pacing and circling the floor. "Yessss, goddammit, Miss Pasha, girl! It's 'bout damn time you got ya ole messy freak-ass over here. We swooped down on this nigga-coon's black, rusty ass the way he did you…!"

Suddenly I am right back where it all began. At the Mall at Short Hills. In the parking lot. Shopping bags in one hand. My other hand stuck down into my handbag searching for my car keys, then pulling them out and disarming the alarm. Opening the back door and tossing my bags in; my hair being violently pulled and my head yanked back before I can close the door. There's a click of a gun as it presses against my temple. My cell and keys hit the ground.

"Bitch, if you so much as flinch, I'ma dead ya ass right here. You hear me?"

"Yes, gawd!" Booty exclaims, snatching me from the memory. I blink her into view. "He ain't know what hit him. I bailed his ass out, all grins 'n' giggles 'til we got his ass up in here for the surprise party." She curls her lip and blows smoke up toward the ceiling. She walks over and roughly snatches the pillowcase off his head. "You still wanna kidnap bitches 'n' put guns to they heads, nigga-coon?"

I gasp at the sight of him.

Blood is leaking out of his mouth and nose. His right eye is swollen shut and bleeding. His left eye socket literally looks punched in.

Yes, he's the one who held the gun. He's the one who punched me in the mouth causing blood to gush out, when I started screaming and trying to fight him off of me. *"Bitch, what the fuck is wrong with you, huh? I told you to keep your motherfuckin' mouth shut, you stupid bitch."* He's the one who hit me upside the head with the butt of his gun, causing everything around me to blur.

Booty slaps his face. Blood and spittle fly out of his mouth. "Nigga-coon, answer me, goddammit! You gonna learn today, goddamn you! I *saaaaid*, you still wanna kidnap bitches?"

He sputters. More blood spews out of his mouth as he tries to speak. Whatever he is attempting to say is inaudible. I glance down at the pool of piss beneath his bare feet, again.

I blink.

Ohmygod! They done knocked three of this nigga's teeth out!

"Miss Pasha, girl," Booty calls out, holding out the extension cord to me. "C'mon on over 'n' take this cord 'n' get you a taste of this nigga-coon's black ass. Do him up right. But don't beat the life outta him, Miss Pasha, girl. He's still my baby. And I ain't tryna see you kill 'im."

Umm, sweetie, I think you're doing a good job of that on your own.

I shake my head. "He's had enough. *I've* seen enough." I slowly walk toward him. I had thought I'd be ready to jump on him, to punch him. Stab him. Or shoot him. That I'd be enraged for what he'd done to me.

But I am not.

What he'd done to me wasn't a personal attack on me. It was a mission. He was only doing what he was instructed, what he was paid, to do.

Kidnap me.

And Booty has already done more to him than I would have ever imagined doing. There is no need for anything more to be done. He has to live with this. As do I. And his scars, his broken bones, his missing teeth, will all be reminders of what he'd done.

I cast my glare over toward Booty. "Untie him."

I hear her son Darius mumbling something under his breath to the right of me. I'm almost certain I hear this nigga say, "This trick-ass." I cut an evil eye over at him. He's standing, glaring at me. Arms folded. His dark lips turned up into a menacing sneer.

Booty grunts. "Mmmph. *Untie him?* Sugah-boo, *boom!* Not tonight. You might run shit down over there at Nappy No More. But you ain't runnin' a damn thang over here, sugah-boo. So, *boom!* This nigga-coon gonna hang there all night 'n' think 'bout what the fuck he done did. He tore his goddamn drawz down to the shitty seams. I ain't havin' no coon-fuckery goin' on with none'a my goddamn kids 'n' they think I'ma cosign it.

"No, goddammit! They know I will bring the ruckus up on they goddamn skulls. I ain't raise his ass to be out there snatchin' up bitches 'n' tryna pistol whip 'em. He's lucky we ain't hang his goddamn coon-ass upside down instead. Oooh, this black-dick nigga-coon lucky he's my son 'n' I'm tryna keep it classy 'n' not do him real gutter tonight. I should dig my nails into his goddamn big, ole, hairy balls. Ole nasty coon-fuck!"

This bitch is really out of control!

I gaze at him warily, taking a deep breath, then slowly exhaling. I glance over at Darius, again. He's smoking a blunt eyeing me suspiciously. I decide he's as ruthless as Booty. They're both cut from the same damn nasty cloth.

I turn my attention back to her. She's staring at me as well with a puzzled look on her face, both hands up on her thick hips. She sucks her teeth. "Umm, is you gonna serve him up a taste or what, Miss Pasha, girl? Or is you gonna stand there 'n' be all flip-floppy? Oooh, I can't stand me no flip-floppin' bitch…"

I roll my eyes. "From the looks of things, you and…" I glance over at Darius. "Darius, right?" He tosses me a head nod in acknowledgment, blowing smoke up in the air. "Well, seems to me the two of you have already given him enough *tastes* for the night. So I had *hoped* to have the opportunity to talk to him. You know. Maybe get some useful information out of him. But that's obviously impossible with his jaw broken…"

I look down at his hands. They are twitching slightly. His knuckles are severely swollen and bloody as if they'd been beaten with an object.

I give him a pitiful look, shaking my head. I shoot Booty an annoyed look. "And having him write out anything is also out of the question since it appears the bones in *both* of his hands are broken."

"Now look," Booty huffs, stamping her foot, "don't do me, Miss Pasha, girl. You damn right his hands are broken. I smashed 'em real goddamn good with a hammer. His coon-ass will think good 'n' goddamn hard the next time he wanna kidnap another bitch at gunpoint, goddammit! You know I don't do—"

I put a hand up, cutting her off. "I don't want to hear any more of this. I *said* he's had enough. Untie him." I reach out and gently touch his mangled, bloody face.

He fights to lift his head, struggles to open his one eye. But, when he finally does, recognition registers on his face. He moves his mouth, attempts to speak. "I-I-I…"

I stop him.

"*You* helped Jasper ruin me," I say, looking him squarely in the face while reaching into my bag and pulling out a napkin. "Did you know that?"

He tries to talk. I raise a hand, stopping him. "Don't. Thanks to *you* and your sidekick—whoever he is, the night the two of you kidnapped me from the mall"—I lightly dab the blood seeping out around his swollen eye—"I was sexually assaulted down in a basement for almost three days, before the nigga who paid you to kidnap me finally came down and beat me half to death, then had his goons dump me in Branch Brook park to die. *You* helped that nigga do that."

He grimaces.

I pause, allowing the weight of what I've said to crush him more. "Did you know that six men took turns skull-*fucking* me? My punishment for sucking dicks behind his back while he was in prison."

He hangs his head.

I gaze at him for moments before saying more. "I hope whatever money you earned that night, *Jah'Mel*, for being an accomplice to what happened to me was well worth it."

Booty huffs. "Hell no, it wasn't worth it...!"

I bite down on my bottom lip. Count to ten in my head. I've had enough of this, her mouth. There's no need for me to be here. With a hanging jaw, unable to talk, to provide me any kind of information, Jah'Mel is useless to me.

If Booty wants to spend the rest of her night beating what's left of his life out of him, let her. His meaningless death will be on her hands, not mine. I have much bigger dragons to slay. And, right now, thanks to James securing the location of that IP address for me, the first nigga to be brought down and slaughtered is, MydickneedsUrtongue2.

I'll have to admit, James really earned himself that wet, sloppy dick suck I put on his ass earlier this evening. By tapping into several databases, he not only secured the address and full name of that nigga, but his social security number, date of birth, as well as his criminal history. The nigga has been in and out of the county jail for nonpayment of child support and disorderly persons' offenses over the last seven years. Mmmph. Anyway, dropping to my knees and sucking and swallowing the hot cream out of James' thick-ass dick in order to finally serve that dirty motherfucker a dose of justice was well worth every damn drop.

So for me, being down in this hot, muggy basement—in this thick-ass cloud of weed smoke, with Booty and her hoodlum-ass son, eye-fucking me one minute, then sneering at me the next—is a waste of my damn time. Besides, it's not where I want to be, any-damn-way. No, I need to be home, thinking out my next move, planning out in my head, how I'm going to taunt, and toy with, the nigga who's been hiding behind the screen name Mydick-needsUrtongue2.

Vernon Lewis.

"His goddamn monkey-ass ain't got shit to show for it!" Booty snaps, cutting into my thoughts. "Where they do that at? All this nigga-coon prolly did was trick up every dime of it on stink-ass bitches 'n' titty bars, instead of payin' his goddamn child support."

I shoot her an irritated look, then quickly bring my attention back to Jah'Mel. He is physically broken. He grunts as he attempts to lift his head and force his bloody eye open. It opens to barely a slit. I look into it the best I can. I think, want to believe, that what I see is remorse. What he's done, what he *did*, to me is not my cross to bear. It's his.

And there is still a price to pay.

Booty starts fussing with Darius about hogging the blunt he has pressed between his thick chocolate lips, stalking over toward him. "Oooh, you stay doin' me, nigga, with ya ole stingy-self. You s'posed to keep the rotation goin', but you wanna be over here playin' tricks. Oooh, I can't stand nothin' ya ass stand for, Darius."

"Yeah, yeah… Aiight. Go 'head wit' that, ma. I rolled you three blunts already. What'd you do wit' 'em?"

"Mmmph. Nigga, don't do me. You know that no-good mother-fucka over there done got my goddamn drawz all soggy. I'm savin' them for later…"

The two of them go back and forth, puffing and popping shit. And it's just the distraction I need.

Jah'Mel attempts to lift his head. "S-s-s-sorr—"

I gently place a finger up to his swollen lips. "Shhh. Don't." I am surprised to hear my own voice softly say, "It doesn't matter. I forgive you." I quickly glance over at Booty and Darius, then lean in as best I can and whisper in Jah'Mel's ear, "But be clear, nigga. The *minute* you're healed, you're going to owe me."

"I-I-I g-g-gotchuuu." He coughs. Blood and spit come gushing out of his mouth.

I quickly step back, shifting my handbag from one arm to the other, glancing over at Booty and Darius. "I'm out of here." They're both looking at me as I head toward the stairs. "You *might* want to get him to the hospital before you end up with another body on your hands."

Booty glares at me, flinging her hand at me dismissively. "Sugah-boo, *boom!* Darius, walk Miss Pasha, girl, up on outta here before I forget my manners 'n' get messy on her. And you *know* I *don't* do messy."

He smirks, taking another pull from his blunt, then passing it to her.

I ignore the bitch. The last thing I hear her say as my foot hits the top landing is, "You see what you done did, nigga-coon?!" *Slash!* "You got me 'bout to get messy on Miss Pasha, girl's ass. Why you do me, goddammit...?"

Slash!

The basement door shuts, muffling out the agonizing sound of his grunts and groans.

Seventeen

Danger and desire are sometimes wrapped up in one...

"Yo, you good?" Lamar asks, noticing the agitated expression on my face as I step out the door and start walking toward him. He quickly goes from leaning up against his SUV to straightening his body, glowering over my shoulder. "You need me to handle sumthin'?"

"No," I say through gritted teeth as he opens the door, helping me in. "Just get me the fuck out of here." He waits for me to slide in, shuts the door, then walks around to the back of the truck, lifting up the cargo door.

Jah'Mel's severely beaten body creeps into my head. Him tied up, hanging naked, and bloody. I glance over at the barbershop one last time. Take in the barber's pole, then the bold red lettering etched across the large window.

Gutter Cuts.

Mmmmph. Gutter is right! I'm going to need to rethink how I engage Cassandra's crazy-ass in any more of this. That bitch is too damn messy, and real reckless.

I fish inside the front flap of my handbag, pulling out my ringing phone and glancing at the screen. I roll my eyes, sucking my teeth. *Oh, no, sweetie. I don't think so. I've had enough of your ass for one night.* I press the END button, fastening my seat belt and settling back in my seat.

The cargo door shuts. A few seconds later, Lamar is behind the wheel, clicking his seat belt in place. He looks over at me. "Yo, e'erything aiight? What the hell popped off in there? You walked up outta that spot lookin' mad tight."

I catch a faint whiff of his cologne. And inhale, breathing in with it the image of Jah'Mel's long, black dick, hanging between his smooth, muscular, blood-streaked thighs. The only part of his body not broken, busted, or bloody.

Thick. Beautiful. Mouthwatering.

My nipples harden at the memory of it. His dick stamped in my mind, causing a slow throb in my clit. My pussy heats.

The nasty dick lover in me wanted to reach between his thighs and grab it, yank it, squeeze it…stroke it. The slutty me wanted to drop down on my knees—right there in his puddle of piss, to sniff it, kiss it, lick it…suck it into my mouth.

I struggled to keep my hot, trembling hand from cupping his balls, squeezing them, manhandling them. Fought to keep from dropping down low and flicking them with my tongue, licking along the thin line across the center of them, bouncing them on my tongue, then sucking them into my mouth.

Oh, I was so tempted, but…no.

I pull in my bottom lip, shifting in my seat.

Mygod! Really, bitch? You're really sitting here thinking about sucking on that nigga's dick and balls. Are you fucking serious right now? Have you no shame? Have you forgotten he's one of the niggas who kidnapped your dick-sucking ass? And you're sitting here fantasizing about gulping that nigga's dick down in your throat. You're out of damn control. Mmmph. How much more slutty can your scandalous-ass get?

I blink the image of Jah'Mel's dick away, looking over at Lamar, swallowing down the saliva pooling in the back of my mouth. "That bitch is fucking crazy."

He turns the key that's already in the ignition. "So," Lamar prompts. "You wanna talk about it?"

I shake my head. "No. I'm not going to put any more energy into it tonight." I swipe my bang from out of my eye. "I have more important things on my plate than getting caught up and dragged into her damn shenanigans."

He eases away from the curb. "I feel you."

I unfasten my seatbelt, scooting over a little and reaching over into his lap, running my open palm over the crotch of his jeans. "What I want you to *feel*," I say low and seductive into his ear, "are my soft lips wrapped around the head of your dick, then sliding deep into my wet mouth."

He grins. "Oh, word?" The truck accelerates, runs a stop sign.

"Don't kill me, though."

He chuckles. "Nah, never that. I'm def not gonna ever let anything happen to you, Pasha. You're special cargo."

I nip his earlobe, then coo into his ear, kneading his stiffening bulge. "Oooh, that's right, lil' daddy. Keep me safe."

He grins. "No doubt. Uhh…"—he glances down into his lap—"you see what you doin', right?"

"No," I say coyly. "I don't see it. But I sure *feel* it. Nice, hard dick. Mmm. My pussy's wet and I'm so…*fucking*… horny."

"Oh, yeah? So what's good then?" His eyes leave the road for a split-second to take me in. "I told you, *any*thing you want, *what*ever you need, I got you. Whenever, however, Pasha."

The way he says this, the way he looks at me, I know he means it. "Right now I *want* to suck this dick." His left hand briefly leaves the steering wheel. "I *need* to slide your dick down into my wet throat and suck out that nut."

"Mmmmm. Damn, ma. You sure know how'ta get a muhfucka rocked."

His seat slides back as my fingers unbuckle his belt. His hand is back on the steering wheel. I inch down his zipper. Pull open the flap of his pants. Lamar reaches his right arm over toward the passenger seat, resting his hand on the headrest while I attempt to fish out his semi-erection. After several frustrating seconds of trying to maneuver it, coax it, from out of his underwear, I rip open the slit of his boxers and it finally pops out. Hot. Eager. Ready.

I gently squeeze it, then lightly graze the head with my fingertips. Blood quickly rushes through it, and his dick stretches, thickens...comes alive. He turns right onto South Orange Avenue.

I stroke him slowly. "You want this throat?"

"Hellz yeah, baby." He runs a red light. I smirk, leaning into his lap, unlatching the hinges of my lower jaw and taking his whole dick into my lipsticked mouth, swallowing it down into my neck until his coarse pubic hairs are tickling my lips. I feel my pussy melting into my panties as I bob my head up and down in long, deep strokes, my lips gliding along the length of his shaft, my tongue swirling, then sliding back down to tongue his balls.

I crane my neck further into Lamar's lap. Slurp his balls into my mouth, then gently roll them around in my mouth, my wet tongue swirling figure-eights over them.

Lamar moans.

"Yeah, baby, suck them big balls...mmmm...aaah, fuck...you got my shit tinglin'..."

I lick his throbbing shaft, slide my tongue over the slit of his dick, then lap up his sweet, sticky pre-cum before fucking him back into my hungry mouth, then back down into my greedy throat, rapidly bobbing my head.

"Aaaah, fuck...damn...mmmph...ya head game is sick, baby."

I pull all the way up from his shaft to the head of his dick, suction my lips around it and suckle, allowing my tongue to twirl over and around it, then plunge back down to the base of his dick. I ease my lips along his length, slurping, gurgling, gobbling, as I fuck him in long, slow strokes in and out of my mouth.

"Aaah, yeah...suck that shit...oooh, that's it...mmmm...that shit feels so fuckin'...good!" He floors the pedal as I swallow him back down in my throat, super-soaking his dick and playing with his wet balls. My lips and tongue are making love to his head, my tongue swirling over its top, my lips milking it. Before long, his wide dick is back down in my neck, stretching and filling it.

His moans get louder as the car speeds up. I imagine down Oraton Parkway. I feel the car jerk to the left, then veering to the left around what I think is the ramp for the Parkway toward Hillside to pick up my car. Lamar's right hand is now on top of my head, his fingers looping through my hair as I deep throat his dick.

The loud slurping sounds I am making fill the SUV, becoming the music to Lamar's moans. The suck-fuck sounds intensify each time the head of his dick pops out of my throat and brushes up against my uvula. The delicious sensation strikes a match inside my pussy.

After a few more seconds, I come up for air, panting, trying to extinguish the sparks in my cunt that will soon erupt into a roaring fire.

"Damn, Pasha...fuck...you know how'ta suck the shit outta some dick."

"Oh, I'm not done, yet, lil' daddy." I swoop my mouth back down over his spit-coated dick, refilling my neck, caging in his cock, and turning up the throat motor, humming, vibrating my tonsils. I flatten my tongue, extend it as far as it will go, then flick it across his head. A molten river of saliva spurts out of my mouth, splashing down around Lamar's balls, soaking the front of his underwear.

He makes a growling sound.

I speed up my neck swab; the head of Lamar's dick rapidly brushing back and forth under my uvula, then back down past my tonsils, stroking the walls of my throat.

I am so wet. The deeper his dick goes, the wetter I get. The sweet, musky heat of my pussy steams the windows. Lamar's right leg shakes, the car swerves, but he quickly regains control of the wheel.

He grunts.

"Ohshitohshit...fuckfuckfuck! Yo...hol'up, hol'up...we got... motherfuckshit...hol'up... "

He tries to pull me up off of him, but my jaws are locked around his cock. I'm in a zone, gobbling him down into my greedy gullet.

I fuck him into my juicy, hot mouth until the head of his dick swells and his thick creamy nut hits the back of my throat, flooding my jaws.

I suck and swallow, suck and swallow until...

Something slams into the back of us, almost tossing me forward, as numerous gunshots ring out.

"What the hell? What is that?" I attempt to lift up, but Lamar forces my head back down into his lap.

"Stay down. We got muhfuckas tryna get at us."

"Ohmygod! *Whaaat?!*"

My heart drops into the center of my cum-filled stomach, knowing whom the culprit behind this shit is. Jasper. And I'm fucking pissed. Again, this motherfucker has niggas trying to get at me. I'm convinced he's not going to quit until he's fucking dead.

I force myself out of Lamar's grip, lifting up and swinging around in my seat to see who is behind us. It's a dark-colored SUV. The windshield is tinted too dark for me to see who's inside.

The vehicle slams into the back of us, again. Lamar swerves over into the left lane, floors the engine, then swerves back over into the other lane, zigzagging in between the few cars still out on the parkway this time of night.

I put my hands on the dashboard and brace myself. There's only one way I wish to die. And that is, in my sleep. Not from being mangled up in some high-speed car chase, or from being shot up by some crazy-ass, gun-wielding niggas. But if we don't somehow get the fuck out of this situation, *quick*, my fate may be sealed by one of the two… or both.

"This motherfucker is really fucking crazy!" I snap, half to myself. *Where are the fucking state troopers when you need them?* "His motherfucking ass is not going to be satisfied until I have him zipped in a fucking black bag!"

"Yo, you know who the fuck these niggas are in back of us?" I tell him I'm certain that they're some of Jasper's goonies. "Oh, word? Is that how that snake muhfucka wanna do it? He really wanna be on this dumb shit. Aiight, bet."

He hits a button on the steering wheel. Within seconds, the sound of a ringing phone is coming through the speakers. "What's good?" the deep, raspy voice on the other end says.

"Yo, real shit. I gotta heavy situation on my ass. Muhfuckas floorin' a nigga wit' heat. I'ma need you to roll out the tank, and be ready in case I can't neutralize the situation."

"Where you at now?"

"I'm getting off exit one-thirty-one on the GSP as we speak. But these niggas are really tryna serve a muhfucka up."

Another round of shots are fired, hitting the back window. I jump. Despite knowing Lamar's truck is bulletproof, my nerves are still rattled. And the only thing I can think about at this very moment is my son, Jaylen. I have to be on the plane in the morning. I have to get to L.A. to see his smiling face and hold him in my arms. So there is no fucking way I'm letting Jasper or any of his goons take me down without a damn fight.

I pull out my phone, making a call. "You crazy motherfucker!" I scream into the receiver the minute Jasper answers. "Call off your motherfucking goons, now, or so help me God you're going to regret the day you were born!"

"Yo, you wanna rock wit' the big boys, right? Yo wanna turn it up in court, right? I tol' ya dumb-ass not to fuck wit' me, but you stay testin' a muhfucka, Pasha. So, what you fuckin' that clown-ass nigga, now? Or suck—"

"Motherfucker, fuck you! You wanna play dirty, nigga? Then let me show you how a dirty bitch does it! See what happens next!" I end the call.

"Aiight, listen," the voice coming through the speakers says. "Handle ya handle. Lure 'em to the spot if you need to. And we'll take care of the rest."

The line goes dead.

Lamar tells me to reach under his seat and grab his Glock.

"Listen. I'ma need you to take the wheel, aiight? While I handle these muhfuckas right quick."

I blink. This nigga is already going over 110 miles per hour. And he wants *me* to take the wheel. Is he fucking serious? *Take the wheel? I don't think so.* It's bad enough I'm on the parkway caught up in a high-speed chase with niggas shooting at us. But there's no time to think, or to be scared. This is a do-or-motherfucking-die situation. And I'm not trying to die. Not tonight. Not with a pair of wet, soggy panties on and a coat of cock cream stained on my lips.

"No," I tell him, climbing over into the backseat, gripping his gun tightly in my hand. "You keep driving. I'll handle the niggas in back of us. Tell me what you need me to do."

He instructs me to push in the release button to the backseats, then lay them flat. I do. "Now crawl into the cargo space and in the middle of the door, there's a lever. I need you to push it in, then slide the panel to the right." I am surprised when I slide the panel back and it creates an opening I can see out of. "Now, aim for them muhfuckas' tires."

Eighteen

There are no limits to how far a pissed-off, vengeful bitch will go…

"Ohmygod, *noo!*" Greta shrieks, her eyes widen and a hand flies up over her mouth as I give her the rundown on the latest turn of events. The first being how Jasper turned it out in court, followed by the uncovering of who one of my kidnappers were, then ending with last night's shootout fiasco. She shakes her head. "This is all too much to digest. You literally have my head spinning."

"Then try imagining what this shit's been like for me these last few days. Wednesday, Thursday, and Friday, three damn days of nonstop drama. I'm fucking drained." I take a deep breath. "You don't know how relieved I was to board that flight this morning to get here and getting the fuck out of Jersey for a hot minute."

I pull in my bottom lip to keep it from quivering. Replaying everything in the last several days, then rewinding back to the shit that popped off the week before that has me feeling emotionally drained. I just want this shit over with. But it won't be. Not until, until…

"Greta, the shit I have been through in the last two weeks…" My voice trails off. I close my eyes, taking a moment to get my thoughts together. I fight back tears. Push back anger. I take three deep breaths, then lift my eyelids and meet the worried look in Greta's eyes.

"I can't believe this shit. Are you for certain it was Jasper? I mean, is he *really* crazy enough to have niggas shooting at you two weeks in a row?"

"Oh, that nigga's good and goddamn crazy." I rock Jaylen, rubbing his back. He's sound asleep in my arms. I pull him into my chest tighter. Breathe him in. "Believe it. I'm positive it was that sonofabitch. When I called screaming on his ass, he didn't deny it. In fact, he practically admitted to it. The nigga was almost gloating. At least that's what it sounded like. So I know, without a doubt, that he had niggas from his goon squad chasing us down the Garden State Parkway like nobody's damn business intent on trying to kill me last night." She wants to know what happened to them. "Oh, them grimy motherfuckers got *got*. Let me tell you…"

I share with her how I'd crawled into the cargo space, pointed Lamar's gun out of the hidden slide in the cargo door, then aimed at that SUV, pulling the trigger. It had taken me seven shots and being tossed around in the back as Lamar zigzagged from one lane to the other before I was finally able to hit the front passenger wheel, causing the truck to swerve off the highway and collide down into a ditch.

Everything was happening so fast. One minute I'm sucking the nut out of Lamar's dick, the next minute I'm shooting his gun. There was no time to think. No time to be afraid. My adrenaline pumped fast and heavy through my veins.

My life was on the line.

Soon after the SUV careened off the side of the road, Lamar slammed on the brakes, threw the truck in reverse, then sped backward on the shoulder of the road. He slammed on the brakes, released his seatbelt, then reached over into the glove compartment and pulled out another gun.

"Stay here," he commanded, swinging open his door, then darted toward the disabled vehicle with two loaded guns in both hands. The only thing I kept thinking as I watched him running was, the police are going to arrest my ass. I'm going to prison. Everything I've worked hard for...gone! My salon, gone! My son, gone! My life, over!

And Jasper's black ass still roams free.

I quickly hopped out of the truck, leaving the engine running, and ran in the direction of the firing gunshots, still clutching Lamar's gun in my right hand. I was scared shitless, but relieved that it was pitch dark and there were no police cars in sight yet. But I knew it was only a matter of time before they'd be swarming all over the place.

By the time I reached Lamar, he was firing continuously, mercilessly unloading his weapons upon our attackers. In a matter of minutes, the situation was handled. Three masked gunmen and a driver...dead.

Half of one nigga's face was blown off.

"C'mon, we gotta get the fuck outta here, now!"

He yanked me by the arm, and practically dragged me behind him back to his truck. We both hopped into the vehicle. Then Lamar sped off like a crazed man before I was able to slam my door shut.

Lamar banged his hand on the steering wheel. "Fuck, yo! That nigga gotta get dropped, Pasha. *Now!* That muthafucka's really pissin' me off. I know you got ya own agenda 'n' shit, but that nigga fuckin' wit' me now. And I ain't 'bout this dumb shit. On my muthafuckin' word, yo. That nigga got it coming...!"

Sweat poured from face. My heart was beating so hard that I thought I would have dropped dead from a heart attack in any second. My hands shook.

He pressed the button on his steering wheel, and less than a second later, a phone rang through the speakers. "Yo, you good?"

"Yeah," Lamar stated, turning off at the next exit. "Punk-ass muhfuckas, clipped me, but I'm good." He let out a chuckle. "Can't say the same for them, pussy-ass niggas. There's a major spill on the side of the road."

I blinked. *Clipped him? Ohmygod, he's been shot!* I wanted so desperately to turn on the interior lights to see, but knew it was an unwise decision.

"Fuck 'em. You know who those roaches were?"

Lamar glanced over at me. I stared back at him. He must have read the look in my eyes, begging him, to not rob me of my moment.

He sighed, shaking his head. "Nah. But I'ma need a crew on lock 'n' ready for some street sweepin' real soon."

"Whatever you need." The call ended.

"Ohmygod! You were shot?" I asked, genuinely concerned. All Lamar had ever been hired to do was to provide extra security for my salon after someone had smashed out the front window in broad daylight with a large pipe. And some silly-ass nigga named AJ—egged on by the same motherfucker who attacked me out in my yard in the middle of the night—came into the salon and aired out my dick-sucking ways in front of a shop full of clients, grabbing his dick and asking for one of my deep throat specials. My indiscretions had slowly caught up to me.

And now Lamar was going above and beyond the call of duty, putting his own life on the line to protect mine. Someone else had gotten into my fight. Thanks to Jasper's fucking ass!

He glanced over at me. "No sweat." He shrugged. "I'll live. "It's a lil' flesh wound." One bullet grazed his shoulder.

I gasped. "You could have been killed."

"Hey, it comes wit' the territory." He caught the worried look on my face. Then smiled, trying to lighten the situation. "Them punk-ass niggas had lousy aim." He hit his chest. "Besides, I got the body armor on lock. But if I ever gotta die, I have no problem dyin' for a worthy cause. I'd take a bullet or two for you, any day."

He winked at me.

And, despite being shot at and almost run off the road, I couldn't help but smile.

I was touched...deeply. I reached over and stroked his cheek, then leaned over and kissed him on it. "I'm so sorry about all of this. I know you didn't sign up for any of this crazy shit."

"Nah, Pasha, you good, ma. This is *exactly* what I signed up for. I tol' you what it was two weeks ago when you were in ya office wit' ya peeps. I already knew what it was wit' you and that nigga. I said I got you. And that's what it is. No matter what it is. But, word is bond, Pasha. Make no mistake. That nigga's gotta go."

I nodded, glancing at the time. It was almost one o'clock in the morning. My flight was in five hours, and mind was racing a thousand miles a minute. Getting sleep was the last thing I'd be able to do.

"I know. Soon."

"Not soon enough. But it's all good. That nigga ain't rockin' no boats this way." He took his eyes off the road and eyed me. "Real spit, I'ma be the one to help you seal that nigga's shit."

I dug into my bag and pulled out a pen and small notepad. Then I scrolled through the MEMO app on my phone and jotted down three addresses. I folded the paper in half, then handed it to him. "I'm leaving for L.A. in the morning to spend time with my son..." He wanted to know who was driving me to the airport. I told him Mel was. Then stated, "While I'm gone, I need you to handle these spots for me. Given what happened last week, he's probably got them all manned up with lots of firepower."

He kept his eyes locked on the road ahead, seemingly unfazed.

"Them muhfuckas not built to fuck wit' my team. Same scenario?"

"Yeah. Then burn 'em down to the ground."

By the time I finish telling Greta everything—well, um, except the parts about me dick-swabbing a computer geek for information on one of my assailants, giving Lamar road head, and having him burn down another three of Jasper's stash houses—all of the blood from her face has drained.

"My, God!" she exclaims, collapsing backward, sinking into the plush leather chair. "*Un*fuckingbelievable. Thank God, you weren't driving alone. There's no telling how it woulda played out. This shit sounds like something straight out of a damn movie. That nigga really wants to kill you."

I sigh, relieved that I finally listened to Lamar, letting him and Mel drive me wherever I need to go. "Or scare the shit out of me. Either way, I'm not going to let him get the best of me. The days of Jasper fucking controlling me are over."

She smiles warily at me, her eyes wet with tears. "And that's what's probably driving him crazier than what he already is."

"Mmmph. Crazy or not. I'm done. One of these days, trust. Jasper's going to be put down like the rabid animal he is."

"I'm just glad you're all right."

"Yeah, tell me about it. So am I." I shake my head. "And then the shit with Cassandra…"

I fill in the details. Leaving out, *of course*, how I had a moment of sluttiness and started lusting over Jah'Mel's dick.

"For the love of God!" she says, leaning forward and holding her forehead in her hands. She takes several deep breaths, then slowly lifts her head from her hands, looking up at me. "Can this shit get any more crazier than this."

Girl, if you only knew…

I stand, excusing myself so I can lie Jaylen down. Once I get him settled in his bed, I go into my room, then unzip the inside storage compartment of my carry-on, pulling out a burner phone. I fish through the side compartment of my handbag. I frown when I can't find what I'm looking for. *Now where the hell did I put that thing? I know I brought it with me.* I keep searching until I locate the phone device I need, then plug it into the cell's headset jack. I adjust the settings, pulling out a sheet of paper with the information I need written on it.

My eyes zoom in on the phone number highlighted in yellow. I dial the number, then wait...

"Hello?" the female voice on the other end says.

Instantly my voice goes from feminine sounding to deep and raspy. "Yo, what's good, ma. Let me holla at Vernon."

"Who the fuck is this?" the chick snaps nastily.

"Bitch, don't worry 'bout who dis is. Put that dick-suckin' pussy, Vernon, on da line, yo. I gotta nut I need him to suck outta dis hard-ass dick."

"Whaaat?! Who the fuck you callin' a bitch? Bring ya punk, pussy-ass over here 'n' say that shit to my face. And what the fuck you mean you gotta dick for *my* man to suck?"

I laugh. "Yo, chill. I ain't got no beef wit' you, boo. But I got some beef for dat nigga, Vernon, yo."

"Oh, yeah? Well, nigga, you callin' my motherfuckin' phone. This ain't Vernon's shit. So say what the fuck you gotta say, then get the fuck off my line."

"Ya nigga suck dick, ma."

"Say, *what?* Oh, hell naw! I know you ain't callin' here with no bullshit like this. Ain't no way in hell the Vernon I know is suckin' no nigga's dick."

"Well, then you a fool. What you think he be doin' when he's up in the county?"

"I know he ain't suckin' no goddamn dick. Not the Vernon I know."

I laugh. "Well, obviously you don't know the Vernon I know. Because the nigga sucked mine."

"Vernon!" she yells in my ear. "Get yo' black ass in here!"

I hear a man's voice in the background. "Yo, what da fuck is you screamin' out my name like that for?"

"Who the fuck you been suckin' in the county?"

"What?"

"Nigga, you heard me. You got some muthafuckin' shit-packer callin' my goddamn phone talkin' 'bout you his dick sucker?"

"Say what? Who da fuck is that on da phone?"

"How the fuck I know. I tol' you it's some nigga callin' here talkin' 'bout you suckin' dick…"

I smirk.

"Give me that shit. Yo, who da fuck is this?"

"Yo, what's good, pussy? When you gonna let me push dis dick down in ya neck? I gotta nut for ya throat, nigga."

"Say what, muhfucka? Run dat shit by me again? You said, when am I gonna let you do *whaaat…?!*"

"Nigga," the chick screams in the background, "I know one goddamn thing. Let me find out you out there suckin' on some nigga's dick 'n' I'ma have you fucked up. I mean it, Vernon! I put up wit' you fuckin' all ya skank-ass baby mothers, but I ain't puttin' up wit' no shit like dis. The only bitch suckin' dick up in here better be *me*. I ain't havin' no down-low shit up in dis here motherfucker…"

"Yo, shut da fuck up wit' dat dumb shit. Ain't no body suckin' no fuckin' dicks. Yo, son…real shit, muhfucka, don't let me find out who da fuck you are. Comin' at me wit' some gay shit. I'ma bust yo' shit open, nigga. My word, muhfucka. I'ma light yo' shit up."

"Nigga, eat my dick!"

I disconnect, falling back on my bed laughing hysterically. I laugh so hard that I am now in tears. *Oh, yes, motherfucker. I'm going to fuck you real good.*

I slip the headset off my head, wrap its cord around the cell, then tuck it under one of my pillows. A few minutes later, I return to the living room and find Greta standing at the bar, fixing a drink for herself. "Would you like one?"

I saunter further into the room. "I don't mind if I do." I sink into one of the leather chairs, crossing my legs. "Sooo. Now that we've gotten all caught up with my drama. What would you like to do today? I was thinking we could drive out to Venice Beach and, maybe, grab a bite to eat."

"That sounds good." She grabs another crystal flute, fills it with champagne, then walks over with both glasses. She hands me one. I take a sip.

I take a quick sip. "Or if you'd like. We can do something else."

She sinks into the chair next to me, placing a coaster down on the marble table that's positioned in between both chairs. "Well, it's so gorgeous out. I would *love*..." Her voice trails off as Mel and Sophia walk through the door, carrying bags of groceries. Greta's voice drops to a sultry whisper. To *fuck* the shit out of *him*. But seeing that he only has eyes for *you*..."

Champagne slides down my throat the wrong way and I cough, trying to keep from choking. My eyes start to water. It takes me a few seconds to pull myself together. "Girl, stop. He's my bodyguard."

She takes a slow sip of her drink, then eyes me over the rim of her glass. She smirks. "Uh-huh, bitch. Play stupid if you want. Trust me. *Guarding* your body isn't the *only* thing on that sexy-ass man's mind."

Nineteen

A good hard dick is a terrible thing to waste…

The annoying sound of my buzzing cell jolts me from a light, restless drowse. I sit up, feeling disoriented, wondering when I'd finally nodded off. For most of the night I'd tossed and turned, a smoldering fire lit between my legs. An aching, burning need to have the flames fanning along the inside of my walls pounded out of my pussy overwhelmed me. Masturbation hadn't brought relief. A cold shower—with the detachable shower-head positioned between my parted thighs, barely grazing my spread pussy lips, and its pulsing water beads beating up into my smoldering cunt—only managed to soothe the boiling heat once I slid a dildo in and fucked into the wet inferno. Only then was I able climb into bed and doze off.

To only be awakened, three hours later, to *this*. I blink.

It isn't my personal line. It's the burner phone. I reach over, my fingers fumbling toward the glowing light, then press the TALK button, bringing it to my ear.

"Hello?" I answer groggily.

"Yo, it's done. We hit 'em all at once."

I rub my eyes, glancing over at the window. Streaks of dawn creep their way through the slits of my custom blinds. "All three? And no problems?"

He lets out a slight chuckle. "Nah, nothin' real niggas can't handle. We lit the sky up. Turned it into a Fourth of July celebration out that muhfucka. Fireworks e'erywhere. The news will be hot 'n' poppin' first thing in the mornin'."

I lean up, propping up my pillows in back of me. I lean back, a smile easing over my lips. *This now makes six of Jasper's stash houses gone. Poof! Burned down to the ground. How you like me now, motherfucker?*

I don't bother to ask how many casualties there were. Don't care to know how many niggas got dropped. The only thing I care about is crippling Jasper's flow, shutting his ass down. Niggas like him have to get hit in their pockets, hard. I may not know where the rest of Jasper's spots are, but it doesn't matter. Right now, I know his ass is feeling it. Crushed. In less than a week's time, I've managed to shut down business and jack his paper, his product, and his manpower.

"Thank you."

"No doubt, Pasha. You already know what it is. So you good?" I tell him I am. Then I tell him that I need for him to handle something else for me. "I got you. Let me know what you need and it's done." I give him the address to the two-family dwelling in East Orange. Tell him I need someone to monitor the comings and goings there. "Say no more. Anything else?"

"Bust out every damn window."

The call ends. Facing the nightstand, I reach over and turn on the light, then place my feet on the carpet, my toes sinking into the plush fibers as I stand to make my safety checks—more so out of habit than necessity; especially now with Mel being here.

Mel.

Snatches of Greta's comments about him ring in my ear as I slip into my robe. "Trust me. *Guarding* your body isn't the *only* thing on that sexy-ass man's mind."

I dismiss the thought from my head, checking the security panel, then double-checking the locks on the doors and windows despite the high-tech system indicating all areas are properly secured.

I check in on Jaylen, walking into his room, then leaning down and kissing him on the side of his head. I watch him sleep for several seconds, breathing in everything he is, lightly rubbing his soft curly hair. *I love you so much.* I take one last look at my sleeping prince, then head down the hall toward Greta's room. Her door is shut. I lean in, pressing my ear slightly to the door. There is nothing but silence on the other side of her door. I move along, stopping next at Sophia's bedroom. I press my ear to her door. All is quiet.

I walk further down the hall to the last room on the right. Surprisingly, the door is half-open. I can hear light snores coming from inside the room Mel is in. I peek inside.

The room is aglow from the two wall nightlights. I wonder why he hadn't turned them off. Then scold myself for caring one way or the other as I inch the door open further.

I take in his muscular frame—six feet, seven inches of hard-body manliness, stretched out in the center of the bed on his back, bare-chested and delicious-looking. The goose-down comforter is rolled down at the foot of the bed, the top sheet, twisted around one muscled leg. A thick forearm is lifted over his face, covering his eyes. His free hand rests on his stomach.

I lick my lips.

My eyes blink. Blink again. Then narrow, zooming in on... *My-god! Is that what I think it is?*

It is! The imprint of his dick, a huge mouthwatering lump,

wrapped, restricted, confined, beneath a pair of burgundy boxer briefs.

The sight of it almost snatches my breath away. My clit twitches as I lose myself in the mental image of stalking over to him, yanking his underwear down over his hips and his colossal cock springing out and smacking me in the forehead.

Mygod! I just want to reach out and touch it.

I bite down on my lower lip to stifle a moan.

My heart stops for a split-second as he shifts in his sleep. Then disappointment sweeps over me as his hand languidly rests over the thick lump in his underwear, blocking my view, robbing me of the rest of the show. He presses the heel of his hand into his dick, then rubs the length of it, before finally lingering at the head. He squeezes.

My right hand slips into the opening of my robe. I lightly pinch my left nipple.

Shamelessly, I stand in the doorway and watch. Wait. Wonder. I know I should walk away and tiptoe on back down the other end of the hall to my room. But I can't. I won't. No, no...can turn away. But I don't want to.

Not yet.

Bitch, you are really out of fucking control, standing here watching this man in his sleep, prying into his personal space like some horny, cock-hungry stalker.

Well, shit! I am horny. I am cock-hungry. And I am stalking his cock!

Pasha, stop this shit, girl! Take your ass back to bed!

The rational side of me wins. I decide it's best to slip back into the comforts of my own room, behind a locked door, then fuck myself to sleep. But as I start to back away from the door, Mel's body shifts again. And he does the unthinkable.

He reaches into the opening of his boxers, pulls out his enormous dick. I have had more dicks in my hands and mouth than I can keep count, but there's one thing I can guesstimate—and be almost ninety-nine-point-nine-nine-percent certain of—and that is, the size of a dick. And Mel's long, juicy, Monster cock is at *least*…thirteen inches long. The biggest, the thickest, I've ever encountered.

Mmmm, I want some of that.

I stay rooted in place. My hands caressing my breasts as he strokes it, alternating from slow deep strokes to fast fist-pumping hand strokes; his long dick gliding in and out of his hand; its large plum-sized head, popping in and out.

I pull in my bottom lip. Imagine my tongue flicking over the head of his dick, catching the clear, stringy fluid as it oozes from his piss slit.

I hold my breath. Strain to hear the low smacking sound of him masturbating as his wide, thick hand rapidly slides up and down his shaft. "Get on your knees, baby," I think I hear him whisper. "Crawl ya sexy ass over to me, *bitch*, and come suck this dick…"

My right hand dips between my thighs. In my head, Mel's dick enters me, then pounds into my pussy, into my wetness. And I arch into the sensation. My pussy quivering and quaking with every stretch-aching thrust.

Oh, yes, fuck me…

But I know that isn't what he wants. Pussy. No, no, he wants this neck—my other pussy. He wants what all the others want, what they crave, what they've been willing to cheat and lie for—and possibly kill for. He wants wet, sloppy, throat-gurgling, lip-smacking head. He wants his dick lodged deep down into my throat. Mel wants to crush my windpipes fucking into my neck.

That's what he wants.

In my head, I hear Mel moaning low in the back of his throat. "Yeah, baby, open ya mouth and take this big-ass horse dick," His strokes quicken. "You think you can handle all of this big, thick dick?"

My wet mouth opens. My soft lips wrap around the head of his dick. I suck. Then use both hands and stroke his shaft, teasing him with my tongue, while cupping his drool-slick balls. Mel spreads his legs slightly. I imagine his big balls hanging perfectly low, touching the sheets beneath him, hiding the crack of his ass.

Yes...

I grind onto my hand, my fingers sinking deeper until my fingertips find it. My spot. Swollen. Sensitive. Full. I rhythmically move my fingers inward, pressing against its spongy curve. My body shudders. Ecstasy ripples through every inch of my flesh.

I bite down on my tongue to keep from screaming out as the image of Mel lifting me up over him, then slowly guiding me down onto his humongous cock—the monstrous head stretching open the mouth of my pussy, then inch by-slow, sweet, torturous inch, widening the passage, splaying my pussy lips beyond my imagination—becomes vividly real in my head.

Yes.

Oh, God, no, this is so wrong. But my pussy is so wet... so very fucking wet.

Still, I make one last weak attempt to break free from the vision in front of me; all six feet, seven inches of his thick, muscular frame. But his dick beckons me. It calls out to me. "Come suck me, boo." As I watch Mel's large hand pump up and down the shaft of his dick, the plum-sized head emerging with each stroke. The sight of it taunts me. "Sneaky bitch...come get this hot load outta this dick…filthy whore…cum slut… You know you want this long, thick dick fuckin' ya mouth, pluggin' ya neck 'til I clog ya throat wit' this nut."

God, yes…

Before I realize it, I am fucking into the surging heat, three-fingers, knuckles deep. The lips of my weeping pussy opening and closing around the stretch and pull of each thrust, matching the rhythm of Mel's thrusting hand. Knees bending, pelvis rocking, my breathing becomes frantic as the wet-clickety sounds my fingers are making become demanding as they slick in and out; a foam of cream seeping out and rimming the edges of my horny, cum-soaked cunt with each thrust.

Mel's motions are deliberate, his jacking off, his fluid stroking. Or at least that is how it seems, intent on bringing him to orgasm. I fuck myself furiously, watching, lusting…waiting. Oh, how I wait. For the flow of his cum to spill out of his dick, to shoot up in the air—hot ropes of white lust, spurting onto his chest, under his chin, over his head, or wherever else it may land.

My free hand slinks up to the swell of my breasts. I caress my nipples, then slide my hand back down over my trembling belly, down to my throbbing clit, where it stays—my fingers firmly moving in slow, circular motion over it.

The faster his hand moves up and down the never-ending length of his dick, the wetter I am, the closer I am to coming.

Clickclickclickclick…

The wet sound of my fingers rapidly stroking between the folds of my pussy becomes louder, urgent, desperate; a wave of liquid heat expanding in my belly, fanning itself along the walls of my cunt, ripping its way through. Blood and heat pound in my clit, in my pussy, in my chest.

Oh, God, yes…

I choke back a moan.

I think I see Mel's right leg trembling along with my own wobbly leg. He grunts low, startling me. His hand strokes become quicker, shorter. My breath hitches as my hand, my probing fingers, match his dick stroking. My pussy pulses and pulls with every stroke. Heat and steam of a budding orgasm hissing out of my slit slow and steady, then…

"Aaaah, fuck…"

Mel's strokes become lightning fast.

"Aaaaaah, shiiiit. Fuck, baby…"

The wet *clickclickclickclick* of my tightening cunt match the slip-slap of cock and fist, the light thud of balls. The sounds become more audible.

"Fuckfuck…aaah, shit…"

I moan and groan along with Mel in my head. My lust-filled gaze locked onto his pumping fist. Flames erupt in the center of my pussy, then burst out in fiery heat. I rock back on the heels of my feet, thrusting my pelvis.

I am coming.

"Here it comes…uhh, uhh…"

Mel is coming.

He grunts, then growls low and throaty.

The air around me seems to get thinner. My eyes blur as dizzying waves of intense heat gush out of me, flooding my fingers, soaking my hand, as Mel growls, his hips thrusting up off the bed, the mattress beneath him springing up and down.

"Here it comes, Pasha, uhh… Come get this nut, baby…"

Thick ropes of white cum shoot out of his dick, up into the air. I blink several times, trying to be certain I heard him correctly, him whispering my name, him calling out to me. I know I heard him say my name. Heard him tell me to come get his nut. Or had I imagined it all?

I blink again.

Then all I see are Mel's smoldering eyes as he lifts up on one forearm, his chest heaving, his fist still clenched around his spurting cock, his nut now spilling out over his hand, like warm buttermilk, thick and rich.

I do not wait for an answer. I untie my robe, stepping into the room and letting it fall off my shoulders to the floor. I quietly shut the door. Then saunter over toward the bed, climbing up on it, inching between his legs. I lick the sweat and cum drizzle from around his balls. My eager tongue journeys along the curve of his fist, lapping up his nut. Not once does he take his eyes off of me. I remove his hand from around his cum-sticky dick, sucking each of his fingers into my mouth, cleaning them, then laving his stomach with my greedy tongue, tasting him, savoring him.

I lick his thick cock clean, my tongue eagerly sweeping over his balls, then along the shaft, traveling upward to his sticky, swollen head, its slit still leaking his man juices. I squeeze the head, opening the eye, then dipping my tongue in deeply. I think of sweet custard with a pinch of salt as I lap him with my tongue, then envelop the head of his dick into my mouth. His dick stretches and thickens, stretching my mouth. Mel rolls his hips, slowly, pushing his throbbing cock deeper into my mouth.

No words are spoken. None are needed. Gulping is the only sound being made as I take him all the way into my mouth as he pushes the cockhead to the back of my throat, clogging my airway passage. His dick is humongous. And I am determined to master every thick, delicious, throbbing inch of it. Unlatching my jaws, my head bobs.

I will gag to death, die with this nigga's dick lodged down in my throat before I claim defeat. I start humming, caressing my pussy as I suck and hum, suck and hum, my sucking mouth getting wetter. I purr, maneuvering, mastering, my mouth, my neck, my tongue up and down the length and width of him; my throat relaxing and stretching like never before, the ache and burn causing my pussy to cream.

Finally there's another sound in the room besides the ones coming from out of my throat. Mel starts moaning. His hands are in my hair, squeezing and palming my head, fingers digging into my scalp.

In seconds, Mel's bulky body is shuddering, his brain melting inside his head, as hot dick milk splashes the back of my throat, flooding my mouth. I continue sucking, my lips only easing back from his dick when I have sucked his forehead in, until the only thing I see when I look up at him are the whites of his eyeballs as they roll to the back of his head.

I gulp and swallow everything he feeds me.

Not wasting a drop.

Feeling powerful. Feeling in control. Once again, conquering.

It is the dawning of a new day when I finally slip out of Mel's room, leaving him snoring, his head slumped to the side, and drool sliding out of his mouth as I saunter back down the hall, gliding my tongue over my cum-glazed teeth, savoring the moment. Basking in the knowing that Mel, like all the others, has been captivated, captured, and now…is under the spell of this juicy deep-throat.

Twenty

*Toying with your prey before going in for the kill
is a much more delicious thrill...*

"Watch ya back, pussy-ass nigga," I say deep and low.

"Yo, word is bond, muhfucka!" Vernon barks into the phone. "I'ma split yo' muthafuckin' shit! Who da fuck is this?"

I use some of the lines he's said to me, my subtle clues to him, when he was calling and harassing me down at the salon. "You'll find out soon enough, pussy. I can't wait to fuck you in dat tight lil' man ass of yours. I'ma gut ya hole real wide, nigga, then—"

"Muhfucka, say *whaaaat?!* I'll put a bullet in ya shit before you or any other muhfucka ever try some homo shit on me. Now how da fuck you get my number 'n' why is you fuckin' wit' me, nigga?"

I laugh. "Whatever, Cock Eater! It ain't ya shitty ass I wanna fuck, anyway. I wanna fuck dis long dick down in ya throat, trick-ass bitch."

The nigga goes ballistic, yelling and screaming and threatening to body a *nigga*. I imagine him pacing the floor like a rabid animal, teeth gnashing, eyes wide, foaming at the mouth.

The line goes dead.

I change cell phones, plugging in my voice changer, then calling back. "Watch ya back, nigga. I'm comin' for you."

"Yo, real shit, muhfucka. Who da fuck is dis?"

"Ya worst fuckin' nightmare!" I end the call. "Bastard," I mutter, tossing the phone into my bag.

Mel glances over at me, chuckling. We landed about an hour ago. And now we're cruising in his SUV—with its thick ballistic-proof glass and panel systems, radar scrambler, run-flat tires, and anti-explosive system—up the parkway heading toward the salon.

I swear. I hated boarding that red-eye late last night, leaving Jaylen behind. I fought back my tears most of the drive to LAX. I had to keep reminding myself that it's only temporary. That, for now, it's what's best for him. Yet, no matter how many times I have to say it in my head, it still never feels right.

"Damn, that nigga gotta be one dumb muhfucka if he can't even figure out by now that you're hittin' him upside the head wit' his own shit."

Early this morning, I had gotten word from Lamar that all the front windows of the two-family house where this nigga's shacking up at—with some flat-ass, dog-faced chick—were bust out in the middle of the night. And, sometime tonight, his Lexus will make its way to a local chop shop, courtesy of Lamar. Then every night thereafter, up until the grand finale, he'll be fucked with, even jumped and a row of his fronts kicked in.

I shake my head. "Stupid niggas like him think with their dicks, which is exactly why he thought it was okay to harass—no, practically *stalk*—me, all because I didn't want to suck his damn dick again. Mmmph. He brought this shit on himself."

Mel's eyes dart over to me, then back on the road ahead. I keep my gaze straight ahead, pretending to not notice. "Muhfuckas real crazy out there these days."

"Yup. And so are some of the bitches they *think* they can fuck with and get away with it."

I feel his eyes on me, heating my flesh. When I look over, I catch him staring at my lips. He smiles at me, then quickly looks away, his eyes back on the road.

God, I hope I haven't gotten myself way in over my head.

My cell rings. I fish it out of my bag, glancing at the screen. It's Cassandra. I purse my lips, contemplate answering or letting it roll into voicemail. I haven't seen or spoken to her since Friday night. And I've ignored her calls and text messages.

The bitch is too impulsive. And, as far as I'm concerned, she's reckless. And definitely not someone I'm going to have help bring down any more of the niggas on my list. She's already done enough. From exposing Felecia and killing JT to practically beating her own son to death, Booty's contribution to my cause has been duly noted.

Nothing more is needed. Cassandra Simms can stand on the sidelines from here on out. I let the call go into voicemail. Two minutes later, my phone *pings*, alerting me that she's left a message. Four seconds later, there's another *ping*. It's a text from her. MISS STANKADANK U NEED 2 GET UR GDAMN MIND RIGHT!!!! IM AT DA SHOP N U AIN'T NOWHERE 2 B FOUND, GDMMIT! WE GOT SHIT 2 DO...PLAYN GAMES. U STAY TRYNA DO ME GDMMIT!! CALL ME

I take a deep breath, deleting the message.

"Yo, e'erything good?" Mel asks, taking his eyes off the road for a quick second.

I nod. "Yeah." I shift my body in my seat, reaching over and turning on the radio.

K. Michelle's "Fallin'" floats through the speakers. I lay my head back on the headrest and close my eyes, getting lost in the lyrics. I hadn't heard this song in years. *Ooooh, this bitch is singing my shit!*

Behind my shut lids, Jasper's face flickers in and out. Everything he is, everything I thought he was, everything I wanted him to be, all tightly coiled in a ball of blazing fire. His crooked grin. His sculpted nakedness, the tattoo of my name etched over his heart. His arms pulling me into him, protecting me, holding me close; his heartbeat and breaths becoming my own. His thick tongue caressing my clit and lower lips. His thick, veiny dick fucking into wetness and heat, stretching into the depths of my soul, delving into everything I was, everything I wanted to be to him… for him.

Until…

Promises were broken. Games were played. Lies were told. Lines were crossed.

Until…

Fists replaced hugs. Loving words turned threatening. Lustful gazes metamorphosed into contempt. Compliments became criticisms.

Until…

I slid another nigga's dick into my mouth.

Bullets replaced kisses.

Nothing else no longer mattered.

Revenge became the only thing I wanted.

My eyes snap open when Mario's "Somebody Else" starts playing. I glance over at Mel bobbing his head to the beat. My gaze flutters to his thick hand gripping the steering wheel. I turn my head toward the window and peer out through the tinted glass. Memories of Jasper quickly fade. My mind flits along the borders of debauchery, finding its way back to late Saturday night, early Sunday morning, my fingers hungrily strumming in my wet pussy while watching Mel masturbate. His horse dick…thick, long, and beautiful!

I cut my eye back over at him on the sly, my gaze dipping to his lap, remembering how his gigantic dick throbbed in my hand, how it pulsed in my mouth, how it stretched my esophagus and shut off my airway, making me lightheaded. I pull in my bottom lip. Shift in my seat. My pussy starts to tingle as I hark back to the way I sucked Mel, fucked him into my mouth, filling my gullet with his thick creamy nut...*Mygod!*

Not once, not twice, but three times The night at the condo, then last night en route to the airport, eleven of his twelve-and-a-half-inch anaconda sucked, slurped and throated. Then, again, this morning in the short-term parking lot, section A-1. And each time I spun Mel's top, I made him moan. Made him grunt, and call out my name as his nut rolled up in his balls and shot out of his dick slit. But I will not be satisfied until I'm able to suck every last inch of him down to the base, until my nose is pressed deep into his pubic hairs.

God, how I love a big, clean dick!

And there aren't many dick suckers out there who can put in the kind of throat and spit work the way I do. Oh, sure there are lots of chicks out there sucking the skin off a nigga's bone, professing to be on top of their head game. But they damn sure aren't sucking the nut, the snot, and the guts out of his ass. And they're definitely not serving up that wet, sloppy throat heat and making his ass see stars, or feel like he's having an out-of-body experience the way I do.

Only one-and-a-half more inches of snake meat to conquer, I think, pulling out my ringing cell. It's a call from my realtor. I put my house on the market two weeks ago, shortly after the shit between Jasper and me hit the fan, eager to be rid of it. So far, the house has been shown to six couples. My fingers cross, hoping like hell she's calling to tell me someone has put in a bid.

"Hello."

"H-h-h-hello, P-P-Pasha?" she says, sounding frantic. "This is D-D-Dana Lamb. W-w-we...h-h-have...ohgodohgodohgod..."

My heart drops. "Dana, girl, please. What the fuck is going on? You're making me nervous, hon."

"I-I-I…" She starts hyperventilating. "Ohgodohgodohgod… you h-h-h-have…t-t-to…g-g-get…ohgodohgodohgod…t-t-there's b-b-blood… e-e-everywhere…"

I swallow back the realization that it had finally come to this. "Blood where, Dana?"

"T-t-the…p-p-p-police…are on t-t-their w-w-way…"

I try to keep calm. "Dana, the police are on their way where?" Mel looks over at me with questioning eyes. I shrug, giving him an I-have-no-damn-clue look. "Where is there blood everywhere?"

I hold my breath, wait for her to tell me what I already know. What I've been expecting. It was only a matter of time.

And still I wait…

"At t-t-the estate," she pushes out. She takes a deep breath, steadies the shaky rattling in her voice. "They're d-d-dead, Pasha! Everyone!"

Someone else takes the phone from her. A man. He says the guard at the gate to my estate was found shot in the head. That there are two more guards also dead. One lying facedown in the middle of the circular driveway, shot in the back of the head. The other inside the foyer of my home, shot in the chest multiple times.

The house has been ransacked.

My nose flares.

"Shit! Please tell Dana to stay put. I'll be there as soon as I can."

I glance over at Mel. But before I open my mouth to say anything, he's already making an illegal U-turn, wheels angrily spinning as he presses down on the pedal, hitting a hundred.

I immediately dial Jasper's number. The nigga answers on the first ring as if he'd been anticipating my call. "Did you find what the fuck you were looking for, motherfucker?"

"Where the fuck is my paper, Pasha?"

"Up in flames with the rest of your shit, nigga! Stupid mother-fucker!"

"Oh, you wanna be funny, right? You think I'm fuckin' wit' you, huh? Bitch! You lucky I didn't burn that muhfucka down. I want my muthafuckin' paper, yo!"

"Nigga, you'll *burn* in hell before you *ever* see a motherfucking dime of that money! And the *only* thing that's getting burned down are your stash houses, motherfucker!"

Silence.

"Oh, what, nigga? Did I hit a nerve? You thought I didn't know? Yeah, *bitch*, I know all about those six houses going up in flames. I told you, nigga. Every time you fuck with *me*, I'm gonna *fuck* with you. You want war, motherfucker. You got it!"

I end the call, narrowing my eyes to thin slits of rage. Not be-cause he's broken into my home because the truth is, I had Lamar handle having all of my personal belongings and anything of value moved out last weekend while I was in L.A. I knew Jasper would be trying to kick the doors in at some point. I'm just surprised he waited as long as he did.

No. I'm pissed the fuck off because I wasn't there to greet his black ass at the motherfucking door!

And now...

The motherfucker has gotten away with three murders!

Twenty-One

There's always a sign of danger long before the eye of a storm hits...

"Miss Pasha, girl," Cassandra yells into my ear over loud music I hear playing in the background. "You need to c'mon down to the club tonight 'n' toss back a few Clit Lickers..."

I glance up at the clock. It's a little after nine in the evening. I should be in my car by now, heading to my hotel suite. Instead, I'm here.

On a Friday night.

With Mel up front, and a bottle of Rémy back here with me as I shuffle through pages of inventory. Truth is, my nerves are still rattled from pulling up into my estate—which officially became a crime scene three days ago for triple homicide, then being greeted by yellow caution tape, multiple red and blue lights flashing, a huge white Medical Examiner's van, two homicide detectives, and blood everywhere from where my three guards were gunned down. Murdered.

In the middle of my foyer, there was blood all over the marble tile, and splattered on the walls. My realtor was a hysterical mess by the time I got to the house, and rightfully so. The whole scene was traumatizing. And, of course, there were no witnesses. Of course I have the surveillance footage, but I told the police there was none. That the cameras weren't working.

When the detectives asked if I could think of why anyone would want to break into my home, as if on cue, I burst into tears, sobbing uncontrollably. Then told them, "My husband and I are in the middle of a messy separation. He's been violent toward me in the past. Although I don't think he'd go as far as killing anyone, I can't be certain." I pulled out my final order of protection and showed it to them. "All I know is, he was very angry about being out of our home. Now, after seeing all this, I don't know what he might be capable of. I'm so scared."

Oh, my whole performance was complete with collapsing into Lamar's arms. Then, when I finally calmed, I kindly offered up the numbers to all three of Jasper's cell phones when they asked if I had a number where he could be reached for questioning. He wasn't a suspect, but the seed had been planted for him to definitely be considered someone to pay close attention to.

Later on that evening, I called Lamar from my hotel suite and told him to torch everything. That's right. I told him to burn my estate down to the ground. The call ended. And six hours later, the job was done. Firefighters were called to the scene of the blaze at approximately 5:42 in the morning.

Pictures of the crime scene and the news of the triple homicide, along with captions of the roaring blaze that took firefighters almost three hours to contain, have been splattered all over the local news. Other than the names of the three victims, reporters had very little to report. News captions highlighting the tragedy, which struck the affluent, gated-community with their sprawling estates, have been plastered on every newspaper.

Once it was discovered that the crime scene plastered all over news was my home, my phone has been ringing nonstop. Although the murders are still under investigation, as of this morning the cause of the fire has been determined as…electrical. All I need to

do now is, wait for the insurance company to complete their investigation, cut the check, then I'm free and clear. Poof…just like that.

Mmmmph. Motherfuckers can keep sleeping on me if they want.

I finish off the rest of my drink, allowing the smooth burn to heat
my insides.

"…Oooh, yes, goddammit… Slick 'n' Chunky are doin' me right
on the ones 'n' twos, sugah-boo. Owwwww…motherfuck you,
Chunky! Motherfuck you, goddammit! You tryna do me! Yessss,
goddammit…! Miss Pasha, girl, get ya mind right! And c'mon
down here so we can turn these niggas out. These thug coons will
love you, sugah-boo. You ain't got shit else to do unless you got
some dingaling you 'bout to wrap ya lips on…"

I frown. "Listen. I already told you that I'm *not* coming down
there tossing back drinks at some damn Crack House. So let it go.
I know you mean well, girl. But I can't stand a bitch who tries to
impose her social life on me."

"Oooh, yessss, do me right, goddammit! Give it to me dirty,
sweetness! Oooh, yesss, goddammit! I love it raw, sugah-boo. You
talkin' my talk, Miss Pasha, girl! Yes, gawd! I like it when a bitch
talks that talk. Cuss me, sugah-boo! Wet my drawz, goddammit!
But you know I ain't *ever* messy! I don't give a goddamn what you
say! Now is you comin' down here to have some'a these Clit
Lickers with me or what?"

I huff. *This bitch is really out of control!* "Look, I need to—"

"Ooooh, yes goddammit!" she yells, cutting me off. "This is my
shit! Chunky Monkey, niggah-coon, *boom-boom!* You tryna do me,
goddammit! Oooh, Miss Pasha, girl, excuse me…this nigga is doin'
me right with the music. Oooh, wait…hold on one minute…"

I roll my eyes, getting up to use the bathroom, listening to Booty
go off. As tempted as I am to disconnect the call, I hold on. Intentionally or not, she can be very entertaining. And whether I want

her to be or not, she's a distraction from my own craziness. Shit I have no interest in sharing with her.

"Nigga, where's my muthafuckin' child support money? See, nigga-coon, you stay tryna do me… What I gotta do, huh? Beat that fat bitch's ass you fuckin' to get my money?" I can't hear what he's saying, but whatever it is, she isn't having it. "You know what, coon-fucker? You ain't shit! Can't stand nuthin' ya long-dick ass stand for. I don't know why I ever fucked with your no-good ass any-goddamn-way. Big-dick fucker! All you was ever good for is fuckin'…uh-huh, whatever, nigga-coon…eat the inside of my ass, Vernon…"

Vernon? I blink. *I wonder if…ohmygod, no…it can't be the same nigga. Or could it?*

I strain against the backdrop of loud music to catch a hint of his voice, a trace of gruff, a tinge of anything, to confirm or refute the nagging in my gut. That he is in fact one in the same.

Vernon Lewis.

My antagonist.

And…

One of Booty's deadbeat baby daddies.

"Oooh, Miss Pasha, girl. I'm back. These niggas stay tryna do me. Be glad you only got you one baby fahver you gotta deal wit', even though the one you got is 'bout as messy as they come. But these no-good, big-dick niggas ain't worth no more than the nut they bust up in ya guts… Ooooh, yesssss, goddammit! Fuck you, Chunky! Miss Pasha, girl, let me go 'n' get my drop 'n' pop on. I'm done with ya stuck-up ass tonight. It's time to turn it up on these nigga-boos. Somebody come wet my throat! I need this neck coated, goddammit…!"

I shake my head. *What you* need *is to take your ass home and be with your kids. This bitch stays posted up in the bar.* "Go, get your dance on," I say, staring at my reflection in the mirror while washing my hands. "We'll talk later."

"I'ma be down to the shop tomorrow after I get the kids off to school, then stop by Dickalina's to get my damn pressure cooker back from that bitch before she starts boilin' her nigga's shitty drawers up in it."

Ugh! Dickalina's a chick I'd personally never be caught dead with. I twist my lips up in disgust, letting Booty know tomorrow's Saturday; that's there's no school.

"Ooh, I better ease up off these Clit Clickers. I done forgot what day of the week it is and I ain't even sauced good. Ooooh, goddammit! Yesssss, Chunky, yesssss! This is my shit... Owww...! Look, Miss Pasha, girl, let me go. I gotta turn up the booty heat on these niggas. I'll see you..."

"Go on and turn it..."

She yells into the phone, "Oh, yesss, goddammit! Waaaaait, waaaait, Miss Pasha, girl! You there?!"

I sigh. "Yeah, what now?"

"Oooh, yesss, goddammit! And the shit in the pot thickens, Miss Pasha, girl! You not gonna believe what the wind done blew up in here tonight, goddammit! Hol' one minute, sweetness..." Her voice fades from the phone. I can barely hear what she's saying now. After a few deafening moments, she's back in my ear. "...sent you a picture. Tell me if you've ever seen this black nigga-coon before..."

I tell her to hold on, pulling my phone from my ear, placing her on speaker while switching apps. "Okay, I got it," I say, opening the text she's sent.

"Tell me what you see, sugah-boo. Tell me what *you* see, goddammit!"

It's a picture of a *fine*, dark-chocolate nigga. He's wearing a dark-colored pullover and there's a thick—what looks to be either white gold or platinum—chain hanging from his thick neck with an emblem hanging from it. He's wearing a Brooklyn Nets fitted cocked to the side of his head. From what I can see in the picture, he looks muscular. I've never seen him before. "Girl, all I see is a dark-skinned nigga flossing. Who is he? One of your sponsors?"

"Look again, Miss Pasha, girl. *Look....again*, goddammit!"

I sigh. "Look, I don't have time for the guessing games, Cassandra."

"Oooh, don't do me, goddammit. *Look* at the picture closely, sugah-boo. Now tell me what you *see*."

I stare at the snapshot again. I squint, then blink, moving my face closer to the phone screen. I look at his eyes again—something is very familiar about them. *Omygod!* I stare at the emblem hanging from his chain. My eyes widen in shock. A rush of anger shoots through me. I grip my chest. I feel myself shaking from the inside out.

It's him.

"I can't wait to tear that throat up...you wanna live, bitch..."

His huge, hairy balls zoom into my mind's eye. I feel faint. And sick to my stomach.

"It's the nigga whose balls I tried to bite off," I push out.

"Yesssss, goddammit! Let's get this nigga-coon *tonight*, Miss Pasha, girl. Oooh, wait...let me go into the bathroom, so I can hear myself think, goddammit."

"A nigga like me doesn't take no for an answer. I take the fuck what I want...dick-teasing, cum slut..."

"Did he see you?" I glance up at surveillance monitor and see Lamar coming into the salon, holding what looks like a manila envelope in his hand. He gives Mel dap. I watch as they talk, wondering if either of them shared with the other how I've made their toes curl and their heads loll to the side with my dick-swallowing skills. If so, had they swapped stories? Had they huddled over a blunt and reminisced how I sucked the nut out of them, rolling the sweet, salty spunk around on my tongue before swallowing.

My mouth and pussy start to juice at the thought of them barging through the door with their hard cocks in hand, demanding to stuff them deep into my mouth, at the same time.

"Yessssss, goddammmit!" Booty screams into my ear, rudely snatching me back to reality. I press my thighs together. "Now what you say to me, sugah-boo?"

"I wanted to know if he'd seen you?"

"Yeah, the nigga-coon saw me; that's why I hurried up into the bathroom before he could come over 'n' get all up in my face again..."

There's a light knock at the door as it slowly creeps opens. Lamar peeks his head in. And I wave him in. I watch as he walks in, my gaze gliding down to his groin, momentarily reveling in the memory.

My pussy grows wetter.

Lamar takes a seat in front of me, sliding the large envelope in his hand over to me. I give him a puzzled look.

"Open it," he says, easing back in his seat; legs gapped open.

"Oooh, goddammit, Miss Pasha, girl. I feel like takin' a bottle to his goddamn fine-ass face. Mmmph. Here I was thinkin' 'bout givin' that nasty, no-good nigga-coon a lil' taste of this cootie-coo the next I saw him..."

I rip open the envelope.

"Before you tol' me all this shit 'bout his black-ass fuckin' in ya throat-box. Ole nasty fucker-bitch...!

My heartbeat quickens.

Inside is an eight-by-ten photo.

It's *him! Legend!*

His dark-brown eyes stare back at me—mean and menacing. His masked face flashes in my head. His deep voice plays over in my head. *"I can't wait to tear that throat up..."*

I open and close my hands a few times to steady them from shaking as I hold the picture up and study it. Lamar has handed me the key to the golden opportunity I've needed.

"I take the fuck what I want..."

On the lower-right corner, his stats are listed: *six feet, four inches, 245lbs.*

I peer over the edge of the photo at Lamar with thankful eyes.

He acknowledges the gesture with a nod, smiling.

"Goddammit!" Booty snaps. "It's time, Miss Pasha, girl! Let's fish this nigga!"

"I..."

"Wait a minute, Miss Pasha, girl... Umm, 'scuse me, bitch. Why is you all down in my goddamn mouth? What, booga-coon, you tryna see how long my throat is...?"

I cringe.

Whoever she's checking must have said something slick back to her. The next thing I know, the sound of glass is smashing. "Bitch, next time I won't miss. Now get the fuck up outta here 'n' wait 'til I'm done handlin' my goddamn business..."

I drop the photo on my desk. Taking a deep breath, glaring at it.

The butt of his gun tucked in his waistband flashes in my mind.

"Suck my balls, bitch..."

"You a dead bitch...you a dead bitch...you a dead bitch..."

The threat plays over and over in my head.

I quickly swallow the rage rising in my throat.

"Oooh, I can't stand me no messy-ass, nosey bitch," Booty says, slicing into the mental recording playing in my head. "Now tell me, Miss Pasha girl, are you ready to start scratchin' niggas off the list?"

I pull open my top drawer and reach for my gun, looking over at Lamar as I lay it on top of the photo, over his face.

Lamar's head nods slowly in agreement.

"Yes," I say, narrowing my eyes at the nigga's snapshot. "Tell me where you want to meet?"

Twenty-Two

A smart bitch uses her foes as her footstool...

At a quarter to one, Lamar and I patiently sit in wait discreetly parked outside of the Crack House—across the street, watching obnoxiously loud patrons stumble drunkenly in and out of its doors, allowing snatches of bass from the club's speakers to thump and vibrate its way out into the night air.

Lamar shakes his head. "Damn. Sounds like you'll fuck 'round 'n' end up walkin' up outta there deaf the way that bass is vibratin'."

I grunt, eyeing four hood-hoochies as they climb out of a black gypsy cab all dolled up in their best matching hooker getups—ultra-short, one-shoulder mesh dresses with fishnet stockings and silver-glitter, eight-inch platform sandals that they can barely walk in.

"Mmmph. Trickin' ain't easy," I say sarcastically, shaking my head as one of the chicks' dresses is sucked up into her big bubble ass. She shakes her booty a few good times and the dress frees itself from her crack. The door opens and the bass pushes out sounding louder, heavier.

"So you ever been up in that spot?" Lamar wants to know, gesturing toward the club with his chin.

I shake my head, curling my lips in disgust. "Ugh. Never." I keep my stare fixed on the door determined and ready to finally face one of my attackers, once and for all.

When Booty called me earlier in the evening, after all of her prodding and badgering, to meet her here to reel the nigga *L* into his own trap, we agreed on the time. Midnight. Then an hour after our conversation, I sent a text telling her I'd changed my mind. That something else came up. That we'd have to get at him some other time.

Truth is, I now have my own plans for Mr. Legend. That doesn't include her.

I frown when I see Shuwanda stepping out of the club in some one-piece jumper and wedge heels. She crosses the street, walking toward the parking lot packed with luxury cars and SUVs. For a second I think she can see me through the tinted glass when she looks over in the direction of the truck as she passes by. But all she sees are two dark outlines.

"Bitch," I mutter, narrowing my eyes. I fight back the urge to hop out and punch her in her damn throat.

"What's her deal?" Lamar asks, reclining back in his seat.

I snort. "The messy bitch is one of my ex hairstylists." I give him the rundown on how she used to slick about me to her customers, thinking the shit wouldn't get back to me. And how the bitch was stealing from me. Then when I confronted her ass about it, she tried to break fly and pop shit. I fired her. Then I had her ass black-balled from working in any of the surrounding black-owned salons.

Lamar nods, rubbing his chin. "Damn. That's fucked up. But when you doin' it like you, haters come wit' the territory."

I shrug. "It is what it is. Them bitches don't validate me." I glance at the digital clock. 1:27 a.m. *I wish this nigga would hurry the fuck on out of there.* I look over toward the club as a couple arguing comes staggering out the door. He's tall, thick and very muscular.

And obnoxiously fine. She's petite with big titties and no ass. They're both clearly lit up. And the chick's pissed off about something. A hand is up on her narrow hip. Her neck is zigzagging from left to right. An angry finger is waving up in his face.

He says something to her, then slaps her hand down, spinning off from her, heading in our direction toward the parking lot across from the club. Chick is hot on his heels still talking shit.

Mmmph. Hot trash, I think, frowning at their matching wears. She's wearing a green-and-brown scooped-neck Camo mini-dress with a pair of dark-camel wedge sneakers. Her long fingernails are painted in bright multicolors and match the colorful yarn braids she has crocheted in her head.

Her boo-thang's hair is parted down the middle and pulled up into four sections of ponytails. He's wearing a pair of green-and-brown Camo cargo pants, a green long-sleeved T-shirt with orange lettering sprawled across his wide chest. I squint, trying to make out what the shirt says.

I blink.

"Ugh, I know his shirt doesn't say what I think it says," I say more to myself. Lamar leans up in his seat, looking over in their direction.

He chuckles, reclining back in his seat. "Yup, it says what it says."

PUSSY EATER.

He stops at the curb, spinning around to face the motor-mouth in back of him, who has apparently punched him in his back. Now I'm curious to know what they're going at it about. I inch my window down until I can hear them.

"I don't appreciate you bein' up in some other bitch's face all night. That's why, nigga! I know that baldheaded bitch ain't suckin' your dick like I do. You all up dat musty bitch's face at da bar 'n' buyin' her drinks 'n' you know the cable bill ain't even been paid, yet! So, what she doin', huh, Knutz? Lickin' your ass when I don't wanna lick it?"

Knutz?

I blink, then squint, taking in everything about him. His menacing voice, his body, his bulging muscles, the way he's manhandling and smacking up that Dickalina chick…my eyes widen. *"Yo, ma, you pretty as fuck. But I will beat you the fuck up…"*

I swallow back a wad of uncertainty.

"I'm tired of this shit wit' you, Knutz! Don't I let you use my EBT-card whenever you wanna buy your beers 'n' shit. You know dat shit's illegal 'n' I can lose my benefits doin' dat. But I love you. And all you wanna do is run 'round stickin' ya dick in these ole skank-ass, dirty bitches! You done brought me home five STDs already! And I ain't goin' down to the clinic for no more gawtdamn shots. And da last time you really had me all fucked up when I had da gonorrhea in my throat! I'ma good loyal bitch to you 'n' all you do is shit on me! Why you keep cheatin' on me, huh, Knutz? Don't I give you all the pussy you want, huh?"

"Mygod," I say, pressing my face to the window. "This better than going to the movies. These two ghetto-ass fools are out of control."

Lamar grunts. "Stupid-asses."

"Yeah, you let me pound dat shit out when ya shit ain't all stank wit' yeast 'n' shit." She tries to slap him. But he grabs her wrist, pushing her backward. "Yo, Dickalina, don't have me buss yo' ass out here. I ain't fuckin' playin' wit' ya retarded ass!"

She stamps her heeled foot, yelling at the top of her lungs unconcerned about who overhears. "I ain't playin' wit' you either, nigga! My pussy be stankin' 'cause you keep fuckin' them stankass sewer rat bitches! And I ain't fuckin' retarded! I'm just a lil' slow, nigga! I tol' you 'bout callin' me dat shit! I can't help it my momma was tryna cook up her work 'n' dropped me on my head when I was a baby. You ain't shit, Knutz! I shoulda listened to Booty 'n' never fucked wit' ya ass in da first place after I tol' her I met you in the visitin' hall when I was goin' to the prison to see my other boo.

"She said you was a no-good bum-ass nigga. And she right! All I do is let you use me, nigga! I let you 'n' ya bum-ass nephew Killah lay up on my Section-8 'n' you know all I got is a two-bedroom. I'm packin' ya shit 'n' tossin' you 'n' his trifilin' ass out tonight! Candy and Clitina ain't got no gawtdamn business havin' to see him layin' up on my sofa playin' wit' his big dick e'ery night. And I shouldn't have'ta be on watch e'ery fuckin' night tryna make sure Clitina's ass ain't in there tryna suck that ole long nasty dick!"

Lamar sucks his teeth. "Yo, them muhfuckas is wildin' out wit' this shit. They need to take that bullshit home."

I can't lie. Watching these two is like watching a horrible train wreck, but you're too damn stuck in disbelief to turn away from it. She says something about the chick in the bar probably having a dick between her legs because she looks like a man. Then she adds, "For all I know, nigga, you prolly suckin' it or lettin' her fuck you in da ass wit'—"

She doesn't get the rest of her words out before he takes his big hand to her face, smacking the shit out of her. In a flash, his free hand is around her neck, lifting her feet up off the ground. She screams at the top of her lungs, swinging her arms, punching and clawing at him to no avail as he violently shakes her.

I gasp. "Ohmygod, that crazy nigga's really trying to crush her neck." I look over at Lamar. "Don't you think we should do something?"

Lamar frowns. "Hell nah. She's used to that shit. Let them niggas fight. Tomorrow that broad'll be right back suckin' his dick again wit' her sockets all punched in."

He punches her in the mouth, then upside the head. Her head snaps with each blow, snot and spittle and blood flying everywhere. But he doesn't knock her out. For a tiny chick, she surprisingly takes her ass whipping with grace as he punches her again, then throws her to the ground. Her body hits the concrete, hard.

She screams at the top of her lungs for help. Pleads with him to leave her alone. Makes all kinds of crazy-ass promises to suck his dick, let him piss on her the next time he wants it, as long as he stops hitting her. But the nigga is too far-gone to be reasoned with.

I literally feel sick. Regardless of what I think about Booty's special-needs girlfriend, she's still a woman, first. And I'm still my sister's keeper whether I want to be or not. I dig down in my bag and pull out my stun gun.

Lamar raises his seat. "Yo, where you goin'?"

"I can't just sit here and do nothing. He's going to kill her if I don't stop his ass." I unfasten my seatbelt and reach for the door handle. Lamar reaches over and grabs my arm. Tells me to fall back. That it isn't my fight. Reminds me of why we're out here in the first place. But I'm not interested. I can't idly sit and watch her get beat down like this. The nigga is stomping and kicking the shit out of her.

I glare at Lamar, snatching my arm back. "Look. If you want to sit back and let a nigga beat on a woman, then do you. But I—"

"Chill," he says, pointing over at them, "ya people's is already on the scene."

"What?" I glance back over at them as Booty is charging toward them in her heels, swinging a nightstick in the air.

I blink.

She hits him in the back of the head. And he spins around and punches her dead in the mouth. I gasp as Booty stumbles back, then charges at him; fists in full blaze connecting blows to his face and chest.

Then out of nowhere the Dickalina chick springs to her feet and jumps on Booty's back. "Bitch! What da fuck is you doin'?! Ain't no body ask you to jump in my shit, bitch! Stay outta my shit, bitch! You stay mindin' somebody else's gawtdamn business!"

Booty swings her off of her, ripping her blouse open. The two of them start fist fighting. Ass and titties are all on display as they go at it like two jailhouse bitches. Knutz is now trying to break the two of them up. Then out of nowhere the two of them turn around and start fighting him.

"Ohmygod!" I huff as I watch on. "I don't believe this shit. That bitch is real twisted. And now she's attacking him alongside Cassandra."

"You see *why* I said fall back."

Niggas start pouring out of the club. Booty yells out something to a young-looking thug who steps up to Knutz and hooks off on him. The two of them go at it. Someone throws a bottle at someone else, then like a wildfire several more fights erupt. Big, burly bouncers in black T-shirts and black slacks race out of the club to break up the mayhem, tossing bodies off of each other. I look on in total disbelief. Right here before my eyes the club's parking lot turns into a damn battlefield and in the center of it all is Booty and her ghetto-trash friend Dickalina.

After several more excruciating minutes of watching, I decide I've had enough of this hood circus. It's already a quarter to two in the morning and the nigga *L* is still nowhere in sight, although his shiny-new Jag with the personalized license plates is parked over in the VIP section of the club's parking lot.

"Let's go," I say, fastening my seatbelt into place. "Before this place starts swarming with police."

"Nah, chill. Not yet. Police ain't rushin' to come out here." I shoot him a look, raising a brow. He shrugs. "Trust me. A buncha muhfuckas stabbing' 'n' fuckin' each other up isn't an emergency." He thrust his chin toward the mayhem. "Look. Here comes ya boy now."

I look over and there he emerges in the thick of the crowd.

Cocky.

My pulse quickens. A renewed sense of purpose surges through my veins. Followed by disgust. The dark-chocolate nigga is fine as hell. And most likely can have more than his share of pussy whenever he wants it. Yet, this dirty nigga would rather force his dick down in a bitch's throat.

Arrogant sonofabitch!

The image of his hard dick pounds its way into my head. My brain starts reeling. Suddenly, I feel my anger swelling inside of me, pushing up against my chest as he swaggers toward the VIP parking. I grab the black case lying on the seat beside me, clutching it to my thudding chest.

Lamar reaches over and touches my arm, temporarily calming the storm brewing somewhere deep inside of me. "Yo, you aiiight? I already tol' you, I can have this nigga handled for you."

I slowly shake my head, my eyes trailing my target as he disarms his car. Opens the door, then coolly slides in. "No. He's mine," I say as he shuts the door of his Jag, starts the engine, pulls out of his space, then peels out of the lot down Halsey Street, the tag LEGEND staring back at me.

Lamar pulls out from the curb and trails a safe distance behind as swirling red and blue lights and the frantic whir of sirens finally approach the club.

The silence between Lamar and me allows me to get lost in my own head, thinking and scheming, as he follows six cars behind. The Jag makes its way toward University Heights, traveling along Martin Luther King Boulevard, before making a right onto a side street, then a left. He drives over a few speed bumps into a well-hidden new housing development. Then pulls into an assigned parking space as Lamar pulls into a space in visitor parking, near a large dumpster. A few minutes more, Legend steps out of the car, the door shuts, the lights flash as he sets the alarm, then he's walking up the short walkway to his front door. An end unit. He slides his key in, opens and shuts the door, disappearing inside.

Lamar pulls out of the space and circles around the block before parking over on the next block, directly in back of Legend's end unit. Nervously, I tuck my hair under a black skull cap, then slip my hands into a pair of black Nomex flight gloves as Lamar slips on his. I am an emotional wreck. But I don't let on. I take slow deliberate breaths to keep my insides from shaking uncontrollably.

Seconds later, lights flick on upstairs. *That must be his bathroom,* I think, looking up at the small window in back of his unit. My stare hardens at a silhouette.

Lamar and I sit and wait. Watching and waiting, waiting and watching until all the lights go out. Finally…

At three a.m.

Twenty-Three

No wrongs go unpunished when you become the judge, jury, and executioner…

My heart is pounding, and my gloved hands are drenched with sweat. As Lamar swiftly opens his backpack and pulls out two glass suction cups, creating a vacuum in the center of the sliding glass patio door. In part awe and part terror, I watch him smartly remove a roll of duct tape and cover the entire glass, save an area wide and long enough for us to step through.

In a hushed tone he explains the tape is used as a shock absorber. Then, with skilled precision, he uses a diamond-tipped glasscutter, tracing and retracing the area to be cut out until the lines deepen and the glass thins.

Every little sound out here seems to have become magnified, heightened by my paranoia. I find myself looking over my shoulder and glancing at my watch every several seconds. Sweat is trickling down my spine.

I don't realize that I have been holding my breath all this time until Lamar grabs the handles of the suction cup and slowly removes the cutout portion of glass. He leans it up against the building. Then within minutes, we are slipping into the two-level townhome through the opening.

Panic sets in when Lamar signals with his finger for me to stay here while he locates the alarm panel. My insides start shaking uncontrollably.

Ohmygod! What the fuck am I doing? On top of all the crazy shit I've already done, or been behind—murder, arson, harassment, assault—I can now add…, even though I'm not here to steal *anything of value, per se—to the list. Me? A criminal, a murderer!*

In a two-week period this is what life has become for me. One vicious fight—for survival, for my freedom and, most importantly, for…retribution.

Lamar is a few paces in front of me, his Glock drawn, his steps catlike, one foot in front of the other, and the weight of his body sinking into his thighs as he moves about the kitchen with purpose and a strange…familiarity.

As if he's been here before.

He mentioned, after he'd slid me the envelope with *L*'s photo and I'd hung up with Booty, that his *peoples* had been keeping a *visual* on Legend over the last few days watching how he moves. He'd offered to handle him for me. Said he'd have him stomped out, tell him I sent my regards, then have a bullet put in his dome.

But, *noooo!*

I refused. Told him that a beat down and a bullet were too easy. That none of them, particularly this nigga, was worthy of a quick death. That I needed for him to *feel* my humiliation. Needed him to *see* the fire in my eyes. Wanted him to *know* how it felt to be violated. Wanted him to *hear* the chill in my voice when I leaned in and whispered my final words in his ear.

I need to be the first person he sees standing over him when he opens his eyes. And there's no time for mistakes or mishaps. Finally, Lamar reappears, waving me over with a hand. And as I'm trailing behind him through the kitchen, then the dining room, heading up the carpeted stairs in this sparsely furnished, weed-scented den of sin, I start thinking, wondering...what if?

What if, in the end—after I've doled out my street justice—something unforeseen happens and things go awry and I end up... *dead?*

What will the headlines read?

Successful Hairstylist to the Hood Rich and Fabulous Found Murdered!

Owner of the Posh & Trendy Nappy No More Hair Salon Tortured and Burned!

Pasha Alona-Nivea Allen, Cum Lover & Loving Mother Found with her Throat Slit!

Deep Throat Diva Sucks in her Last Breath! Body of Salon Owner, Pasha Allen, Found with Unknown Man's Dick Stuffed in her Mouth!

What if this is all a setup? What if Lamar is luring me to my own demise?

What if...?

No, no. It can't be. He wouldn't have burned down those stash houses, or brought me any of the money found in them, if he were playing me.

"*Any*thing you need me to handle for you, Pasha. I got you." That's what he'd said to me, on more than one occasion. He offered up his services to me. I didn't seek him out. Just like when he stepped to me after one of my practice shoots down at the firing range and stated, "I'm diggin' how you handle a weapon. What's a beauty like you needin' protection from?"

I looked him up and down, then cocked my head. "From no-good niggas."

"Then how 'bout you let one'a the good ones protect you? I'd love to be at your service." He reached into his back pocket and pulled

out a cardholder, then handed me a white card with SECURITY/
BODYGUARD SERVICE, LLC, written in bold black letters. Two
weeks later, I called to inquire about guard service for the salon.
And instead of him sending someone from his staff, *he* showed up
for duty. That was over ten months ago. Still, maybe that was the
plan all along. To have me let down my guard. Get me to trust
him. Then *bam!* Do me in. Turn me over to the wolves.

But why would he wait until now?

I switch the leather case from one hand to the other, then slip
my free hand down into my jacket pocket, pulling out my .45-mm.
I aim the Ruger at his back, just in case. *If I'm going down, nigga,
you're going down with me!*

I glance over my shoulder, checking to make sure no one is
creeping up the stairs behind me, or us. My gut tells me I can
trust Lamar. I want to trust him. At this moment…*need* to.

My instincts are all I have.

I relax a little, pushing the disturbing thoughts of being ambushed
into a recessed corner of my racing mind as Lamar and I hit the
top step and ease down the hall. I tighten my grasp around the
case's handle.

My bag of tricks.

There are four doors, one of them closed. Three bedrooms.
One bathroom. Slowly, we make our way to his bedroom. I feel
like I am floating. Beads of sweat line my forehead. My racing
heart and jittery nerves cause me to overheat.

The closer I get to the door, the harder my heart pounds.
Adrenaline surges through my veins. The moment is here. Judgment day is finally upon us.

Lamar reaches the door. His gloved hand is on the doorknob. He pauses, glances over his shoulder at me. His eyes asking the question his mouth doesn't. "Am I ready?"

I nod.

Slowly, he opens the door, then quietly steps in, his nine-millimeter leading the way. I stay in the back, standing in the doorway, waiting. Watching.

The room reeks of alcohol and weed. Suddenly, a beam of bright light illuminates from a mini Lumen flashlight. Lamar is standing near the bed—a queen-size, four-post bed, shining the light in the face of the snoring figure.

Legend.

"Rise 'n' shine, dirty muhfucka," Lamar sneers, poking him in the head with the barrel of his gun. "Look what the Boogeyman brought ya...?"

Legend jumps, clearly startled. "Yo, what the—"

In one swift motion Lamar raises his gun and viciously brings it down on top of Legend's head, then follows up with a barrage of blows to his face and head, knocking his lights out.

Twenty-Four

If you want to strip a nigga of his manhood, slice off his dick,
then fuck him in his ass with it...

The lids of Legend's eyes finally flutter open. And I'm leaning directly in his face when they do. He blinks a few seconds, still dazed from being knocked in his head. There's a deep gash over his eye. His arms are stretched out and bound by rope on either end of his headboard's bedposts. His legs are also spread open wide and tied at the ankles to the posts at the foot of his bed.

"Remember me?" I say real low. "I'm the bitch you heard had niggas begging for this throat. And now I'm about to become the bitch that has *you* begging for your life."

His eyes widen, confusion and shock, then realization swimming in his pupils. His body jerks, tightening the ropes around his wrists and ankles as he tries to break free.

"Where you think you're going, boo?" I jeer, lightly running the tip of my blade in my hand over his left nipple. "You all mine tonight, sweetie. And I have a special night planned just for you. I'm going to give *you* what you gave me. Remember?" I lick my lips. "Mmm. I can't wait to tear that throat up. Let's see who the slutty cum-slut is after I'm done with you."

He tries to speak, but everything comes out garbled. A black leather ball gag is strapped tightly in his mouth. He grunts and growls.

I grab him roughly by his face, digging my nails into his cheeks.

"Bitch," I hiss, bringing my face inches from his, my eyes narrowing to slits. "*Shut* the fuck *up*! You have *no* fucking idea what you and the rest of them grimy niggas did to me down in that basement." I can smell the liquor and weed seeping from his panic-stricken pores. "But tonight, you're going to find out. And to ensure you do…" I let go of his face, stepping away from him. I quickly glance over at Lamar as I grab the leather case at the foot of the bed. My gaze shifts back to Legend. "I brought along some party favors to make the night memorable for the both of us."

He lifts his head. His eyes shift from me to the case, then over at Lamar, then down at his body. Fear floods his pupils when he finally realizes he's stretched out butt-naked, his long dick limply resting over his huge, hairy balls.

I unzip the case, then slowly pull out his treats—one at a time. I wave a chocolate-colored, ten-inch dildo in the air. "I brought you some cock, boo. A party ain't a party unless I can run hard cock all up in you."

Legend grunts, wildly shaking his head, his eyes pleading. He's sweating now. The veins in his neck are bulging.

I glare at him, then cock my head to the side. "You want to know why I'm letting you see what I look like, don't you?" He blinks. "See. Unlike you pussy-ass niggas hiding your faces behind masks, I want you to see me when I fuck your whole world up, like you did mine. You and the rest of them dirty niggas sexually tortured me when you motherfuckers kept me locked down in the basement tied up. So I'm going to give you a little taste of what torture really is."

I smirk, pulling out a Taser. "And this is for when I need to zap your balls." I grab at his balls, motioning with the Taser as if I'm about to put the heat to them. "I should Tase these big motherfuckers right now."

His body wriggles helplessly on the bed.

Next comes the blowtorch, then the bolt cutters. Finally, I pull out a nine-tailed flogger. Barbed wire is attached to the tails. Frantically, Legend tries to flail his arms and legs, each time the ropes cutting into his circulation.

I drag the Cat O' Nine Tails along his left leg, then his right leg; the sharply pointed barbs clawing into his skin. He writhes, groans loudly. A sadistic grin eases over my lips as I run my hand up along the shin of his leg, then over his muscular thigh.

"If you haven't figured it out, yet, I'm going to slowly torture you, dirty sonofabitch...you piece of shit, until you beg me to kill you. You let Jasper get you caught in a fire that didn't have shit to do with you."

I drag my finger along the frame of his body until I'm back at his side again. I shift my body, swing my hand all the way back, then slap the shit out of him. His head snaps to the left. "You really thought you could put your motherfucking hands on me..." I slap the other side of his face. "Thought you could ram your dick in my neck..." I slap him again. "And get away with it. Didn't you?"

He tries to speak.

"Nigga, save your breath. No one can hear you. You fucked with the wrong bitch, sweetie." I slide my hand over his stomach, then allow it to linger down over his cock. "You have no idea how long I've waited for this day. How long I have prayed for this day." I cup his balls, then gently squeeze. "Mmmm. These big balls." I start rubbing them seductively. "You remember when I tried to bite these big motherfuckers off, don't you, boo?"

I have the nigga spooked. *Good!*

He grunts, his chest heaving.

"Oh, don't worry. I'm not going to bite them off. Oh, no..." His eyes frenziedly follow me as I walk to the foot of the bed and pull out a scalpel from the case. I hold the sharp instrument up for him to see, pointing it at his groin. "I'm going to slice them off. Then feed them to your boy, Jasper."

His eyelids snap open and close. He rapidly shakes his head.

I glance at my watch. Its 4:20 a.m. I'm consciously aware that I must administer his dose of justice before dawn.

"Yes, nigga. I *am* going to castrate you." He bucks and thrashes, shaking the headboard. "Oh, don't worry. I've read up on it and watched several videos on how to properly gut your nut sac. The whole process is much the same as castrating a bull or pig. So, you"—I drag the scalpel up the bottom of his right sole, slicing open his foot—"are going to be gutted like the dirty pig mother-fucker you." His body lunges forward in pain. "Then I'm going to sauté your balls."

I walk back over to him, placing the scalpel beside him and picking up the switchblade. I press a gloved finger in the center of the ball. "Shhh. No need to fight it, boo. It's just you and me, no one else. So you might as well relax and enjoy. If not, I'm going to take the fuck what I want." I flip the blade open, then press the tip of it into his nipple until I draw blood. He flinches. "Isn't that what you said to me the night you came down into that basement and tormented me, beat me, threatened my life, then forced your dick into my mouth? You take what the fuck you want, right? Isn't that what you said?"

He groans and thrashes, causing the ropes to cut deeper into his skin.

"You wanna live, *bitch?*" He grunts, nodding his head. He reminds me of a Bobblehead. "Then stop trying to break loose. You're not going anywhere."

I can tell Lamar is getting impatient. If he had his way, he'd already have a bullet in Legend's head and we'd be on our way. He doesn't say anything. But I can see it in his eyes, willing me to hurry the hell up. He wants me to rush what I've waited, for what seems like forever, to finally do. No. I'm not rushing shit, for him or anyone else.

I have at least an hour and fifteen minutes before sunrise. And I plan on using every damn minute, every fucking second, of it in a slow, sweet, torturous way, all in the name of psychological warfare.

I look over at Lamar. He's standing, gun in right hand, face expressionless. But there's a glint of amusement in his eyes.

I pull out a bottle of Masterjack men's massage lotion.

"See, nigga. Because I'm so forgiving, I'm not going to just fuck you up. I'm going to make sure you get a sweet release, first, before I punish you for what you did to me. I'm going to give you the best and the *worst* handjob of your life."

I squirt a generous amount of the lotion all over his cock and balls. Something delightfully frightening stirs inside my pussy as I take his meaty dick in my hand and begin massaging it.

As much as he tries to fight it, tries to struggle against it, his dick has a mind of its own. And in deep, languid strokes it gives into the slippery sensations as I bring it to life. Legend writhes and groans, his toes opening and closing.

"Yeah, big-dick motherfucker." I quicken my strokes to match the sudden throb between my legs. He grunts. I bite down on my tongue. His eyes flutter. Mine narrow to slits. His cock thickens and stretches and pulses in my hand. My clit aches.

"All this big juicy dick and you want to go around stuffing it into bitches' mouths, huh? You like raping bitches, huh?" He shakes his head. His eyes widening as I yank his balls. "Lies! That's what you did when you forced me to open my mouth, so you could fuck your dick into my mouth. *You* sexually assaulted me, nigga."

Against his will, his hips begin to thrust as I stroke him. He shuts his eyes tight. Throws his head back. A muffled growl emits from the back of his throat. I reach for the bottle, squirt more lotion over his cock, then resume stroking him with one hand, gliding over the head of his dick, teasing it, while taking my free hand and massaging his balls, rolling them around. He flinches. His eyes pop over.

I smirk. "Relax. I'm not going to bring it to your balls, yet."

He looks over at Lamar as if he's going to save him. "Muhfucka, don't be lookin' over here at me. She's the one who won't let me body ya worthless ass."

I inch my finger near his asshole. His head snaps back in my direction. His hips lift off the bed as he attempts to clench his ass cheeks shut. I wedge my finger inside, then ram it into his hole.

Whatever pleas for help or mercy he's making come out mangled and choked. His groans sound like a wounded bear as I stroke his cock and finger-fuck him in his ass.

"C'mon, boo," I taunt, swirling my hand over the head of his dick, "bust this big dick for Deep Throat Diva. That's what they call me, nigga. The bitch that sucks a nigga crazy." I ram another gloved finger into his ass. My anger rises like bile. "The bitch you told to either suck, 'or you gonna die tonight, ho,' remember that?"

He grunts. Horror washes over his face as I force a third finger into his manhole. "Dirty motherfucker, how does it feel to be violated, huh? You like it, huh?"

More pained grunts, more anguished groans. His dick gets harder. I stroke it faster. "Yeah, pussy-nigga, rapist, no-good sonofabitch… let me see you bust that nut…you want me to wrap my slutty lips around the head of this dick, don't you, nigga…? You want some of this deep neck, huh…?"

Another muffled growl pushes out from the back of his throat. My pussy juices, overheats. His manhole heats and swallows in my fingers. Legend groans and lolls his head back. He squeezes his eyelids shut. Pressing back tears of what I hope are of embarrassment, of violation, of degradation. Ramming my fingers in and out, my own tears begin to surface.

"This is only a piece of what it feels like to be violated, nigga. I am no way near done with you."

He's sweating. I'm sweating. My knuckles rub the rim of his hole. The nigga's eyes snap open, glossed and practically crossed. Seconds later, his body thrusts. His legs shake. A thread of stringy precum drips out of his dick-slit. His slippery dick becomes harder than the proverbial rock. I egg him on. Goad him. Edging him to an unwanted orgasm.

His head rocks back and forth. He is growling, growling, growling. I have the nigga in a glazed frenzy as I rapidly stroke his dick, finger-fucking into his ass, hitting his prostate each time. He makes a strangled noise. His body convulses.

My pussy is tingling and twitching. I have to fight back my own whorish urge to lean in and swallow down his dick, milk it into my throat. I can feel it. He's on the verge of exploding. Vibrating waves shoot up his swelling dick as my fingers continue to stroke his spot.

Another growl, his body thrashing, ropes slicing deeper into his flesh, a gusher of thick, white nut bursts out of his slit, launching into the air, then splattering down on his shoulders, his chest, his stomach, his face.

"Yeah, motherfucker, bust that dick milk…give me all that hot nut, nigga…mmmm, that's right…get it all out…because this will be the last nut you ever bust…"

I keep stroking his dick and fingering his ass, talking dirty, calling him names. His dick explodes again, spurting out a rope of creamy nut that hits the ceiling, then over his shoulder, his abs, then finally spilling over my gloved hand. I pull my fingers out of his ass. Legend looks like he's ready to pass out.

I press my ass-scented gloved fingertips over his nose. "You smell that, nigga?" He grunts, trying to jerk his head away. I grab his face with my cum-coated hand. "Stay still and sniff, motherfucker!" I roughly push my fingers all up in his nose. "That's the scent of a nigga who's about to get fucked real deep…"

I smear his nut over his face, then reach for the flogger. "Now it's time to really get this party started…" He thrashes and bucks, his head snapping from side to side as I bring the flogger down over his cock and balls; the barbs clawing into his prized possessions. Lash after lash, I remind him of everything he ever said down in that basement to me. I remind him of how he choked and punched me. Remind him of the pain he caused me. "Motherfucker, you're going to regret the day you pulled your dick out on me!"

His bloodshot eyes plead incessantly.

Lash after lash, the barbs bite into his thighs, his groin, and his stomach, shredding and ripping into him, drawing blood, inflicting pain. By the time I'm done with this nigga, every day for the rest of his life, every time he drops his drawers, he'll be forever reminded of what he'd done to me.

When I am satisfied with my flogging, I reach for the Taser as his head lolls backward, forward, then over to the left. He's drunk with pain. His dick and balls are bloody and stripped raw. I light fire to his scrotum with one zap of the Taser, causing his head to snap back and his eyes to pop open as if he's possessed.

In my peripheral vision I see Lamar flinch and turn as a blood-curdling noise escapes the back of Legend's throat. His face is contorted. Tears spring from his eyes before he passes out. I wait. Give it time for the electrical flames to subside, then slap his sweat-soaked face. "Wake the fuck up," I hiss. His lids rapidly flutter, barely opening. "I'm going to ask you some questions. And you only have one shot at giving me the correct answers, before I light your balls up again. You understand me, fucker?"

He slowly nods. I ask him if he knows the nigga, AJ. He nods again. I ask the same about that nigga, Vernon. He looks away, slowly shaking his head. It doesn't matter if he's lying or not since I already know where to find him. Next I ask him if that crazy nigga Knutz was down in the basement, too, with the rest of them niggas. He hesitates, but gets his mind together and nods his answer when I move the Taser back toward his balls.

I step back from him. He looks as if he wants me to end it all right here. Put him out of his misery once and for all. Something buzzes. Lamar and I shoot each other a look, then cast our eyes in the direction of the sound. I walk over and pick up a pair of True Religion jeans, fishing his cell from out of his front pocket, then glancing at the screen. It's some trick calling, most likely either for some pussy, drugs, or both. I toss the phone over to Lamar. He scrolls through the phone.

I pull out my gun, screw on the silencer, then shoot this nigga in his left knee. He tries to scream out his agony, but it's all a garbled mess of grunts. "See, I shot you in your knee because I can't trust you not to try and kick and fight when I untie your leg. And if you keep it up, I'm going to bust you in your other knee."

I grab the dildo and lube it up. Legend's eyes pop open. He's grunting, again, thrashing his head. I ask Lamar to help me. Tell him I need for him to untie this nigga's left leg, then pull it all the way up to his chest. Then I ram all ten inches of the dildo into him, tearing the seam of his asshole open, fucking him mercilessly.

I leave the dick lodged into his ass, reach for the scalpel. I watch his bloodshot, tear-filled eyes flood with panic and pleading desperation.

"Too late for apologizes," I say, climbing up into the bed between his legs. "You're a nut too late," I grab his nut sac, "and now two balls too short..."

I slice down into the center of his scrotum. His body jerks. His wrists and ankles are badly cut and bloody. His jaws tighten around the gag. "You were a pussy for doing what you did to me..." He is sweating profusely. The agonizing pain ripping through his body as I slice him open, then pop out one of his large, slimy balls. "And now I'm going to give you one..."

Twenty-Five

Nothing's sacred in the pursuit of street justice...

Seven a.m., Saturday morning, my vibrating phone awakens me. Without looking at the caller ID, I answer groggily.

"I knew I shoulda never trusted ya slut-ass..."

I blink, jolting up in bed. "Are you *fucking* kidding me? Nigga, why are you fuc—"

"Nah, shut the fuck up 'n' listen. You duped a muhfucka, got me all caught up in the matrix believin' you was different from all them other bitches I was fuckin' wit'. Outta all the bitches, I gave *you* my muhfuckin' heart, Pasha. Gave *you* all'a me, yo. You..."

"Do you see what the hell time it is?"

I take a deep breath. Push it out slowly. I am too exhausted to argue with him. Too emotionally drained. I literally climbed into bed with a banging headache—the image of Legend's convulsing body, wire-clawed genitals, and sliced open balls all stained into my memory—less than forty minutes ago.

I am still trying to absorb everything that happened last night, everything *I* made happen with the help of Lamar. The memory of the blood and the jagged clawing into his skin and the pained expression on his face and the fear in his eyes and his fingers—all ten of them cut off at the first knuckle, scattered about the room, leaves a bittersweet taste of justice served to that nigga *L* in the back of my throat.

Out of all the niggas who were down in that basement that night, I loathed him the most. Torturing him aroused me. Watching him suffer excited me.

"Fuck outta here, yo," Jasper snaps, cutting into my reverie. "Fuck what time it is! You a fuckin' smut, yo. This is me 'n' you, Pasha. Drop the bullshit, yo. You fuckin' shitted on me! You a fuckin' dick-suckin' bitch, yo." His voice cracks. "Why you have'ta be a fuckin' smut, yo, 'n' be out there suckin' niggas dick 'n' shit, huh? Fuckin' slut-ass…"

He sounds like he's high out of his mind. Sounds like the nigga's been up all night somewhere, smoking and drinking, and doing God knows what else. He sounds desperate, like a nigga on the verge of snapping.

I hold my breath. Close my eyes. My grip tightens around my cell. I know I should hang up on him. But I don't. I want to hear him out. Need to hear him out—for me, maybe for him.

But why?

"All the bitches I coulda been wit' 'n' I end up wit' ya scandalous ass. And you end up bein' the fuckin' messiest outta e'ery last one of 'em broads, yo. You grimy as hell, Pasha. You know that, right?"

I have another call ringing through. It's Stax.

I sigh. "Jasper, we've already gone over this. Yes, I know. I know all about how *I* fucked *you* over. I am very much aware of how scandalous I am; how messy I've become. *Yes*, I'm a cum-guzzler. Yes, I'm a no-good, dick-sucking bitch. I cheated on you, Jasper. I hurt you. I know this. I've heard it more than enough times from you to never forget it. There's nothing I can do about it. It's done. I can't change it.

"So why are you calling me *now*, at *this* time of the morning with the *same* shit? It's already been established that you're hurt. At least I've admitted to what I've done to you. I take full responsibility for what I did then. And for what I'm doing *now*. But you still refuse to take responsibility for your shit. Sign the divorce papers so we can both go our separate ways. I don't even care about the names of them niggas anymore. All I want is for you to let me go. You can have every dime of your money."

"Fuck that muhfukin' paper you stole from me, yo. I wanna see my fuckin' son!"

I take a deep breath. "I didn't steal shit, Jasper. I simply relocated it for insurance."

He blows a breath into the phone, sounding as if he's smoking a blunt.

"Nah, you stole from me, yo. You stole my trust. My fuckin' heart. You a fuckin' thief, yo. You even tryna take my fuckin' son away from me. You a real fuckin' heartless, snake-ass bitch, Pasha. You've fuckin' takin' e'erything from me, yo. E'ery-fuckin'-thing I thought *I* was comin' home to *you* sucked out through some muhfucka's dick. I fuckin' *hate* you for doin' that shit, Pasha. Fuckin' bitch, yo!"

I swallow.

"Jasper, I'm hanging up on you. I'm—"

"Fuck outta here, Pasha. Fuck you hangin' up for, huh, bitch? What, you got some nigga's hard dick in ya hand you tryna swallow, huh? You did this shit to us, yo. You stabbed me in the fuckin' chest. You're the worst fuckin' bitch I've ever had!"

I squeeze my eyes shut, shaking my head. I feel myself starting to unravel. "No, Jasper. I'm the *match* you've never had. I'm no more scandalous or messy than *you*. You're a ruthless nigga, Jasper. We *both* did this to *us*. *We* stabbed each other using the same knife. I know I hurt you. But what about how you've hurt *me*, huh? Do you *still* think having me kidnapped and locked down in some fucking basement to be sexually tortured by a bunch of goons was justified, huh, Jasper?

"Did *I* fucking *deserve* to be attacked and almost beat to death for cheating on you? You could have just beaten me, Jasper! I could have handled the physical scars. What *you* did to *me* cut deep into me, Jasper! Every nigga you commanded to shove his dick into my mouth helped *you* strangle my spirit. I've spent almost a year-and-a-half of my life, dying inside because of *you*, nigga."

"Then it won't fuckin' matter when I take e'erything that's ever mattered to you before I fuckin' kill you."

The line goes dead.

"Nana, please. I'm begging you. Jasper is crazy. I didn't want to tell you. But if something happens to me, I want you to know that Jasper's behind it. He's responsible for what happened at the estate. He had those men murdered, Nana."

She gasps. "Dear God! And the fire? Are you saying he burned down your home, too?"

"Yes, Nana. That's exactly what I'm saying."

It's another half-truth to add to my basket of lies. But I'm desperate. I need Nana safe. And I'm willing to say whatever I need to in order to get her to understand that it isn't safe for her to be over there in that house alone. Although I have hired someone to be parked outside at all times to keep watch, it's not enough. I want her as far away as possible. Out of Jasper's reach.

"But why?"

I tell her because he wanted to get inside of the house to get things out of his safes, but I refused to let him. Then I share with her bits and pieces of what I've been dealing with, like the drive-by shooting in front of the salon a few weeks back.

"Lord God! Then why isn't he arrested?"

I don't want him arrested, Nana. I want him tortured. But...not yet!

The light turns green. I sigh. "There's nothing linking him to either crime, Nana. But that doesn't mean he's *not* the one who's behind them. And after his threat to me this morning, I don't know what he's liable to do next."

"I fear no evil..."

I massage my left temple, stopping at a traffic light. *This shit is ridiculous!* I've been on the phone talking to her for the last ten minutes pleading with her to go to Arizona to stay with her niece, Fanny, until this shit with Jasper is over. I've even offered to fly her out to California to stay at the condo with Greta and Jaylen. But Nana is being her usual stubbornly determined self and refuses to budge.

And it's really starting to piss me off.

"I'm not letting the devil or none of his followers run me out of my home." I check the rearview mirror to make sure Mel's truck is still behind me. It is.

Lamar's SUV is in front.

I am boxed in the middle. Sandwiched between two men willing to do whatever they need to in order to protect me. After that phone call from Jasper this morning, my nerves were rattled. They still are. However, I wanted to drive *myself* to the salon, not be chauffeured today.

Reluctantly, they gave in.

The light turns green.

"Nana, I know how much stress you've been under lately. A getaway—"

"I won't hear of it," she snaps, sounding annoyed. "I said *no*. And that's what I mean. Now hush up all this foolishness. I'm not going *any*where; do you understand me, Chile? Not until the authorities bring home my grandbaby."

She's not coming home, Nana.

I tighten my grip around the steering wheel. "Nana, don't."

"Don't *what*, Pasha? *Remind* you that you still have a cousin— who you somehow seem to want to forget about, still missing out there?"

Without getting caught up in my own feelings about Felecia, I manage to mumble, "I know *she's* missing. But she's not my concern, Nana. *You* are."

She huffs. "Well, she *should* be your concern, Pasha. She's mine. And so are you. What in the world has gotten into you? This in-difference you have toward Felecia all of a sudden has got to stop, you hear me? She needs your prayers right now. Not your hostility."

Lamar pulls up in front of the salon. I turn into the side parking lot with Mel behind me. My jaw tightens. I pull into my parking space, practically slamming the car into PARK. And before I can filter my true feelings, before I clear my thoughts, I snap, "I beg your pardon, Nana, but my *indifference* toward Felecia stems from her not only talking about me behind my back and breaking my confidence, but from sleeping with Jasper, okay?"

She huffs. "Pasha! Have you no shame? Lord, God! You'd be-lieve that ole heathen husband of yours over your own flesh and blood? Felecia would *never* do anything like that to you."

I blink, disbelief and hurt and disgust flooding my eyes. "Nana, please. All you've ever done is take up for Felecia. Even when she stole your checks out of your checkbook and forged your name for all that money, you swore up and down she'd never do anything like that. And when the truth came out, you *still* made excuses for her. I'm sick of it. Believe it or not, she *did* sleep with Jasper. Not once, not twice, but multiple times. Why? Because she was jealous and hateful and wanted the life I had. And I know all this because she admitted it. So, don't talk to me about indifference, Nana."

Nana huffs. "You hush your fresh-ass mouth, Pasha! Spewing the devil's tongue at me. I raised you better than this." She sighs, then gets silent. I roll my eyes, knowing what's coming next. Prayer. "In the name of Jesus," she finally says. "Right now, Pasha, whether Felecia did or didn't sleep with Jasper doesn't matter. What's important is, *you* forgiving her as I continue to *forgive* you."

I shut the engine, yanking the key out. I gather my things, swinging open the car door. "*Forgiveness* went out the window the day Felecia laid on her back and *screwed* Jasper, so her hatin'-ass could turn around and *screw* me. I love you, dearly, Nana. But I pray that *that* bitch is somewhere burning in hell."

Twenty-Six

Suspicions run high when bitches can't keep their stories straight…

"**G**irrrrrrrrrrrrrl, let me tell you," this string-bean-thin, high-yellow chick with small titties and an apple-bottom ass says, plopping down in Kendra's chair. "The Crack House was *turnt* all the way up Friday night. It was wall-to-wall niggas up in there." She tosses her honey-blonde, shoulder-length hair to the side. "I met me this fine-ass chocolate nigga who kept buyin' me drinks all night, too."

My ears perk up at the mention of Friday night, and The Crack House. I tilt Bianca's chair back, placing her head under the spigot, then begin running water through her hair.

Kendra sucks her teeth, snapping the cape around her client's neck. "Dang, I knew I shoulda threw on my clothes and came out. But, none of my corny-behind girls wanted to go. Mmmph. The Crack House keeps it turnt up."

"Chile, please. Turnt up is right. You missed out on a damn good time. The music was right. The dollars were right. The drinks were plentiful. And, baaaaaabeee, there was a buncha hard, horny niggas up in there tryna get them some wet-wet."

I roll my eyes, applying shampoo and lathering up Bianca's hair, lightly massaging her scalp. "Mmmm, girl. That feels good," she says, closing her eyes. "You know the only reason I keep coming back is for your scalp massages, right?"

I chuckle. "Well, I aim to do whatever it takes to keep clients like you coming back. Besides, you tip good, boo."

She laughs. "Girl, fingertips like yours are worth every penny…"

"I was backin' this thang all up on him on the dance floor," I overhear Honey Blonde saying to Kendra. "Oooh, and you know I had to get me a lil' sampler of some'a that beef when I felt how big he was."

"Ohmygod, heifer, you're such a skank," Kendra says, laughing. "But do tell. How big was he?"

"Yes, do tell," another client says as she's getting up from Kenyatta's chair to go sit under one of the dryers. "I ain't getting none at home, so I need something good to fantasize about while I sit under this dryer."

I quickly glance over toward the front area when I hear the bell to the front door chime as it opens. I immediately recognize her as one of Kenyatta's clients. She stops at the counter to say something to Trish, one of my manicurists, who's covering the desk until her appointment arrives. The music fades as her voice comes over the intercom, requesting for Kelli, one of the salon's eyelash technicians to the front.

I finish washing and rinsing Bianca's hair, then wrapped a towel around her head and sit her up. "Girl, when are you going to hire another office manager?"

I shrug, drying her hair. "Who knows, girl. I haven't really been looking. With all this stuff I have going on right now, an office manager is the last thing on my mind."

"Girl, you know I understand." She shakes her head, chuckling. "I thought I'd walk in today and find your protégé at the desk, again, giving us another mini-show."

She's talking about the day I walked up in here and Booty had taken it upon herself to cover the front desk area. She had the music blasting and was in the middle of the waiting area about to drop it down low to some song playing, talking about she was on break.

I almost passed out seeing all that ass of hers bouncing and clapping. Bianca starts cracking up. "Pasha, girl, you should have seen your face when you walked through the door and saw her performing."

I shudder, waving her on. "Ugh, please. No, thank you. My stomach was in knots the whole time she sat up there at the desk. All I kept thinking was how much money I was losing. Every time the phone rang, I cringed."

"Girl, I was sick for you. Another few hours and she would have turned this place out."

"Ohmygod, yes. Tell me about it. She's many things, but customer-service friendly is not one of them." We share a hearty laugh. "I don't even want to entertain the thought."

Kenyatta's client finally makes her way to the back. She greets everyone. I smile and say hello. She takes her seat. "I think I'm going to get the lash extensions after I finish up with you," she says, setting her purse up on her lap as Kenyatta snaps a cape around her neck.

"Oh, them lash extensions are the business," Kenyatta says. "And Kelli is no joke. She'll have you walking up out of here runway ready, girl."

"She sure will," another client chimes in from another station, getting braids. She's brown-skinned with doe-shaped eyes. "She did mine last week." She bats her lashes, grinning wide. She has a wide gap between her two bottom teeth. "I love 'em. I don't have to worry about putting on mascara or eyeliner. These bad boys are *every*thing."

I remind her to make sure she comes in next week for her three-week eyelash touch-up to replace any lashes that might have fallen out, which turns into a mini tutorial on hair and eyelash growth and the eyelash-extension process. By the time I've finished breaking it all down, three more clients have decided to endure the two-hour process for longer, more luscious lashes.

"Ooh, yes, long and luscious, like my new boo's dick," Honey Blonde says. She clucks her tongue. Then she sticks her tongue in her cheek and starts bobbing her neck.

I frown. Bianca gives me a look through the mirror as Honey Blonde starts going into detail how she gave him head in the club. I glance over toward the lobby and see Mel handing Trish something. A few minutes later the CD playing on the stereo stops, then K. Michele's "My Life" comes through the speakers.

Kenyatta grabs a comb and points it at her. "Ooh, no you didn't, girl!"

Honey Blonde laughs. "Girl, yes, I did. Right there in the club."

"Trick, lies! Shut your mouth!" Kendra says, shaking her head.

"Lies nothin', boo. You know I don't ever lie 'bout no sex. I sucked him in a corner off from the dance floor while a Meek Mill track was playing. I was good 'n' drunk. And he was good 'n' hard. And mmmph. He got to talkin' all this freaky, rough stuff in my ear 'bout how he wanted to take me outside 'n' fuck the shit outta me."

"Girl, did you swallow?" Gap Tooth wants to know.

Honey Blonde smacks her lips. "I sure did. I don't play when it comes to giving head, boo, especially when the nigga is fine 'n' talkin' a buncha freak-nasty shit. And he was really givin' it to me good 'n' dirty, sayin' how he wanted to knock my tonsils out, then bend me over 'n' rip off my panties, spit in my booty hole 'n' pound his dick in it." She starts fanning herself. "And, mmmph... was tanked up off them Wet Drawz."

"Ooooh, yes, girrrrl," Gap Tooth chimes in, waving a jeweled hand in the air. "Them Wet Drawz will do it."

Honey Blonde laughs. "Uh-huh, sure will. Them Wet Drawz had my own drawz soaked 'n' had me soakin' him up real good, too."

Kenyatta frowns, holding the flatiron in her hand, shaking her head. "I'm done. You sucked off some nigga you just met in the club *and* swallowed his babies?"

"I sure did. And it was damn good, too."

I shift my eyes around the floor and start humming along to K. Michele singing about her life struggles while everyone on the floor starts talking about dick sucking and dick sizes. I want no part of this conversation.

As I'm putting the finishing touches on Bianca's wrap, she finally gets around to asking about the murders and fire. "You know I don't like asking you too much out here on the floor," she says, giving me an apologetic look. "I know the walls have lots of ears."

I wave her on. "Girl, please. It's been all over the news. Police still have no leads. It's a mess."

"Thank God you and Jaylen weren't there when that happened."

I close, then open my eyes, slowly shaking my head. I feel myself getting choked up. "Bianca, girl. I don't know what I'd do if anything were to happen to my son. I don't believe in coincidences. Everything happens for a reason."

She gives me a questioning glance through the mirror.

"Had we been home," I elaborate, feigning distress. "There's no telling..." I pause, shaking my head. I blink back tears. Fight to keep my composure here on the floor. "Girl, I don't even want to think about what would have happened."

Her eyes soften. She reaches for my hand and squeezes. "You know I'm here for you, always. And so is Garrett."

I nod. "I know. And I really appreciate the both of you."

"Do they at least know what caused the fire?"

I nod. "It was electrical." Well, that's how Lamar's fire *specialist* made it appear.

"Oooh, wait, wait," Honey Blonde says all animated. "And I ain't even tell you how I was leaning up against him on the wall, letting him finger me in my butt."

All the chatter on the floor stops. All eyes are back on Honey Blonde.

"Girl, I can't with you," Kendra says, shaking her head.

"See now," Gap Tooth says, wagging a finger at Honey Blonde. "You doin' too much right there, girl. You suckin' dick one minute, then gettin' fingered in yo' ass the next."

Honey Blonde shoots her a dirty look. "Umm, do I know you, boo? Did I ask you? Yeah, I let him finger-fuck me in my ass. And *what?* Ain't no shame in my game, boo. My name is Raynora Clemmons. I suck dick in the club. And I like fingers in my ass."

Everyone laughs.

"So Miss Nasty Wet Drawz," Kendra says. "Does this Mister Fine who you sucked and let finger you in the club have a name?"

"Girl, his sexy ass's name is Legend." I eye her through the mirror. Kendra wants to know if she went home with him. "Mmmph. You think I didn't. And he tore this wet-wet up real right. I didn't limp up outta his place until the sun came up."

I blink. *Bitch, lies! You wish you were somewhere getting done right. That was probably your delusional ass calling him for some dick while I was slicing out his balls.*

The client in Kenyatta's chair says, "Chile, you sound like my husband's trifling BM. That whore loves anal. She'll pull a butt-plug out of her behind in a heartbeat and doesn't care where she does it. She stays in The Crack House. You probably know her. Cassandra Simms."

Ohmygod!

Everyone on the floor says, *"Big Booty?"*

She grunts. "Ugh, yes. Don't remind me."

I literally am in shock. Then again, Booty has so many damn baby daddies, it's hard to keep track of them all. Besides, she's never talked about any of her kids' fathers. And the only one I know of is Julius, a police officer—a fine one, I might add. But I'm not sure which of her kids is his.

Kenyatta spins her around in her chair. "LaQuandra, girl. All this time you were coming down to the other shop I was at, I did not know that your stepson was *her* son. Girl, get out! It's a small world. He's a lil' cutie-pie, too. Looks just like your husband. Wait. Doesn't she have like fifteen kids or something like that?"

"No, ten. But they all wild and bad as hell."

"Ten kids?" Kendra says, looking up from Gap Tooth's head. "Wait. That chick that comes in here wearing all the hotness with the bangin' body has *ten* kids?"

LaQuandra rolls her eyes, shaking her head. It's clear she's jealous.

"Well, damn," Kenyatta says, tapering the back of LaQuandra's neck with the clippers. "Which baby daddy is your husband?"

She sucks her teeth. "Isaiah is number seven."

"I remember you saying how you couldn't stand her," Kenyatta states, glancing over at me. *Oh, okay, I see you like to be messy, too.* I shake my head.

"Chile, I can't stand her. She is so damn ghetto it's ridiculous. You know she came up into my school trying to turn it up. School hadn't even gotten started good and there was already a problem with her son. She came up into the school trying to bring the ruckus…"

"Girl, noo," Kenyatta says.

"Chile, yes. I had to forget I was a professional for a minute and step out of my heels and serve her up a real good beat down. We tore my office up. The police dragged her out in handcuffs." She shakes her head. "It was a mess. I tell you. Chicks like her don't need to have kids."

"Girl, speaking of hot messes," Honey Blonde says. "A fight broke out outside the club Friday night and that chick you talkin' about 'n' like twenty or thirty others all got locked up that night. Somebody said she took it to some nigga's head wit' a club. I didn't see none'a that. But I saw when she pulled out a can of Mace 'n' maced the shit outta some chick who was supposedly her friend."

The LaQuandra chick sucks her teeth. "Mmmph. I'm not surprised. Cassandra's a damn rattlesnake. She'll turn on you in a New York minute. You didn't hear it from me. But that messy bitch stays in the middle of shit. She got lucky when that lil' young girl only sliced her face for messing with her man. But it's only a matter of time before someone slices her damn throat."

I cringe when I see Booty walking through the door. The last thing I need is this escalating into another salon brawl. I hand Bianca a mirror, glancing around everyone's stations. "Okay, y'all let's switch our channels to something a little more upbeat." My cue for when a client someone is talking about is walking through the door. Booty says something to Mel, then leans over the counter, flipping through the appointment book, like she's running shit.

"Girl, this looks good." Bianca hands me the mirror back. I unsnap the cape. Booty stalks over toward my station as Bianca is getting up.

"Ooh, hey, Miss Cutie-Boo," Booty says to Bianca.

"Hey, girl."

It gets quiet. Booty looks around the salon, then frowns when her eyes zero in on the LaQuandra chick. She swings her neck in my direction, raising a brow. "Umm, Miss Pasha, girl, I need to have a word wit' you." I tell her I'll be with her when I finish up with Bianca. I glance up at Lamar. He gives me a head nod knowingly. Keep an eye on her ass. "Uh-huh. I'll be right here, too," she says as she plops down in my chair, slowly turning it, facing the mirror.

Bianca follows me up front, handing me a hundred-dollar bill when we get to the counter. "Girl, you think it's safe leaving her back there?"

"If not, she'll be out of here in handcuffs." She tells me to keep the change. We embrace. She tells me she'll see me in three weeks, then heads toward the door. I race back to my station to find Booty taunting the LaQuandra chick.

"So what lies you been tellin' today, Miss *Quaaaaandra*, huh?"

"Cassandra, please. You know I'm not doing this with you. So let's leave it at that. Please and thank you."

"Coon, *boom!* You can't do shit wit' me. But Isaiah, on the other hand…" She toots her lips up. "Mmmph. Do me a favor, nigga-boo. Tell Isaiah his baby muhver said she's ready to give him another baby since yo' empty ass can't give him one." She pats her crotch. "Let 'im know this cootie-coo misses him. He's 'bout due for his late-night feedin' anyway."

"Bit—"

Kenyatta places her hand on the LaQuanda chick's shoulder to keep her from hopping out of her chair. "Don't, girl."

Lamar comes down the stairs from the pedi-mani loft. Mel comes to the back from the lobby.

"Cassandra, you wanted to see me," I say, cutting in before they turn it up.

She tilts her head, placing a hand up on her hip. "Uh-huh, Miss

Pasha, girl. I sure do. I gotta bone to pick wit' you, sugah-boo."
She follows behind me, then stops. "Ohhhh, and *Quaaaaaandra*,
wit' ya dog-faced self, since I know you like keepin' my name
rollin' off ya tongue, how 'bout you tell 'em how I came up in ya
school 'n' yanked ya scalp clean off ya' head. I tore ya ass up, real
good, didn't I? You want round two?"

Twenty-Seven

Ignorance isn't the problem. It's a stupid bitch that refuses
to be aware...

"Mmmph. How long that coon-bitch been comin' here?"

I frown, shutting the door behind us. "Cassandra, don't start. This is like her second time. Why?" I walk around the desk, pulling out my chair. "Her coming here to get her hair done should have nothing to do with you."

"Oh, trust, sugah-boo. That rotted bitch can be here all she wants. But I know one thing, if you ever hear her talkin' slick 'n' greasy 'bout me, you better check her, then let me know, so I can take it to her face. That bitch real lucky I ain't wear my figthin' heels up in here today."

I tilt my head. "Yeah, like how you were checking Felecia every time she talked shit about me?"

She bucks her eyes. "Miss Pasha, girl, *boom!* Don't do me. I'm still kinda hot in the drawz wit' yo' ass for how you carried on down at the barbershop. I had Jah'Mel strung up good 'n' right for yo' ole coon-ass 'n' you ain't even bring no heat to his ass. Mmmph. Then last night I tell yo' ass let's get it poppin on that nigga-coon *L* 'n' you go 'n' get all flake-flake on me, textin' me back some ole coon-fuckery. What you had to do that was more important than handlin' yo' business, huh? You need to get ya goddamn mind right..."

I feel a headache piercing its way through the front of my head. And Booty's loud-ass mouth and theatrics aren't helping any. I eye her with mounting tension coiling through every nerve in my body as she sits here talking shit about what I *need* to be doing.

Usually when shit spews out of her mouth, I can laugh it off, brush it off, or let it go over my head, because it's Cassandra. And Cassandra is who Cassandra is. But, today, I don't give a damn *who* this bitch is. And I couldn't care even less about laughing at, brushing off, or letting anything she says go over my damn head.

"I ain't 'bout to keep tryna help a bitch who ain't even tryna help herself. I done brought the horses to ya ole stank-ass 'n' all you gotta do is hop on up 'n' ride 'em out. But you on some ole other shit. What is you waitin' for, huh, Miss Pasha, girl? This shit wit' you don't make no damn sense…"

I count to ten in my head. Try to let the slick shit she's saying go over my head. Keep trying to remind, convince, myself that she doesn't mean any harm. But this bitch stays coming at me sideways. I'm all for someone speaking their mind and expressing themselves. But I'm sick of her thinking she can say whatever the fuck she wants, whenever she wants, however she wants, to whomever she wants and *not* get called on it. It's the same shit with her coming up in here always talking out the side of her neck to clients and staff whenever the hell she feels like it. She breeds drama. The shit's toxic. And I'm sick of it!

So today is *not* the day that I'm in the mood for Cassandra Simms' shit!

I blink.

Masking my thoughts, I calmly say, "You know, Cassandra, it seems like every time you have something to say about someone, anyone for that matter, it's always followed by some kind of snide remark, or slick dig on the sly. And it comes off messy. You're entitled to your opinions. And I've always appreciated your direct-ness, and brutal honesty. However, people don't always need, or want, to hear your thoughts or feelings about them, especially when it's not solicited. Sometimes it's simply best to keep what you're thinking to yourself."

"Wait a minute, Miss Pasha, girl," she snaps defensively, giving me an indignant look. "I ain't *ever* been messy, goddammit. I don't even 'preciate you tryna do me. You know Booty don't bite her tongue for no-goddamn-body. I call it like I see it, sugah-boo. What you see is always gonna be what you get. If a nigga-bitch don't like it, then she can eat the inside of my ass. I'll gladly bend over 'n' pull open these big, fluffy ass cheeks for her to have at it, goddammit."

Okay, let me try this one more time. My headache is now pounding at the front of my skull. "Cassandra,"—I pull open my top drawer for my bottle of Advil, catching a glimpse of my 9mm—"it's not what you say, it's how you say it. You need to learn how to be tactful."

She makes a face, bucking her eyeballs and yanking her head back like she's about to have a fit. "*Tact?* Sugah-boo, *boom-boom!* I ain't got no time sugah-coatin' shit for some sensitive-ass nigga-bitch. Like I *said*, I call it like I see it. And *who*ever don't like it can suck my goddamn thong…"

I take a deep breath. Bite down on my bottom lip. This time I count to twenty in my head as I gape blankly at her. She takes my expressionless stare and silence as an open invitation to continue offering up her unsolicited remarks about *me*.

"Now back to you, Miss Pasha, girl, with ya ole slutty-self. I swear I hope you done learned ya lesson, messin' with that Inter-net shit. 'Cause if you ain't, ya ass is on ya own the next time a nigga stomps ya lights out. 'Cause I can't be tryna run no Save A Ho campaign when I'm tryna keep Day'Asia's ho-ass from fuckin' the whole damn county before she gets her lil' hot ass outta high school."

I can feel the heat of anger rising. I consciously, purposefully, try to talk myself out of going in on her. But the heat surging through me has ignited a fire that is now becoming a burst of roaring flames.

"See. Miss Pasha, girl. You need to get ya goddamn…"

Before she can finish the rest of her sentence, I rip into her ass. "You know what, Cassandra? You don't know what the fuck I've been doing, bitch. I've been biting my tongue, holding back from lighting you up. But—"

"Booga-bitch, boom-boom! You wait one goddamn minute…"

"No, *bitch! You* wait a goddamn minute!"

"No, *goddammit! You* better *wait!* You have me confused, booga-bitch! Now I like you, Miss Pasha, girl. But I will beat yo' ass a new goddamn heartbeat! You *not* gonna sit here 'n' talk shit to me, after *all* the shit I done for ya snotty-ass! I beat the skin off Jah'Mel's coon-ass for you 'n' this how—"

I stand up. Hand on hip, a little piece of the old, neck-rolling me from long ago, emerging. "Bitch, you haven't done shit for *me* that you didn't want to do for *you! You* have *me* confused, sweetie! I haven't asked *you* to do *shit* for me, bitch. So don't sit there acting like you've done me some goddamn favor, like I'm some fucking charity case. Bitch, please!"

"Booga-bitch, *boom!* Don't do me, goddammit! I ain't have to do shit for you, so do—"

"Bitch, *you* jumped in the middle of my shit without an invitation. *You* stuck your motherfucking nose in my business where it had no business being; shit, you are always somewhere doing. Why? Because you're a messy, nosey, gossiping-ass bitch who loves motherfucking drama!"

"Coon, *boom!* Mother*fuck* you, goddammit!"

"No, bitch! Motherfuck *you*! I've had it with your mouth, Cassandra! You wanna call it like you see it, then let's call it like it is. Yeah, bitch, I sucked dick! And got my ass beat for it! Yeah, bitch, I'm in all the mess I'm in because of it. But *you* need to look your whore-ass in the mirror, *first*, before you try to read me. You think you're the baddest bitch out there doing it big? Bitch, please.

"All you are is some dusty, trick-ass, gutter-bitch who sucked and fucked her way up off the streets and pushed out a bunch of babies by a bunch of different big-dicked niggas who didn't give a fuck about you because *you* didn't give a *fuck* about yourself. Yeah, bitch, I sucked a bunch of dicks. But I'm damn sure not tricking for the next come-up.

"The difference between what I do and what the fuck you do is that I *suck* dick because I *want* to. You *fuck* and take dick every which way it'll fit in your ran-through slut-holes because you *have* to. Because tricking and being a loudmouth bitch are the only skills your dumb ass has. So the *only* bitch in the room who needs to get her mind right, is *you*! Ten years from now all you're going to be is some washed-up wannabe with a closet full of handbags and heels walking around with a goddamn pamper strapped on your ass because you spent your whole life letting no-good niggas fuck you in your ass. Don't judge *me*, bitch! Judge your-mother-fucking-self!"

I guess after saying all this, I should see it coming, should know Booty would take this to another level, because she's a street bitch. But I don't. And the next thing I know, the bitch is up on her feet, lightning-quick, and her fist connects to the side of my head, almost snapping my neck off my shoulders, causing my knees to buckle.

The bitch almost drops me! And in that instant, I'm *right* back down in that horrid basement tied up and being beaten and slapped and whored around by a buncha niggas.

I'm *right* back where I was twenty-three years ago—fourteen years old, with a bloody blade in my hand—giving a jealous bitch a hundred-and-sixty-three stitches for putting her hands on me.

In a flash, with one closed fist to the side of my head, Booty knocks me, resurrects me, *right* back to the bitch I've spent the last seventeen, eighteen years of my life trying to keep buried.

She bangs her fist on my desk. "Miss Pasha, girl, goddamn you, bitch! I didn't wanna take it to ya goddamn head. But, bitch! Don't you *ever*, talk to me like I'm…"

Before she can finish her sentence, leap, lunge, dig into her clutch, or do anything else a bitch like Booty does, my hand is gripping the gun in my drawer and she's staring at the barrel of a 9mm, aimed at her face.

"Bitch, jump if you want and I'ma splatter your goddamn head open. You put your motherfucking hands on the wrong bitch!" I pull the trigger, purposefully shooting slightly over her head. Her eyes buck wide open. "Make no mistake. The next one won't miss! Don't you *ever* as long as you breathe, *bitch*, put your motherfucking hands on me!"

Her jaws tighten. "Booga-bitch, *boom*, goddammit! You done tore ya goddamn drawz off! This is how you gonna do me, goddammit?!? Huh, booga-bitch? Pull a fuckin' heater on me, then shoot at me, like I'm some gutter-bitch…?"

"You *are* a *gutter*-bitch!" I snap, stamping my heeled-foot. The side of my head feels like it's about to cave in. "And your gutter-ass mouth and you putting your hands on me is about to cost you your goddamn teeth if you don't figure out a way to *think* before you *open* your motherfucking mouth when you're speaking to *me*, or about me. And I mean that shit, bitch!"

"Bitch!" she yells, one palm planted on the desk, the other pointing in my face, spit spewing out of her mouth. Her eyes are wide and crazed. "Do me right, goddammit!" She bangs the desk with her fist. "Put that motherfuckin' burner down 'n' do me right, booga-bitch! Make me nut, booga-bitch 'n' *fight* me like a *real* bitch! I love me a good goddamn fight! Give it to me good, booga-coon-bitch! Let me see you with the hands, goddamn you, Miss Pasha, girl! Cum-suckin' bitch! You gonna do me, goddammit…!" She lunges toward me, both fists balled tight. "Fight me wit—"

I swing my arm back and hit this crazy bitch upside the head with the gun, knocking her off balance. I hit her again; this time she topples over and hits the floor. But she's quick on the drop and doesn't stay down long. She's back up on her feet, tilting her neck from side to side, cracking bones.

"Oooh, you dirty bitch! Do me right, goddammit! Bitch, I was born *built* for a good goddamn street brawl! Fight me with your hands, Miss Pasha, girl!" She starts pounding her fist into the palm of her hand. "Drop the gun, booga-bitch, 'n' let me see *you* hand-to-hand, like real bitches do it, goddammit! Let me see the bitch you used to be!" She goes into a boxer's stance, starts bobbing and weaving. "Don't play no goddamn games with me, Miss Pasha, girl. You ain't no pussy-bitch, like the rest of them coon-bitches in the streets! Fight me, goddammit! Do me riiiight, bitch!"

"Oh, you really wanna fist-fight?" I spit furiously. "Then you got it."

Booty charges me, again. She's strong as a damn man, swinging her arms wide and connecting with heavy punches. She's on me and we tussle over the gun. I don't want to shoot this bitch because I don't want to leave the State stuck with taking care of her bad-ass, ghetto-ass brats. But I will. One of us is going to have go down. And I'm damn sure not trying to let it be me. Not after everything I've fucking been through.

The gun points sideways, up, down, sideways, again, then goes off, a slug going into the left wall, followed by another bullet hitting the right wall on the other side of the room.

"Get the fuck off me, bitch!"

"Do me…right, god…dam… mit!" She's trying to manhandle the gun out of my hand, but I keep my grip wrapped tight. "Put the…gun…uhh…down…'n'…uhh…fiiiiiight…*meeee!*"

"Bitch, you getting dropped today. Them bad-ass kids of yours…is about…to be…orphans…"

That sends Booty over the edge. She starts punching me with one hand while still trying to get the gun out of my hand with the other. Scrapping with this bitch has my lungs on fire. We're both sweating. Pain is knotting the muscles in my thighs, my calves slowly burning from wrestling her in heels. But I refuse to go down. And so does she.

Another round fires out, hitting the wall again. I'm not sure how long we're in here scuffling before the last bullet finally dislodges. But when it does, I let go of the handle and the gun goes flying across the room. Now it's me, and Booty…and our hands.

"Yessss, *goddammmit!*" Booty shrieks, her fist connecting to my face. "You mine now, boog—!"

I throw a right punch that snaps her jaw shut, causing her to bite down on her tongue. I hit her again. Blood gushes from her nose.

"Do me, goddammit!!!! Wet my drawz, bitch! Yesssssss, god-dammit! *This* is the ole, dirty street bitch I know, goddammit! The bitch who ain't take no shit from no-goddamn-body!" She punches the shit out of me. "Welcome back, booga-bitch!"

Now it's on like never before. Blow for blow, she and I go at it like two wild bitches with something to prove to the other. Heels snap off shoes, buttons pop off, shirts rip open. Hair gets yanked. Nails break. Titties spill out of bras. Lips get split. And for the first time—in like, years—I fight with *everything* that's in me. I fight Booty in a way that I've never fought any other bitch when I *used* to fight in the streets. I fight her in a way I didn't fight Felecia—in a way I've *never* fought Felecia—before I blew her fucking brains out.

No. I fight Booty the way she wants it, the way she loves it. Because the bitch crossed the line when she put her hands on me, because the bitch asked, *begged*, for it. And, crazy as it sounds... because I respect the street bitch that she is. And I'm *not* letting her whip my ass—not today. And definitely *not* up in my office.

I pull from all of my life experiences, tap into everything I've learned over the last year in my Muay Thai kickboxing training, and give Cassandra the fight of her life. I give it to her the way a street bitch is supposed to get it—*good and goddamn dirty!*

Twenty-Eight

The walls will close in and have a nigga scrambling long before the floor drops...

"What the fuck, yo?!" Jasper screams into my ear the minute I answer my phone. "You still wanna play this muthafuckin' game, huh? You know I ain't have shit to do wit' our fuckin' crib gettin' burned the fuck down, yo. So why the fuck is you tryna have that shit pinned on me, huh? You been on some real crazy bitch-type shit. Real shit, yo. Why the fuck you give them muhfuckas my numbers 'n' shit, huh?! What the fuck is wrong wit' you, man? Is you muthafuckin' outta ya fuckin' head? Got them crab-ass muhfuckas askin' me 'bout some dead fuckin' bodies. I ain't touch them muhfuckas. *You* got them niggas bodied wit' ya fuckin' bullshit, yo. All you had'a do is run me my muhfuckin' paper 'n' we wouldn't be goin' through none'a this bullshit. But, no. Ya dumb-ass wanna let some hoodrat bitch get all up in ya ear 'n' got you tryna be on some gangsta-type shit."

I glance at the time, sighing. It's a few minutes past eleven, Sunday morning. *Enough is enough with this nigga. It's time to get this motherfucker off the streets.*

I remove the icepack from the side of my swollen face, lifting myself up from the damask lounge chair. I wince, holding my right side. I have huge bruises on my side, neck, and back. My left eye is swollen. That bitch lumped me up real good, but she got hers, too.

The two of us fought as if we had something to prove, as if we had been longtime archenemies, rolling around on the floor, punching and slapping and choking one another, clawing at hands, arms, necks, titties, tossing each other into walls, doing whatever we had to do to take the other out.

Hairdos tore up, heels broken off, blouses ripped open and stained, we fought until we were too exhausted, too sore, and too damn beat up to keep going. Finally, when the last punch was thrown, the last face was slapped, the last dirty insult hurled, we were both collapsed on our backs, sweating, stretched out, breathing all hard and crazy, our hearts pounding in our chests.

We had to literally drag ourselves over to a chair and pull ourselves up from the floor. Then the crazy bitch turned to me on her way out of my office—with her handbag tucked under her arm—and said, "Nigga-boo, make sure you got yo' ole messy, cum-suckin' ass here on Monday 'cause I'ma be here bright 'n' early to get my goddamn hair did. And you better do me right, goddammit! Or I'ma fight yo' ass again."

"Fuck you!" I snapped, still trying to catch my breath. "You ghetto bitch! You better let…that hot trash…Dick…alina do your… knotty shit because I'll burn out…all your fucking…scalp…before I do…shit!"

"Booga-bitch, *boom!*"

"Bitch, come get your lashes from off my motherfucking floor!"

"Eat my ass!"

I reached for the broken heel of my eighteen hundred-dollar shoe and threw it at the door as she hobbled on her one heel out the door. All I could do when I finally got back here to my suite yesterday was slip out of my clothes, then ease myself down into the Jacuzzi tub and allow the heat, steam, and Himalayan Pink bath crystals to soothe me… and take me away.

"Pasha! What the fuck is you doin', yo?!" Jasper barks, snapping me out of my reverie. "You hear me muthafuckin' talkin' to you…?"

I blink away the memory of my fight with Booty, groaning as I slowly attempt to stand. Jasper's incessant tirade goes on for another two minutes before he finally realizes I haven't said one word during his whole rant.

I limp over to my vibrating phone on the nightstand. It's a text message from Lamar. TURN ON CHANNEL 2! SHIT JUST GOT REAL!

I reach for the remote, sitting on the edge of the bed and turn on the television. My eyes widen at the news caption. There's an inset photo of Legend behind anchorwoman Anna Rose Lopez has she begins reporting today's breaking news.

"Newark police were called two o'clock this morning to one of the most shocking and gruesome crime scenes in the city's history, leaving investigators shaking their heads in disbelief. A local Newark man was found in his University Heights townhome sometime last night by a longtime friend and housemate; naked, gagged, tied to a bed, and brutally tortured. The victim had been sodomized, his genitals severely beaten, and his scrotum cut open and his testicles removed. His fingers were cut off at the first knuckle and found strewn about the room…"

I close my eyes, then slowly open them. "Jasper, do you still love me?"

The question clearly catches him off guard. "Say what?"

"Do. You. Still. Love. Me?"

Silence.

"Hello?"

"What?"

"Answer the question."

He huffs. "Yo, why is you askin' me that shit for?"

"It's either a yes or no."

"That shit doesn't matter, yo…" His voice cracks. "Did that shit matter when you was out there suckin' them muhfuckas' dicks, huh? Did you give a fuck then if I loved ya muthafuckin' ass or not?"

"Yes, it mattered."

He snorts. "Yeah, *right*. But not enough to keep ya muhfuckin' ass off ya fuckin' knees."

"Fuck you, Jasper, okay. Did it matter to you when *you* were out fucking them bitches on *me*, Jasper, huh?"

He sucks his teeth. "Whatever, yo. That shit's different."

"Different? Are you serious? How? Please explain that shit to me."

"I wasn't eatin' none'a them bitches' pussies. I wasn't out lettin' bitches bust in my mouth, yo. You was out there lettin' a muh-fucka coat ya muthafuckin' tongue 'n' neck wit' his nut 'n' shit. You've fucked me over, Pasha. That shit doesn't sit well wit' me, yo."

I shake my head, bringing my attention back to the television. The reporter's grave expression and laden voice as she delivers the horrifying news sends a chill through me.

"… A sharp instrument gouged out the victim's eyeballs and his tongue was cut out. In addition, both the man's ears were sliced off. Investigators report there was an extremely graphic sexual comment burned into his upper torso, along with the saying: 'hear no evil, see no evil'… There are no suspects at this time. Authorities are asking anyone with any information regarding this heinous crime to please call Crime Stoppers at …"

"Mmmmph. That's too bad. You might want to turn on the news."

"What?"

"Turn on the news."

"What for?"

"To see your fate." I press END. If he *thought* I was playing when

I said he and every last one of them niggas he had attack me were going to drop, he'd better think again. I *meant* what I said.

"Do you think you'll be able to get at him?" I ask, sitting across from Lamar and Mel. Mel is quiet, observing. Watching Lamar, watching me. I shift in my seat. *Mmmph! He's so fucking fine!*

They both are.

Am I wrong for wanting to suck them both, right here, right now?

My mouth starts juicing. I swallow back the neck-juice pooling in the back of my throat.

"Yo, that nigga's toast," Lamar says, leaning back in his seat. He drapes an arm over the back of the sofa. "We got that nigga's every move on lock. Been waiting for you to give the word, Pasha. Real spit, I've been clocking that nigga for a minute. I just didn't say anything."

I nod understandingly. "Are you sure he won't get away? You know ever since his spots got hit, he's been armored up real heavy. And now with the shit that just happened Friday night all over the news, I'm sure his goon count is going to be up. We're only going to have one shot at getting him. I need him shut down before he tries to do anything else."

Like have my grandmother killed.

"That nigga ain't ready for us." Lamar's brown eyes are intense, filled with fire, as he looks at me. "Trust me. That cat doesn't have enough manpower to stop us from gettin' at him. I'm not about to let nothing happen to you."

"Nah, *we're* not," Mel states authoritatively, his gaze locked on mine, "going to let *anything* happen to you. Lamar and I got this."

I nod pensively. I know, I believe, they will do whatever they can to keep me safe. They've already proven so. Still, even with a plain-clothes guard down in the lobby, two standing guard at my suite's door, I'm not out of harm's way, I will never be out of danger, until Jasper is handled.

Yet, I have no idea what I'm going to exctly do to him when they snatch him up. But what I do know is, he's going to pay. And this shit with him, one way or the other, will finally be over. Still, my emotions are torn. My heart is hurting. I'm mentally exhausted. I am overwhelmed.

I literally feel as if, in a matter of weeks, my whole world has been swept up in a tsunami; a tidal wave of lies and deceit and betrayal and multiple murders; a downpour of conniving, treacherous schemes, which I have manipulated, orchestrated, or carried out.

Torturing that nigga Legend had given me some reprieve. But it frightened me. I got off on it. I wanted to…I don't know. Fuck. I felt…dirty, but morbidly turned on. No, no. Extremely turned on. My pussy was soaked.

Dripping.

And then I had the sick, twisted nerve to ask Lamar to eat my pussy when we finally pulled up into the hotel's parking lot. And he did! Tongued my cum-flooded hole with greedy need, with an unbridled fervor that almost had me wanting him to push his rock-hard dick inside of me. Almost.

I've ached for revenge. I've thirst for retribution. And vengeance is finally mine. They say Lady Justice is blind. Maybe she is. Maybe she isn't. All I know is, in my case, the bitch isn't blinded by shit. She sees it all. She remembers it all. And she's not dishing out fairness. She's inflicting pain. She's wreaking havoc. And the bitch isn't going to stop until…

I run my fingers through my hair. "I want Jasper alive."

Lamar sighs. "Damn. I'm not even gonna front, though. I'd love to pop a bullet in his biscuit. Dead that nigga on the spot."

"And Stax is not to be touched, either." They both give me a confused look. I narrow my eyes, sweeping my gaze from Lamar to Mel. "*Nothing* happens to him. Nothing."

Lamar leans forward, resting his arms on his knees. "C'mon, Pasha. We can't guarantee he won't catch it wit' the rest of them niggas. If he's poppin' off rounds, he's gonna have'ta get put down. It goes wit' the territory."

"Do you have the location already secured?" I inquire, referring to the site where Jasper is to be taken once he's gotten. Lamar nods. Tells me it's been read. I take a deep breath.

"My peoples are all ready 'n' set to move on this," Lamar says, glancing at his watch, "like now. Give the word. And it's a go." He pulls out his cell, then answers. "Yo, what's good? You got that shit for me? Oh, aiight aiight…that's wassup. Good lookin', fam…oh, no doubt. That's what it is… One." He ends the call, looking over at me. "That was my peoples. We found two more of that nigga's stash spots."

My eyes light up. *Ohmygod! I can't believe this shit!* "Get out. Where?" He tells me Jasper has a spot in East Orange, up the street from Elmwood Park, and another stash house in Irvington. Shutting these two spots down would officially cripple his flow. Last week, while I was in L.A., three were burned down. And the week before that, three others were shut down. I didn't need to know the specifics of how Lamar's connects handled the situations. I still don't. All I care about is the cash found. The drugs and whatever weapons they find go to Lamar to do whatever with.

He stands, holds his arms up over his head and stretches. "Let's shut the rest of that pussy-muhfucka's shit down tonight."

I nod. "Fine by me." I glance over at Mel. He spreads his legs, sinking back into his seat.

"Bet." Lamar looks over at Mel. "Yo, you rollin', son?"

"Nah, I'm good."

I toss my bang from over my eye. "Good. Because I need for you to handle something with me tonight." I let him know of my plan to try to set up a time to finally meet MydickneedsUrtongue2 tonight.

"Oh, word? Aiight. Bet."

I look over at Lamar. "We might need to bring him to the warehouse, too."

"Cool. So what 'bout that nigga, Jasper? When you want my peoples to get at him?"

I mull the question around in my head. Consider the implications, the possible outcomes. Fucking Jasper! He started this. There's no way of getting around it. No matter what, there are going to be casualties. Still, I have to figure out a way to keep Stax out of the crossfire.

I sigh. "Do it all tomorrow tonight; the later, the better."

I tell him this, hoping like hell I can lure Stax away from Jasper long enough for them to snatch his ass up the same way he had me snatched. With a fucking gun to his head! Then I want him blindfolded and duct taped, and tossed in the back of a van.

But, for later this evening, I have something in mind for someone else.

My nemesis.

MydickneedsUrtongue2.

"Yo, whaddup, pussy-ass nigga?" I say into the phone the moment Vernon picks up. My voice comes out souding deep and raspy. It's three o'clock in the afternoon. Mel looks up from the magazine he's reading, shaking his head. "When you suckin' dis hard-ass dick, yo?"

I smirk, pulling out my laptop. I wait for it to boot up, then log into AOL. I am immediately alerted that I have mail. Two emails from this nigga. YO WAT'S GOOD? WHEN WE LINKIN' UP? U READY 2 EAT DA NUT OUTTA DIS DICK OR WAT? OR U STILL ON YA BS? CUM SUCK DIS DICK, YO. DIS HARD DICK READY 4 U

"Muhfucka, what the fuck?! Why is you still comin' at me, nigga? You must really want me to put a bullet in ya shit, yo. Word on my seeds, muhfucka, the minute I find out who da fuck you are, it's on, nigga. I'ma handle ya punk-ass."

I laugh. "Blah, blah, blah. All I want muhfucka is my dick sucked."

I hit REPLY and type: IM SO READY FOR YOU. EVERY TIME I GET EMAILS FROM YOU MY THROAT GETS SOOOOOOOOO, SOOOOOOOOO WET. CAN WE MEET TONIGHT? THIS NECK NEEDS YOU TO FUCK IT DEEP. LET ME KNOW.

"Nigga, is your muhfuckin' *crazy?!*" he shrieks in my ear as I open the next email from him. "I ain't suckin' ya muthafuckin' dick, yo. I ain't no dick sucka, muhfucka!"

I...TILL PLAY'N DEM PUSSY ASS GAMES!!! U SUCKIN' DICK OR WAT? HOLLA BACK!

"Then let me suck yours," I say, lowering my voice. "I've been checkin' for you on the low for a minute, yo."

"Say what, muhfucka?"

HI. I KNOW YOU THINK I'M PLAYING GAMES. I'M REALLY NOT. I'M READY TONIGHT. I'M SO HORNY FOR YOUR HARD DICK. I WATCH YOUR VIDEO OVER AND OVER WHILE I PLAY IN MY PUSSY. I NEED THAT HARD DICK IN MY LIFE.

I grin. "I wanna suck ya dick, nigga. You got that big-ass dick, yo. I want some'a dat. What I gotta do to get some'a dat thick chocolate?"

"Muhfucka, you wildin', yo. You comin' at me real reckless, for real for real, yo. What's really good wit' you, nigga." He lowers his voice. "How you know I gotta big dick, anyway, muhfucka, huh?"

"I peeped it in da county, when you was comin' outta da shower one time 'n' another time when you was in da weight room. I used to beat my shit, thinkin' 'bout havin' ya shit in my mouth, boo."

"Nigga, I ain't ya muthafuckin', *boo*, yo. I ain't wit' dat gay shit."

I purse my lips. *Yeah, whatever, nigga. But your motherfucking ass is still on the line. So what does that say?*

"Ain't nobody sayin' you gay, big daddy. I know you think you *straight*, muhfucka…"

"*Think?* Nigga, you outta ya rabbit-ass mind; ain't no *thinkin'* shit! I'm a hunnid wit' mine, muhfucka! I ain't suckin' dick 'n' I ain't gettin' fucked, muhfucka."

I chuckle to myself. "Uh-huh, if you say so, pa. Shit. I'm mostly straight, myself. When I'm in da mood to beat da pussy up, I go in, yo." I bite into my lower lip to keep from laughing. "I'm sittin' here now, playin' wit' my shit, now. I wanna suck dat dick, muhfucka."

Mel gets up from his seat; his arousal evident by the long, thick lump hanging along the inside of his left thigh. I swallow, eyeing him as he heads to the bathroom.

"So you gay?"

I roll my eyes. "Nah. I'ma real-live freak-type nigga. I love pussy. But I dig suckin' dick on the low, too."

"I ever suck ya shit, nigga?"

"Nah, yo."

"Then why da fuck you call my girl wit' all dat crazy shit, tryna disrupt my shit, huh, muhfucka?"

I laugh inside. *Good motherfucker!* "My bad. I was on some foul shit. I'm sayin', though. Let me get on dat dick, yo. My dick stay hard thinkin' 'bout you, nigga. I can't get dat shit outta my head. I wanna watch you fuck ya bitch's pussy, then let me suck her pussy juice off ya dick. Then I wanna stick my tongue in ya asshole. I wanna taste dat man-booty, nigga."

I bite down on my fist to keep from laughing. Mel shifts in his seat, chuckling to himself.

"Oh, word? You want dis dick in ya ass, too?"

Ohhhhhhmymotherfuckinggod! Oooooooh, you dirty motherfucker!

I click open the video he'd sent of him jerking off. His dick is big. It's thick. Dark. Delicious. His balls hang like chocolate clackers, waiting to be clicked, clacked, and sucked into a mouth.

I take a deep breath. "Yeah, I wanna feel you in my ass, too. This asshole mad tight, muhfucka. I'm horny for dat dick, though. So wat's good? You lettin' me suck da nut outta dat shit or wat?"

"Muhfucka, you ain't gettin' shit 'til I know who da fuck you are. Comin' at me on some fag shit, like we mad familiar."

I have a new email. MydickneedsUrtongue2. I click it open. IMA BUST DAT THROAT OPEN. MY SHIT HARD AS BRICK! WAT X YOU TRYNA LINK UP? WHERE? IF U SERIOUS, HIT ME UP @ 973-444-5555 SO I KNOW U AIN'T FRONTIN'. IM HORNY AF! GET AT ME ASAP!

I smirk. *Yeah, I bet you are. Down-low motherfucker!*

I quickly type back. MMMMMM. I LOVE A HARD DICK! I'M VERY SERIOUS. WAIT UNTIL YOU SEE HOW I HANDLE YOU!

"Muhfucka, fuuuuck you," I say, flipping the script on him.

"Yo, what da fuck you say?"

"Don't drop da soap, nigga. I'm da muhfucka that's 'bout to take yo' shit, punk-ass bitch!" I end the call, shutting off the phone and removing the voice-changer device.

I lick my lips as Mel walks back into the room. "All that talk about sucking dick has me ready to slurp down on something hard."

He grins. "Oh, yeah? What you have in mind?"

I stand, sauntering over to him, pussy wet, mouth even wetter. I reach for his belt buckle, then run my hand along the inner part of his thigh. "Drop your pants and I'll show you."

Twenty-Nine

Seducing the enemy is like sucking a nigga with a small dick;
just pretend you love it...

"Yo, who da fuck is dis?"

Down-low motherfucker!

Hearing this nigga's voice again really makes my skin crawl, yanking me back to the dreadful day my world started to unravel. My dick sucking had finally caught up to me. Thanks to him.

Vernon Lewis.

"Those sexy-ass lips of yours were all I thought about when I was in the county. I beat my dick every night, thinking 'bout you suckin' my joint, again..."

"Who is this?"

"The nigga you dissed a few days ago. I bet you didn't think I was gonna figure out who you were, did you, you dick-suckin' bitch?"

He'd found me. A photo of me plastered in the local news section of *The Star-Ledger*, recognizing me for donating time and staff to the needy and homeless, offering a day of spa pampering at Nana's church's community day event is what led him to me. With the press of three digits...*4-1-1*...this nigga immediately had a direct link to *me*—the real me.

The bitch that gobbled his dick in the front seat of his Lexus, stroking his balls, then milking him to the edge of an orgasm; teasing him, toying with him, until he begged me to swoop my mouth all the way down on his cock and suck the nut out of it.

Yes, me. The dick-sucking master; the bitch that sucked the nigga nuttier than he already was.

"You got me wanting to bust a few rounds of nut down in that nasty-ass throat of yours...'ma 'bout to be your worst fuckin' nightmare. Check ya mail, baby. And if you don't do what I want, there'll be more where that came from."

Among the stack of mail on my desk, there—with my name typed on it—was a manila envelope with no return address. Inside, there was a sheet of paper with a color copy of the photo of me from the newspaper on it.

I unfold the sheet of paper I've kept hidden. The one sent to me by this nigga to torment me. Its caption: BUSINESS OWNER, PASHA ALLEN, STYLIST AND OWNER OF NAPPY NO MORE HAIR SALON IN ORANGE, NEW JERSEY, GIVES BACK TO THE COMMUNITY. Underneath, in cutout lettering, glued to the white copier paper, reads: PASHA ALLEN (AKA DEEP THROAT DIVA) IS THE COMMUNITY DICK WASHER. DICK SUCKING BITCH!

I narrow my eyes, swallowing back rising anger as I glare at the paper in my hand. I take a deep breath. Slowly blow it out. Then go into script.

It's showtime.

"Hi. It's Deep Throat Diva."

"Oh, word. Dat's wat it is. So wat's good? 'Bout time ya freaky ass hit me up. We linkin' up or wat? You got my dick harder than a mutha; real shit, baby. Wit' ya slut-nasty ass."

I cringe. "That's why I'm calling. I'm real hungry for some of that big, black Mandingo dick."

"Cool, cool. Dat's what a nigga tryna hear. I want you ta suck da nut outta dis snake 'n' swallow dat shit. You got me, yo?"

I get up from the bed, half-limping, half-walking, into the bathroom. I flip on the light, taking in my reflection in the mirror. I wince at the sight of my bruised face. Cold, angry eyes are staring back at me. "Oh, I got you, big daddy." I reach for my brush from off the vanity, run some water over it, brush my bang, blending it in with the rest of my hair, then slicking it back with gel.

"Yeah, aiight," he says, sounding skeptical. "So why all of a sudden, out da blue, you hit a muhfucka up tryna get at dis dick? You wasn't beat for a muhfucka before, 'member dat, yo?"

I roll my eyes. "I know, I know I was such an idiot for brushing you off like that. I was cleaning out my email inbox and came across the email you sent with the picture of your big dick." I keep the lies rolling trying to keep him from becoming more suspicious than he already is. "You already know I'm a dick sucker who loves sucking big dick. I kept kicking myself, even after all that shit you did to me, for not sucking your dick when you wanted me to. All I do is play the video you sent of you stroking your dick. God, your dick is so big."

"Oh, word? You like dat big dick, huh? So you ain't tryna set a muhfucka up for some payback-type shit then?"

I smirk. "No. I got what I deserved. I should have never tried to get brand-new on you. I should have been your personal dick-sucker all along."

"True, true," he says, sounding justified for stalking me. "You fucked up, but I ain't gonna hol' it against you. Just glad you ready to put ya cum suckers to work on dis dick. I ain't wanna bring it to you like dat, but you had'a muhfucka feignin' for dat shit. Shit got kinda outta hand."

I blink. *Nigga, really? Shit got kind of out of hand? Are you fucking kidding me?!* I roll my eyes up in my head. *This motherfucker is nuts!*

"Hands down, I ain't ever had a bitch suck my dick the way you sucked it. My girl can't suck dick for shit. But three of my baby mothers know how to suck dick good, but they still ain't got shit on you. Ya head game's bananas. So wat's good, you suckin' on dis dick or wat?"

I glide a coat of MAC Red satin lipstick over my lips, then pair it with Kiss Me Quick lip liner. I pucker my dick-suck-ready lips. Looking in the mirror, I blink several times, barely recognizing who I am.

Murder, torture, and being an accomplice to burglaries and arsons have a way of changing a bitch. The face staring back at me is still very beautiful. There's something in my hazel eyes that is both mesmerizing and haunting.

The look of a cold, heartless bitch.

"Yes. I'm sucking your dick, your balls and every drop of your thick, hot nut. I hope you're not going to cum quick."

I step out of the bathroom, walking out into the sitting area where Mel is. He's sitting on the sofa; his long legs stretched out in front of him, reading the latest edition of *Black Enterprise*. I swallow the lingering aftertaste of his nut as the thought of his humongous dick stretching down into my neck—only two hours ago, flashes in my head. My hand cupping his heavy balls, gently massaging them as I coated his cock with a bunch of spit, super-soaking it, gagging on it—being the nasty, slutty dick-sucker that I am.

"Nah. I'ma lock ya jaws. Damn. My shit's hard as fuck, yo. So when we doin' dis?"

I blink the memory of Mel stuffing my mouth, filling it with his cock cream, out of my head…for now, bringing my attention back to this crazy nigga on the other end of the phone.

I glance at the time. It's five mintues to eight. "Let's meet now."

"Damn, you real hungry for dis nut, huh?"

I will myself to keep from sucking my teeth. For some reason Booty pops in my head. To think this is the nigga she let fuck her raw and nut all up in her insides. A part of me almost feels like I should at least tell her about this dirty nigga. After all, messy or not—and regardless of the fact that I didn't ask her to—she provided me with names and information I wouldn't have probably gotten any other way.

My plan for revenge wouldn't have come together as quickly as it has had it not been for Booty's meddling ass. So whether I want to admit it or not, she lit the fire. And a part feels as if I owe her.

Yeah, maybe you do owe her. But you don't owe that bitch shit tonight! Tonight, this nigga's all yours.

"Mmmm-hmm. I don't have any good dick in my life, so I'm real hungry for yours."

Mel shoots a look over at me, shaking his head and grinning.

"Oh, word? What, you ain't cock-whorin' over on da freak-nasty site no more?" I tell him no. Tell him it was too dangerous. That I no longer want to be perusing online sex sites like Nastyfreaks4u for randon dick anymore. That the only dick I'm interested in sucking is his. I tell him I want to be his personal cum whore; to suck his dick whenever, however, he wants it. I can tell by the way he's grunting that I've got him reeled in. His heavy breathing lets me know I got the nigga turned on by the idea of having me as his personal dick-sucker.

"Mmmmm. My pussy's so wet. I wanna suck your dick in the backseat of your car."

"Yo, you lick ass?"

I frown. Not that I'm opposed to tossing a nigga's salad. Hell, I've run my tongue all up in Jasper's ass plenty of times when we were together; and *not* because he was pressing me for it. It's what I wanted to do. Turned that nigga out for the tongue lap on the sly. Had him feeling some kind of way about it, but the nigga never stopped me, either, whenever I did bless him with this tongue.

I decide to fuck with this slimy sonofabitch even more. Tell him that I don't only want to lick his ass, but that I want him to smear his nut on my tongue, then bend over his car seat, pull his ass open and let me tongue him in his hole.

"Damn, yo. Ya freaky-ass got me goin' through it. Where you wanna meet?" I tell him the location. Then stress the importance of keeping this between us. "No doubt, no doubt. I ain't tryna put shit out there like dat. Wat we do is wat we do. But, yo…if you front on me…"

I smirk. *And what, motherfucker?!*

"You have no idea how long I've thought about getting at you. You and that big, black cock are all I think about."

I unzip my leather travel case, running my hand over the assortment of goodies: duct tape, Gorilla glue, bolt cutters, a black leather Gag Blinder mask with removable snap-on blinders and removable muzzle, a four-way leather hogtie binder, and three dildos—one six-inch, an eight-inch, and a twelve-inch.

"Trust me," I continue, zipping the case up. "Fronting on you is the last thing on my mind. I'll be there in twenty mintues. Alone. Make sure your dick is clean, rock-hard, and ready for me."

Motherfucker likes stalking bitches for a good dick suck, then I'ma give his black ass something to stalk!

"My shit's always clean. And I stay hard 'n' ready."

I glance over at the portable spanking pad with restraints leaning up against the wall near the door. "Then buckle up, big daddy. Tonight you're going to be in for the time of your life. I promise you. It'll be one night you'll *never* forget."

Mel and I are only seconds away from the designated location when one of my phones starts vibrating. It's a text. I roll my eyes, opening it. Yo WHERE U AT?

I suck my teeth. "This thirsty fucker," I mumble. I don't bother to respond. We roll up a few feet behind where his Lexus is. Mel is in the backseat. He crouches down when I put the SUV in PARK. He knows to wait a few minutes, then once I'm inside this nigga's car, creep up and handle the rest.

"You good?" he wants to know as I take a deep breath, shutting off the engine.

I shudder, reaching for my Taser and the bottle of Wet in my handbag, then sliding them into the front pocket of my jacket. I avoid looking at him through the reaview mirror. But I can feel his brown eyes on me, unnerving me. "Yeah. I'll just be glad when this shit is finally over."

"I feel you. I know this shit's startin' to get to you, but you one more muhfuka closer to the finish line; remember that."

I nod, flashing my high beams, signaling that I'm there. I slip on my black leather riding gloves, then open the door and step out into the night air.

Ready to take down one more nigga.

I can see the dark shadow inside the vehicle reaching over and opening the passenger side door as I near the car. The interior light comes on as I quickly hop in, shutting the door. The inside reeks of weed and alcohol and a hint of cologne. Bulgari, I think.

I quickly drink him in with my eyes. The nigga's tall, at least six-three. His jet-black skin shines in the darkness. The nigga has the nerve to be well groomed. Sideburns amd mustache trimmed to perfection. Waves, thick and deep. He's fine. Real fine. Damn him!

No-good, dirty bastard!

Flashes of the night he jumped out from behind the bushes in my front yard and attacked me pop in my head. The gloved hand that quickly covered my mouth to mute my startled scream; the voice growling low in my ear, "I've been following your every move, slut. Now open ya fuckin' door…" Then we're wrestling and we're down on the ground, his hand around my neck until I am clawing at him, screaming and kicking and punching him until he finally lets me go and starts running down the street. "This ain't over, bitch!"

Oh, you were so right, motherfucker. This shit is far from over. But it's about to be. Real soon.

"Yo, wat's good?" he says, eyeing me and licking his lips. His dick is already out, his left hand slowly stroking it.

"You and that big dick is what's good," I say, shifting in my seat and reaching over and grabbing it. "Oooh, it's so thick."

"Yeah, dat's wat it is. You got my muhfuckin' shit hard as fuck, baby. Now get up on dis dick 'n' suck it like you in love wit' it. I ain't tryna hear a whole buncha chitchat, just suckin'." He eases his seat back, then lays it all the way back. He reaches over, tries to pull me by the back of my neck down into his lap. "C'mon 'n' wet dis dick wit' dem pretty cum-suckers."

"Mmmmm, you wanna feel my slutty lips on the head of your dick?" I coo, reaching into my pocket for the Taser. I grip it in my right hand while using my left hand to stroke his dick, hoping like hell Mel hurries the fuck up and gets over here before I have to put my mouth on this nigga's big, juicy dick.

God, his dick is so thick. I fight to keep from drooling. I wonder why I didn't suck him more than once. *I must have known his ass was a fucking loose screw.*

He lifts his head up from the headrest. "Yo, wat da fuck, ma…?

Why is you playin' wit' my shit? Stop teasin' me. I ain't come out here for no handjob. I can jerk my own shit at da crib."

"Relax," I say real low, eyeing him seductively. *What the fuck, Mel?! What the fuck is he doing back there?* "I'm going to give it to you real good, nigga."

I lean into his lap, and flick my tongue over the head of his dick. "Yeah, dat's wat da fuck I'm talkin' 'bout..." He lays back in his seat. I flick his dick again, then slowly lick it like it's a chocolate-dipped popsicle until his whole body relaxes.

I ease the Taser out of my pocket, then in one swift motion connect the contact probes to his neck, pressing the trigger and sending electric bolts of fire through his body, causing him to scream out.

The driver's side door swings open just as he passes out.

Thirty

A ruthless bitch will stop at nothing to quench her thirst for revenge…

His eyelids open and close slowly, struggle to focus, then widen in shock. He tries to speak, but syllables are unable to connect to words and the only things coming out of his mouth are gurgling grunts. "Aaaah, aaaaah, aaaah…"

His naked body jerks wildly, looking around the large, open garage space, then down at the leather restraints around his wrists and ankles. He's strapped to an inversion table in the middle of the cement floor. "Aaaah, aaaaaah, aaaaaah…"

I lean into his face, opening a tube of Wet and squirting a glob all over his flaccid dick. "You like your dick sucked, don't you, Vernon Lewis?" His eyes widen in surprise. "Yeah, I bet you didn't think I'd ever find out who you were, did you, Mister My Dick Needs Your Tongue Too? You thought you could torment me, sending niggas into my salon to call me out in front of customers, and post fliers about me sucking dick all over my salon door and windows, then attack me in my yard…"

He grunts, shaking his head. Attempting to speak to no avail.

"I'm the one who called your girl's phone and told her you were a dick sucker. I was the one calling and telling you how I wanted to suck your dick. All the while had you thinking it was a nigga." I lean back into his face, lowering my voice. "Down-low motherfucker. I wonder what your baby mother, Cassandra Simms, would say knowing one of her baby daddies was willing to let another nigga suck his dick."

He shakes his head. "Aaaaaah, aaaaaah, aaaaaaaah…" He tries to shake himself out of the restraints. "Aaaaaah, aaaaah, aaaaaaaaah…"

"Nigga, I couldn't care less who you let suck your dick on the low. And I'm not telling Cassandra shit. That bitch'll find out soon enough, along with everyone else. So no worries, Miss Honey Boo-Boo, your secret's safe with me."

He grunts again.

I reach between his legs and grab his dick. I stroke it. Glide my hand up and down his shaft, swirling my fingertips over the head. "Aaaah, aaaaah… "

"You love this big dick sucked, don't you, Miss Downlow?" I increase the speed of my strokes. Against his will, it begins to thicken, stretch, and come alive. "You like stalking and harassing and threatening bitches to wet it for you, don't you, pussy-ass bitch?"

He shakes his head, grunting.

"Don't worry, boo," I taunt, cupping his balls. "I'm not going to slice out your balls, or whip up this big, pretty dick like I did that nigga, Legend's." He rapidly blinks, fear shoots through his pupils. "Yes. That was all my handiwork. I sliced that nigga's tongue out and cut off his ears, too. And you want to know why I cut out his balls?" He grunts again. "Don't worry. I'll tell you, anyway. I cut out that nigga's balls because the disrespectful motherfucker put his hands on me. Cutting them out of his nut sac was his punishment for what he'd done to me. And then…"

I whisper in his ear, "I left him to bleed to death." I glance at his dick as it starts to throb in my hand. "Ooooh, your dick feels so good in my hand. I love big dick. But you already knew that; isn't that right, you dirty motherfucker? I had you feening for this throat, didn't I? I guess you want to know what I'm going to do to you, huh?"

He grunts, his eyelids flutter; I'm sure in response to the way I'm jerking him off. "Uggh, ugggh, uggggh, ugggggh..."

"Yeah, you dirty fucker, you wanna cum for me, don't you?" I abruptly let go of his aching cock. "You want to know what your punishment's going to be for coming into my life and wreaking havoc, huh? You see them niggas over there?"

His eyes dart frantically around the room again.

I smirk when he turns his head toward the noise coming from the right side of the garage. There are six tall, masked niggas— thugged out and tatted up, sitting at a rectangular table on the other end of the garage, watching porno on a flat-screen television. There are bottles of Hennessy and Cîroc on the table, and a thick cloud of weed smoke encircling them. They're getting lit for the festivities to come.

My cell vibrates. I pull it out of my pocket, turning my back, leaving Vernon to suffer in silence. "Hey."

"Everything good?"

"Yes."

"How long you gonna be out there?" I glance down at my time-piece. It's already a quarter to ten. I'd like to be home by midnight, if I can help it. I tell him probably another hour or so. "Cool, cool."

I glance over at Vernon. I want this shit over. Now. I turn my gaze from his. Tell Lamar to hold on, then pull out my personal cell and call Stax.

"Yo," he says smoothly into the phone. I can hear niggas in the background talking. I think I hear Jasper's voice, but can't be for sure.

"I *need* to see you."

"When?"

"Tonight."

"I'm kinda tied up with…"

"Have I ever called you and asked for anything?"

"Nah."

I breathe in, then out. My voice comes out a soft whisper. "I *need* you *tonight*, Stax. *Please*."

It gets quiet around him. He's moved away from the loud voices. "Talk to me, Pash." I swallow. There's something in the way he shortens my name. *Pash*. His voice is gentle, caring. I try to recall if it's always been there. His concern.

"Not over the phone. I need to…*see* you."

He pauses.

"I got you. Give me like three hours." I tell him where I'll be. Tell him not to leave me waiting. "I'm always a man of my word."

"Make me a believer," I say before ending the call. I place the other phone back up to my ear. "Go ahead and handle those other spots tonight, but not until I send you a text. Be ready."

"Aiight. What about…?"

"If you still have eyes on him, get him, too."

I tell him I want that piece of Felecia I had him put on dry ice to finally be displayed. I give him the address in Maplewood where I want it put on show for all to see. I know I'm raising the stakes. But it's time. The only thing I can do now is brace myself for whatever comes in the aftermath. And there will be plenty.

"I got you," he says. "It's almost over."

"Yes, it is." I end the call, walking back over to Vernon. He starts grunting and shaking his head, clearly trying to say something.

"Aaaah, aaaaaaah, aaaah…"

"You know Jasper, don't you?"

He nods. "Aaaaaah, aaaaaah, aaaaah…"

"Is there something you want to tell me before I give you a taste of what you put me through?" He nods his head again. "Good." I walk around him, then unfasten the gag. He opens and closes his mouth, tries to work out the ache from having his jaws forced open.

His voice comes out hoarse, "W-w-why are you...doin' dis, yo...?"

I slap his face. "You don't *ask* questions, motherfucker! You *answer* them. Now, *why* did you harass and practically stalk me after I told you I wasn't sucking your dick again?"

He shuts his eyes, sighing. "I was dead-ass wrong."

I slap his face again. This time, my nails graze his cheek, breaking skin. "That's not what I asked you." I stalk over to my black case and pull out the bolt cutters, then back over to him, opening and closing the blades. His eyes pop open in panic. "Motherfucker, know this. What happens to you *tonight* depends on *you*. If you haven't noticed, I'm a bitch on a mission. So *don't*. Fuck. With. Me."

"I-I-I'll tell you w-w-whatever you wanna know; just don't cut none'a my s-s-shit off." I lean into his face, grabbing his dick. "N-n-no. P-p-please, not my d-d-dick." Fear and panic and horror all coils around him, like a python; slowly squeezing him. He starts crying like a little bitch. "D-D-Don't c-c-cut off my d-d-d-d-dick."

"Pussy, you harassed the shit out of me, remember that? All because you wanted this neck work, well, tonight you're going to get all the neck you want." I slap him upside his head with all my might. "That night in my yard, when you attacked me, you slapped me. No man had ever put his hands on me until then." He tries to apologize and I slap him again. "Save it, nigga."

I narrow my eyes. Tilt my head, reaching for the lube, then squirting more over his dick. "You like niggas sucking your dick, huh?"

His eyes buck. "Nah. I-I-I a-a-ain't ever have no nigga s-s-suck my s-s-shit." I stroke his dick. Make it hard for him to concentrate. "Mmmmph... uh...-I..."

I tighten my grip around his thick shaft, rapidly stroking him up and down, until my fingers are coated in precum. I start moaning, running my tongue over my lips. "So you've never fucked with a nigga."

He shakes his head, stuttering out another "no."

The more I stroke him, the more precum he oozes. And I am becoming aroused. My pussy moistens. My lace panties dampen. "No worries, boo. Tonight, you will. I'm going to make sure all of your fantasies come true. Mmmm. This big, long dick."

He sucks in air, tries to fight back a grunt of pleasure. "N-n-nah, I'm g-g-good."

I let go of his dick. Take my wet fingers and smear them over his lips. "Lick your lips." He frowns. "Lick your motherfucking lips. Or"—I pull out a blade, pressing the tip to his bottom lip— "I'll slice these motherfuckers off."

Hesitantly, he licks them.

"That's right. Taste yourself, nigga." Next, I step out of my juicy panties, placing the crotch up to his nose. "Smell that? That's my excited pussy, nigga. Knowing you are finally getting what you deserve has me so wet. Lick my panties, motherfucker."

I narrow my eyes when he hesitates. Stick the tip of my blade into the head of his dick, threatening to slice it open. His tongue extends and he laps in long strokes.

I nod my head over toward a video recorder on a tripod. "To-night, you're going to get your first starring role in a home video for the viewing pleasure of that fat bitch you're with, all of your baby mothers, your boys, and whomever else *I* decide to send it to. So you better start talking."

He breaks out in a sweat, then sings like a bird. Tells me the night he responded to my ad on Nastyfreaks4u.com and met me at Weequahic Park, he didn't know who I was. All he knew is, he wanted to see me again. Wanted another round of head. But got snatched up by the sheriffs for not paying child support and sat in the county for three months thinking about how good I sucked his dick until he was finally released.

He swallows, then licks his dry lips. I reach for a water bottle filled with a chilled golden liquid. Tell him to open his mouth. Then squirt a stream into his mouth. He coughs. Gags. I tell him it's piss.

"The sooner you tell me what I need to know, the sooner you get out of here. Dead or alive…it's up to you."

The realization that he may end up bodied quickly motivates him to get his mind right. He tells me he sent me an email the first chance he got his hands on a computer, in hopes to get his dick back down into my throat. But when I turned him down, he felt dissed and got pissed.

I roll my eyes. Let out an impatient sigh. Tell him to fast-forward this shit. All I want to know is, how Jasper fits into all of it. He tells me he didn't know Jasper personally. That he knew of him through some other niggas in the hood. But he wasn't the one who paid him to harass me, or attack me. That Jasper never even stepped to him. It was a chick.

"I swear on my kids, I ain't know who you was until the day I was at my man's crib 'n' I peeped you in dat news article. I was like, 'oh, shit. Word is bond. Dat's da bitch who sucked my dick.' I tol' him how bananas ya head game was."

I cringe.

"My peoples hipped me to who you was. Then tol' me he used to fuck ya peoples on the low." I ask him who. He tells me he can't remember her name, but knows she worked at my salon 'n' used to answer the phones when he'd call there for me. He doesn't have to say anything more. I already know whom he's talking about.

"Felecia," I mumble. All along that bitch knew. She played the shit out of me.

"Yeah, her. My mans hit her up 'n' tol' her what I tol' him. A few days later she had him hit me up 'n' said she wanted to holla at me."

I blink. Feel myself getting sick as he tells me how that grimy bitch fucked him and his nigga that night, then offered him five grand to stalk me. That bitch was behind my windows being smashed out. Behind that nigga AJ walking up into my shop and calling me out. Behind him attacking me. For five grand, that dead bitch tried to have me done in.

I glance at the time. It's 11:37 p.m. I have to hurry out of here. Need to get back to my suite to freshen up before I meet with Stax. I had no intentions of fucking him when I initially called him. I only wanted to get him away from Jasper. Wanted him away from the fire. But, now…want to *fuck*. Him.

One last time.

Before it's all over.

I walk behind Vernon. Tell him to open his mouth. He initially refuses, until I threaten to saw off his balls. His mouth snaps open wide, allowing me to fasten the mouth gag back on. I flip up the inverted table he's on, so that his head is now upside down.

He grunts.

I squat down, take the leather strap in my hand, then secure his head with the strap to keep it from moving around. "Don't worry. You'll get out of here alive."

"Aaaah, aaaaah, ugggh, ugggh!"

His eyes roll around in their sockets as he tries to see what I'm doing next. I walk over to my case. Pull out a deluxe chastity anal plug from my case, then walk back over to him.

His eyes widen. "Aaah, aaaah, ugggggh, ugggggh…"

"Stop all that noise, bitch!" I reach down and punch him in his eye. "You're not getting your dick sliced off. You're not getting bodied. You're not getting your tongue or ears sliced off. You're not getting whipped with barbed wire or having your fingers cut off. All you're going to get is a little ass-play and some cum, then get dumped out on your front lawn. So why the fuck are you carrying on, huh?"

I lube the plug. "I'm going to stick this in your ass." Unlike most ass plugs you just slide in, this one lets you expand its size up to almost three inches, stetching your ass nice and wide, then allowing you to lock it in place. I let him know this.

He grunts and groans louder. Tries to break free from the restraints.

I glance around the space. The masked niggas are good and lit up, loud-talking and laughing about some chick in the video they're watching not being able to handle a dick in her ass, throat, and pussy at the same time. Each one bragging about what they'd do to her if they were there.

I catch Mel's attention as he's walking out of some kind of back office area and talking on his cell. I give him a hand signal, letting him know that it's time for his hood stripper/escorts his *peoples* recruited to be ready for what's next. But first…

I return my attention back to Vernon. "I'm going to piss in your fucking face for making my life a living hell." I lift my ankle-length skirt up over my knees, then slowly lower my bare pussy over his head. "You see all that pretty pussy?" I taunt. "Look up into my pussy hole, nigga, or I'm going to gouge your eyes out."

"Aaaaah, aaaaaah, arrrrrrrgh, arrrrrrgh, arrrrrrrrrgh…"

I piss all over his face.

When I'm finished soaking his face with a golden shower, I use a feminine wipe to clean off, then wipe his face with it. "Now, for the grand finale." I wave Mel and his freak crew over. "Those six niggas over there wearing those masks are going to come over here with their big, hard dicks and use your face and opened mouth as a cum dump."

"Arrrrrrgh, arrrrrrgh, arrrrrrrgh…"

The hard, horny thugs, who will all walk out of here two grand richer than they were before stepping in here, make their way over toward us. "Here they cooooooooome," I jeer, reaching between his legs and working the four-inch plug into his tight, hairy man-hole. His growling becomes more intense, excruciating, as I twist the rubber bulb stretching him open. The widening of the plug is supposed to be done in slow increments, but I am pressed for time. And I'm not interested in making this fucker comfortable. So I stretch him open to full capacity.

Then lock the plug in place, smiling as I toss the small key down into a drain in the cement floor. "When the party's over," I add, walking off to pack my leather case, "you'll need to have that plug cut out of your ass."

I stand. Watch three hard-body, chocolate thugs—horned up from weed, booze, and watching porn—position themselves over Mr. MydickneedsUrtongue2's piss-stained face, rapidly stroking their rock-hard dicks, while the other three look on in back of them—watching and waiting for their turns, slowly edging themselves to climax.

My pussy starts to pulse. My nipples harden.

"Arrrrrrrgh, arrrrrrrgh, arrrrrrrgh…aaaaaaaah, aaaaaaaah, aaaaaaah…"

I lick my lips.

One by one, thick ropes of white cream spew out of their cocks, coating Vernon's face, his chest, and filling the open space in his gag with cum until he gurgles and grunts, practically choking on a mouth overflowing with man seeds.

I close my eyes, taking a deep breath.

Another nigga scratched off the list.

Tears begin to well in my eyes, but I refuse to let any fall.

Not here. Not now.

Thirty-One

Money isn't the root of all evil, pussy is…

Twelve forty-five a.m., Stax lets me know he's in the hotel lobby. I quickly send Lamar a text to proceed with the plan as discussed, then quietly slip through the door of the adjourning suite from the watchful eyes of the two guards standing watch over me, and wait for Stax.

Lamar texts back. Says everything is a go. They are moving out now. And like the two times Jasper's six other stash houses were seized and burned down, his team will spill out of unmarked vans—donned in black Kevlar, gas masks and firepower held in ready positions, fingers resting on trigger guards—to the front and back of each spot as hundred-pound door busters swing into action, splintering locks and knocking wooden doors inward. Point men will toss flash grenades into the front and back, then permanently shut shit down.

My only hope, there isn't a lot of blood shed.

Within minutes, there's a light knock on the door.

He's here.

Pushing back the scenes playing out in my head, I quickly glide a coat of cherry-flavored lip gloss over my lips, then open the door, stepping aside to let him in. He smells as if he's freshly showered. I breathe in his scent, shutting the door behind him.

"I'm glad you came," I say as he crosses into the room. He's wearing a navy blue designer sweat suit with a navy blue Yankees fitted hat and a pair of crisp white Air Max.

I gesture with my hand for him to have a seat on the sofa.

"Nah, I'm good," he says; his tone clipped. He's looking at me, but seems distracted. *Shit must be getting real hectic.* He studies me. "What happened to ya face?"

I give him a dismissive wave. "A disagreement with a disgruntled bitch turned ugly."

He gives me a questioning look, then shrugs it off. "So, what's up? You said you needed to see me." I blink. His aloof demeanor takes me aback, only for a brief moment, though.

"Yes." I sit on the sofa, crossing my legs and allowing my robe to spill open, revealing my thigh. I clasp my hands over my knee. His gaze slides down to my hardened nipples pressing against the fabric of my robe, then to my thigh. "Does Jasper want you to set me up?"

His eyes narrow slightly. "Where'd you get that from?"

I shake my head, sighing. "Stax, you promised you wouldn't let anything else happen to me. Did you mean that?"

"C'mon, Pash. Of course I did. I keep tellin' you, I say what I mean."

"Then be honest with me, *please*. Does Jasper want you to kill me?"

He removes his hat. Runs his hand over his head. Then glances at his watch. *Nigga, I don't know what you looking at the time for. I'm not letting you out of here anytime soon.* I tilt my head, waiting.

He decides to sit next to me, his leg barely touching mine. "Hell nah. He knows not to ever come at me wit' some shit like hat. Yeah, Jasp came at me a minute ago wantin' me to get at you, but

I told him I wasn't beat. I've snatched up a few muhfuckas 'n' muscled 'em up when needed. But all that extra shit, I'm not wit'."

I ask him if that was his reason for coming down to the salon after Jasper had his goons shoot at me in front of the salon two weeks ago. He told me it wasn't when I asked him then. I'm asking again to see if his answer changes. It doesn't. He says Jasper only asked him to get me to him. Then he'd take care of the rest.

"And do what, *kill* me?"

The grim look on his face says volumes.

I clench my teeth. "That bastard's going to get everything he fucking deserves."

He eyes me, not so much in suspicion as in confusion, then realization. "I need you to keep shit a hunnid wit' me, Pash. Did you have anything to do wit' what happened to that cat *L* they had plastered all on the news?"

I bat my lashes, feigning shock. "Why? Was he one of the nigga's Jasper had assaulting me?"

"Answer the question, Pash. Yes or no?"

I narrow my eyes. Stax is smart enough to know—at least I hope he is—that flat-out admitting to what he already knows to be true is not going to happen. But I won't deny, either. "There were six grimy motherfuckers that I recall who were all wearing colored basketball shorts, stampeding down the stairs into the basement, then taking turns fucking into my face, coming in my mouth, because of Jasper's ass. That is a fact. So, Stax, the truth is, I intend on making it my business that *every* last one of them niggas pay. One by one, they will all drop, including Jasper."

Stax massages his temples. There's a long pause. A deafening silence as if he's trying to find the right words to say. He seems to be thinking. "And the fires?" he asks, finally.

I blink. "What fires?"

"C'mon, Pash. Don't front like you don't know what time it is. Those six spots that got ran through, then set fire to, were stash houses. Those were big hits, Pash. Some real major losses."

I shrug, slowly shaking my head. "Karma is a bitch, Stax. So I need for you to fall back for a while, please."

He frowns, giving me a strange look. I glance at the time. He's only been here for ten minutes and it feels like forever.

"I'm *not* asking, Stax. I'm *pleading* with you. It's the only way I can keep you safe."

"Safe? Safe from what, Pash?"

I take a deep breath. "From…" My chest tightens. All of a sudden, I am feeling overwhelmed. My emotions are swelling. Pushing up against the floodgates.

This isn't scripted; isn't part of the plan. No. No crying.

"Me," I whisper, choking back tears. I am gripped with anger. My voice is strained with hurt and sadness. "From me, Stax. I have to keep you safe from *me…*"

His intense stare starts to unnerve me. I shift in my seat. Turn my head from him. My bottom lip quivers. The floodgate snaps open, the dam breaks. And the tears come in a rush, crippling everything inside of me. Jasper's pushed and pushed and pushed. Now he's pushed too far. He's turned me into *this*… this blood-thirsty bitch. And I won't stop, can't stop, until I've fed it, until it's sated.

And now I'm afraid…*very* afraid for anyone who gets in my path. My blood pounds through my veins. My head starts to throb. I become a ball of snot and tears and slob, holding my face in my hands, shaking my head and rocking.

My wrenching sobs come from somewhere deep. From peeling

scabs, and unstitched emotional wounds; from fists and threats; from multiple niggas taunting me, fucking into my mouth, jeering and sneering, egging each other on.

To disrespect and degrade the dick-sucking bitch.

To break the cum-slut's spirit.

Stax moves closer. His arm is around my trembling shoulder, and he's pulling me into him. "C'mon, Pash. I hate seein' you cry. It fucks wit' me. Shit's real crazy right now, Pash. Give Jasp his paper 'n' he'll leave you alone. That's my word, Pash. I'll handle this shit, aiight? You gotta trust me. He'll sign the papers."

Eventually I quiet. The tears subside. I lift my head, finally looking up at Stax. I am surprised to see the pained look on his face. His eyes are red. But there are no tears. Still, I am aware with aching clarity the depth of his feelings for me. The ones he's kept hidden from me.

Feelings I've been oblivious to.

I stare into his brown eyes. He takes a hand and using his gentle fingers to wipe tears from my face. He holds the back of my head, pressing his head up against my forehead. "God, you're so fuckin' beautiful…" He draws back to look at me. "I have to stay away from you, Pash. This shit between us is too dangerous."

I close my eyes, rubbing my neck. We're both quiet for several moments. I turn to him, taking a deep breath. Finally he asks, "What the fuck are we doin', Pash, huh?"

I touch his face. My fingers tremble over the outline of his jaw, then over his thick brows, then his lips. I am unraveling. Becoming undone again. His heated gaze unhinges me. I look away from him. Before the guilt finds its way home and comes rushing to the surface.

Before the tears come again.

Thirty-Two

Seduction and surrender can be the ultimate forbidden pleasure...

"Answer me, Pash," Stax demands, his mouth near my ear. "Why am I here?" He nips my lobe. "And don't bullshit me."

"I'm using you," I admit, sitting up on my knees on the sofa, pulling loose the tie of my robe. I part my thighs. One hand massages my breast, the other slips between my legs. I dip a finger inside of me. "My pussy's wet, Stax."

"C'mon, Pash. Don't." He takes a deep breath, getting up from the sofa. His arousal evident by the thick lump in his sweats.

"Don't you want to be inside this tight pussy? I know we have to stop this. But I don't want to. Not tonight. I want you to fuck me one last time." I pull open my robe. Allow it to fall from my shoulders. Stax tries not to cast his gaze down at the eager fingers, slipping in and out of my slick cunt. "Give me that dick, Stax. Fuck me. Pound the life out of this pussy."

I can tell he's fighting against his subconscious. Struggling to keep from caving into his heated desires for me. He lets out a groan.

Tears spill down my cheeks. "I didn't ask for this, Stax. This aching want for you. Jasper did this, Stax. He fucked Felecia. Fucking you, Stax, numbs the pain. It helps me block it all out." I ease off the sofa, baring my nakedness; baring my wounded soul—desperate and desolate—as I walk over to him.

I move in closer to him. Our bodies meet. And he doesn't back away.

I ask, "Do you love me?"

"Fuck, Pash! Shit." He shakes his head. "We can't do this shit, ya heard?" He cups my face in his hands. He leans in and brushes his lips against mine. "This shit's fucked up, Pash. You fuckin' got me goin' crazy. Shit."

Still…he doesn't answer the question.

"I know it is." I move my wet pussy against him. Break his resolve. My hand reaches between his legs, grabbing his dick, stroking and squeezing it over his sweats. I feel it twitching as it swells. "Mmm. Let me feel this big dick inside of me."

"You playin' wit' fire, Pash. We could both both end up gettin' burned."

"I'm already in the flames." I ease my hand up under his sweatshirt until my fingers find his nipples. I pinch them, lightly, causing Stack's breath to hitch. His tongue is in my mouth, his left hand gripping my ass. My skin burns where his fingers are—his touch, his body, fusing into my own.

I am smoldering with need. I step out of his embrace. Lie back on the sofa, my legs bent at the knees and spread, waiting…wanting. My pretty pussy wet and swollen, I peel my dew-slick lips open, showing him my pink insides.

Without prompting, Stax pulls his sweatshirt up over his head, tossing it carelessly to the floor. I lick my lips, taking in his flat stomach muscles. He pushes down his sweatpants and boxers until they are wrapped around his ankles.

He stands like this, unmoving, his swollen dick pointed straight as an arrow, bouncing up and down, his hands fisted at his sides, watching me watching him.

He tortures me. Slowly, he kicks off his sneakers, then steps out of his sweats and underwear. Naked. His dick is thick and sturdy and ready as he reaches down and pushes my legs further apart, the head of his dick stretching through a wet, welcoming warmth that engulfs him.

He fucks into me deep. Plunges into me hard and fast. His dick is buried so deep. So damn fucking deep. I curse him for the delicious burn. He curses me back for the delicious squeeze.

I groan. He groans.

My pussy dissolves into his strokes. His arms curl under me, then he's lifting me. We're standing. "Wrap your legs around me. Let me get all up in this pussy, baby."

My legs take on a life of their own and wrap around his waist, my arms clasp around his neck, and we are moving. Slow, intense. His eyes on mine, burning into my soul.

"Uhhh…don't know what the fuck you're…mmmph…doin' to me, Pash…uhhh…"

Stax thrusts into me, his dick fucking into my heat, fucking into my heart, fucking into the hollowness of my soul, filling it with everything he is.

Thrusting and grunting again and again, pulling out to the crown of his dick, then thrusting back in balls deep.

I am fighting a rushing wave of pleasure. *Ohgod, noooo! Please, Lord God!* "Uhhh…"

I am bouncing up and down and around the length and width of him, the slick-click of my pussy soaking his dick with hungry need and greedy want. Stax's dick grows bigger inside of me, his ten inches swelling into a part of me I'd hidden, forgotten existed. But Stax finds it, strokes it; shoves it open with every stroke.

That space…*OhsweetFatherGod, nooo!* I am coming and I am forgetting. Forgetting everything, letting it all go, as he fucks me. Forgetting my hate, my anger, my lies, my secrets as he fucks me deep and deliberate. I forget I am only using him as he kisses my mouth, bites my lip, my throat, leaving his mark, stamping my body, my pussy, with fiery passion.

I gasp his name as he pounds into me. *LordGodJesus!* My fingernails dig into his shoulders, grazing his heated skin.

"Mmmm, this pussy's so wet for me," he murmurs, his eyes becoming slits of boiling lust. His voice comes out a husky whisper as he says, "Oh, fuck...mmmm..." His big hands grasp my hips as he slams himself up into me. "Take it all, baby. Don't hold back. Fuck me back, Pash...show me what you got for me, baby..."

The harder Staxs fucks me, the wetter I grow around him, allowing him to go even deeper.

"Yeah, that's it. Fuuuuck! You got my head up all fucked up, baby..." His hands move all over my back. "Shiiiiit...mmmmmph... you feel so good on my dick..."

An image of Stax kneeling in front of me, his hands holding my thighs apart and him loving my pussy with his mouth, pops into my mind, causing me to moan out in pleasure. The sheer memory of how he stroked my clit and sucked at me as if I were a ripened sweet fruit floods my senses.

I throw my head back. I am moaning louder. I am getting lost in the swirling heat. Getting lost in the memory of the night I seduced him in my office, manipulated my way between his legs. The taste of his cock in my mouth, the sweet, salty tang of his nut as he emptied his balls down into my neck. The firm-soft wet of his tongue pushing its way into the slit of my pussy, fucking in and out of my wetness, flicking and toying with my clit, sucking on my swollen cunt lips. The sizzling sensation of the memory and the way his dick is feeling inside of me at this very moment has me reeling.

I arch into the blaze.

Stax's dick hits all the right spots, the way his tongue had licked all the right ones. Each stroke steals another piece of something inside of me, robbing me of my senses, raiding my pussy with strong, powerful thrusts.

I am mewling. Then catlike sounds seep out from the back of my throat as Stax's mouth finds my left breast, sucking in the rigid sweetness of my dark nipple. Then, without warning, he bites into it, causing bolts of pleasure to shoot through every nerve in my body. The sudden ache pushing out a steady flow of juices. His dick slipping in and out of wet heat, pumping in and out in a steady rhythm.

I am coming.

No, no, no, no!

Oh, God, yesssss…

His tongue is now licking; his mouth now sucking, the spot he's just bitten, his wet tongue exploring the distended tip of my thick nipple.

I bite down on my bottom lip, groaning. Bucking my hips. Fucking him back. I fight from growling, from gnashing my teeth and biting into his flesh, like a wild beast in heat.

He backs me up into a wall. I find his mouth again, and this time it's my tongue that pushes its way inside. Stax allows it, welcomes it, showing his voracious need in the eager way his tongue greets mine. He loops a hand in my hair, pulls me deeper into our kiss. And fucks me mercilessly against the wall.

He moans my name over and over again. We both know; we feel it…the electricity zapping through my walls, the current rising. I know. He knows. He should pull out...*now*. Before it's too late. But he doesn't. He wants more from me. Wants all that I am offering him. And I give it as fast as he takes it.

My pussy becomes a fist, a wet glove of muscles clenching him tightly. Stax bucks and thrusts into me, and I go wild with fiery hunger, throwing my head from side to side, screaming his name. I am coming.

He is coming, nearly howling as a burst of wet fire shoots out of his dick and empties deep inside of me, engulfing us both into the flames.

Thirty-Three

*Hatred can be as blinding as love; not seeing the thin line
can be deadlier...*

"Ohhhhhhmygod! *Nooo!*"

"Sssh, sssh. Somebody turn that up...!"

"Ohmygod! Who would do something like that...?"

These are the responses of patrons and stylists in the salon, first thing Monday morning, as the air around the room freezes solid while everyone looks on in horror and shock at the three flat-screen TVs airing the morning news.

"This is Channel 4 News reporting live from Maplewood, New Jersey. Authorities were called to this home on Prospect Street at approximately five thirty-seven in the morning on what is one of the most grueling, horrific crime scenes. A decapitated woman's head with its tongue cut out was found placed upon a stake in the middle of this lawn. *Cheating Whore* was carved into its forehead..."

My eyes widen. And, of course, I gasp and my hand flies to my mouth as I stand in the middle of the floor and feign shock.

"Reporting live from Channel 2 News...a quiet Maplewood community is shaken to its core and in shock at a decapitated woman's head found placed upon a stake in the middle of this family's front lawn early this morning. The young woman, who had been reported missing a little over two weeks ago, was identified by one of the grandsons of the woman who lives at the residence where the decapitated head was found. Investigators at the scene..."

I choke back an Oscar-worthy sob, clutching my chest as I collapse into Lamar's arms.

My cell and office line rings nonstop with an outpouring of condolences, and shock over the news of Felecia's head up on a stake. Calls from my cousins Paris, Porsha and Persia, followed by their aunts Fanny, Lucky and Penny, then their mother, Priscilla; followed by Bianca and Garrett.

Now I'm on the phone with Mona, who's asking what everyone else has asked, "Where's the rest of her body?"

"In an urn," I want to say. But I don't. My lips are sealed. Lamar and Mel are the only two who know that the rest of her body was cremated. That her ashes are kept locked in a safety deposit bank, waiting to be served up at the right moment.

"How you holding up, Pasha?" Mona asks, sounding genuinely concerned. I tell her I'm doing the best I can. "What happened to her is horrible. It's on every news channel nonstop. I don't understand who in their right mind would do something like that. I only hope she wasn't alive when whoever did that to her. MyGod! How barbaric, cutting off her head and carving *Cheating Whore* into her forehead like that? And then"—she blows out a breath— "to put her head up on my grandmother's lawn like that. Who the..." Her voice trails off as if a light bulb has gone off in her head. "Pasha?" Her voice is above a whisper. "Did you...? Oh, God, no. Please tell me..."

"Ohmygod, no," I lie, glancing up at the television in my office. I glance up at the television. Another newscaster is reporting on the bitch's head being found. How her front teeth were knocked out and all the rest of her teeth either yanked or twisted out of her mouth. Felecia's decapitated head is the hot topic for every newsroom today, so much so, that no real extensive coverage is being given on the two suspected drug dens burned down to the ground last night—well, early this morning, and how all the niggas in each spot were found outside naked with their hands and feet tied together and drugs and stolen guns in their laps.

There were only two bodies. And that's because they popped off their weapons first, trying to protect their beloved drug king's work. They fought for the cause, and are now dead for the cause.

"I hate the bitch for what she did to me," I say, reaching for the TV remote and shutting it off. I've had enough. "But I'm no monster, Mona. I can't believe you'd even think I'd..."

She quickly apologizes. "I know, girl. Even I know you're not capable of being *that* vicious. There's no way you could ever do some gory shit like that. It's just that, well...whoever did this knew her. And it was very personal for them, like they wanted to send a message."

"Well, sounds like I'm not the only one she crossed."

"Stax is really messed up behind it."

"Yeah, I bet," I say, rolling my eyes up in my head. Stax is the one who first saw the head in his grandmother's yard when he pulled up into her driveway five o'clock this morning after fucking me all through the night.

"And now no one seems to be able to get in touch with Jasper. Stax and Sparks have been calling him all morning."

I smirk. *And they won't be getting in touch with his ass until I'm done with him.* Lamar's *peoples* were able to snatch his ass up last night an hour before his drug spots went up in flames. I guess he called himself slipping out for some sidepiece pussy in the middle of the night without any of his goons and got got before he could get his dick wet.

"Mmmph. I haven't talked to him; not since the day he shot up my security staff and kicked in the doors to my house. And I bet you anything that nigga was behind having my home burned down." I throw that lie in for good measure. She knows how ruthless the nigga is, so it isn't inconceivable for him to have done it.

I eye Lamar as he walks into my office carrying a box of supplies. I reach into my desk drawer and hand him the key to the closet. He stacks the supplies in the closet for me, then shuts the door and relocks it.

"No one still has heard from Jasper. Sparks said he was trying to reach him late last night and he still hasn't gotten back to him."

"Mmmph. Not my concern," I say dismissively. "Whatever happens to him, he brought on himself."

"This is such a fucking nightmare, Pasha. Mygod! When will this shit end?"

"I guess it'll be over when the last hand is dealt." Lamar hands me the key. I gesture for him to have a seat. "You know Karma plays no games. When it's time to go around, it hits hard. And it's always when you least expect it."

"I know," she states bleakly. "And, sadly, they all deserve to get what they get. I just wish that whoever did that shit to her wouldn't have put her up on my grandmother's lawn like that. I mean, how the fuck disrespectful was that?"

"Well, like you said, whoever did it was obviously trying to send a message to someone. Sounds like it was meant for Jasper's ass if you ask me."

"I guess. But it still doesn't make any sense."

"Nothing that bitch did made sense. I found out she was the one who hired niggas to smash out my windshield and the salon's front window."

"*Whaaaaat?!*" she shrieks. "You have *got*. To. Be. Kidding me."

"Mmmph. I wish." I fill her in on everything else that bitch did, leaving out—of course, all the details of where and how I got the information.

"Oh, Pasha, that bitch was real dirty."

"*Exactly*. And that's why her damn head was found up on a damn stick for all to see just how fucking messy her ass was." We talk several minutes more, then end the call.

Greta calls a few seconds later to express her condolences and shock as well. I fill her in, then let her know I'll be flying out over the weekend. She wants to know if I'd rather her fly back with Jaylen instead, particularly if Felecia's service is this weekend. I tell her absolutely not. I don't tell her how I'll begrudgingly pay my respects for appearance's sake, but my son isn't coming anywhere near Jersey or Felecia's fucking casket. Besides, as far as I'm concerned, as long as Jasper is still breathing, my son is still in harm's way. And I won't risk it—for anyone.

"Okay, well keep me posted," Greta says. "If you need me to do anything, let me know. You know I'm here for you."

"I know." A few more words are said, then I ask her to put Jaylen on. The minute he hears my voice, he starts getting excited, talking a mile a minute. I close my eyes, pinching back tears. I miss my son so much. I tell him how much I love and miss him at least six times before finally ending the call while doing everything in my power to keep from breaking down. Hanging up, ending our FaceTime moments, and leaving him in L.A. are always hard. And the longer he's away from me, the more difficult it's becoming.

Each call after that becomes increasingly more difficult to keep up the façade of being the grieving cousin/sister when I really don't give a fuck about the bitch being dead. When I'm the one responsible for the bitch's head being found up on that spike in the first place.

I did that shit. Hacked off her head and took a carpet knife and carved into her forehead. That bitch is lucky after what I heard from that nigga Vernon that I didn't douse her fucking head with gasoline, then toss a match up on her scandalous ass.

Still, out of the calls this morning, all the pretending I'm doing, the hardest conversation I've had to have is with Nana. Over and over she kept saying how I got my wish. "You wished my gran'baby dead. God have mercy on your soul."

"No, Nana," I countered before I got the dial tone in my ear. "May God have mercy on *hers.*"

I grab my neck. Tension courses all through my body, wrapping itself tightly around my neck, like a noose. Nana's hurting, rightfully so. She has to bury a bitch she raised and loved as if she were her own child. And all she has to put Felecia to rest is…her head.

"So what now?" Lamar wants to know, leaning forward in his seat. I get up and walk around my desk, closing the door shut, then walking back over and leaning up against my desk, folding my arms.

I take a deep breath. "Is my package all secured?" I ask, referring to Jasper. He tells me it is. "And what about the cum dump from the night before?"

He laughs. "Oh, them niggas still poppin' off in that nigga's mouth."

"Good. And the pictures?"

"No doubt. Got his face and mouth flooded wit' nut."

"That'll teach his ass. I want his asshole filled with the Gorilla glue, then when it dries, toss him the dumpster with the rest of the trash."

"Daaaaaayumn." He smirks, rubbing his chin and nodding his head.

A brow arches. "What?"

He shakes his head. "Nah, nah. I'm sayin'...you're more ruthless than I thought."

I shrug. "It's definitely not what I aspired to be."

"But it's in you, Pasha. My peoples really wants to holla at you 'bout that proposition I came at you wit. You give it any more thought?"

I let out a nervous laugh. "What, to be a hired killer?" I shake my head, covering my face, then looking back at him. "Ohgod, no. I'm not interested in being on anyone else's payroll except my own. What I'm doing, what I've had to do, is personal. But once this shit is over, I'm done. So tell your *peoples* I said no thanks."

He smiles. But doesn't say anything. I tell him I need to go to Nana's. That I'm not being chauffeured or going over there with a bodyguard at my side. He gives me a worried look. Tries to advise me against it. But my mind is made up.

He opens his mouth to say something, but is stopped by my ringing cell. I reach for it, glancing at the screen. It's Stax. *I can't. Not now.* I take a deep breath, pressing IGNORE.

Jasper's face pops into my head and I get a thought. I want that nigga JT's frozen dick from Booty. *But how? I'm not speaking to the bitch.*

Lamar looks at him. "What's on your mind?" I share my thought with him. "Oh, daaaaaayumn. That's some real cold shit." He laughs. "No pun intended. I know y'all rocked it out in here a couple'a days ago, but you should call her."

I shake my head. Tell him I have no interest in dealing with her. But that it still doesn't mean I don't want that nigga's dick.

He nods, a sly smile easing over his lips. "There's always more than one way to get what you want. If askin' doesn't work, takin' it always does. Where she got that shit?"

My eyes widen with mischief as I tell him. In her deep freezer, in a freezer Ziploc bag, placed inside a Tupperware bowl with a red lid, under slabs of ribs and family packs of chicken.

Thirty-Four

You want to keep a secret, learn to keep your mouth shut...

"Umm, Pasha," Kendra says when she buzzes me through the intercom. "There are detectives here to speak with you."

Lamar and I look at one another. "What the fuck?" I mouth to him. "Okay, can you send them to my office?"

Lamar stands. "You aiight?"

I nod. "Why wouldn't I be?" I tilt my head. "I've done nothing wrong."

He grins. "You need me to hang around?" I shake my head. Tell him it isn't necessary. "Aiight. I'm going to make sure those packages are being handled with care. I'll be back in an hour or so."

He opens the door as the two detectives approach. I grab a handful of tissue from a box on the desk, gesturing them in while summoning up another flood of tears from somewhere deep.

"Mrs. Tyler?" a deep voice belonging to a short, robust white man with a receding hairline says. I nod, dabbing the corner of my eyes with tissue as Lamar shuts the door behind him. I glance at the wet stain in the center of his navy blue tie. "I'm Detective Wertzul." I blink up at him as he smoothly flashes his badge. "And this is Detective Howardson," he adds, gesturing with his hand to a tall, light-skinned man sporting a navy blue suit, white dress shirt and blue pinstriped tie. I take in his smoothly shaven bald head and neatly trimmed goatee wrapped around big, juicy red lips, then down at his long loafer-clad feet, before finally locking on to his gaze.

"Yes," I say with a disarming smile. "How can I help you gentlemen?"

Detective Wertzul clears his throat. "We'd like to talk to you about the murder of Felecia Allen. As you are aware, her head was found decapitated early this morning."

I tilt my head. "Okay. What does that have to do with me?"

"Mind if we have seat?" Detective Wertzul asks while his partner eyes me all crazy like. Whether part intimidation or part pissed with the world, it's not going to work. Not on me. If this skinny nigga was looking to shake me or get me to loosen my lips with his eyeballing, he had better try again.

I glance at my watch. "I have somewhere to be, so you'll need to make this quick," I say, ignoring the question. "Now what's this about?"

"Mrs. Tyler," the skinny, eyeballing fucker interjects, pulling out a notepad and pen. "When's the last time you spoke to the victim, Miss Allen?"

"Like three weeks ago." I keep my eyes locked on his penetrating gaze. *Nigga, you aren't about to work me!* "Why?"

"Do you mind telling us what the two of you talked about?" Skinny Fuck wants to know. I tell him the phone call was brief. That she called wanting to meet with me. That the plan was for her to come here that Sunday evening at nine.

"And did she ever make it here?" Detective Wertzul asks. I tell him. Tell him I waited around until after ten on her to show up. That I called her leaving a scathing message on her cell for being inconsiderate when she hadn't called to say she wasn't going to be here. I am tempted to offer to allow them to review the tapes on that day, but decide against it. *Fuck 'em. They don't have shit on me, so let them have their little goose chase.*

Skinny Fuck stares into me, then says, "We're aware that you and the victim worked together…"

"No, she *worked* for me. And before you ask, I fired her because she was bad-mouthing me to clients behind my back." Then he has the audacity to ask if I fired her before or after I learned she was having *an affair* with Jasper. I laugh. "If that's what you want to call it. She was sucking his dick and swallowing his nut while he was incarcerated and smiling in my face."

The Skinny Fuck shifts his weight on his feet, looking over at his partner, then snidely says, "The ultimate treachery."

A hand goes up on my hip. "And the perfect recipe for murder," I say sarcastically, *"if* I gave a damn about her *fucking* my soon-to-be ex-husband. Now, unless I'm a suspect in your little investigation, I think it's time the two of you get the hell out of my office." My lips quiver. "How dare you"—I point a finger at the both of them—"come up in here and insinuate or interrogate me as if I had something to do with what happened to my cousin. She was like a sister to me."

On cue, I choke back a sob.

"We've had our disagreements and, yes, we've fought over the years. And, *yes*, that bitch hurt me, okay? It's no secret. I slapped her face and told her to get the fuck out of my salon. And I would have beaten her ass if I felt it necessary. But it wasn't. I fired her instead."

"Mrs. Tyler," Detective Wertzul quickly says apologetically, "we didn't mean to upset you. We're only doing our job, trying to cover all of our bases, and look into every lead possible, so that we can find whomever is responsible for the victim's murder."

I allow tears to fall unchecked. "Then how about you *follow* the yellow-brick road and let it *lead* you to her fiancé, Andre. It wasn't the first time she cheated on him."

I blow my nose, then grab more tissue and wipe my face. They both look at each other, then at me. Skinny Fuck keeps staring at me. "Your husband went to prison for drug dealing, isn't that right?"

I blink. My temper kicks up a notch. "What does that have to do with what the fuck happened to my cousin having her head chopped off?"

"It's just ironic that *your* cousin's decapitated head with the words *cheating whore* carved into her forehead winds up perched up on a stake on the lawn of *your* husband's grandmother's home."

I shrug. "Must be coincidence. Like I said, *detectives*, let the road lead you to her fiancé." I walk toward the door, swinging it open. "Now if you gentlemen don't mind, I'll see the two of you out."

Detective Wertzul makes a feeble attempt to smooth things over. "We appreciate your time. And, again, I apologize for any undue stress our visit might have caused you."

"Well, it's caused me a great deal of stress. I have a husband who I have a restraining order against, but refuses to sign divorce papers. Then last week, three of my guards were murdered on my property, then less than twenty-four hours later, I lose almost everything I owned, including my home, to an electrical fire." I start sobbing. "And n-n-now…a week later, my cousin is dead. And her head is cut off. And you insensitive bastards come up in here grilling *me*, like I'm guilty of something."

Now all of sudden Mr. Skinny Fuck wants to change up. "Mrs. Tyler, forgive me. I apologize if I've offended you in any way. I'm sure this is a very difficult time for you and your family. We'll see ourselves out." He extends his hand. I give him a dirty look, dismissing it. "Okay, then. We'll be in touch."

I ignore him, dabbing at my eyes as we walk out into the salon area. I'm relieved it isn't packed in here today. And given the circumstances, I'd cancelled all of my clients earlier. There are only six clients under the dryers and three clients in stylists' chairs. Up in the mani-pedi loft I spot four women sitting in massage chairs getting pedicures.

I walk the two plainclothes detectives up to the front, walking around the counter. Detective Wetzul reaches into his suit jacket pulling out a business card. "Here's my card if you hear anything." He lays it on the counter. I eye his partner. His hand is on the doorknob, but he's facing me, staring.

I spot Lamar as he pulls up in front of the salon. Mr. Skinny Fuck turns the knob and pulls open the door, glances at me once last time, then steps out. I eye him as he stands in front of the salon's window. Lamar steps out of his truck and two black Yukons with tinted windows roll by as he heads up toward the door.

It all flashes in front of my eyes in slow motion. Then everything stops. The snapshots in my head become freeze-framed. It's happening. Unfolding right before my eyes. I see Lamar suddenly spin around, reaching for his weapon, but he isn't fast enough. He drops. Before I can open my mouth, bullets are flying out of the front and back windows of both SUVs.

I see the bullets coming. Aimed at Lamar. Aimed at the salon's window. None are meant for Mr. Skinny Fuck with the shitty attitude in the cheap suit. Everything speeds up as I quickly scramble from around the counter, chest pounding, dropping to the floor as glass explodes everywhere into tiny pieces. Mr. Skinny Fuck's entire head is burst off his shoulders, his brain and skull now bloody fragments among shards of bulletproof glass that isn't so bulletproofed for an AK-47.

All I hear are my screams echoing around in my head as Mel

throws himself on top of me, before rolling over and scooping me up into his arms. It is then that my heart sinks. And the only thing I am thinking—as the lone white detective scrambles outside with his weapon drawn while yelling for everyone inside the salon to stay back—is, *"Ohgod, please don't let Lamar be dead!"*

Thirty-Five

Settling scores doesn't always end in death…

Five days later, with Legend's tortured body being found, Felecia's decapitated head spiked up on Jasper's grandmother's lawn, and Vernon being found late Tuesday night in Weequahic Park blindfolded, naked, and gagged with a locked anal plug in his ass filled with Gorilla glue—all within the same week of each other, the newspapers and newscasters have been having a field day speculating a possible connection between the trio while investigators desperately continue to search for leads.

So far, there are none.

And Mr. Vernon Lewis aka MydickneedsUrtongue2—who is laid up in a hospital bed after needing emergency surgery and the only breathing victim—is keeping his cum-glazed lips sealed about what truly happened to him during the two days he was MIA in fear of the photos and video of him having six niggas nutting in his mouth and face from being leaked.

So word is he's told police and everyone else who's asked about his ordeal that he stayed blindfolded and never saw who buttonholed him. All lies, of course. But, as long as that's his story and he's sticking with it, he doesn't ever have to worry about having his dick sliced off or being outed as the down-low nigga that he really is.

"Pasha, I'm so so sorry to hear about what happened to Felecia."

I blink out of my thoughts and up into the face of Shuwanda. "I *know* how close the two of you once were. It's a shame how you turned your back on her."

I stand up, giving her a tight smile, sweeping my bang over my forehead. I remove my shades and glance around the church. "No, bitch," I hiss in her ear, looking to see who's within earshot. "What you *know* is, how messy she was. And what's a shame is your ugly face and pathetic existence. Now get the fuck out of my face. Before I tear your ass up in here."

Her eyes snap open wide, shocked. But before she can open her mouth to say something sideways, she is being gently ushered out of the church by my cousin Penny's twenty-one-year-old son who's tall, solid and built like a linebacker.

How dare that two-faced bitch come over to me!

"You good, cuz?" one of his other brothers asks walking over to me. I nod. He wraps his arm around me. "When you comin' out to Arizona, so I can show you off to all my boys?"

I tell him when all of his boys are no longer in college or living at home with their parents. He grins, teasing me about probably not being able to handle a young stud. I shake my head, waving him on. His two older brothers, ages twenty-six and twenty-eight, come up and give me a hug and a kiss before dragging him off to go sit in the back of the church—where I'd rather be.

I glance at my timepiece, sighing. I want this day over with. Sitting here, in this church, forced to look at the closed mahogany casket that contains Felecia's tooth-and-tongue-less head, while listening to Nana wail one minute, then sing praises of how wonderful her darling *gran'baby* was, is making my insides turn.

That whore was a dirty bitch.

I was loyal to her and she backstabbed me. But I'm at peace with it now. The snake is gone. Its head cut off. Still, I'm annoyed for having to close the shop on a moneymaking Saturday just so salon staff can come pay their respects, if they want to. Even in death, this bitch is costing me time and money.

Andre leans in and kisses me on the cheek. I glance up at him. His handsome cocoa-brown face is etched in pain. His eyes are swollen and red. I reach for his hand and squeeze. "She's really gone, Pasha. Felecia. She's r-r-really gone." His lips quiver. I can see him straining to keep it all together. I stand and give him a hug. It's the least I can do.

He clings to me a little longer than I think necessary and I pull back. "You know she really loved you, Pasha," he says, his eyes brimming with tears. "She never stopped loving you."

I give him a blank stare. Then decide to give him another hug. "Andre," I say in his ear real low, "you're a good, hard-working man. Felecia didn't deserve you. I understand you're grieving. But that bitch didn't give a damn about anyone except herself. So you hold on to whatever lies you need to to help you get through your loss."

I sit back in my seat, then glance around the massive church, before casting my eyes over at the sixteen-by-twenty-four photo of Felecia propped up on a gold easel. Nana is sitting in the first pew with her nieces Fanny, Lucky, Penny, and Priscilla. And, of course, Andre, who is beside himself with grief is sitting up there with them.

Of course the hushed whispers and questioning glances from relatives as to why I'm not sitting up front beside Nana swirl around the church. But I don't give a damn. I'm not serving up sympathy for Nana toward a bitch that stabbed me in the back, and fucked my damn man. So sitting directly behind her is good enough.

I sigh.

"Oh, there, she is," I hear someone say. I smell Mona's favorite perfume, Signorina, before she even leans in and her lips brush my cheek. She wraps an arm around me, pulling me into her. "Hey, girl. How you holding up?" I tell her I'm fine. She rubs my back. I thank her for coming.

Stax is right behind her. I glance at him, giving him a weak smile, thanking him for being here. He looks stressed. When Mona steps back, he leans in and kisses me softly on the cheek. Then whispers into my ear, "Have you talked to Jasper?"

Truth is, even though Jasper was snatched up early Monday morning, I haven't seen him since court. Right at this very moment, he's down in a basement blindfolded and tied to a chair, his hands bound behind his back...the same way he had me. The only difference is no one is forcing his dick into his mouth. But they are going upside his head. And he knows who's behind it. Me.

I've made it no secret. Unlike him, I want him to know that I'm coming for him. That I'm going to serve his ass. And I want him on edge—waiting.

I shake my head. "No. Why?"

"No one's seen or heard from him in five days."

I shrug, turning to him, my face void of expression. "Not my problem."

He eyes me, furrowing his brow. "I'ma holla at you later, aiight? We need to talk."

I nod. He acknowledges Paris, Porsha, and Persia who are sitting in the same pew with me. Stax squeezes my shoulder, and I'm instantly flooded with unwanted heat. I shift in my seat, eyeing him as he follows Mona over to the other side of the church, taking a seat.

I take a deep breath.

Mygod, all he did was touch my shoulder and my pussy is churning. This is so not good.

Lamar leans up in my ear, his hand on my shoulder. "You cool?"

I nod, closing my eyes. I reach for his hand, squeezing it. He's not even supposed to be here. He's supposed to still be in the hospital recuperating, but he insisted on being here with me. I thought he was dead the day of the shooting. But when the doctor came out of surgery and assured me that he was alive and had only suffered a bullet in the back of his right thigh and shoulder, I broke down in tears. Real tears. Mel had to console me. Lamar's taken three bullets on account of me.

Although the first one grazed his shoulder, he still chooses to put his life on the line for me. And all I keep hearing him saying is, "It comes with the territory. I'd take a bullet or two, for you any day…"

Still in all, the shooting on Monday turned out to be a bigger blessing than I'd imagined. And after almost two hours down at the precinct giving my statement, disclosing the number of events leading up to my obtaining an order of protection and the murders on my property while sobbing like a nutcase, I walked up out of there with Jasper Tyler being a "person of great interest."

I glance over at Mel who smiles at me, then gives me a sly, conspiratorial wink. Thanks to him, Jasper's fresh fingerprints are now the only prints on one of the guns that were used to shoot up my salon Monday. With his gloved hand, Mel placed the weapon into Jasper's limp hand, closing it around the weapon while he was drugged up.

Having my salon shot up was part of a plan to set up Jasper. *Not* killing anyone; particularly a damn cop. How was I supposed to know they were coming to the salon that day? But they did. And they stayed longer than they should have, even after I tried rushing them along. So an asshole detective's head got blown off instead. In the end, his untimely murder is going to help me in ensuring Jasper's demise. And his fingerprints are all over the gun that pulled the trigger.

At least the detective's death isn't going to be in vain.

Yes, I'm framing his ass for murder, as a backup plan. I'm covering all of my bases. If Jasper somehow gets out of this without a bullet in his head, he'll crawl out, instead, with a warrant for his arrest. They'll put his ass under the prison. Lucky for him, Jersey no longer has the death penalty. Mmmph. What a sinful shame.

I glance back at Mel again. I can't help but smile. He's another one loyal to the bone. Willing to do whatever he has to in order to keep me safe *and* satisfied. It's amazing what a good dick suck and fifty grand—of Jasper's money—for a job well done can get you. I still wonder if he and Lamar have discussed with the other how I've handled their dicks down in my throat. Not that it matters. Neither of them are my man.

Pasha gasps, squeezing my knee. "Oh, God, no."

"What?" I say, looking over at her, then in the direction of her gaze.

I cringe. *This bitch!*

It's Booty laid out from head to toe. Her body is wrapped in a form-fitting, black designer dress with the back cut out, black sheer stockings cover her legs, and six-inch, black Louboutins are on her feet. She has on a pair of black shades and a wide, black, floppy hat is on her head. In the crook of her arm hangs a black Hermès in calfskin leather.

"Who in the world comes to a funeral dressed like that with their back cut out practically down to their tailbone?" Paris whispers, leaning into me.

I have to give it to her, the bitch is slaying the wears. Still, she's way overdressed and over-the-top with it, but it's so her. She's wearing, from my modest guesstimation, well over ten thousand dollars' worth of high-end fashion, and her backward ass would rather trick her money up in malls and boutiques instead of owning her own home.

I bite the inside of my bottom lip, hard, practically breaking skin to keep from laughing at the absurdity. I can hear her saying something like, "Don't do me, sugah-boo. I came here to steal the show, goddammit!"

I shake my head.

Standing beside her wearing a cute, little, black one-piece is a pretty, dark-chocolate teenaged girl. She favors Booty, but has a flat-ass and big, bouncy titties.

"See, Day'Asia," Booty says with no regard for filtering what comes out of her mouth, "this the dirty ho I was tellin' you 'bout. Ole Miss Messy FeFe. The one I wanted you, Clitina and Candy to jump up on for me. But looks like somebody else done got to the ole Bobblehead, first. Mmmph."

For the love of God!

The air around me is practically sucked out of the room as all eyes within earshot of what she said snap over in her direction.

My cell vibrates. It's Mona texting me. WHAT IS THAT CRAZY BITCH DOING HERE?

I shift in my seat, letting out a sigh of relief when Cassandra Simms makes a beeline around the other side of the pews where Stax and Mona are. I look over at her and shrug, catching Stax staring at me. I hold his intense gaze for a few minutes, then quicky break away when my phone vibrates, again. It's Lamar. U WANT THAT FREEZER SITUATION HANDLED?

I nod my answer as the pastor finally enters the pulpit and begins his eulogy. I drift in and out of most of the long, drawn-out encomium on the life of a shady bitch gone too soon. Whatever. Felecia is right where she should be. In a box. Out of her misery. And the only thing on my mind now is finally handling Jasper, so that I can close this chapter of my life and move on.

I still have no idea who the *Calm One* is since no one seems willing or able to tell me. And I still don't know for certain if Desmond was also down with Jasper and the rest of those niggas or not. And at this point, I don't care. That nigga Legend's newstory got the message out loud and clear. And if it hasn't, after I'm done with Jasper, it'll be clearer.

I look over at Paris. She smiles at me, grabbing my hand. I squeeze it. Then glance over my shoulder at Bianca and Garrett. Then Mona. She catches my eye and gives me a wry smile. She knows. It's in her eyes. I smile back. Stax's gaze is locked on me, again. I shift my eyes before he sees more than he should.

Before I allow him into that part of me more than he already is.

I lean my head on Paris' shoulder and close my eyes as the soloist takes the mic and belts out, "Father Can You Hear Me."

Thirty-Six

Where there is smoke, there's always a blazing fire…

"Ooooh, you dirty, stink bitch," I hear in back of me as my six-inch stilettos click against the concrete toward the waiting Range Rover. I toss my hair and continue stepping as if I don't hear her. "Oh no, Miss Pasha, girl. Don't do me. Don't have me jump on ya goddamn back out here on church grounds. And you know I'll do it. I know ya messy ass hear me. Don't take me there, Miss Pasha, girl. You know I don't do messy."

I take a deep breath, stopping dead in my tracks and turning to face her. If I weren't pressed for time and still annoyed with her ass, I'd laugh. I shift my Balenciaga handbag from one hand to the other, letting its straps hang in the crook of my arm.

"How can I help you, Cassandra?" Yes, I'm serving her attitude. I'm still not over her for putting her damn hands on me. "I don't have time for your messy ass today."

"Now, you wait one hot goddamn minute, Miss Pasha, girl. Don't do." She glances over at her daughter and tells her to go sit in her truck, handing her the keys.

Her daughter rolls her eyes, sucking her teeth. "I'm ready to go, now. This place gives me the creeps."

Booty gives her a dirty look. "Well, maybe if ya ass wasn't creepin' out in the streets bobbin' for dingaling all the time, you wouldn't be all creeped out 'bout bein' at a church. Now I'm tryna keep it classy out here, Day'Asia. Don't muthafuckin' press me to get messy. And you know I don't do messy. Now go on 'n' take ya ass to the truck. I'ma take you shoppin' when I'm done wit' my business wit' Miss Pasha."

"I'm out here tryna keep it classy, comin' to you as the bigger woman but you already tryna take me to the other side. And all I'm tryna do is share my condolences."

I toss my bang. "Then send me a card." I turn on my heel for the SUV when what she says next stops me dead in my tracks.

"What ya ole cum-lovin' ass do after you sliced that nigga's balls out, huh? Lick 'em, then eat 'em?"

I glance around the to see who else might overhear this bitch recklessly flapping her jaws. "Excuse *you*?"

She pulls her shades down to the bridge of her nose, eyeing me. There's still a bruise around her right eye where I punched her. "I don't know how you did it, Miss Pasha, girl. But I know ya sneaky ass is the one who had a hand in doin' that nigga Legend in. And I *know* you the one who made Miss Messy FeFe a permanent Bobblehead. And ya sneaky ass doin' it all wit'out me when I'm the bitch who got shit poppin'. Mmmph. You'se a real dirty bitch. You knew I wanted me a lil' taste of the action. But, mmmph. Motherfuck you, nigga-boo. It'll be real messy if some lil' birdie chirps in the wrong ears, now wouldn't it?"

I cock my head to the side, stepping closer to her. "Bitch, know this. I don't know what you're talkin' about. But I don't take kindly to threats. So think what you want. But don't *you* ever forget that I *know* you're the one who bodied JT, and *your* son Darius and his boy, Beetle, are the ones who disposed of the body, then dumped his car."

She blinks.

I glare at her, crossing my arms. "Yeah, sweetie. I did my homework, so don't *you* try to do me." It was actually Mel who told me about JT's car being brought to a scrap yard in Newark; the one his *peoples* owns. Apparently, the nigga Beetle is the one who drove it there. My guess, while Booty's son dumped JT's body somewhere.

I glance over her shoulder and spot Stax and Mona walking out of the church.

I decide to stir the hornet's nest. I step in a little closer. "And I *know* where *Darius* dumped the body *and* the gun used to finish him off, so let your little birdies chirp if you want." It's a bluff. Well, about knowing where the body and weapon is. Still, she doesn't know that. And judging by the way she's standing here looking at me, she believes the lie. Dropping the bait is one thing. Now waiting for the sharks to bite is another. Eventually, Darius will lead me to where that body is. When he does, I'll be there to reel him in.

"Wait one goddamn minute, Miss Pasha, girl. You ain't about to finger-fuck me or…"

"And I *want* that nigga's dick," I say, cutting into her sentence. "*Today.*"

"Nigga-boo, *boom-boom*, goddammit!" she hisses, swinging her bag from one hand to the other. "You ain't gettin' shit. You threaten me, then *think* I'ma just give you somethin'. Booga-coon, *boom!* What, you done sucked up all the live niggas' dicks out here that ya desperate ass gotta take to suckin' a dead nigga's frozen dick now?"

"You fuckin' bitch," I jeer. "You're the one keeping the shit for a souvenir, so what does that say about you? I want. His. Dick, Booty."

She smirks, planting a hand up on her hip. "Oh, no, sugah-boo.

I ain't givin' you shit. You want that dingaling. It's gonna cost you, sugah-boo. You gonna pay me for all my pain 'n' goddamn suf-ferin' 'n' for havin' me go almost a whole week wit'out gettin' my hair 'n' nails did. And you ain't ever s'posed to let personal shit get in the way of business. Real bitches fight, tear each other up, then go out 'n' get they drink on. But, noo. You wanna be an ole messy bitch, Miss Pasha, girl. So you ain't gettin' a goddamn thang from me 'til you do me right, goddammit."

I smirk, glancing at my watch, then over her shoulder. "Suit yourself. Look, I have somewhere to be. But you might want to get your daughter home before she ends up missing with a *dick* in her mouth."

"Say what?" She glances over her shoulder at Day'Asia standing over by a black Benz all grins and giggles talking to Fanny's twenty-two-year-old son who's clearly way too old for her hot ass. But I can tell his hormones and her big, juicy titties are getting the best of him. "Day'Asia!" she snaps, stamping her heel into the concrete. "Day'Asia!"

"Whaaat?!"

"Bitch, don't you *whaaat* me! I tol' you to take ya black ass to the truck! Not be out here tryna get you no goddamn dingaling. Now don't have me get all ghetto 'n' ugly out here on church property! Get yo' stank-ass in that damn truck 'n' wait for me to get there, like I tol' you to do! You know I'm grievin' 'n' you got me out here ready to turn up the gas on yo' ass. NOW get ya ass in that goddamn truck, Day'Asia! You muthafuckin' kids stay tryna do me. I can't even have a goddamn moment 'n' come out to a damn funeral to grieve. And I tol' you…"

I don't stand around for this mess. By the time she finishes her tirade and turns back to me, I'm already at the truck, sliding into the backseat with Mel shutting the door. He hops into the driver's seat and drives off. The last thing I see is Booty stepping out of her heels and storming over toward her daughter.

I shake my head, sighing. "Lamar, were your *peoples* able to handle that?"

"No doubt. It'll be at the spot when you get there tonight."

I pull out my phone, then compose a text. U MIGHT WANT 2 CHECK UR FREEZER WHEN U GET HOME.

These bitches gonna learn today. Don't fuck with me.

I press SEND just as an incoming call rings in. It's Stax. "Hey."

"I need to see you. Now." I tell him no. "*No?* Nah, man. I'm not tryna hear that, Pash. We need to talk." I tell him I can't. Not now. Maybe later. "I'm not tryna hear that, either. You're not 'bout to play me to the back, like some crab, Pash. Make time for me."

I blink. He isn't asking me. He's telling me. And the nigga's tone strikes a match to my clit, lighting a slow flame.

Damn him!

I press my thighs together, knowing if he comes to the hotel, we're going to end up fucking each other down into the springs. I can't let him and his good dick or the sweet throb in my wet pussy distract me.

"Pash, don't deny me, ma. You owe me this."

I swallow back the memory, the taste, of him inside of me, and give in.

"But not at my hotel," I quickly say, shifting in my seat, feeling heat shoot up my spine. "I'll meet you at Lincoln Park. We can walk and talk there."

"Cool. I'll be there in twenty minutes."

I smirk, shutting my phone off. I lean up in my seat and tap Mel on the shoulder, letting him know there's a change in plans. I scoot back, laying my head back against the headrest, trying like hell to figure out when shit changed with me. And Stax. When did he get into my head and start chipping away at my thoughts? Was it after the second, or third, or fourth time I sucked his nut down into my mouth? Or did it happen right after he slid his dick into my pussy?

No. It happened the first time I *really* looked into his eyes. And saw him.

And me.

Ohgod, no! Stax's purpose in my life has been served. Fucking him was more so for revenge than for pumping him for any more than what he'd already told me. So then why is my pussy smoking hot thinking about him?

I shake the answer out of my head. Bottom line, I can't ever be left alone with him again.

Thirty-Seven

Hidden desires can sometimes cloud and conceal
one's true intentions...

"Keep shit a hunnid, Pash. You know where Jasper is, don't you?"

I look away from him, closing my eyes. My heart tells me I can trust Stax, which makes me want to give him the truth. But my head is telling me some other shit; that his loyalty is to Jasper. Good dick or not, blood is always thicker than water. No matter what I think I see every time he looks at me, it'll never change shit.

He knew what Jasper planned to do to me and did nothing.

My silence is his invitation to continue.

"Pash, look at me, ma." I don't. "I know what my fam put you through really fucked you up. And, word is bond, Pash. I'm fucked up over it, too. You already know that. I know he hurt you. And I know I hurt you, too, for letting him hurt you like that. That shit still fucks wit' me, Pash."

"You already said all this," I say, blinking back tears. I still don't look at him when I say this. I can't. "I *meant* what I said, Stax, when I said I'm trying to keep you safe."

He sighs. "You don't have to worry 'bout me, Pash. I'm protected even when it looks like I'm not." He blows out another breath. "Do what you gotta do, Pash, aiight. I already know what it is. And I'm not tryna take that from you. So handle your business. But I want his body when you're done."

Now I am looking at him. I tilt my head. "Who said *anything* about a body?"

"C'mon, Pash. Who you think you talkin' to, ma? I see where this is goin'. First, my fam JT goes missin'."

I give him an incredulous look. "*JT?* I didn't have anything to do with that. I didn't even know he was involved in what happened to me until *after* he went missing."

His eyes stay locked on mine as if he's trying to catch any indication of deceit. There is none. He shakes his head, sighing. "This shit is crazy. Them retarded muhfuckas stay wildin' 'n' doin' dumb shit. And I'm always the one cleanin' they shit up. Ain't no tellin' where that nigga is rottin'. So, you didn't have shit to do wit' JT's situation. But that nigga Legend, tortured then bodied. Felecia's head chopped off. Now Jasper's missin'. You see how this is all startin' to look?"

"Yeah, like they fucked over the *wrong* bitch."

He smiles at me, shaking his head. "I used to tease that nigga Jasper when he'd be on his bullshit wit' you. I'd be like, 'Yo, you know she's the Boogey Man's daughter, so you better quit sleepin' on her before you find ya ass hangin' upside down somewhere. That gutter grit is in her blood.' I kept warnin' his ass. Mmmph. Nigga ain't wanna believe me, though. Now look." I blink. "What, you ain't think I knew who ya pops was? Anyone in the game knows who the infamous Ralphie Allen is. Ya pops was a real beast in these streets, Pash." I nod knowingly. The man was treacherous if crossed. And wouldn't think twice about tossing gasoline up on someone, then setting them on fire.

"Real shit, Pash…" He pauses, shaking his head. "You're dangerous as fuck, ma. And I knew if you got pushed far enough that same beast would be awakened in you." He rubs his hands over his waves, then covers his face, before looking back at me. "I done got myself caught up in some shit wit' you, Pash. Fuck. I gotta stay away from you, man. And I'm tryin', Pash, real shit. But it's like..." He shakes his head. "You got this hold on me or some shit. I let you get all up in my head."

I shift my eyes from his. I look down at the ground, over at the couple walking their dog, over toward the street...anywhere except at him.

"On my life, Pash, I meant e'ery word I said when I tol' you I'll never let Jasp hurt you, again. I put that on e'erything I love. Jasper's my blood, Pash. But the nigga been mad reckless for too long. Him, JT, Des...all them niggas."

"What about Des?" I ask, practically easing up on the edge of the bench.

He lets out a frustrated sigh, shaking his head. "Nah, nothin', yo. I'm tired, man. Those stash houses that somehow got raided, then burned down..."

My stomach lurches. "Yeah? What about them?"

"Those weren't Jasper's spots, Pash. He ran 'em. But they were a *few* of mine." I blink. I catch the emphasis on a *few*. My eyes widen in disbelief. All these years I thought *he* worked for Jasper. Thought *he* was one of Jasper's henchmen. That Jasper was the one who put his family on. And Stax is the real top-dawg nigga.

I'm speechless.

"That was *your* work, wasn't it?" I shift my eyes. "You ain't gotta admit to it, Pash. I'm impressed." He lets out a laugh. "You got that off, Pash. When the first three got hit, I thought it mighta been some snake niggas tryna muscle in on my flow. So I had cats sweepin' the streets 'cause niggas in the game always talkin'; someone always flossin' off a come up, or yappin' at the mouth tryna earn stripes 'n' shit. But shit came back quiet. Then I thought maybe it was some outta-town muhfuckas, but that wasn't it, either. I was like, 'Nah. Whoever's behind this shit is out for blood. The shit's real personal.' And I know I haven't shit on no one. But I still didn't connect *you* to them hits 'til Sunday night when you hit me up mad pressed for me to get at you."

I shift my body on the bench. All of a sudden it's starting to get hot. I feel beads of sweat gliding down my back. Stax hasn't shifted his gaze from me once since he started talking. Nor has his tone changed.

God, I just want to poke his damn eyes out! And slap his beautiful face! He's extremely calm. I don't know if I should jump up now and start running and screaming for my life, try to fast-talk my way out of him doing me in right here, or simply let him end it right here, right now.

"You sexed me up real right, Pash. Put it on me like no other. Had me creepin' outta ya suite mad early in the mornin' to only fire back up my phone to see mad missed calls 'n' texts about two more of my spots gettin' hit 'n' Jasper bein' MIA. Then I get greeted by Felecia's head propped up on a stake in my fam's yard. That's a lil' more than coincidence, feel me?"

I feel my chest tighten. My bang falls over my left eye. I toss my head, clearing my one-eyed view of him. "Look, Stax," I say, preparing to stand. "I think we should wrap this up. I don't like where this is…"

He reaches for me. "Nah, chill. I'm not done. You owe me, Pash." His brow arches. "Do you know how much paper 'n' product I lost from those eight spots you had hit up tryna get at my fam, huh? Millions of dollars, Pash. You 'n' Jasper cost me mad paper, aiight. But I ain't sweatin' that shit."

I swallow. He's so calm that it's frightening me. My eyes dart around the park. "C'mon, Pash. I'm not gonna hurt you. Damn. I'd *never* hurt you, man. I tol' you, yo. You gotta special place in my heart."

I pull in my bottom lip. My heart is beating heavy against my chest. I can hear its pounding in my ears. I feel myself getting dizzy. I close my eyes and take a deep breath. And when I open them, I ask, "Do you love me, Stax?"

It's the first time his gaze shifts from mine. He clears his throat, then narrows his eyes. "I want Jasp, Pash. Do what you gotta do wit' him, feel me. But when you finish, he's mine. He's my blood. And I want him. *Dead* or *alive*."

He gives me a look that lets me know he's serious. This is a side of him I've never seen.

"Stax…"

"This isn't a negotiation, Pash. Until JT's body is found, my fam, none of us, have closure. I'm not lettin' another member of my fam go missin', Pash. Whatever happens, they, *we*, deserve closure; feel me?"

I slowly nod.

He stands, taking me by the hand and helping me up. "C'mon. Let me get you back to ya peoples." An electric current shoots through me. "Them some real thorough cats you got on ya team, Pash."

I look up at him. "Yeah, I know. I really lucked up." He smiles at me. "What?"

"Nothin,' Pash."

"No, say it."

He stops walking and reaches for my hand again. "You're a beautiful woman, Pash. Don't let what Jasp 'n' the rest of them grimy muhfuckas did to you turn you into somethin' ugly, ma. That's not you, ma. Don't let them have ya shine, Pash. What they did was some real pussy-ass shit. But don't let that shit control you. Take back what they took from you. Do what you gotta do, then let it go.

"I don't want anything else to *ever* happen to you." He steps in and pulls me into his arms, giving me a tight embrace. I feel myself melting into him. "Fuck, Pash." Silence drifts in between us. And in those several moments, I feel him growing against me. I fight the urge to reach between his legs and grab him. I want to drop to my knees and throat his cock right here, right out in the open. "Why the fuck you do this to me, huh? This shit is fuckin' crazy," he finally says, snatching me out of my lusty thoughts. "I gotta stay away from you, Pash."

I nod my head into his chest, feeling safe in a way that I've never felt with anyone else. Yet, understanding all too well what he's saying. "I know, Stax."

He steps back from me. "When you gettin' at Jasp?" I tell him tonight. "Hit me up when you're done." I tell him he'll be dumped where he dumped me. He nods, pulling me into his arms again. "You in my heart, Pash. Don't *ever* forget that."

"Do you love me, Stax?" I ask, again, not really sure if I even want to hear his response. I don't realize I'm holding my breath until he cups the side of my face in his hand, then lightly brushes his fingertips over my lips.

He pulls in his bottom lip, then says, "C'mon, Pash. What you think?"

I roll my eyes. "Why can't you just answer the question? It's either yes or no."

He kisses me on the forehead. "Go handle your business. Then let me handle mine."

Nothing else is said as he walks me back to my SUV. Mel gives him a head nod, opening the door for me. I climb into the backseat, and he shuts the door. Stax stands there with his hands stuffed in his pocket, staring into the window. I feel his eyes burning through the tint, warming my skin and heating my pussy.

Even as we drive off, I can still feel him, smell him, all over me. The reply to my question still unanswered with words. Yet, spoken in the intensity of his gaze.

I cover my hands in my face. *Mygod, what have I done?*

Thirty-Eight

It's finally over when it's over…

August 27, 2011, in front of a hundred-plus designer-clad guests all gathered on three acres of sprawling, manicured property—under a huge white, air conditioned tent with its white plush carpet, flickering candles, torches, and hundreds of gorgeous white roses everywhere—I sauntered down a red-carpeted aisle a shaky, nervous, nail-biting mess on the inside, but was every bit the blushing, glowing, beautiful bride on the outside as I made my way to the altar, smiling wide, pretending… picture-perfect and ready to exchange vows with a man who less than six months prior had had me tied up down in a basement being tossed around and manhandled by a bunch of no-good motherfuckers whom he'd recruited and paid to *force* their dicks into my mouth.

Because I had cheated on him.

Because I had betrayed him.

The price for my indiscretions, my punishment: rape her soul and let her do what she does best—suck dick. Then for the grand hoorah…flick off the lights and beat the life out of her, then toss her naked body in a park, bloody and unconscious.

And still…said, "I do."

And still…pretended.

And…waited.

For the day I could, I would, finally savor the sweet, bitter taste of retribution.

With smiles and beguiling eyes, I sucked and fucked a ruthless, cold-hearted nigga, playing my position and being the bitch that learned her place, all the while, plotting and planning and preparing for my moment. To exact revenge against the one nigga who stripped my spirit and left me for dead.

Jasper.

The bad boy I gave my heart to.

The ruthless nigga I once loved and feared.

The grimy motherfucker who tried to have me killed.

And tonight, less than four months into a sham of a marriage, after eleven-and-a-half years of history together...this is where it all ends.

Down in a basement.

Six masked niggas.

And Jasper.

Naked and tied up with his face covered in a waiting for the Mistress of Ceremony. Me. The bitch he crossed; his judge, his jury, and the executioner of his miserable fate.

I reach for my flute of champagne; careful not to mess up the talons I've put on and painted over my own nails, and take a slow, deliberate sip. I swirl my tongue around the wet coolness of the bubbly elixir, then swallow. I take another sip, then set my glass on the table.

I breath in a deep breath. Shyne's "Bad Boyz" plays again on the portable stereo. The song that blared through the speakers the night I met Jasper. The song I have locked on repeat, playing over and over as I prepare myself, as I get ready for the most explosive performance of my life.

Tonight, all eyes will be on me. And I, along with the show I am going to put on, will be stained in every onlookers mind.

If Jasper survives tonight, he'll be haunted, tormented, and painfully turned on by tonight's special delivery. Unlike the way that nigga had his goons toss me around, crawling on my knees, getting slapped in the face with their dicks, like some dirty gutter whore, I'm going to fuck his world up sensually.

As sick and twisted as it may be, I'm going to straddle Jasper and ride his thick, nine-inch, condom-wrapped dick one last time until he floods it with his cock milk. Then I am going to turn on the sixty-inch flat-screen TV and play the video footage I secretly recorded of me fucking Stax and of him eating my pussy and fucking him in his ass. I want Jasper to feel violated and dirty and hurt the way I felt finding out he'd fucked Felecia. I want him to know I fucked his right-hand man, that I fucked Stax. That his own cousin snaked him, the way mine snaked me.

Without thought, I bounce my ass and snap my fingers, getting caught up in the "Bad Boyz" beat, staring at myself in the mirror. I glance at the time, strutting over to my chirping cell alerting me I have a text. I glance at the screen. It's a text from Booty. OOOH U NO GOOD DIRTY BITCH!!!!! MOTHERFUCK U, GODDAMMIT! WHERE'S MY SHIT, BITCH?

FUCK U 2, SWEETIE, I text back, tossing my phone into my bag, then applying another coat of coconut shimmer body butter over my skin. I slip into a diamond-studded black satin bustier, then strap on a black leather harness with detachable flap. I step into a pair of red five-inch Gucci platform pumps. Then for the final touch, I open a silver box and pull out a black masquerade mask adorned with glitter and ruby rhinestones, carefully placing it on. I apply a coat of red lipstick over my lips, then glide a coat of gloss on them.

When I am done, I refill my drink, then stand before the mirror. My breath snatches as I stare at the reflection in front of me. What I see is breathtaking. Sexy. Seductive. Scandalous.

And…sadistically sensual.

I am pleased at what I see. Very much so. Beautiful shimmering skin that glistens just so under the lighting. A gorgeous body. And a gleam in my to-die-for hazel eyes that I haven't seen in almost two years.

I glance at the time again. A quarter to nine.

I take a deep breath as I lift my flute. "Well, this it. The moment you've been waiting for. Here's to a night they will soon never forget." I take a big gulp of champagne, then another, then another, finally setting the empty glass down.

I slip into a black robe, grab my black leather case, then head out of the makeshift dressing room/office I used to prepare myself. As soon as I step into the hall for a patiently waiting Mel to escort me down to the basement, his eyes practically pop out of their sockets.

"Damn." It's all he says. It's all that's needed to be said. His roaming eyes say the rest.

It's showtime.

So let the seduction and torture begin.

Thirty-Nine

*When the trap springs shut, a caged nigga will feel the wrath
of the bitch he's fucked over…*

There he lies. In the center of the basement, on a table, strapped down naked. His face is covered with the black gag mask wth snap-on blinders and removable muzzle I'd decided not to use on Legend the night of his demise.

I have no idea who any of these six masked niggas standing around drinking and smoking are. And I don't need to know. All I know is, they've smacked Jasper around for the last few hours under my direction. And now they're only here as props to add to the humiliation.

All talking stops when they spot me. You can almost hear a pin drop as I walk by, the light scent of coconut trailing behind me. All I hear is, "Oh shit… Goddaaaaayuum she's bad as fuck… Damn, *that's* who that nigga fucked over…?"

Mel positions himself over by the stairs, sitting on a pleather barstool.

Lamar limps over to me, leans in and whispers, "You sure you want all these cats down here watchin' this?"

I nod, turning my back to him as I unfasten my robe and let it slide off my shoulders. He takes it, folding it over his arm. I turn to face him as his eyes drop down to the slow rise and fall of my breasts. Subconsciously, he licks his lips.

"They stay," I say, walking toward the table, feeling their eyes on the sway of my bare ass cheeks. I swallow, hard, taking in Jasper's nakedness, drinking in the ripped body I once adored. I place the case at the foot of the table between his spread legs, opening it, then pulling out a six-, eight-, and twelve-inch dildo, laying them down on the table. Next I pull out a XL stainless steel chasity cock cage, then a deep throat gag.

I hear someone say, "Daaaaaaaaayum, that nigga 'bout to really catch it."

Jasper grunts.

In the right corner, I spot the portable spanking pad with the restraints all set up and ready for use.

Lastly, I pull out a bottle of Pjur Eros lube, then squirt it all over his flaccid dick. The dick I once sucked and loved and couldn't get enough of.

I take it in my hand, stroking it.

Japser grunts again, his legs twitching. He lifts his head up from the table but is unable to see anything with the blinders over his eyes. I keep stretching and stroking his dick; it isn't cooperating. It needs a little motivation, I think, letting it go and reaching up and yanking off Jasper's blinders so he can. See. Me.

He blinks. Tries to adjust his eyes to the light, until he finally blinks me into focus. "Remember me? The bitch you threatened and forced to marry you. The bitch you had kidnapped for cheating on you." His eyes widen. "Don't look shook now, nigga. *Everything* you had done to me, I'm going to do to you. But, first, I'm going to fuck you one last time, Jasper. You want this pussy one last time, nigga?"

He grunts, shaking his head.

I slap his face, blocking out everyone else in the room. "Shut the fuck up, nigga. I'ma fuck your dick, bitch. So I need you to relax, so it gets hard for me. Otherwise"—I reach for the scalpel strapped to my thigh, placing it up to his neck—"I'm going to slice into you inch by inch until you bleed out. You wanted to fuck with me? Now I'm going to fuck with you, bitch. I'm going to show you what type of bitch I really am. So give me a hard dick, Jasper, so I can fuck you into my pussy. Understand?"

He grunts, his eyes filling with what looks like pleas. I ignore them, reaching for his dick again. Stroke it. Feel my pussy start to churn as it finally begins to thicken. When it bricks, I tear open the Magnum, then roll it down on his dick. "Yeah, motherfucker, this is the hard dick you liked forcing inside my pussy, isn't it?"

He grunts again. A chill passes through my skin as I climb up on the table and straddle him. Blood rushes down through my veins, making its way to my clit as I reach in back of me and press his dick into the back of my pussy. But it isn't his dick I'm fucking when I close my eyes and gasp. It isn't him stretching me open as he groans into the warmth as I slowly roll my hips.

I don't look at him. I can't. Not yet. "You miss this tight pussy, don't you, nigga? Big black dick feels so good in my pussy…"

Ohgod, the dick really does start getting good and I am moaning, loudly now, gripping it as I ride up and down on it. "Yeah, mother-fucker, this is the pussy you was ready to kill for, isn't it? You kept stealing this pussy anytime I didn't wanna give it to you, didn't you, nigga?"

He grunts.

I am oblivious to the peering eyes in back of me.

I open my eyes and blink in Jasper. I slap his face.

He grunts. He bucks his hips upward. He doesn't want this. He does. But not like this. He's trying to fight it, but this pussy's too wet, too juicy, too hot, for him to resist, for him to hold out much longer.

I reach in back of me for his balls. They slowly tighten as my skilled fingers slide behind them, moving in slow circles. He grunts again, his hips bucking frantically now.

I hear the niggas in back of me groan. Perhaps in aching frustration having to sit through this, watching my ass clap around Jasper's cock, breathing the heated scent of my wet pussy.

I know this nigga's body like the back of my hand. I pinch his nipples, the triggers to his balls.

I ignore Jasper's knowing eyes. Five days with no pussy, no ass, no throat, he's about to explode.

And he does as I maliciously coo, "Oooh, yessss, Stax... give me all that thick, hot nut. Flood my pussy, big daddy." His eyes widen as I lift my hips up off his dick, smirking.

He violently jerks his head up, growling and groaning. I slap his face again. "Yeah, I fucked him, and what?" He grunts, shaking his head. I reach for his sticky dick, pulling off the cum-filled condom, then stuffing it into the opening of his mouth. He gags, jerking his head, then shaking it side to side, trying to dislodge the condom.

"What, you don't like the taste of a condom in your mouth? Shut the fuck up, bitch! You fucked Felecia, motherfucker. So I fucked Stax." I tilt my head. "All is fair in the art of love and war, isn't it? How does that shit feel, nigga, knowing Stax had his big, thick, ten-inch dick all up inside this good pussy, huh? Had I known he was so damn good in bed, I would have been fucking him your whole bid, nigga, instead of creeping out sucking all them niggas' dicks."

He grunts, shaking and jerking the table trying to break free.

I slap the shit out of him again. "You could have beat the shit out of me, motherfucker!" *Slap!* "You could have left me, nigga!" *Slap! Slap!* "But instead you had niggas violate me!" *Slap!*

I stop myself, taking a deep breath. I snatch the six-inch dildo. Jasper eyes me as I unsnap the flap in my harness, then slide the silicone cock through the hole, then snap it back into the harness. "I want you dead, bitch! But that'd be too easy. I'm not letting you off the hook that easy."

My cock juts out from the harness ready for what's next. I wait for Mel and four of the masked niggas to untie Jasper and get him off the table. He tries to fight, but they overpower him, giving him swift body shots as necessary until they finally get his arms and legs securely strapped. I walk in back of him, his ass bent over—open and ready—and remove the muzzle and mask from his face.

He spits out the nut-flooded condom, then starts spazzing, his voice hoarse and raspy. "What the fuck is you doin', yo? This shit ain't over, Pash, real shit! You better muthafuckin' body me, bitch! 'Cause word is bond all of you muthafuckas are boxed, yo!"

I smirk. "What goes around comes around, nigga. I told you, you should have killed me when you had the chance. But you didn't. And guess what? Them niggas out there aren't checking for you. Not tonight. But don't worry. They'll be there to pick your naked body up at Branch Brook Park. You remember where that is, right?" I don't wait for him to respond. I reach for the deep throat gag. "It's where you dumped me, nigga. So shut the fuck up."

I have Mel hold his head back. Tell Jasper to open his mouth. He refuses. I ask him again. "Fuck you, Pash! I ain't openin' shit, bitch!" He spits at me. "Fuckin' snake-ass, bitch!"

I smirk, walking back over to my case and pulling out the bolt cutters. "You can call me whatever you want, nigga. But I'm not fucking with you. Open your fucking mouth." He still refuses. I hand Mel the gag, then bend down, open the cutters and cut off his pinky toe. He grits his teeth, grunting. Still refusing to open his mouth. I cut off three more toes, leaving him only with his big toe before he passes out from the pain and Mel is able to secure the gag around his mouth.

Then I kneel in front of him and stuff his sticky dick inside the stainless steel cock cage, open the XL steel cock ring and secure it around his balls, securing the cage to the ring with a small carbon steel lock, which will be extremely difficult cutting off. Then I take the bolt cutter and cut the key in half, tossing the pieces into two separate trash bins.

When Jasper finally comes to, his cock is tightly caged in. And the stainless O-ring attached to the gag holds his mouth open nice and wide, so he can't close it while I fuck into his face. I let him know why I caged his cock. "You like to fuck and get your dick sucked, well, let's see how wet them bitches get it now."

Mel has his head in an armlock to keep him from jerking his head around while I serve him. "Now, you're going to know what it feels like to have a dick rammed into your neck, motherfucker." He grunts, his eyes open wide enough to pop out of his head as I ram the six-inch cock into his mouth and fuck his face. He gags and grunts. His eyes fill with tears as I pound in and out of his mouth. I talk all kind of shit to him. Call him all kinds of dirty cock-sucking whores and sluts, slapping his face. "Swallow that cock, bitch!"

The niggas in the room taunt him. Talk shit, egging me on. "Yeah, baby, choke that pussy motherfucker with that dick...give that nigga something big...beat that motherfucker's throat up, ma..."

I go from the six-inch to the eight-inch to finally the twelve-inch mercilessly tearing into his mouth, my pussy juices leaking out from the friction of the base. I abruptly stop and pull out. Mel lets go of Jasper's head and he violently gags up a bunch of spit. "Oh, you didn't like having a bunch of dildos in your mouth, huh?"

He angrily grunts. Tears streaking down his face.

"No worries," I say as Mel walks back over to us, handing me the Tupperware bowl from out of the freezer. "I got something a whole lot better than a silicone dick." I lift the lid, pulling out the Ziploc freezer bag. "I got the real thing for you, nigga. I want you to taste what a real cock tastes like…" He grunts, growls, trying to jerk himself free from the spanking chair to no avail. I pull out JT's thick, black frozen dick.

He grunts, again.

I hear, "Oh, shiiiiit, son, is that…? Oh, hellllll, nah, that's a nigga's dick she 'bout to serve him! Ohhh, fuck…! Daaaaayum, she wildin'… that's some real gangster shit…"

I wait for Mel to hold his head for me, again, then push JT's frozen dick into Jasper's mouth, easing it out nice and slow. "Yeah, nigga, suck that big black dick." I ram it in and out of his mouth, fucking into his face with it until it starts to thaw out, then I leave it there, tearing off a strip of duct tape, then wrapping it around his mouth.

When Mel finally releases his head, Jasper wildly shakes it from side to side, grunting and growling. His eyes filled with rage. I narrow my eyes. Burn my glare into him. "You fucked with the wrong bitch, nigga. You thought I was weak, huh? Yeah, you had me beaten and broken. But you underestimated me, bitch; that was your first mistake. You got me fucked up in the game, mother-fucker. You should have listened to Stax when he warned you that the same blood that ran through my father's veins ran through mine. But you slept on me. Who's the bitch, now, nigga?"

I reach for the DVD remote, turn it on, then press PLAY. Everyone in the room waits with baited breath as the DVD starts to play. I open with, "If you're watching this video, Jasper, then checkmate, nigga. That means you're somewhere tied up and gagged, waiting the final phase of your fate. You fucked that bitch Felecia. And now watch as your cousin fucks me…"

Jasper grunts, hanging his head, then shaking it. He doesn't want to hear or see anymore. I warn him to hold his head up and open his eyes. Threaten to cut off the toes on his other foot. He slowly lifts his head as Stax's face comes into view, then disappears between my naked thighs, eating my pussy. I smirk as his eyes fill with agony and hurt and hate. I walk off, grab the lube from off the table, then squirt a generous amount all over my cock, walking back over to him.

I ease up in back of him. "You wanted to beat on me and force your dick in me, like I was your motherfucking property or some shit. Well, I'm going to tear your asshole open with this twelve-inch dick, bitch. Let you feel what it's like to be violated. To have something taken from you."

He violently jerks and shakes and tries head butting me to keep me from getting anywhere near his ass. But I'm not deterred. I grab the bolt cutters again, and start cutting off the toes on his other foot. Until the pain is so excruciating that he passes out again. Then I have Mel and four other niggas remove him from the spanking chair and place him into another restraint device that I'd brought along; just in case, to ensure he can't jerk and head-butt me while I fuck into his guts.

This time when he comes to, he's on his knees, his head bent forward, his arms pulled back to his ankles and both secured to The Doggy Style Locking Spreader.

"No use in fighting it, nigga." I push my finger into his ass. He makes inaudible sounds. "I have you locked into position for the ass pounding of your life, nigga. But first, let me tell you whose dick you have trapped into your mouth…" I ease up over his back, pull open his muscular ass cheeks, then ram half of the cock into his hole, causing the veins in his neck to almost pop out of his skin. "I don't even have it all in and you already yelling like a little bitch," I taunt.

Then I lean in closer, and whisper real slowly, "Felecia told me she was pregnant by you, you dirty motherfucker. Lying-ass nigga." He grunts. "You should have seen her face when I slammed my gun into her mouth. The bitch begged me for her life before I pulled the trigger and blew her skull out."

I reach around and yank the tape from around the mouthpiece of the gag. JT's wet, soggy cock drops out of Jasper's mouth, then I unfasten the gag and let it hit the floor.

"That dick you had in your mouth," I hiss real low in his ear, slowly rocking more cock into his ass. "Was Jaheem's, nigga. How did that dead nigga's dick taste in your mouth, bitch? Yeah, that's right. You sucked your dead cousin's dick, motherfucker."

He gags and coughs and vomits, then cries out, before spewing a bunch of profanity. I push more dick into his hole, then pull almost out, then push back in. I gesture with my hand that everyone can leave me alone with Jasper. But only a few of the niggas opt to bounce. Everyone else remains, transfixed as I slam into Jasper's ass. And fuck him mercilessly until I have ripped him open; until I am coming over and over again, and I have fucked him unconscious.

Sweaty and panting and emotionally drained, I slowly pull out, finally feeling vindicated. I glance over at Mel. "I'm done with him. No wait…" I walk over to my case and pull out a bottle of rubbing alcohol, opening it, then walking back over to Jasper and pouring the entire bottle out over his head. He yells and shakes his head wildly, letting out a piercing sound as some of it leaks into his eyes.

"You'll never look at another bitch again, you dirty sonofabitch!"

I curve my ten pointy, two-inch-long, acrylic nails into claws, then hook them into his eyeballs, slicing into his eyelids, some of the nails cutting into his orbs, ripping into his corneas, irises, and pupils. I claw and claw until he's bleeding out of his eyes. I ask Mel for matches. Then set his head on fire. His piercing screams echo throughout the basement as I stand here watching his hair, scalp and face burn off.

"Now I'm done with him," I say when the flames finally die out.

Mel points to the device he's locked into. "What about that?"

"Dump him locked in it."

I grab my robe and slip it on, heading up the stairs. I stop and turn back, walking over to the DVD player and retrieving the DVD of Stax and me. I look over at Mel, then glance down at Jasper—bent over in doggy-style position with his asshole gaping open, knowing this will be the last time I'll ever have to lay eyes on him again. I bite into my quivering lip. Then push out a slow, pained breath.

"Before you get rid of him, cut out his fucking tongue."

Forty

Saying goodbye at the end of the road is always bittersweet...

"Jasper's dead," Mona croaks into the phone.

I snap up in bed, my pulse quickens. *"Whaaat?!"*

Mona's breaths come in heavy bursts through the phone. "Pasha... he's fucking dead. It's all over the news." Her voice cracks. "His body was found early this morning."

"Where?" I ask, closing my eyes and holding my breath.

"Floating in the Hudson River."

I gasp, clutching my chest. *Ohmygod! That's where Stax must have dumped him once he was picked up last night.* I know he wasn't dead when Mel had his *peoples* dump him in the park. Mel had assured me Jasper was still breathing. Barely. But he was still alive.

Mona sniffles into the phone. "The news is saying he was found with his wrists and ankles locked into some kind of device and his..."—her voice quakes—"his penis was in some kind of locked chastity thing. And most of his toes cut off. Whoever had him, tortured and sodomized him, burned his face and head with some kind of flammable, then dumped four bullets into his head."

My eyes pop open in disbelief. "Say, what?" I toss the covers off, jumping out of bed to turn on the television. *Ohmygod!* I race out of my bedroom into the stitting room area where Lamar and Mel are watching the newscaster reporting live from the scene where Jasper's body was found. They both look as shocked as I am.

Mona is sobbing. I don't know what to say to her. So I let her get it all out. When she finally pulls herself together, I ask, "Who identified his body?"

"Stax. He's still there now."

I swallow.

"Pasha." Her voice is barely a whisper. "Did you…" She chokes back more sobs. "I know he had it coming, but…"

"No, no, of course not. I wanted him to pay for what he did to me. Not dead. I didn't kill him or have him dumped in the river."

But I did everything else.

"I didn't think you did. That would make you one… "

"*Ruthless* bitch," I finish for her.

She lets out a strained chuckle. "Yeah, picture that. You *ruthless*. Only a monster could do what was done to Jasper. Now, a bitch like that scandalous-ass Cassandra is a whole other story. That bitch is liable to do anything. I wouldn't put shit past her crazy ass."

I take a deep breath, walking back into my bedroom. I pull back the heavy drapes, lighting the room up. I overhear the weatherman on the television in back of me saying the temperature for today will sunny and cold.

"Mona, you never know what a person is capable of when they've been pushed too far." I pause, absorbing the sweet agony of knowing Jasper is out of my life…for good. "Especially when you're fighting for your life."

"You're right. If it were me in that situation, I'd want him dead, too."

"I wish things could have turned out differently," I say softly. "It hurts knowing Jaylen will grow up without his father. But I'm glad it's over."

Right now I am simply numb from everything. The last several weeks have been the most emotionally taxing for me. It's been nothing—and I do mean *nothing*, but drama. Nonstop. And I'm tired. I'm done. And, yes…so, so, glad it's over.

Still…it's hard to digest the news that Jasper's dead. When I doused him with the rubbing alcohol last night, then struck a match and watched his head go up in flames, a part of me went up in that fire with him. Burning him, although not planned, also burned away something dead inside of me. That part of my spirit he strangled when he fucked into me, when his goon fucked into me, when he'd beaten me and threatened me. And I'd allowed him to do it. I let him kill me. Gave him permission to keep strangling the rest of me until there was almost nothing else left of me.

And now I only hope I'll be able to rise above the ashes.

"I still don't know who the *Calm One* is," I finally say, stepping away from the window and walking over to the bed. I lie back on it. "Sometimes I can still smell being down in that basement with them niggas. Sometimes I still hear them jeering at me. Still see their dicks dangling in my face. The Calm One, whomever he is, kept me safer than I would have been had he not been there. He didn't let any of them niggas go too far."

"And if you did know," she asks, drawing several shaky breaths, "what would you do? What would you say to him?"

I stare up at the ceiling. "Honestly, Mona. I don't know. I think I'd want to know why he was there. He never participated. And I'd want to know why." I let out a sigh. "Oh, well. Maybe I'm not supposed to ever know who he is."

"Maybe," she says, taking a deep breath. "Somethings are better left alone."

I sit up on the bed. "Yeah. I agree."

"Anyway, I think we both have a lot to let go of, Pasha." She tells me she's decided to get into therapy to deal with the sexual abuse and her feelings toward JT. "It's time for healing, Pasha. For the both of us."

I pull in my bottom lip, reflecting on everything I've gone through over the years with Jasper—the good, the bad, and some of the scariest. I have a lot of scarring from what he did to me. I squeeze my eyes shut, trying to keep my tears at bay.

"I think you're right," I finally say.

Mona sniffs back what sounds like more tears. "Jasper was my cousin. And I loved him. But I hated him for what he'd put you through. Now I feel so bad for cursing him out the way I did the other day. I couldn't hold it any longer. I ripped into him, Pasha. Called him everything but the child of God. And now he's gone. I'm just glad it's finally over. Worrying about whether or not I'd one day get a call that you...that something awful happened to you would have killed me. I *know* he wanted you dead. Well, maybe not dead, but he wanted you hurt—badly. He wanted you scared. He was such a fucking ruthless asshole."

I close my eyes, clutching the phone. "Yes, he was." I swallow, blinking back tears. "Very ruthless. But there's always someone more vindictive and more vengeful and more ruthless out there, waiting for the right moment to strike."

"And it looks like Felecia and Jasper both fell into the same fate."

There's silence between us. I can almost see Mona's wheels spinning in her head, thinking, wondering. She knows, I'm more certain of it. She may not know how. But she knows someway, somehow, I played a role in their demise.

Don't ask. Don't Tell. Or simply deny.

"Where's Avery?" I ask, feeling the need to change the subject, glancing at the time. 9:28 a.m.

She sucks her teeth. "Ugh, don't get me started on him. He and Mario left up out of here for some tattoo party or some mess one his boys was having up in Connecticut last night and them fools haven't gotten back, yet." She huffs. "I told Avery don't have Mario coming back here looking crazy with a bunch of tattoos all over him. I told him to let him wait until he's eighteen. But, he told me to fall back and let them have their father-son bonding time. Really? And he couldn't take him fishing to bond? Mmmph."

I chuckle. "I didn't know either one of them were into tattoos."

"Girl, please. Avery has a big-ass tattoo over his shoulder, but you wouldn't know it unless you catch him in a tanktop. After he got that panther on his shoulder, he…"

My heart drops. *Panther? Avery has a tattoo of a panther? Oh dear God, no!*

No. No. It can't be!

My mind quickly scrambles back to the basement. The long muscular legs, the Duke basketball shorts, the white wife beater, the face mask, all come into view. The way he nervously shifted his eyes from me, not allowing me to see them, the way he walked, his body build, were all strangely familiar to me. His left shoulder, the sleek panther stretched across his skin finally flashes in my head.

I blink, again, as a single tear slides down my cheek, then another. I pull in a deep, pained breath. Then ask her what shoulder Avery's tattoo is on.

I hold my breath, slowly feeling myself becoming lightheaded. My knees buckle the second she says what I already feared.

"His left shoulder."

Forty-One

There's always a price to pay…

Sitting behind my desk, I pull out the folded piece of paper from my purse, holding it in my hand for a few moments before finally opening it. I stare at the names on the list.

JAH

KILLAH

JT

LEGEND

AJ

FELECIA

JASPER

MYDICKNEEDURTONGUE2

THE CALM ONE

I close my eyes. Try to erase their images from my mind as I shift through the snapshots. I don't want to forget. But I don't want to remember, either. I shouldn't have to forget. But I don't want to be haunted by the memories. I don't want to be tormented by the ghosts of their dirty deeds.

Or by my own.

When I finally lift my lids, my eyes are blurred with tears. There are still names missing from this list. Still niggas who have gotten passes only because no one was willing to give them up. But I am so okay with that. Really. I meant what I said about the message being sent. And now with Jasper's murder, and the way in which he was found, all on the news, they know. They all know.

And if they don't, shame on them.

I swallow, choking back tears as I reach for my pen, drawing a line through their names. Every name on this list affected my life in some form, disrupted my world in some way. Their deeds stained in my memory. But the ones who hurt me the most, the ones who meant me the most harm, are the ones who were dealt with, most severely.

I reach for a handful of tissue, dabbing under my eyes, then blowing my nose. Pulling out a WITE-OUT correction tape, I white-out the names of those who were exterminated; the ones who had their lights shut, the ones who caused me the greatest pain. Felecia and Jasper.

Then I white-out Legend's name.

Next, I stare at JT's name. Had Booty not bodied him, I would have tortured him slowly with the others. Still, he got what his hand called for just the same. I white him out. Although there's a line drawn through Killah's name, I circle it.

Wait, wait... didn't I hear that name somewhere?

Yes.

My mind goes back to the night I sat parked outside in the SUV with Lamar, across the street from The Crack House. Ugh. The name alone makes me cringe.

"...All I do is let you use me, nigga! I let you 'n' ya bum-ass nephew Killah lay up on my section-8..."

Ohmygod. So that's who he is. Killah. Dickalina's crazy-ass man's nephew. I pull in my bottom lip, taking my pen and circling around and around his name, wondering what I should do with this. Wondering if it even matters. He hadn't really done much the night of my kidnapping. Not like Jah'Mel had. And Booty already handled him. Mmmph. He's lucky he's still breathing. But that may all change if Booty ever learns that it was him who got JT's dick out of her freezer for me. That nigga owes me. And I intend on holding him to it until his debt to me is paid in full. So far he's proven himself redeemable.

I scratch his name out, blackening over it with the pen until it is no longer visible, until the ink bleeds through the paper.

I stare at Calm One's name. *Damn you, Avery!* Since this morning, I've been playing my conversation with Mona over and over and over in my head, sifting through it, dissecting it. Trying to find an answer to my most troubling question: What the hell am I going to do now?

Do I tell her? Then run the risk of having her learn that he'd also answered one of my sex ads wanting his dick sucked. Do I share with her our long email and IM sessions full of sexual confessions? Do I risk her finding out that I'd met him early in the morning at a park and was tempted to climb into his truck and throat his dick, even *after* finding out who he was? Do I tell her I stuck my hand through his window and stroked *her* husband's big, thick dick? That my pussy moistened? That my mouth watered?

No. That would destroy her.

But the question is, "Who am I really protecting? And why?"

There's a knock at the door. I quickly fold the paper, stuffing it back inside my bag, clearing my throat. "Yeah? Come in."

The door opens and Mel pops his head in. "Uh, Pasha, there's a situation out front that's about to get ugly if you don't come handle it."

I frown. "Mel, I can't. Not now. Please. Just handle it. Do whatever you have to do."

He shakes his head. "Pasha, you not hearin' *me*. You need to come out front. This chick is goin' ballistic, yo. And she's *not* tryna hear it. Lamar's out there now tryna calm her 'n' get her to bounce, but she actin' like she's ready to knuckle up. Yo, you need to come out here before…"

I put a hand up, stopping him as my cell rings. "All right, all right. Tell whoever's out there carrying on I'll be out in a minute." I glance at my cell. It's Bianca. "But right now, I need to take this call." I wait for him to shut my door, then answer. "Hey, girl."

"I heard what happened to Jasper. It's all over the news. Just wanted to see how you were holding up."

I rake my fingers through my hair, drawing several shaky breaths. Not out of guilt for my role in Jasper's demise. Now whether or not he was already dead before those bullets were finally pumped into his head is beyond me. Fact is, he was still breathing, though barely, when he was tossed out of the van. Maybe the fire to his head killed him. Maybe those bullets did. Either way, at this moment, it doesn't matter to me. I don't need to know. I don't want to know. I wanted retribution. And I got it.

"I'm torn," I admit, pulling out the list and staring at it. I inhale slowly, my gaze never leaving Calm One's circled name. I choose my next words spoken very, very carefully. "Jasper hurt me deeply, Bianca. A part of me is relieved he's gone. That man put me through—no. Correction. I *let* that man—put me through emotional hell. He was the cause of me being laid up in that hospital bed in a coma for four days, fighting for my life."

Bianca gasps. "Ohmygod, Pasha! Noooo. And *you*…"

"Yes, I stayed," I answer for her, picking up on the question lingering in her tone. "And I still married him. And I never reported it to the police. I did what I felt I had to, for me and for my unborn child, at the time."

She gasps again. Shocked that Jasper had beaten me almost to death knowing I was pregnant with his child. I don't go into any further details, particularly about being sexually assaulted by a string of niggas he recruited. I decide it's best she think it was a domestic dispute gone ugly rather than a jealous-crazed nigga punishing me for cheating on him; for sucking a bunch of random niggas; for posting online sex ads soliciting niggas for their hard dicks—and sometimes their wet tongues on my pussy, behind his back.

I decide she doesn't need to know that I was the infamous Deep Throat Diva on the Nastyfreaks4u website. Not that she would judge me. Still, some things are best kept to oneself. Booty and Mona knows. And those are already two, too many.

"Pasha, I-I," her voice cracks. "I'm so sorry you had to go through all that. I only wish I could have been there for you."

I smile, closing my eyes, crumbling the list in my hand. "You're here now." We talk a few minutes more. I tell her I'll let her know when Jasper's funeral services will be, then end the call. My cell rings again. This time it's Nana.

I sigh, reluctantly answering. "Hi, Nana."

"Looks like you've been given *a ram in the bush*." Her voice is calm, her tone distant and cold. "I saw the news."

I shudder. "Everyone has."

"It's time you make amends, Pasha. Get right with God. You took the word of a lying, cheating, thieving man over the word of your own flesh and blood." She pauses, swallows, then pushes a strained breath into the phone. "*You* let the devil incarnate destroy your relationship—"

Not today, Nana. Not to-fucking-day! I quickly cut her off. "*I* didn't let the devil destroy my relationship with Felecia. She did. And the sooner you get it through your head, the better. But if you want to believe that your precious gran'baby was so wonderful, then do so. She *fucked* Jasper. She *fucked* me over. Not the damn devil. I made amends with that the day her casket hit the dirt." She gasps. Opens her mouth to say something, but I shut it down. "Nana, I love you. But I don't *need* your judgment. And I'm *not* in the mood for your religious soapbox. Now if you don't mind, I have to plan a burial for a man who not only fucked my flesh and blood, but who tried to have me killed. I'll keep you in my prayers as I'm sure you will with me."

I end the call, pushing back from my desk to see who is up front trying to turn it up in my salon and disrupt my fucking day.

Forty-Two

You'll never shake drama when it knows exactly where to find you...

As soon as I walk by the stylists' workstations, all eyes zoom in on me. Kendra slowly shakes her head, mouthing, "Cassaaaaandra."

I roll my eyes, shaking my head, immediately annoyed that she'd have the fucking audacity to show her damn face here after assaulting me in my office. The minute I get to the front area, I spot her at the counter in a pair of ultra-tight jeans, wedge heels and a knit blouse that clings to her flat stomach and cantaloupe-size titties, with a hand up on her hip. She has her head covered in a silk wrap, with a matching scarf draped and wrapped around her neck. From the neck up, she reminds me of a Muslim woman.

I take a deep breath. Not in the mood for her antics. "How can I help you, Cassandra?" I say combatively, tilting my head.

"You can help me, first, by taking all that stank out your voice, Miss Pasha, girl. I ain't here to play no games with you. I'm here to get my hair did. And these ole big, buffed niggah-coons talkin' 'bout I'm not welcomed here. What kinda games you playin', huh?"

I give her an annoyed stare, raising a brow. "Cassandra, were you not asked to leave?"

She huffs. "Don't do me, Miss Pasha, girl. Don't. Do. Me. Yeah, these nigga-coons called theyselves puttin' *me* out. But I ain't goin' *no*...where...until I get my hair did."

I tell her that I'll see if one of the other stylists is willing to fit her in. But that I'm not interested. She shakes her head, banging her fist up on the counter. "Oh, no. Oh, no. Not today. You *not* 'bout to do me, Miss Pasha, girl, 'cause we 'bout to tear it up in here!" She sets her purse up on the counter. "You owe me, Miss Pasha, girl. And *you* better do me right, goddammit! Or we both goin' up outta here in handcuffs. You takin' cocks outta my home…"

Oh, God, no! This bitch is about to really set it off. I cast a glance over at Mel. Everyone within earshot is looking from me to Booty, then at each other in confusion.

"That shit you pulled at Bobblehead's funeral wasn't cute, Miss Pasha, girl. And *you* gonna pay me for…"

I turn to Mel, deciding to get this loudmouth bitch out of earshot of prying eyes of clients, sitting or standing around wide-eyed and slack-jawed, waiting to hear what Booty's going to say next.

"Mel, will you escort Miss Simms to my office, please?"

I walk off, my heels angrily clicking the checkered tile as I quickly head back to my office.

"Don't do me. I don't need this ole big-dick thing escortin' me nowhere, goddammit."

I ignore her.

"Now I came here tryna be classy, but I see you wanna kick it up to ghetto, huh, Miss Pasha, girl? I want my goddamn hair did. I got somethin' for yo' ass if you even try me in ya office today."

The minute she steps into my office, I whip around to face her. "Cassandra!" I snap through clenched teeth. "You *shut* your. *Filthy. Ass. Mouth.* You want to be paid? Hold that thought." I stalk over to my desk, unlocking the bottom drawer and yanking it open. I snatch out my handbag, opening it and pulling out my checkbook. I slam it down on my desk. "*You* want to be paid"—I stab

my pen into the check—"then let me *pay* you to be on your way."
I write out an amount, then rip out the check, shoving it to here.
"Here. This should cover whatever pain and suffering you *think*
I've caused you in that little fucked-up head of yours. Now get
the hell out of my salon." I spin on my heel, walking over to the
door and swing it open. "Now. Get. Out."

She stands in the middle of the room, staring down at the check,
then over at me. "Oh, you a real dirty bitch, Miss Pasha, girl. Your
messy ass really tryna do me, huh, Miss Pasha, girl." She stamps
her foot, pointing a finger at me. "I been goddamn good to you
'n' you really tryna fuck me over."

I blink. Give her an incredulous, confused look. "Fuck you over?
Whaaaat in the world are you talking about?"

She tears the check up into tiny pieces, tossing it up on my desk.
"You writin' me a goddamn check for twenty-thousand dollars
tryna fuck up my benefits; that's *what* I'm talkin' 'bout, goddamn
you, Miss Pasha, girl. Don't do me. You know I can't deposit this
in my bank account 'n' fuck up my section-eight and EBT benefits.
And I ain't cashin' this down at no check-cashin' joint, so they can
eat into my coins wit' their service fees. No. You gonna need to
give me cash. And I want it in hundreds and fifties."

I stare at her for a few seconds, waiting for the punchline, thinking maybe she's joking. When I realize she's dead serious, I burst
out laughing. I laugh so hard that my sides begin to hurt and tears
spring from my eyes. I'm more convinced than ever before. *This
bitch is fucking crazy!*

I grab hold of the edge of my desk, buckling over in more
laughter. It takes me several more minutes to stop laughing. But
the tears just keep falling and now I don't know if it's because I've
been laughing so hard or if it's because I've held so much in and

it's finally nice to let go. I grab a handful of tissue, wiping my face and blowing my nose.

"Bitch, you owe me an apology," I finally say, giving her a dirty look.

She scoffs, indignation all over her face. "*You*. Have. Got. To. Be. *Kidding*. Me! An *apology*? Uh. *You* owe me one. You ain't have no business stealin' shit from outta my home, goddamn you. That cock ain't belong to you."

I start laughing again. "Oh, mygod! And you *think* it belonged to *you*? Full disclosure, sweetie; do tell."

She huffs. "Well, it ain't *belong* to me. But *I'm* the one who sliced it off."

"So you think it was okay for you to keep it as a keepsake, huh?" I start laughing again.

"Oh, motherfuck you." She joins in my laughter. "I can't stand shit you stand for. Now is you gonna do my hair or am I gonna have'ta turn up the ghetto heat up in here?"

I shake my head. Tell her to come back at seven o'clock tonight. "Now get the hell out."

"Eat my ass, Miss Pasha, girl. Ole messy-ass self! And don't even think you gonna do a whoopty-wham on me 'n' sneak up outta here early. " She glances at her watch. "It's four o'clock. I'm gonna be sittin' outside waitin' for ya ole sneaky ass. So don't do me. Matter of fact, I want me some mink lashes, too, today so you gonna need to get me in here *before* seven. And I want you to put 'em in. You owe me, goddammit!"

"Bye, Cassandra," I say, walking her to the door. "I'll see you at five-thirty." She walks out, smirking and shaking her ass, brushing up against Mel. And true to her word, her crazy ass parks her ass outside in a portable beach chair, playing music and turning the front of my salon into a damn block party. I'm too damn through!

Forty-Three

A broken heart can mend…

"See. Miss Pasha, girl. I ain't wanna tell you this 'cause I don't wanna ever have'ta bang you in ya forehead if you *ever* turn on me—'n' believe me, sugah-boo, I'ma beat the drawz off you if you do me—but you the first real classy bitch I ever met...."

I turn her in the stylist chair finishing up the final touches on the thirteen hundred-dollar weave I've installed. She doesn't need weaves. She has beautiful shoulder-length hair. But no matter how many times I try offering her other hair options, like Fusion hair extensions, she's not interested. So, I let her do her.

"Now, I'ma classy bitch, too, Miss Pasha, girl. But I'm hood-classy with my shit. But you elegant with your shit, Miss Pasha, girl; you one'a them high-end, classy bitches who like to do a lil' cum garglin' on the side…"

I cough, almost choking on my spit. "Ohmygod, girl! You're really pushing it. Don't have me burn your face with one of these flat irons. Is that supposed to be some kind of underhanded compliment?"

She gives me the eye. "What you think, Miss Pasha, girl? And don't even part ya cum-suckers 'n' say I'm bein' messy. 'Cause you *know* that's not how I do mine with you. And I wish you would burn this beautiful face. We'll tear this shop up, sugah-boo."

I slowly shake my head. "Girl, not a word."

"Mmmph. Anyway. Wit' ya ole messy self. My only good friend

is Dickalina, 'n' she don't know shit 'bout classy. Shit, her ass can't even spell 'class.' Who you know spellin' 'class' with the letter *K*? But she the only bitch I fuck with. And I know she kinda retarded 'n' I don't judge. You know what I'm sayin', Miss Pasha, girl? But lately I ain't really even beat to fuck with her like how I used to. It hurts my eyeballs watchin' her be okay with what she got 'n' her not wantin' more for herself. I mean I know she slow 'n' all 'cause she got dropped on her head when she was a baby, so her skull all fucked up on the inside."

I blink.

She sighs. "Miss Pasha, girl, I go over to Dickalina's tryna get her to move on up outta there. I tell her she can apply for section-eight 'n' get her a nice house with a yard instead of comin' outta a dusty-ass buildin' to a buncha concrete 'n' broken glass e'erywhere 'n' the bitch don't wanna upgrade. All she wanna do is be right where she at, stuck in the projects with a buncha wild nigga-coons. It's depressin', Miss Pasha, girl.

"I hate goin' over there. I tell her ass to go to school 'n' get her GED, then go to beauty school 'n' get her paperwork so she can do hair at a shop somewhere 'n' all this bitch wanna do is do wash 'n' sets in her nasty-ass kitchen with all them damn dirty dishes in the sink 'n' roaches crawlin' around, like they payin' rent. And this bitch talkin' 'bout 'c'mon down to Dickalina's *Swish 'n' Swirl*'..." She grunts, shaking her head. "Who the fuck wanna get they hair did at some damn Swish 'n' Swirl? That mess sound like she suckin' the nut outta dicks 'n' swishin' the shit 'round in her damn mouth. Nasty bitch! What she doin', cock wash 'n' balls curls? Mmmph. Dickalina so stuck in bein' ghetto. Like she just don't wanna get her mind right. But I don't judge, you know what I'm sayin,' Miss Pasha, girl?"

I blink, deciding to not even address the "I don't judge" comment. It isn't worth the energy. "Listen, Cassandra. Sounds to me like what you're saying about your friend is advice you really should consider for yourself. Maybe for once you should *stop* focusing on what others aren't doing, and spend more time focusing on what *you* should be doing to improve who you are."

She frowns. "Don't do me, Miss Pasha, girl. There ain't nothing wrong with *me*. See. Here you go tryna be messy."

"I'm not *doing* you. And I'm *not* being messy. I'm being a friend—a *real* friend." She grunts and I start laughing. "Cassandra. I can't with you. I don't know what the world would be like if there were more than one of you."

"Mmmph. You sure can't, sugah-boo. And neither can the world. They ain't ready for a bitch like me. That's why there's only *one* Big Booty, okay? Don't do me. All the rest of them bitches might got them some big ole asses, but they ain't ever gonna be me. They just a buncha raggedy bitches with big asses."

"You're a mess. Anyway, back to you," I say, grabbing a flat iron, "stop being so defensive all the time, Cass. I'm not your enemy. I'm not trying to hurt you, girl. And, trust, hun. There *are* some things that *are* wrong with you, like some of your thinking. But there are also so much more that's right with you. And those are the qualities you should enhance. You're a little"—I shake my head—"uh, scratch that. There's nothing *little* about it. You're a whole lot rough around the edges. But I've seen that softer, vulnerable side of you, too. Underneath that hard exterior is a really sweet, kind-hearted woman who's afraid to let others in. But I'm really glad that you've allowed me to get a glimpse of that part of who you are."

"Oooh, goddamn you, Miss Pasha, girl. Booga-coon, *boom!* I hate e'erything you stand for right now." She turns her head away from me, dabbing the corners of each eye. I eye her, letting silence fill the space around us. "You the first bitch," she finally says, keeping her gaze away from mine, "who got me wantin' more, Miss Pasha, girl...." She pauses, pressing her palm to her eye. A few seconds pass, then she sniffles. "Ooooh, I need me a lil' get right, goddammit. I need to get my mind right. Fuckin' with you gotta bitch feelin' all soft 'n' gooey. Ooh, I can't stand no cryin', weepy-ass bitch, goddamn you, Miss Pasha, girl."

She shifts in her seat. "And ya stank ass still owe me for puttin' me through all kinda stress. What was you gonna do, turn ya back on me 'cause we had a lil' sisterly fistfight? Mmmph."

I blink. "*Sisterly?!* Cassandra, stop! You can't be serious. Not the way we were going at it in my office. We fought like two bitches trying to kill each other."

She shoots me an evil eye through the mirror. "Like I said, *sisterly.* Should I spell it? Don't do me, goddammit. We sistergirls, Miss Pasha, girl. And sistergirls tear each other's ass up when they get messy. But they don't ever turn they backs on each other. You might not wanna forget it. Don't ever turn ya back on me, Miss Pasha, girl."

I choke back a rushing wave of emotions. I set the flat iron down and grab the comb to finish styling her hair. "I'll be sure to never forget that." I lean in and wrap my arms around her. "Messy or not, you're all right with me, Cassandra."

"Oooh, you'se a real dirty bitch, Miss Pasha, girl. I can't stand shit you stand for." She turns her head from the mirror, casting her gaze downward as she rummages through her handbag. She pulls out a tissue and dabs her eyes. "Finish up my goddamn hair, so I can get the hell on up outta here. You ain't even 'bout to do me, goddammit. And mess up these four hundred-dollar mink lashes."

I can't even... mmph. I shake my head, spinning her around in the chair one last time. She turns her head. My heartstrings tug as Booty fights to keep me from seeing this side of her. I unsnap the cape from around her neck, handing her a mirror and glancing up at the clock. Nine o'clock at night.

"See. You shitted ya drawz, Miss Pasha, girl. Lashes right, weave right. Mmph. Can't a bitch serve me, but you, sugah-boo." She gets up from her seat, opening up her clutch, then counting two grand. She hands it to me, telling me to keep the change. I shake my head. "I think I'ma collect on the rest of that debt you owe me, Miss Pasha, girl." She tucks her purse under arm.

I blink. "Oh, you want me to write you that check after all. Why don't I just give you back your money? I already told you everything'd be on the house for a year."

She toots her lips, giving me the evil eye. "Don't do me. And I tol' you I got me sponsors to maintain my upkeep. And, no, I don't want a check. I want them dead presidents. But tonight, we goin' out to celebrate, goddammit!"

I frown. "*Out* to celebrate what?"

She bucks her eyes. "To the death of a no-good, dirty nigga; that's what we celebratin'. You free, Miss Pasha, girl. You can suck you a lil' dingaling now wit'out that ole crazy coon tryna do you. You can suck you down a nut wit' peace of mind now, sugah-boo."

I roll my eyes, sucking my teeth. "Oh, whatever." I tell her she can have a whole year of salon services for free as my way of repaying what she thinks I owe her, but I'm not interested in going anywhere near The Crack House.

She tilts her head. "You'se a lie. Don't do me, Miss Pasha, girl. What I need free goddamn salon services for when I keep me sponsors to keep my nails 'n' hair did? You ain't makin' no sense,

Miss Pasha, girl. Think 'n' stop tryna be messy. You goin' out wit' me for stealin' JT's cock, *tonight*, 'n' that's that, *so* you might as well get yo' mind right. You owe me. Now go get yo' wears right. And don't play no games, Miss Pasha, girl. Be ready by ten thirty. Matter of fact, I'ma sit right here 'n' entertain"—she points over at Mel—"that big ole hunky, chunky six-stacks of sexy man meat sittin' over there while you clean up. Then we gonna all walk outta here together wit' yo' ole sneaky-ass."

I shake my head. I can't help but chuckle at her ass as I straighten up my area, then move toward the back to my office. I shut my door, then go to my closet, unlocking it, then rolling a trunk out and pulling up a floorboard, which hides the customized floor safe. I slide all the receipts and earnings for the day inside, then lock it, putting everything back. I go into the second safe in the wall where I keep emergency cash, pulling out four stacks of hundred-dollar bills totaling ten grand. I stuff the money into my handbag, then lock everything up, shutting off my light and locking my office door.

Forty-Four

There are no coincidences; only moments of opportunity...

"**S**ugah-boo, I *knew* I was a bad bitch when I was young and hot in the ass, goddammit," Booty says, peering at me over the rim of her Gucci wraparounds. It's pitch-dark out and I'm still trying to figure out why she has on shades. But, okay.

Anyway, we've been sitting out in her truck, talking. Well, she's talking. I'm listening as she confides in me things about her childhood and life that she's never shared with anyone else. Like how every nigga she ever let run up in her raw wasn't because she wanted *him* to love *her*, but that she wanted him to *leave* her with *something* she could love even when he was long gone. How she wanted lots of babies she could love and know they'd love her back no matter how fucked up she felt inside because she'd always do her best by them. And she knew babies and kids loved unconditionally. How she'd never turn her back on them the way her mother and grandmother had done her, which is why she's hard on them and overprotective of them at the same time.

She's shared all of this and more. Things I never knew about her. Or never really cared to ask. Or never cared about...until now. Booty isn't the type of chick I would have ever aspired to be with, or get to know, outside of the salon.

But here I am.

And here we are sitting outside, at almost midnight, two unlikely souls, somehow bonding, forming a very strange—yet, endearing—friendship that I never would have guessed, or imagined, possible.

I look over at her and smile. "Girl, you're *still* a bad bitch."

She snaps her head back, smacking her lips. "Miss Pasha, girl, don't do me. I *know* I'm still a bad bitch, sugah-boo. I ain't need you to remind me. But, thanks, I guess. Annnnyway, I was real grown back then with real grown titties 'n' a real grown juicy ass. And a bitch couldn't tell me shit, especially after I started fuckin'. Oooh, yes, gawd, Trigger—Jah'Mel and Darius's *fahver*—that no-good, big-dick, gun-happy nigga-coon, showed me how to make this cootie-coo skeet. Yes, lawd, he fucked my drawz inside out, Miss Pasha, girl." She clutches her chest, shaking her head and waving a hand in the air. "Ooooh, I was so hot-in-the-ass for the dingdong back then, Miss Pasha, girl…"

I shake my head, laughing. "Cassandra, girl. I can't with you. You *still* hot-in-the-ass."

"Ooooh, Miss Pasha, girl. I can't stand *shit* you stand for, god-dammit. You stay tryna do me, sugah-boo. You know I *love* me some good goddamn dingaling, yes, lawd! But don't even get cute, sugah-boo; you like you a whole lotta cock-a-doodle-doo, too. So don't do me with ya ole cock-washin' ass. That's what got ya sneaky-ass in all that shit in the first place. But I ain't even goin' there with ya ole sensitive-ass 'cause you know I don't do messy."

I feign insult. "Ohmygod, Cass, I am *not* sensitive."

She toots her lips, raising a brow. "Sugah-boo, *boom-boom!* You'se a lie. The last time I said somethin' 'bout ya dick-suckin' ways, ya ass turned up the gas 'n' took it to a bitch's head. Oooh, you did me right, goddammit! But you really ain't have'ta do me upside the head with that gun like that. You had'a bitch seein' stars. Oooh, it made me nut my drawz, goddammit. Now *that's* how a bitch s'posed to bring it, if she gonna do me. You gave it to me rough 'n' dirty. And, sugah-boo, you the *first* bitch who *ever* wet my drawz right in a fight!

"But, yes, gawd, you ain't the only cum-guzzler on deck. I can suck a mean dingaling, too, Miss Pasha, girl. Prolly not as good as yo' ole dick-swallowin' ass. You prolly make a nigga-coon's asshole whistle when you suckin' that thang-a-lang-a-lang. And don't think I ain't see how Stax was droolin' 'n' lookin' all cross-eyed 'n' googly-eyed at you at Miss FeFe's funeral. His eyeballs stayed bouncin' 'round the room tryna act like he ain't seein' you. I *know* you done had them ole fluffy dick suckers wrapped around his dingaling. You prolly done fucked him, too. Ole nasty stank-ass."

I crack up laughing. "You know what, Booty, motherfuck you, goddammit. No comment. Your ass is a hot damn mess."

"Uh-huh, but you know I ain't *ever* messy. But, annnnnyway, Miss Pasha, girl, as I was sayin' before you cut me off..."—she takes a long pull off her blunt—"... you sure you don't want you none'a this, sugah-boo?" I shake my head. Tell her no. She twists her lips, blowing smoke out of the cracked window. "Mmmph. Don't think I'm givin' up on ya ass. One'a these days I'ma get ya ole high-class ass to roll 'n' burn with me. I'ma get ya ass lit up like a damn torch."

"Um, *sugah-boo*," I say jokingly. "Good luck. Let me know how you make out with that."

She grunts. "I ain't goin' there with you right now 'cause we on a mission." She bangs the palm of her hand on the steering wheel. "Yes, gawd, Miss Pasha, girl. Them nigga-coons gonna fall out 'n' shit they drawz when they see us two bad-ass, classy bitches step-pin' up in this muthasucka tonight, goddammit. I'ma turn up the gas on them nigga-coons, goddammit. Yes, fahvergawd!"

I groan.

She pulls her shades down, peers over the rim. "Don't do me. Anyway, back to Trigger's ole grimy-ass. If he didn't get his dumb-ass locked up and get them football numbers, ain't no tellin' how I woulda turned out. A bitch prolly woulda been wild 'n' crazy…"

I shoot her an incredulous look. "Uh, and you don't *think* you're already wild and crazy?"

"Sugah-boo, *boom, boom!* Now, I might kick up the gas 'n' light a nigga-coon up when he tryna do me 'n' I might even snatch a bottle or two off the bar 'n' take it to a booga-coon's head when she tryna be messy, but I ain't hardly wild 'n' crazy. Shit, Miss Pasha, girl. I was on my own way before Beulah's ole rotten ass ever tossed me outta her house. Shitty-bitch! Oooh, goddammit!

"E'ery time I think 'bout that ole nasty bitch, leavin' her ole crusty, pissy-ass drawz in the middle of the bathroom floor, wantin' me to cook 'n' clean 'n' rub her ole nasty, swollen-ass feet, lookin' like goddamn pig hoofs, then the bitch callin' me all kinda names, callin' me all kinda ugly bitches 'n' sayin' I ain't ever gonna be shit 'cause I ain't shit, tellin' me I ain't ever gonna be nothin' but an ole junkie crack-whore like my momma. That hateful-ass bitch tried to tear my spirits, Miss Pasha, girl. Mmmph. Let a bitch keep tellin' her babies they ain't shit, that they ain't worth shit, that ain't nobody gonna ever love 'em, 'n' see how fast they start eventually believin' that shit.

"So, Miss Pasha, girl. All my life I been fightin'. And I'm still fightin'. Fightin' to prove stank-ass Beulah wrong, that *I am* some-body. The bitch's dead 'n' I'm still tryna show that bitch that I ain't none'a the shit she said I was, or was gonna be. Oooh, I wish that bitch was still alive. I'd beat her ass dead, goddammit!"

I reach over and grab her hand, choking back upsurges of sadness as she shares. "You don't have to prove shit to her, or anyone else."

"I know I don't. But I still do 'cause I'm so mad at the bitch for dyin' on me before I could show that bitch that I ain't a junkie, crack-whore…" She gives me a sly grin. "Well, I *do* do me a lil' whorin', but I ain't whorin' for no damn crack. And I ain't somewhere doin' molly-whops 'n' drinkin' syrups 'n' all other kinda dumb shit. I do my weed. Do my drinks 'n' my hard damn dingaling. And I ain't givin' none'a that up. Maybe the weed one day"—she takes another pull from her blunt, then shakes her head—"no, gawd, I ain't givin' this good shit up, either. And I'm definitely not givin' up on no dingaling, no, gawd! Hard dingaling makes this cootie-coo go *boom-boom*, Miss Pasha, girl!"

"Anyway, I been fightin' to keep niggas from tryna do me. Fightin' to keep bitches from tryna do me. Fightin' to keep all my kids together. Fightin' to make sure they stay clothed 'n' they black asses in school. Fightin' to keep from ever goin' hungry or bein' on the streets. All I know how'ta do is fight. And, yes, *Fahver-Gawd*, I'll take it upside a nigga-coon's head if they fuck with me, my kids, or any-damn-body I got me some love for."

I turn my head toward the window, quickly dabbing the tear that escapes from my eye as I watch people spill out of luxury cars, blinged-out hoopties, and gypsy cabs all piped out in their wears to get their party on. I say a silent pray.

Booty quickly flicks the rest of her blunt out the window, then flips down the visor, sliding open the lighted mirror. She digs into her purse and pulls out a designer compact.

"And bitch," she starts as she glides a fresh coat of lipstick over her plush lips, "you *still* ain't said shit 'bout how you got into my house 'n' got JT's dingaling up outta my freezer. And you *still* ain't say whether you sucked it or sautéed it." She pauses, smacking her lips together, then fussing with her bang. "But I ain't even gonna press. You owe me, goddammit."

"And I'm paying up now, aren't I?"

She grunts, tooting her lips up. "Mmmph. Legend dead. Felecia dead. Jasper dead. And JT's cock gone. But *you* ain't had nothin' to do wit' nothin', huh, Miss Pasha, girl?"

I glance at her, feigning insult. "Ohmygod. How could you think such a thing? That would make me the judge, jury, and executioner. And you know I don't have it in me to be any of those things."

She twists her lips up, pulling her shades down and crossing her eyes. "Uh-huh, if you say so. And my ass is flat. I know you an ole ruthless bitch underneath all that cuteness 'n' finery, sugah-boo. So don't do me."

I don't say a word, turning my head and glancing over at the club. I blink several times as if I'm hallucinating when I spot someone who looks like Stax behind the wheel of a metallic-silver Benz G550, but I quickly dismiss it as silly because I've never known him drive anything flashy, let alone an SUV with that kind of six-figure price tag.

Booty snaps her compact shut, tossing it back into her bag. "Miss Pasha, girl, c'mon, let's go up in here 'n' turn the booty heat up on these coons." I suck my teeth, sighing. "Mmmph. Suck all you want. But I tol' you, you owe me. So time to pay up."

My stomach knots as I get out of her truck. *Okay, girl. It's only one night. You got this*, I think, as she sets the alarm. *It won't be that bad.*

Booty comes around and links her arm through mine, our heels clicking against the cement in sync as we make our way up the sidewalk toward The Crack House. "And Miss Pasha, girl," she says, rolling a piece of gum in her mouth. "You gonna have some Clit Lickers or a few Wet Drawz wit' me, too, goddammit!"

I shake my head. "Ohgod, no. Not Wet Drawz, please. I'll have me a Cosmo."

She sucks her teeth. "Don't do me, sugah-boo. They aint servin' none'a that dainty shit up in here. But don't worry. I'ma have Big Mike do you up right. I tol' him all about you, so he gonna have a special drink on deck for you."

I groan. "Ohgod. What is it?"

She laughs. "The Dick Sucker, Miss Pasha, girl. What else. Don't play, sugah-boo. Isn't that what you do best?" I can't help but join in her laughter as the glass doors open and I'm smacked in the face by the loud, booming sound of bass pumping out of massive speakers as Jay-Z and Kanye West's "Welcome to The Jungle," their latest song, bounces off the walls.

"Yessssss, goddammmmit!" Booty screams, throwing a hand up in the air and bouncing her ass, zigzagging her way through the crowd. "Ohhh! Ohhh! We gonna light some candles 'n' do some fuckin' tonnnnnight…yesssss, yesss! Welcome to the jungle, welcome to the jungle, goddammit!" She dips down low, then pops back up and grabs my hand, pulling me along. "Yesss, gawd! It's packed up in here wit' dicks 'n' hoes!"

I blink. The crowd is wild. It's so packed in here. We're not even through the club good and niggas are all up on Booty, likes she's a goddess or hood celebrity. And she turns it out right in the middle of the floor. She's in her glory. And they're even trying to press up on me, licking their lips, and eyeballing me like I'm the Last Supper.

"Oooooh, Miss Pasha, girl! Mmmph. Look at Stax's ole fine, big-dick self all jeweled up 'n' juicy over at the bar! Yessss, goddammit! Verrrrrry special! Fuck the flowers 'n' gifts; you gonna get you some dingaling tonight! Yesss! Yessss! Yesss, goddammit, welcome to the jungle!"

Mygod, it's a zoo in here! And booty's the Zookeeper. I clutch my purse to my chest, feeling so out of place. I spot Stax with his back to us. Whomever he's with, nods their head in our direction, causing him to crane his neck. Our eyes meet. And his butter-soft, pussy-eating-toe-sucking lips ease into a sly grin.

Yeah, I'm going to need me something real strong to drink to get through tonight. And a Dick Sucker isn't it!

Forty-Five

There is deliverance in death…

Another funeral. Another closed casket, I think staring at the portrait of the man I had loved, then hated, then wished dead. And eventually tortured.

When Stax saw me in the club with Booty three nights ago, he'd asked if I wanted anything special for Jasper's funeral. I told him no. Still, as his wife there were things that I felt obligated to tend to, like handling the obituary and the programs, and making sure there were flowers here from his son. And me.

I kiss Jaylen on his head, breathing in his innocence. Grateful he is too young to know, to understand, that he'd had parents who went to great lengths to hurt and destroy the other. And feeling justified in doing so.

And, no, it wasn't always bad. Life with Jasper was fun. It was spontaneous. Intense. Exciting. Explosive. Adventurous. Then somewhere toward the middle of our relationship, it became hectic. Obsessive. Controlling. Demanding. Stressful.

It became full of jealousy, drama, and lies.

Until what we had finally became frightening. Destructive. Violent. Fatal.

Finally ending in death. One of us had to go. I'm glad it was he instead of me.

He was beyond redemption. So, as far as I'm concerned, who-ever dumped their clip in his head did him, and *me*—and *maybe* the next bitch, a favor.

I peel my gaze away from the man I once loved, blinking away his haunting smile, glancing around the funeral home. It's packed with the hood rich and fabulous—young and old, hustlers and hoes, wannabe crooks and gangsters, pimps, players, shakers and movers, ex-lovers, and jump-offs, all congregating here to pay their final respects to the man many of them admired, respected, loved and—I'm sure for some, feared.

Everyone, except me and…Stax, interestingly, sit or stand in a fixed state of shock, their minds still reeling from the tragic news of Jasper's expiry. All of his relatives, mostly from Connecticut, pack the pews mourning the loss of their revered loved one, shaking their heads in disbelief. Speaking in hushed whispers how tragic, how unfortunate, how untimely, his death is. "The streets done took another one of ours," I overhear a very pretty older, brown-skinned woman saying to her male companion as they walk by. "Such a pity. Jasper was one of the good ones."

I raise a brow, puckering my lips. Mmmph. Not a word.

Glancing at my Harry Winston Lattice, I check the time. Eleven o'clock. *One more excruciating hour and this dog and pony show will finally be underway.* I keep my gaze on my wrist getting lost—no matter how brief, in the brilliance of the nine-carat diamonds. "Hey, Pasha, girl," Bianca says, leaning in and kissing me on the cheek. "I love you dearly. But we really have to stop meeting like this."

"Ugh. Tell me about it. If I have to sit through another funeral, I'm going to slice my wrists." I smile up at her. "Thanks for coming."

She strokes the side of my face. "I had to be here for you." She hands me an envelope. "You know I love you, girl." I smile again. Let her know how much I appreciate her in my life. She and Paris greet each other, then she excuses herself to go over to express her sympathy to Mona.

I glance over at Avery, catching him eyeing me. I tilt my head, purposefully looking over in his direction. My shades hide the glint of burning. He quickly averts his gaze.

I shift in my seat as Jasper's grandmother wraps her arms around the portrait of him, wailing. It takes Mona and three of her cousins to help pry the eighty-seven-year-old woman's frail fingers away from the frame. She faints in front of his casket, pulling down with her the half-couch casket spray, my all-white floral tribute to my dead husband, the nigga who wreaked havoc in my life; the nigga who violated me in the worst way imaginable.

Mmmph. Four-hundred-and-fifty dollars' worth of white carnations, gerberas, gladioli, asters, orchids, and roses all toppled over. I strain to keep from rolling my eyes as Mona tries to reposition the spray on Jasper's casket.

It's no secret to most of his family that we were separated, that I'd obtained an order of protection, and wanted a divorce. So the fact that I'm sitting here staring into space, emotionless, should be of no surprise to any of them. Jasper had been dead to me, emotionally, long before his body ever hit the bottom of his steel box adorned with platinum finish.

Still, many of the mourners come over to me, offering a warm hug, a few words of heartfelt sympathy, or an envelope stuffed with Hallmark gibberish—and, some checks and dead presidents. The best I can do is offer back a tight-lipped smile and, perhaps, a gracious head nod.

I rock Jaylen in my arms, thankful he's asleep. I lift my black shades from my face and dab the rim of my left eye with the handkerchief clutched in my hand. Not because of tears. There's something in my eye. I blink, then drop my shades back down over my eyes.

"Pasha, you okay?" Paris asks, sitting to the right of me. I nod. Once again, I sit in the second pew behind a wailing grandmother, burying one of her own with Paris right by my side. The only difference this time, I'm not flanked with Mel and Lamar sitting in the back of me. Lamar is still recuperating from his gunshot wounds, while Mel is sitting outside in my stretch limo, waiting on me to walk out of here.

I'm headed for the airport to L.A., where I'll be for the next month in preparation of my grand opening of Nappy No More II, which will be an exclusive, extremely upscale salon and spa in Beverly Hills, catering strictly to the true elite clientele, wealthy and famous. I have to say, I really lucked up with a wonderful realtor out in L.A., Katrina Rivers, who located this prime piece of real estate property for me. While Nappy No More I continues to serve the hood rich and ghetto-fabulous, I've hired Greta to manage it.

Stax, Sparks, Desmond and Avery—Jasper's blood, confidants, partners in crime, and now…pallbearers, all stand overwrought with grief.

Stax, Sparks, and Desmond stand at Jasper's casket, an arm around the other's waist, linked together by sadness and loss, remembering Jasper for who he was to them. Sparks' head is bowed. My heart aches for them when I see tears squeeze from the corner of Stax's closed lids.

Mona walks over and squeezes herself in between Desmond and Sparks, their arms wrapping her into the fold. She is crying profusely, for many reasons. Love and guilt being the two I knew of. Jasper was her cousin, yes. But she also knew what he was capable of. She knew of, overheard, many of his dirty deeds. She'd covered for him in her youth. Made excuses for him.

The pastor opens with, "Vengeance is mine, sayeth the Lord…"

From across the church, I catch Booty eyeballing me over the rim of her Guccis with her lips twisted up. I roll my eyes, turning my head as someone gets up and begins singing "Amazing Grace," followed by a solo of "Precious Lord."

When the second song ends, the pastor gets up and finishes his eulogy, saying something about forgiveness and letting go, and letting God, but I'm so disconnected from this whole ordeal that I'm not really paying attention. It's not until a young girl—who looks to be no more than twelve or thirteen—takes a seat at the piano and belts out "It's So Hard to Say Goodbye to Yesterday" sounding like a mini Lauryn Hill while taking me back to an eleven-year-old girl who sat at a piano and sang this same song in this same church at her father's funeral, that a wave of emotions overcome me. I was that little girl.

I choke back tears as Paris wraps her arm around me, knowingly, pulling me into her and whispering how much she loves me.

And, without warning, I start to feel my body shaking from the inside out. Start to feel my chest tightening. Then I am sobbing.

Not for Nana.

Not for the scandalous bitch who betrayed me. Felecia Travonda Allen. The bitch I murdered.

Not for the nigga whom I once loved with everything in me. Jasper Edwin Tyler. The nigga I married, had a child with, then did whatever I could to make him pay for what he did to me.

Not for Legend or JT or the other ruthless motherfuckers who fucked their dicks into my mouth and pumped their seeds down into my neck.

No.

I am wailing…for me.

Pasha Nivea Alona Allen-Tyler.

For my wretched soul.

For the bitch with the broken spirit.

I cry for forgiveness.

Not for me.

Not for my sins.

But for all those who've trespassed against me.

I stretch out my hand, tears and snot, mourning the loss of the woman I once was. I clutch my son to my chest, sobbing. Shedding the shell of the old me.

Jasper did this to me. Felecia did this to me. Legend did this to me.

But, most importantly, *I* did this to me.

I remove my shades, wipe my eyes and blow my nose. Finally, I look at Jasper's portrait one last time. My cherry-red-painted lips curl into a sly grin.

Yeah, motherfucker, look at you. Boxed and beaten, ready for your final resting place. You thought I was a weak bitch, huh? Now who's the fool?

I hand Jaylen over to Paris and get up as the pastor says whatever he's saying. All eyes are on me as I lift his coffin. I want to see him. I need to see him.

One last time.

I hear the gasps around the room as I lift the lid. Down at the foot of his casket, scattered all over his feet with the eight missing toes, are Felecia's ashes. The rest of her pregnant body cremated. They deserve each other. She wanted him. Now she has him. They can burn in hell together.

Revenge is most definitely a dish best served cold. I spit in his face. *I hope you burn a thousand deaths, nigga!*

I slowly close the lid, feeling weights dropping and shackles unsnapping. Everyone in the room is mortified, stonestill, as I grab my son from Paris and saunter down the aisle with my head high, feeling light, feeling free.

I step out into the brightness of day; the crisp air cooling my cheeks as I make my way toward my waiting limo, sliding in the backseat with my son. I breathe a sigh of relief as Mel slides in across from me, shutting the door.

"You good," he wants to know, his gaze warming my skin.

I toss my bang from over my eye. "I couldn't be better."

The driver pulls off. And I close my eyes, not once looking back. It is finally over for me.

And justice was served mercilessly to all those who crossed me.

My way.

Epilogue

There's a price to be paid and joys to be gained when we finally let go…

FOUR MONTHS LATER…

Despite the dust of Felecia's and Jasper's deaths finally settling, up until two days ago—the day I stepped off the plane at Los Angeles International Airport in preparation for the Nappy No More II Grand Opening, I had been feeling… I don't know. Restless. My spirit was still unsettled. My nerves still rattled.

I had wrestled with the knowledge of Mona's husband being the one I referred to as the *Calm One* ever since I'd learned of his tattoo of a panther over his left shoulder.

For weeks, after Jasper's funeral, I played the news over and over in my head to the point I was practically obsessing over it. Then, finally, I decided to let it go. I had to. Avery had caused me no real harm. So there was no reason for me to cause him any. Ruining his marriage or destroying Mona's world, like mine had been destroyed, wasn't an option. I love her. And I didn't want to risk losing Mona's friendship.

So I had come to terms with letting it go.

And I had.

Until three days ago.

Until I pulled out my laptop and logged back into my Deep Throat Diva AOL email account, pulling up an old email from Ready2nutInU, then emailing him. WE NEED TO TALK. Four hours later, he replied back. I'D HOPED WE'D NEVER NEED 2. WHERE?

The next morning, at seven o'clock, we met where it all began. Mountainside Park. I slide into his SUV. And although flashes of his beautiful curved dick popped in and out of my head as I sat in the front seat looking at him, there was only one thing on my mind. "Why, Avery?"

His cologne wafted over to me. I breathed him in and watched as he fidgeted in his seat, searching for words to explain, to express, his regret for his involvement in what happened to me.

"On my family and everything else I love, Pasha, I wanted no part of that shit Jasper had planned for you. And I refused to get down with it. But, then, I was asked to be there to make sure shit didn't get crazy. To make sure none of them niggas got way out of pocket and tried no extra shit. I tried to keep you safe the best way I could, Pasha. It hurt like hell to watch them do that shit to you."

"But you did nothing to stop it."

"I did what I could," he offered solemnly. "I can't say any more than that. I hope, one day, you'll be able to forgive me."

I swallowed back the sordid memories of those nights tied up down in that basement, feeling a hole being slowly eaten in the pit of my stomach. Still, I had to be honest; if not for him, for myself. "There's nothing to forgive, Avery. I wanted to be mad at you. I swear I did. Wanted to hate you like I hated all the rest. But I couldn't. And I still can't. Because, as crazy as this sounds, you were the only one giving me hope that I'd get out of there alive. How much money did you earn for that?"

He quickly shifted his gaze from mine, then landed his eyes on me again. "I didn't do it for the paper, Pasha. I did it because I had to. I needed to."

I gave him a quizzical look. Wanted him to elaborate on his need to, on why he had to. Yet, I didn't push when he didn't say more. It wasn't that important. If for nothing else, meeting with him face to face was more about letting him know that I knew. The few times I'd seen him since my attack, I thought his uneasiness around me was because of our online encounter, thought it had to do with his secret desire for me to wet his dick. And here it was because he'd been there. And guilt was eating away at him.

I eyed him. "Tell me something, Avery. How many times did you get off after standing around watching me being forced to super-soak all those niggas' dicks? Did the images stay in your head? Did they brick your dick? Did you go home afterward and fuck Mona?"

He nervously opened and closed his legs. Ran a hand over his face. I was tempted to fuck with him. Curious to reach between his legs and grab his dick, to see how hard it'd gotten. I burned into him with my glare, waiting, smirking.

"What now…?" he said. All of a sudden, he'd gotten concerned I'd expose him to Mona. I wanted no part in that. But he didn't need to know that. I let the possibility dangle over his head, allowing an ominous silence to fill the space around us.

"Pasha," he softly called out to me as I opened the door to leave, my body shifted, both heels already planted into the ground. I craned my neck, glancing at him, meeting his pained gaze. "I really do love Mona. I'm just not sexually satisfied."

JT's face flashed in my head. And my heart ached for what he'd put her through. "Mona needs you, Avery. Talk to her."

He looked away. When he returned his gaze, there was a glint of sorrow in his eyes. "I've given her all I can. I have nothing else for her. I'm tired of talking."

"Then leave her. Get out before she gets hurt. Before she realizes everything she's believed in was a lie."

"I'm not leaving what we've built together."

I felt a tinge of sadness bubbling up inside of me—for him, and Mona. "Then my advice, Avery: Be *very, very* careful." I narrowed my eyes. "You have *no* idea exactly what lengths a scorned woman, a woman with nothing to lose, will go to in order to make someone she's loved suffer for hurting or betraying her." I tilted my head, kept my eyes locked on him. "You see where Jasper is, don't you?" He gave me a blank stare, then blinked as my words finally registered. Despite myself, I leaned back into the truck, giving him a light kiss on the cheek. "You take care of yourself, Avery. And be safe."

I eased out of his truck, shutting the door, never looking back. Mona would find out on her own, in her own time, what type of man she was married to. It was only a matter of time.

The die had been cast.

"Paaaaasha, *daaaaahling*," Zeus, my newly hired, seven-inch-heeled, gender-bender office manager for the salon here in L.A., drawls out as he sticks a wiry head of sandy-brown curls through the door. "Let's not keep the guests waiting."

"I'll be out in a sec," I say, slipping my diamond studs into my ears, screwing on the backs, then gliding a coat of gloss over my freshly painted lips. I smile at the reflection staring back at me in the mirror. Pleased, no…*happy*, with what I see.

Jasper had tried to break me. I *thought* he had broken me. I believed he had destroyed me. But, no, I wasn't broken. I was beaten. I wasn't destroyed. I was damaged. But I am not the one who ended up dead.

I'm the last bitch standing—stilettos on my feet, diamonds around my neck, stepping over the bodies with over ten million dollars of Jasper's money, an insurance policy worth a half a mil that I'd taken out on him a few months before we were married, and the insurance check from a house I had someone else burn down.

And here I am. This is what I've become: a *ruthless* bitch that has emerged from the clouds of gun smoke and ashes, a bitch that will deliver your head on a silver platter and your tongue on a pitchfork without blinking an eye.

Fuck what anyone says. Vengeance was/is *mine*.

I pick up the folded piece of paper lying on the vanity, and open it, staring at the only visible name left on it. *Killah*. He'll have his own hell to pay one day. But it won't be by me, I think, as I reach for a pack of salon matches, striking a match, then setting a corner of the paper on fire. I toss the burning paper into the toilet, then flush.

Taking a deep breath, I shut off my light, and finally step out of my private bathroom, wearing a flowing black V-line dress with a cutout back and high/low hemline and a pair of six-inch stilettos. I decided to keep my look simple, yet classy.

He snaps his fingers in a zigzagging motion. "*Fiiiiiiierrrce*, I say. You serve it. You *weeeeerk* it." I smile, taking in his smooth, honey-coated skin, long lashes, and pouty glossed lips. He licks his lips at my shimmering bare legs. "And you are giving me legs for *daaaaaaayz*, Miss Honeeey, okay. You give me life."

I smile. Not only is Zeus beautiful to look at, he is a refreshing breath of air, and a no-nonsense kind of guy. He's a true godsend.

With flying back and forth to Jersey, I need someone I can trust to hold things down here for me. Still, I felt I should warn him before I hired him to not ever cross me. His response sealed the deal. "Diva, the only thing I cross are these long legs. Now when can I start?"

So far, he is more than I could have ever hoped for in an office manager. And I am falling head over heels in love with his energy. I follow him out front.

Dozens of white roses, calla lilies, and lilacs are situated throughout the salon in tall, sleek crystal vases. I glance around, smiling. Yes, I truly have arrived. I'm a young, beautiful, successful, and *very* wealthy woman surrounded by love, and lots of fine, hardbodied men. Life couldn't be any better.

Everyone claps. And then I welcome and thank them for sharing in my success. Nappy No More II is more than a hair and body salon. It's an experience.

From the moment you step through the sliding glass door into the reception area and are greeted by a stunning rain curtain that flows from the ceiling to the black lava stones in the marble floor and the floating suspended mirrors, you know you have stepped into ten-thousand square feet of sleek sophistication. And the floor-to-ceiling windows, which allow natural light to enter throughout the salon, add to the ambiance, while the concierge desk and retail displays and open color bar offer optimum service and products.

The Steinmetz diamonds around my neck and wrists come alive under the recess lighting as I step into the center of the salon, a flute of sparkling scrumpy in my hand, glancing around the elegant space, smiling. Everyone is here: Paris, Porsha, and Persia; Mona; Bianca and Garrett; Cassandra; and, Greta, who was my savior during my most trying moments. I owe her so much. They are all milling about, sipping on their choice of Armand de Brignac or Krug while nibbling on shrimp, caviar, and an array of other hors d'oeuvres.

"Ooooh, Miss Pasha, girl," Booty says, sauntering up to me dressed in a showstopping nude Emilio Pucci gown with a scalloped hemline. "You snatched ya damn drrrrawzzz, sugah-boo, 'n' showed ya fluffy ass wit' this right here. Oooh, you so goddamn high-class. You done made me shit my drawz wit' all this elegance…"

I cringe inwardly. But Booty is Booty. And I'd never want her to change. Well, okay…maybe just a little here and there. I give her a wide smile. "Thank you. I'm glad you decided to come. I am really happy you're here."

"Well, you know I ain't never been on no plane, Miss Pasha, girl. But ain't no way I was gonna miss a chance to see how the rich 'n' famous do it. And you did me right, putting me in first-class. Yes, gawd. I could get used to this, sugah-boo. I wonder if I could transfer my section-eight out here 'n' get me one'a them big ole mansions I seen drivin' through here. Mmmph." She sees the blank look on my face, chuckling. "Miss Pasha, girl, you know I ain't leavin' the hood, sugah-boo. But I hope to get me some celebrity dingaling before I leave." She reaches for another flute of champagne. "I shoulda brought my flask 'cause you know I ain't wit' all this fruity-tootie drinkin'. I need somethin' wit' a lil' more thug juice in it. I'm glad I packed me some get right in my clutch, though. I'ma go outside in a minute 'n' get mind right."

Despite myself, I can't help but laugh. I give her a hug. "Cassandra, thank you."

"Ooooh, now hol' on, Miss Pasha, girl? You know I ain't wit' all this huggin' mess. Now what you thankin' me for?"

I smile at her, cupping her face, and looking her in the eyes. "For being your incredibly ghetto-fabulous self, for having my back, and for becoming a very special part of my life. You forced your way into my heart. And I love you, girl."

She rapidly flaps her extra-long mink lashes. "Motherfuck you, Miss Pasha, girl. Goddamn you. You stay tryna do me." Her lips quiver. "You ain't gonna be stayin' out here, is you? 'Cause I need to know how I'ma get my hair did. You know I can't let no other bitch lay her fingers through my scalp but you."

"Cass, I'll *always* be here for you even when you piss me off... to do your hair. I'm not going to ever turn my back on you."

I'm caught completely off guard when she grabs me in an embrace, and bursts into tears. It doesn't take long before we are both crying. She backs out of our embrace. We pull ourselves together, drying her eyes. "You ole ugly bitch. I hate...ev-v-eryt-t-thing... you stand for."

Dabbing under my eyes, I laugh. "I love you, too, Cass."

She grunts. "You ole messy bitch. You lucky I'ma keep it real elegant 'n' not show my..." Her voice trails off when a celebrity rapper steps through the sliding doors with an entourage of ballers in tow. "Yes, lawdgawd, I think I done found my next...let's see, one, two, three, four, five, six sponsors. Heeeeey, sugah-boos," she coos when she catches their eyes. I eye her, shaking my head, as she sways her hips in pursuit of her next victims.

I dab under my eyes again with the back of my pointer fingers. I smile warmly when I spot my realtor, Katrina, walking through the doors holding the hand of a deep dish of tall, dark chocolate. *Mygod!* My knees almost buckle. She throws me a wave, walking toward me, smiling. "Girl, you are fabulous," I say as we air kiss. "So glad you could make it."

She lifts her Cartier Paris shades, resting them atop her head. "Boo," she says warmly. "I wouldn't have missed it. The place is fiiiyah, girl. I love what you've done to it. You are servin' me life. I can't wait to get my hair laid for filth up in here." She turns to Mr. Fine Chocolate. "Oh, babe. This is Pasha, the owner. She's from Jersey, too. Pasha, this is my boo, Alex."

"Yo, what's good?" He extends a wide hand. And my hand gets lost in it as he shakes it. "Congrats on ya spot. It's mad classy."

I smile. "Thank you." Katrina grabs a flute of champagne off a silver tray as a waiter walks by. "There's also a juice bar," I say, looking at Mr. Fine Chocolate, "around the corner. Please. Mingle. Make yourselves comfortable." He excuses himself, kisses Katrina on the cheek, then makes his way through the salon. "Girl, he's fine. When's the big day?"

She sucks her teeth, waving me on playfully. "Girl, he's aiight. I think I'll keep him around for a while." She smiles, glowing. "We're tyin' the knot in the fall. October, if I don't have to body him."

I cough almost choking. "Ohmygod. I can't. Katrina, you're a mess."

She laughs. "Hon, I'm dead-serious. I love my Alex. And I know he loves me. But trust. That fine muthafuh…man, is *still* a man. But I've already warned him. If he ever crosses me, I'ma have him toe tagged."

I blink. She tilts her head. And there's something in her eyes that lets me know she means every word she's said. She chuckles. "You know my girl called me poppin' mad shit…ooh, excuse me, I'm still tryna work on my gutter mouth." I laugh. Tell her to be who she is. "Hon, I'm from the streets of Brooklyn. You don't really wanna see the real me. But anyway, my girl, Chanel, was *haawt* when you tossed her up outta ya salon in Jersey." She leans in, lowers her voice to a conspiratorial whisper. "I *know* her. And Trust. If she was googly-eyein' my man, I woulda cracked her face up wit' a flat iron, then tossed her out, too. I keep tellin' her gold-diggin' ass to stop trickin' for the next come up." I smile, shaking my head. I keep my comments to myself. We chitchat a few minutes more before she moves on to join the others.

Three hours later, the festivities begin winding down. Guests are saying their goodbyes. Booty has gotten her claws into her prey, tooting her lips up as she saunters out the door with him and his entourage. Katrina and her fiancé are long gone. Paris, Persia, and Porsha tell me how proud they are of me, giving me hugs before making their way to their suite at the L 'Ermitage. Porsha stops and reminds me to save the date for her upcoming wedding to her fiancé, Emerson, in the fall. I tell her I wouldn't miss it for the world. She blows me a kiss, tells me she loves me, then is out the door, climbing into the limo with her sisters.

Mona, Greta, Zeus and three of my new stylists, along with Mel, are the only ones still here when the one person I am shocked to see strolls through the doors with his swag on ten, carrying two magnums of Dom White Gold.

"Ohmygod, Stax! What are you doing here?"

"C'mon, Pash," he says, giving me a hug and kiss on the cheek. "Why you think? You know I was gonna be here. Even if you didn't hit me wit' an invite. I know I'm mad late." I smile. Tell him it doesn't matter that he's late. He's here and that's what truly means the most. Mona eyes me, then Stax.

He walks over and gives her a hug. Greets everyone else, setting the bottles of bubbly on the juice bar. He's seemingly unfazed by the fact that Zeus and the three stylists are eyeing him, practically drooling; seconds away from trying to pounce on him.

I grab another glass of sparkling cider while the rest of them drink and chatter. Finally, an hour after everyone is finally gone, Stax and I are in my office. I haven't seen him in three months. And prior to that, I'd only seen him a few times after Jasper's funeral. This is really the first time we've been alone.

"You lookin' real good, Pash. You glowin' all over, ma."

I smile. "Thank you. You're not looking so bad yourself." *No, you're looking fine as ever. Sexy as fuck!*

"I've missed you, Pash."

"Awwww. You didn't have to fly way out here to tell me this," I tease. "You could have simply called, or sent a text."

"Nah, I wanted...*needed*, to see you."

I swallow, feeling my skin heat.

"I've had you heavy on the brain the last few weeks, Pash." He pauses, takes a deep breath, then reaches for me. "This thing between us, Pash. I don't know what it is. I don't know what it means. All I know is..."

I stop him before he says more than he should. "It *doesn't* mean anything, Stax. It *didn't* mean anything." I turn away from him. Not because I am done with our conversation, or with him. No. I am afraid of what I'll say or do if he keeps talking, if he keeps staring into my eyes, trying to dig his way any deeper than he already is into my soul.

He reaches for my hand, pulling me to him. I immediately feel a pulsing in my pussy. I try to pull away. He refuses to let me.

"You know you don't mean that. Tell me you don't feel it every time we touch. Tell me you don't see it when I look at you. I see it when I look at you, Pash. I saw it the night I made love to you. The night you gave me all of you."

I turn my gaze from his. *God, no...please.* How dare he fly all the way out here, barging his way into my life on one of the most important days of my life, thinking there's some unspoken bond between us? The gall of him to think, assume, I'd seen it, felt it, too! Damn him!

Truth is, he's right. I saw it in his eyes the first, second, and third time, he fucked into my pussy. I felt it the night in my hotel suite. Felt the electricity, felt the heat. I inhale. In an instant, waves of memories wash over me, moistening the lips of my pussy.

"Maybe I shouldna flown way out here. I coulda waited for you to get back to Jersey to holla at you. But, nah, I hopped up on a whim and snatched up a last-minute ticket. I know I should let this shit go, Pash. Know I should just keep it movin'. But I can't, man. It's somethin'. And it's fuckin' wit' me, Pash. I need to know why I can't shake you, baby."

I feel like I am melting inside as he eyes me. His arms tighten around me. His mouth is on mine, his tongue slipping in. And I let myself get swept up in the heat until he finally breaks away.

"This shit is mad crazy, Pash. I already know tryna fuck wit' you is a dangerous game. But I'm ready to play it."

"Stax, I used you," I blurt out, reminding him of what I told him months ago. "I wanted to hurt Jasper, the way he'd hurt me. I told you this."

He shakes his head. "Yeah, I know what you tol' me. But, nah. I wanted to be used, Pash. I *wanted* you. I *still* want you. I've tried to put distance between us. Shit's fucked up, ma. I know what it is wit' you. I know how you get down. Still..." He shakes his head, again. "You gotta muhfucka open. And I'm man enough to admit that shit."

I blink.

He can't be serious? Not now. What was there really between us?

Nothing, except for a few good—uh, correction...*great*—dick-sucking moments; some delicious tongue work; and ten, thick, glorious inches of deep-dick fucking. Other than that the only common link between Stax and me is Jasper. And he's dead.

"So, what's the real problem, Pash? Talk to me."

"The problem is *me*, Stax." He looks surprised, but I continue. "I've loved everyone else except for me. I've loved niggas more than me. I've loved all the trappings of the fast life more than me. I've loved dick more than me. And I almost lost my life, risked my reputation, everything, with my impulsiveness. I was selfish, Stax. And while Jasper was locked up, I let loneliness morph itself into recklessness. If I am nothing else, I have to be true to myself. I told you once how I loved dick, Stax. Lots and lots of it. That hasn't changed. I'm in love with a big hard dick, Stax. I love sucking big dick—deep throating it, more than being fucked by it."

"C'mon, Pash, don't."

I hold up my hand to silence him. "Please, Stax. Let me finish. You are a good man. God, where were you fifteen years ago?" I shudder at the thought. "You're Jasper's cousin, for God's sake, Stax. I can't go there. *We* can't go there."

He smirks. "We already did, Pash. The match was struck the night I walked in ya office and scooped you up in my arms. I know it's all fucked up, yo. But that shit don't matter now."

"For *who*, Stax? You? Me?"

He looks at me, then narrows his eyes as if he's studying me; as if he's seeing me for the very first time. I quickly move from his view, darting over to my desk, putting a safe space between us. Subconsciously, I knew the moment would come: a day, a night, a time of reckoning.

I feel the walls closing in on me as he keeps his gaze trained on

me. He stalks over to me. Plants his palms flat on the desk, leaning over, inches away from my face.

I cast my eyes downward, then around the room. Anywhere
except back at him. In fear, they'll reveal more than I am willing
to share. Not now. Not yet.

"Don't run from me, Pash." The tenderness in his voice burns
into my pores. The blaze is starting from the inside out. "Don't
run from this. From us, yo. You want big dick? Is that it? I got
more than enough dick to keep your jaws busy, Pash. So don't let
that be ya excuse."

I swallow.

He touches the side of my face with a hand. "I ain't Jasper. This
dick is yours, Pash. I'm yours. *All* yours. But I ain't gonna sweat
you. You do what you gotta do to get right wit' you. And I'ma be
waitin' for you. So all that dick suckin' you love doin' so much,
there's a big, ten-inch dick wit' ya name on it. Only when you
ready for it."

I feel the rug being snatched up from beneath my heels. I brace
myself against the desk, steadying my nerves. Scrambling in my
head to find a way to navigate out of this net he is tossing over
me. "I finally know who the Calm One was," I say, shifting the
direction of the conversation. I tell him how I found out.

"Oh word?"

I eye him. Wonder why when I tell him it was Avery he doesn't
blink. Doesn't seem the least bit surprised. "So what do you plan
on doin' wit' that info?" he calmly asks. I tell him nothing. Admit
that I'm torn because I feel Mona deserves to know. But I don't
want her to get hurt. She's had enough losses. He nods knowingly.
I ask him if he knew Avery was there.

"Yeah."

I swallow.

"Pash, *I'm* the one who asked Avery to be there. Jasp asked him to be down wit' that shit and he tol' him he wasn't beat. The only reason why Avery was there was on the strength of me."

The room starts to slowly spin. I feel myself starting to hyperventilate. I can feel the blood draining from my face. "W-why?"

"It was the only way I could keep you safe. Jasper wanted them niggas to go all in on you. I wasn't diggin' that shit. But you were his wife, so I had to let him do him. I tol' you, I wanted no part of that shit. But I had to have eyes 'n' ears on shit. I'm the one who tol' Avery you were carryin' Jasper's seed 'n' to make sure none'a them niggas hurt you. When Jasp finally came down into the basement, he wanted you bodied, Pash—you and his seed. Avery is the one who went down there 'n' stopped him from stompin' you out. You were already unconscious."

I cover my mouth with a hand. *Ohgodohgodohgodohgodohgod...*

Suddenly, I wish I had been the one to put those bullets in that dirty motherfucker's head. Now I have to know, need to know, if Jasper was already dead when he was picked up from the park.

Stax slowly shakes his head. His eyes stay locked on mine. There's a fire burning behind his pupils. "Nah." I ask if he had him killed. He slowly shakes his head again. "Nah. I personally handled that shit. I dumped that heat into his skull, then tossed his body in the Hudson. That was my work, Pash. I finished him off."

There's no remorse, no guilt, in his voice when he says this.

My eyes widen. He walks around my desk. "I tol' you, Pash. I'ma never let anyone ever hurt you again."

Without a thought, my hand rests on my stomach. "But, why?"

"C'mon, Pash." He lowers his voice. The warmth in his eyes is dizzying. I look away. "Why you think?"

After several strained moments, I meet his eyes. I nervously bite the inside of my bottom lip before finally asking, "Do you love me, Stax?"

His gaze drops to my hand and I quickly become aware of what I have been doing this whole time. Gently rubbing my slightly swollen belly. He narrows his eyes. I can see the wheels in his head spinning as he counts back to the night in my suite. Despite the loose-fitting dress I am wearing, I am barely showing. Still, he's noticed. I see the way his expression turns into a question.

"Pash, keep shit real wit' me. Is that my seed?"

I let out a nervous chuckle. Shift my eyes around the room. I am afraid to trust this feeling of comfort and safety, of promise and hope. I'm afraid to become unguarded enough to allow vulnerability to creep in. Afraid to be a part of who he is while being apart from him. Afraid to trust myself enough to be able to love him when I am at a point of finally learning how to love myself; of how to balance forgiveness and letting go.

No. Stax and I can't be together. There is whole lot more to him I am afraid to know. That I don't think I ever want to know. I am not ready for his truths. How can I be? I am barely ready for my own. Still I am accepting them. They are who I am. They are things I have become.

I am a woman. A mother. A widower. A murderer.

I am the infamous Deep Throat Diva.

I have become a ruthless bitch.

And I am falling in love with a man I cannot allow myself to have.

I open and close my eyes. Hoping, wishing, like hell I can blink away these feelings, flash away his body from my mind, his taste from my lips, his touch on my skin. I wish like fucking hell I could blink away the aching need to want to fuck him right here, right now—for the last time.

But I can't.

Stax pulls out a peppermint candy, unwraps it and slides it into his mouth. He offers me one. I shake my head. Tell him no. He reaches for my hand. Holds it with strength and gentleness.

"I need to know, Pash." He asks again, "Is it my seed?" I still do not answer him.

"Do you love me, Stax?"

"C'mon, Pash. What you think?"

There is an intense moment of silence before he wants to know how many months I am. I tell him four. His eyes fill with sudden realization. Still, he is patiently waiting for words of confession to slip from my lips. There are none.

I swallow, reaching up on the balls of my feet and placing both hands on his shoulders. Then I kiss him. He kisses me back, moving into me. And this time when we kiss, it is with the sweetness of peppermint staining my tongue, and the harmony of an answer to his question; and mine to his.

And possibilities start to bloom.

Maybe there might be a chance for a happily ever after, after all.

ABOUT THE AUTHOR

Cairo is the author of *Retribution*, *Slippery When Wet*, *Big Booty*, *Man Swappers*, *Kitty-Kitty*, *Bang-Bang*, *Deep Throat Diva*, *Daddy Long Stroke*, *The Man Handler*, and *The Kat Trap*. His travels to Egypt inspired his pen name.

2005

"Aye, yo, you need to let me know now if you're gonna ride this shit out with me 'cause I ain't beat to be up in this muhfucka stressin' 'bout dumb shit, feel me?"

"I'm not going anywhere. I'm with you, baby."

"Aiight, that's what it is. I'ma need you to hold it down out there. Keep that shit tight, ya heard? Don't have me snappin' out 'cause you done got caught up in some bullshit."

"Whatever."

"Whatever, nothin', yo. I'm tellin' you now, Pasha, don't have me fuck sumthin' up. I didn't ice ya hand up for nothin', yo."

"Jasper, please, I'm not beat for another nigga. Four years ain't shit. I keep telling you that."

"Yeah, and? I'm gonna keep sayin' the shit 'cause I know how hot in the ass broads are when a nigga gets behind the wall. They be on some ole other shit."

"Well, I'm not them."

"Oh, so you not hot in the ass?"

"Yeah, for you. But not for any other nigga."

"You better not be either, yo, word up. Let me find out you done had another muhfucka hittin' that shit and I'ma bust yo' ass."

"Nigga, please. The only thing you're gonna be bustin' is a bunch of nuts in them hands."

"Yeah, aiight. I gotta buncha nuts for ya ass, ya heard? Talk slick if you want, but I'm tellin' you, yo."

"I heard you. And I'm telling you. I'm all yours in mind, body and soul. This pussy and my heart are for you and you only. And I got it on lock until you get home."

"You better."

"I promise, baby. I do."

ONE

Y ou ready to cum? *Imagine this: A pretty bitch down on her knees with a pair of soft, full lips wrapped around the head of your dick. A hot, wet tongue twirling all over it, then gliding up and down your shaft, wetting it up real slippery-like, then lapping at your balls; lightly licking your asshole. Mmmm, I'm using my tongue in places that will get you dizzy, urging you to give me your hot, creamy nut. Mmmmm, baby…you think you ready? If so, sit back, lie back, relax and let the Deep Throat Diva rock your cock, gargle your balls, and suck you straight to heaven.*

I reread the ad, make sure it conveys exactly what I want, need, it to say, then press the PUBLISH tab. "There," I say aloud, glancing around my bedroom, then looking down at my left hand. "Let's see how many responses I get, this time."

Ummm, wait…before I say anything else. I already know some of you uptight bitches are shaking your heads and rolling your eyes. What I'm about to tell ya'll is going to make some of you disgusted, and that's fine by me. It is what it is. There's also going to be a bunch of you closeted, freaky bitches who are going to turn your noses up and twist up your lips, but secretly race to get home 'cause you're as nasty as I am. Hell, some of you are probably down on your knees as I speak, or maybe finishing up pulling a dick from out of your throat, or removing strands of pubic hair from in between your teeth. And that's fine by me as well. Do you, boo. But, let me say this: Don't any of you self-righteous hoes judge me.

So here goes. See. I have a man—dark chocolate, dreamy-eyed, sculpted and every woman's dream—who's been incarcerated for four years, and he's releasing from prison in less than nine months. And, *yes*, I'm excited and nervous and almost scared to death—you'll realize why in a minute. Annnywaaaay, not only is he a sexy-ass motherfucker, he knows how to grind, and stack paper. And he is a splendid lover. My God! His dick and tongue game can make a woman forget her name. And all the chicks who know him either want him, or want him back. And they'll do anything they can to try to disrupt my flow. Hating-ass hoes!

Nevertheless, he's coming home to *me*. The collect calls, the long drives, the endless nights of sexless sleep have taken a toll on me, and will all be over very soon. Between the letters, visits and keeping money on his books, I've been holding him down, faithfully. And I've kept my promise to him to not fuck any other niggas. I've kept this pussy tight for him. And it's been hard, *really* hard—no, no, hard isn't an accurate description of the agony I've had to bear from not being fucked for over four years. It's been excruciating!

But I love Jasper, so I've made the sacrifice. For him, for us! Still, I have missed him immensely. And I need him so bad. My pussy needs him, aches for the width of his nine-inch, veiny dick thrusting in and out of it. It misses the long, deep strokes of his thick tongue caressing my clit and its lower lips. I miss lying in his arms, being held and caressed. But I have held out; denied any other niggas the privilege—*and* plea-sure—of fucking this sweet, wet hole.

The problem is: Though I haven't been riding down on anything stiff, I've been doing a little anonymous dick sucking on the side from time-to-time—and, every now and then, getting my pussy ate—to take the edge off. Okay, okay, I'm lying. I've been sucking a lot of dick. But it wasn't supposed to be this way. I wasn't supposed to become hooked on the shit as if it were crack. But, I have. And I am.

Truth be told, it started out as inquisitiveness. I was bored. I was lonely. I was fucking horny and tired of sucking and fucking dildos, pretending they were Jasper's dick. So I went on Nastyfreaks4u.com, a new website that's been around for about two years or so. About eighteen months ago, I had overheard one of the regulars who gets her hair done down at my salon talking about a site where men and women post amateur sex videos, similar to that on Xtube, and also place sex ads. So, out of curiosity, I went onto their site and browsed around on it for almost a week before deciding to become a member and place my very own personal ad. I honestly wasn't expecting anything to come of it. And a part of me had hoped nothing would. But, lo and behold, my email became flooded with requests. And I responded back. I told myself that I'd do it one time, only. But once turned into twice, then twice became three more times, and now—a year-and-a-half later, I'm logged on *again*—still telling myself that *this* time will be the last time.

I stare at my ring finger. Take in the sparkling four-carat engagement ring. It's a nagging reminder of what I have; of what I could potentially end up losing. My reputation for one—as a successful, no-nonsense hairstylist and business owner of one the most upscale hair salons in the tri-state area; winner of two Bronner Brothers hair show competitions; numerous features in *Hype Hair* magazine, one of the leading hairstyle magazines for African-American women; and winner of the 2008 Global Salon Business Award, a prestigious award presented every two years to recognize excellence in the industry—could be tarnished. Everything I've worked so hard to achieve could be ruined in the blink of an eye.

My man, for another, could…will, walk out of my life. After he beats my ass, or worse—kills me. And I wouldn't blame him, not one damn bit. I know better than anyone that as passionate a lover as Jasper is, he can be just as ruthless if crossed. He has no problem punching a nigga's lights out, smacking up a chick—or breaking her jaw, so I already recognize what the outcome will be if he ever finds out about my indiscretions. Yet, I still choose to dance with deception, regardless of the outcome.

As hypocritical and deceitful as I've been, I can't ever forget it was Jasper who helped me get to where I am today. He's been the biggest part of my success, and I love him for that. Nappy No More wouldn't exist if it weren't for him believing in me, in my visions, and investing thousands of dollars into my salon eight years ago. Granted, I've paid him back and then some. And, yes, it's true. I put up with all the shit that comes with loving a man who's been caught up in the game. From his hustling and incarcerations to his fucking around on me in the early part of our relationship, I stood by him; loved him, no matter what. And I know more than anyone else that I've benefited from it. So as far as I'm concerned, I owe him. He's put all of his trust in me, has given me his heart, and has always been damn good to me. And, yes, *this* is how I've been showing my gratitude—by creeping on the internet.

He won't find out, I think, sighing as I remove my diamond ring from my hand, placing it in my jewelry case and then locking it in the safe with the rest of my valuables. Jasper gave me this engagement ring and proposed to me a month before he got sentenced while he was still out on bail. He wanted me to marry him before he got locked up, but I want to wait until he gets released. Having a half-assed wedding was not an option. But, there'll be no wedding if I don't get my mind right and stop this shit, soon! *I'll stop all this craziness once he gets home.* This is what I tell myself, this is what I want to believe. The fucked-up thing is that as hard as I have tried to get my urges under control, there are times when my "habit" overwhelms me; when it creeps up on me and lures me into its clutches and I have to sneak out and end up right back on my knees sucking down another nigga's dick.

See. Being a seasoned dick sucker, I can swallow any length or width without gagging, or puking. I relax, breathe through my nose, extend my tongue all the way out, and then swallow one inch at a time until I have the dick all the way down in my throat. Then I start swallowing while I give a nigga a nice, slow dick massage. The shit is bananas! And it drives a nigga crazy.

I sigh, remembering a time when I once was so obsessed with being a good dick sucker that I used to practice sucking on a dildo. I had bought myself a nice black, seven-inch dildo at an adult bookstore when I was barely twenty. At first, it was a little uncomfortable. My eyes would water and I'd gag as the head hit the back of my throat. But, I didn't give up. I was determined to become a dick-swallowing pro. Diligently, I kept practicing every night before I went to bed until I was finally able to deep throat that rubber cock balls deep. Then I purchased an eight-inch, and practiced religiously until I was also able to swallow it. Before long, I was able to move up to a nine-inch, then ten. And once I had them mastered, it was then, that I knew for certain I was ready to move on to the real thing. I've been sucking dick ever since.

The only difference is, back then I only sucked my boyfriends, men I loved; men who I wanted to be with. But now…now, I'm sucking a bunch of faceless, nameless men; men who I care nothing about. Men I have no emotional connection to. And that within itself makes what I'm doing that more dirty. I realize this. Still—as filthy and as raunchy and trifling as it is, it excites me. It entices me. And it keeps me wanting more.

As crazy as this will sound, when I'm down on my knees, or leaned over in a nigga's lap with a mouthful of dick while he's driving—it's not him I'm sucking; it's not his balls I'm wetting. It's Jasper's dick. It's Jasper's balls. It's Jasper's moans that I hear. It's Jasper's hands that I feel wrapped in my hair, holding the back of my neck. It's Jasper stretching my neck. Not any other nigga. I close my eyes, and pretend. I make believe them other niggas don't exist.

The *dinging* alerts me that I have new messages. I sit back in front of my screen, take a deep breath. Eight emails. I click on the first one:

Great ad! Good-looking married man here: 42, 5'9", 7" cut, medium thick. Looking for a discreet, kinky woman who likes to eat and play with nice, big sweaty balls, lick in my musty crotch, and chew on my foreskin while I kick back. Can't host.

I frown, disgusted. *What the fuck?!* I think, clicking DELETE.

I continue to the second email:

Hey baby, looking for a generous woman who likes to suck and get fucked in the back of her throat. I'm seven-inches cut, and I like the feel of a tight-ass throat gripping my dick when I nut. I'm 5'9, about 168 lbs, average build, dark-skinned. I'm a dominant brotha so I would like to meet a sub-missive woman. I'm disease free and HIV negative. Hope you are, too. Hit me back.

Generous? Submissive? "Nigga, puhleeze," I sigh aloud, rolling my eyes. *Delete.*

I open the next three, and want to vomit. They are mostly crude, or ridiculous; particularly this one:

Hi. I'm a clean, cool, horny, married Italian guy. I'm also well hung 'n thick. I'd love to put on my wife's g-string, maybe even her thigh-highs, and let you suck me off through her panties, then pull out my thick, hot cock and give you good oral. I'm 6'2", 180 lbs, good shape. Don't worry. I'm a straight man, but behind closed doors I love wearing my wife's panties and getting oral. I hope this interests you.